THE HEEL OF ACHILLES:
THE COMPLETE ADVENTURES
OF THE MAJOR, VOLUME 3

THE HEEL OF ACHILLES
The Complete Adventures of the

Major
VOLUME 3

BY

L. PATRICK GREENE

ALTUS PRESS

2019

© 2019 Altus Press • First Edition—2019

THANKS TO

John Barach, Judy Lloyd & Walker Martin

TABLE OF CONTENTS

GOLD FROM OPHIR

IT WAS very evident to "Whispering" Smith that his capital was diminishing; his hold on the multitude of criminals—great and small—in South Africa, weakening; his field of operations narrowing and his own much-vaunted immunity from arrest was becoming endangered.

Whispering Smith found all this very disturbing and was not at all heartened by the blandiloquent flatteries of the riff-raff who depended on him for everything—including their freedom.

At least Smith, who was dishonest in his dealings with everyone, was honest with himself. Methodical man that he was, he had only to consult his account books to see how many times he—and the criminal organization of which he was the whip-cracking leader—had failed.

It made dismal reading: Six failures in as many months—more than in all the preceding years! And they had all been expensive failures; most of them mirth-begetting failures. It was that which rankled most, for the man with the whispering voice had no sense of humor—not when the joke was on himself.

His last failure—an attempt to control the shares of the big Diamond Mining Syndicate—had made him the laughing stock of Kimberley. Men whispered to each other when they saw him approaching and, though many of them feared him sufficiently to abstain from laughing openly, they could not altogether hide the mirthful light in their eyes or, as they turned away, the convulsive movement of shoulders.

In an effort to save his face Smith announced that he was going north to rest a while. He also let it be known that, on his return, he would personally settle with the man who had been responsible for his six failures. Hearing that threat, not a few well-meaning souls advised the threatened one to leave the country; they recognized that Smith was still a power to be reckoned with.

After supervising the removal and safe storage of his valuable records—Smith had a very complete dossier of practically every "wanted" man and woman in South Africa—and issuing final instructions to the ablest of his lieutenants concerning the management of his saloon, Smith only waited for a favorable opportunity; he thought if he could do a little business on the way north, it would be all to the good.

So it was not altogether by chance that he traveled on the same train as did Sam Miggs who was returning, after a week's vacation in the diamond town, to take up his duties as transport rider for the Ophir Mine.

"Yes, sir," said the dining-car conductor in response to Smith's query as he boarded the train, "lunch is served. There's just one seat vacant. This way, sir."

Smith, somberly garbed, looking like a missionary returning to his savage flock, followed the gold-braided uniformed man into the dining saloon and seated himself in the vacant seat indicated by the conductor.

Smith's *vis-à-vis*—the table was one of the small ones, seating only two—was deeply absorbed in the menu card. Smith noticed that his hands were smooth, yet suggested

great strength, and, failing to get a glimpse of the man's face, glanced around the saloon.

He knew many of its occupants intimately—too intimately for their comfort—and they returned his malicious nod of recognition in a self-conscious, shamefaced manner.

At the table opposite sat a lean, sallow-faced man; his beard was of several day's growth; his eyes were bloodshot. He had demonstrated his contempt for the refinements of civilization by rolling his shirt sleeves above his bony elbows—his greasy, dust-stained coat hung over the back of his chair. He was evidently well-loaded with liquor and, as his constantly shifting eyes noticed Smith, he half-rose from his chair and indicating that man with a grandiloquent gesture.

"Allow me, ladies an' gen'mun, to introduce t'yer my pal Whip—" he then began in a booming voice.

"Shut up and sit down, you drunken fool," Smith interposed harshly. "I'll see you later." This last was barely audible.

The other gulped, his prominent Adam's apple moved rapidly up and down, and he flinched as if he had been struck across the face with the lash of a whip. Three times he essayed to speak, but seemed incapable of articulation; then picking up his coat he shambled out of the saloon.

Smith watched his departure, turning in his chair to do so; his eyes, shrinking to pin-points, were so evil in their suggestion that a woman who sat at a far table gasped audibly and then began to talk in a high-pitched, hysterical voice.

Laughing softly, Smith turned again to face his table companion who had discarded the menu and was regarding him with a bland, disarming smile.

"This is absolutely priceless, isn't it?" he drawled, fixing his monocle more firmly in place. "I was just beginning to feel terribly bored, and now—why here's my dear old bosom friend, er, Whip—Whispering Cut-throat Smith of Kimberley and the gutters of the world."

Smith scowled and he half-rose as if considering changing to the seat just vacated by the departing drunkard. He would have changed, had he not been acutely conscious of a hard glint in the other's eyes and a half-challenging, half-mocking note in his voice.

Instead, he mouthed obscene blasphemies and said in savage whisper, "You damned stinking dude!"

The other spread his hands deprecatingly.

"Come now, old horse," he remonstrated. "No harsh words, I beg of you. I've always wanted to have a chat with you, face to face as it were; and there you are and here I am—what could be nicer than that?"

Smith did not reply; rage seemed to hold him speechless.

"Really, old man," continued the monocled one, his gray eyes twinkling with merriment, "there's no cause for gnashing of teeth and what not. Tell me all about it. Why are you going north?"

"Is that any damned business of yours?"

"Of course it is. A man must live, you know, and if you are going to pull off any little deal—why, er, I'd like to take a hand. You've been a perfect gold mine to me and I've only the warmest feeling in my heart for you—really!"

"Major," Smith said slowly, in a low, menacing voice, "I've had enough of your damned interference. In some way or other you have blundered on to my plans, and spoiled them, several times and—"

"Six times in all, old dear," the Major interrupted complacently. "But I don't think you're doing yourself justice when you say that I blundered on to your plans. You scheme too carefully for that to happen, you know. What's more—" the Major's tone was that of a spoiled child—"I don't think you give me credit for being so deucedly clever. But there! That's always been my cross in life! No one ever gives me credit for having brains—poor things, don't you know, but my own. And yet I do the most surprisingly clever things at times, pull off some ripping schemes. But, just the same, people never give me credit."

He took out his monocle and polished it with a vivid green silk handkerchief. His expression was very self-pitying.

"You talk like a market woman, Major," Smith said patiently, having gained control of his rage and hoping that in some way the Major would expose his hand. Smith could not entertain the thought that this meeting was accidental. "And you *have* brains," he added.

The Major replaced his monocle and beamed happily.

He seemed now to be a good-natured, dudishly attired man who had not a thought in his head beyond his personal comfort and the conventions of good social usage. Certainly there was nothing about him to indicate that he knew the veld and the people of the veld better than any other white man; that he was a good shot, a wonderful horseman and the best all-round athlete in South Africa. There was nothing to show that his keen brain had conceived raids on the diamond mining syndicate—as a protest against what he considered the unjustly drastic laws regulating the industry—which had proved beyond the ability of the police to unravel. His immaculate, well-valeted clothes—in a country where khaki trousers and gray flannel shirt was accepted as full dress—concealed his perfect physique, just as his monocle, his bored, almost inane expression and languid drawl concealed his quick wit.

"No," Smith continued, "I don't think you're a fool," then turned to give his order to the waiter.

"Hot bread and milk," he said.

The Major chuckled.

"I always thought villains drank whisky neat—and you are a villain, you know, Smithy. So I'm no fool?"

"A fool couldn't spoil my plans four times—and live."

"Six times! Pardon the correction, but we must be accurate—a point of honor. Six times! That should be checkmate, Smithy—you play chess, of course?"

"It's not even check, Major. I never lose."

"What, never?"

"Never."

"Oh, come! You don't play fair. You should have said, 'Hardly ever!' But perhaps you don't know *Pinafore*. You know, Smithy, you're a top-hole reformer, really. I've been so busy playing with you that I haven't had time to attend to my own little affairs. Imagine it! I haven't handled an I.D.B. deal for months and months and months. Colonel Carstairs of the police—he's a great friend of mine—tells me that his men are going to present me with an illuminated testimonial. Won't that be bully? Or do you think he was spoofing me?"

The Major looked with great interest at the steaming bowl of bread and milk which the waiter now set before Smith.

"What frightful pap," he murmured. "Are your teeth bothering you or is it senile decay?"

"Major," said Smith in a tense voice, "I think you will die very soon."

"Bless my soul!" The Major looked greatly worried. "I know I'm a little bit tuckered out, haven't been sleeping well lately, but I didn't dream I—"

"Yes. You'll die soon and quite suddenly. Or, no. I think a long term of hard labor on the Breakwater would be a much better method of settling my little debt with you."

"I don't quite understand. You mean that—?"

"I mean that I'm tired of setting fools on your track. I'm going after you myself."

"There's no fool like an old fool, Smithy."

"I'm playing fair, Major. I'm warning you. Better take the first train to the Cape and the first boat home. You'll be safe there—perhaps. Otherwise—I give you three months."

The Major shivered.

"You're a cold-blooded Johnny. But are you a good sport? I'll bet you a fiver your plan number seven doesn't come off. Are you on?"

"Yes, and to show you I'm game I'll give you odds—fifty to one." With a grand gesture the Major produced a dainty notebook and a gold pencil. "Fifty to one," he murmured as he entered the bet. "Sovereigns, Smithy?"

"What?" Smith was endeavoring to decipher the intricate monogram on the cover of the Major's notebook and he looked up with a start to meet the Major's quizzical stare. "Oh, yes, sovereigns. Anything you like."

"Ripping! I'll be two hundred and fifty pounds richer three months from now. How about a stake holder?"

"Don't need one—we are both men of honor."

"Are we? That's news."

Smith was silent and, the Major's fast course having been set before him, seemed to forget the matter. Indeed, seeing and hearing him now one would have thought that he was lunching with an old friend.

"I wonder how you'll do it," the Major mused, reverting to the other's threat, as Smith with a grunt of repletion pushed away from him the empty bowl. "Will you drug me? I know you won't shoot me; you're afraid of firearms, aren't you? That's so funny!"

He chuckled softly as Smith winced. It was one of the queer anomalies about Smith. He was terribly afraid of firearms—never carried them and it is doubtful if he had ever fired a shot.

"There are more ways of killing a dog—" Smith began contemptuously, hesitated and then, struck by a new thought, began again, leaning forward confidentially. "Look here, Major! It's damned silly for two men like us to be at each other's throats. We're both against the police, blast the fools, and, working together, there's not a thing we couldn't do. Come in with me; I can always find a place for a man with brains like you."

The Major pondered this a moment and then he drawled, "Not losing any time trying to win your bet, are you, dear lad?"

"What do you mean?"

"Well, your days are numbered and it looks as if you are trying to end mine by linking my name with yours. But it won't do—really it won't." Then, he added casually, "Who was that drunken bounder who sat opposite? Friend of yours?"

"No! Never seen him before. But never mind him. Come in with me and let me pay my bet now."

He reached for his wallet.

The Major shook his head.

"No. It can't be done, Smithy."

"Better think twice," Smith countered swiftly. "I'm offering you equal partnership with me. There's no risk—we could control everything. Why, man, if I'd someone with brains like you working for me I'd be boss of this whole bleedin' country! And rich! Why the hush money we'd receive from women alone—with you handling them— would be as good as a gold mine."

"I'm afraid I couldn't handle the women," the Major said slowly. "They've always had me up a tree, as it were."

He was silent for a moment, his eyebrows knit in a puzzled frown—indecision, Smith thought.

"Well, Smithy," he exclaimed presently, "I've thought twice—and, second thoughts are best, aren't they?"

"Yes." Smith was eagerly expectant.

"Yes."

The monocle fell from the Major's eye; the flabbiness about his jaws vanished, his eyes ceased to twinkle.

The dude had vanished—suddenly and completely— with the dropping of the monocle, and in his place sat a man of action, stern of purpose, who would permit no tampering with his code of ethics.

"Yes, Smith," the Major continued in a firm," cold voice. "I've thought twice—and my second thought is the same as the first. You're a waster, an abject rotter. There's not a good thing about you; you're lower than the lowest of the crowd of gutter scum who crawl and do what your filthy mind suggests. There," his monocle again gleamed in his eye; his voice changed, was confusedly apologetic, "that's that. Didn't mean to get melodramatic, but the old tongue does wag at an alarming rate at times, doesn't it? At least you realize that we don't run in double harness, don't you?"

Smith seemed to be on the verge of strangulation.

"Why, what's the matter?" asked the other.

"Nothing's the matter, Major—with me," Smith whispered thickly. "But there will be with you."

"If that's the way you are going to talk, breaking up our nice sociable little chat, why—" the Major shrugged his shoulders and rose languidly to his feet.

Smith glowered. He was holding on to the edge of the table, his knuckles showing white from the pressure he exerted, his long, white, diamond beringed fingers tensing nervously. Then, suddenly, he relaxed, his figure slumped and he smiled.

"Where are you going, Major?" he asked.

The Major stared with incredulous admiration at the man's quick mastery of his emotions.

"To my compartment."

Smith made a gesture of impatience. "I mean after you leave the train."

"Oh! On a hunting trip. Jim, my native servant, is going to meet me at Two Tanks siding."

Smith's eyes narrowed.

"I may see you again very soon, then," he said with a well-satisfied smile. "Expect to pull off a little business deal there. Better join me, Major."

"Thanks—but I think not, really. I've already explained why."

"You're a damned fool," growled Smith.

"Toodle-oo!" said the Major, and walked slowly out of the saloon, exchanging happy banter with many of the occupants of the car who knew him and greeted him affectionately.

AT TWO tanks siding—where the only buildings were the two water-tanks which gave it its name, a galvanized storehouse and a few small huts which marked the quarters of the mounted policemen on duty there—a motley crowd I had gathered to meet the northbound train. All the white settlers of the district were there—twenty of them, no more! The women, dressed in faded finery—blatantly not suitable to the climate, but worn for the style and grandeur it once possessed—brewed tea over a smoky fire and discussed in monotonous, spiritless tones the domestic happenings of the past week and the prospect of a trip home—next year, or the next!

Two of the women were openly and unfeignedly envied. They, with their men folk, had ridden over fifty miles since sunrise solely in order to travel on the train to the next siding—where they would meet the southbound train and return on it. They would eat a meal, cooked by other hands than their own, amidst the comparatively luxurious surroundings of the dining saloon.

Most of the men were gaunt and haggard-looking; none had escaped the abnormal strain to which the pioneer settlers of any new country peopled by a savage race, are subjected. Also these men had been through the hell of two native rebellions and devastating cattle plagues which had destroyed ninety per cent. of all the cattle in the country.

That they had the courage to remain and attempt to gather up the threads, still holding the vision before them

of prosperity and a peacefully settled country, was a credit
to the race which bred them.

All carried rifles, even the women, and some of the
men had revolvers in holsters attached to their belts. The
revolver, however, was not a favored weapon among these
settlers; a shotgun, loaded with buckshot, proving infinitely more effective when dealing at close quarters with
native warriors.

The men gave the impression of being constantly on
guard—as indeed they were. They had paid the penalty
twice for allowing themselves to be too easily lulled into
fancied security by the specious promises of the Matabele.
They eyed with suspicion, therefore, the gesticulating mob
of native women, old men, boys and a scattering of powerfully built warriors who—laden with skins, goat's milk in
filthy containers, musical instruments and curios of all
sorts—were also waiting for the arrival of the train.

When a native youngster, boisterously playing the war-
game with other children of the *kraals*, ventured near the
little group of white children, he was quickly shooed away,
and the hands of the white men instinctively tightened
about their weapons whenever their eyes rested upon one
of the proudly self-confident warriors. They realized all
too well that the civilization of the country was no more,
had no greater hold, than the gleaming rails along which
the train would presently arrive, unless—as had happened
before and could happen again—the rails had been torn
up down below. The memory of trusts betrayed, of homes
burned, of friends—men, women and children—tortured,
mutilated and left to pray for death, had left them very
bitter. Things like that could not be forgotten soon or easily.

It was evident that the slightest overt act on the part of
one or other of the Matabele warriors would be the signal

for—as Reamy, the mounted policeman on duty at Two Tanks, tersely put it—"An Almighty big *verdoemte indaba.*" Reamy was a Dutch Colonial. And so, knowing the natives, the policeman walked among them, exchanging hunting gossip with the old men, sharing his tobacco with the warriors, exchanging coarse banter with the women and admiring their babies. His presence did much to relieve the tension.

A little beyond the knot of natives was a Cape Cart to which were harnessed four mules. On the driver's seat was a squat, powerfully built Hottentot who sat regarding the gathering of whites and blacks with an air of irritating superiority.

After a while the trooper made his way toward the Cape Cart, carefully pushing his way through the swarming native children who, with shouts of glee, claimed him as their prisoner.

"Hullo, Jim," he called in the Taal. "What are you doing up here?"

The Hottentot's face became a mass of joyful wrinkles. "Greetings, Baas Reamy," he answered. "I wait for my baas—the Mahjah! We go a-hunting. He comes on the train, having first sent me to make ready."

Reamy shook his head. "It is bad business, Jim, to hunt up here now. You see—" he pointed to a warrior who, seated on the ground nearby, was scowling fixedly at the white men. "Hate is still there, and where there is hate there is—"

"No sense, Baas," the Hottentot interrupted.

"True! But death is there, also."

"My baas will hunt just the same," Jim said complacently! "He'll know how to deal with these black ones. Besides," Jim, with a flourish of his long whip, indicated the white women and children, "if they are safe, then we are safe."

"Who says they are safe? Only the men who do not know the Matabele. I say to all these men, 'Send your women and children away for one, two years.' But they won't—and so we have to watch very carefully."

Jim grunted agreement.

"Your mules look well, Jim," the trooper said presently. "And the Cape Cart, is it new?"

Jim grinned. "Ten days ago my baas sent me up here. I was to travel slowly—arriving today. But the mules were fast and for five days I have been camped by the river back there, waiting. The mules have done nothing but eat while I painted the Cape Cart. My baas will be pleased."

"He may *sjambok* you for disobeying." They both laughed loudly at the thought. "And you have been here five days—yet I did not know it?" continued Reamy.

"Who can see Jim when Jim does not wish to be seen?" the Hottentot said with a chuckle. "And there are ways of stopping the chatter of people."

The policeman looked as if he would like to question Jim further, but was called by a white man who wanted his advice on some obscure native-labor technicality.

As he departed another Cape Cart, drawn by six mules, drew up alongside of Jim's. It was driven by a tall, sinister-appearing half-caste. The mules were hollow-flanked and in obviously poor condition, the Cape Cart in sad need of repairs, the harness mended by string and bits of twine.

"Hullo, nigger," the half-caste called derisively to Jim, and then, when Jim did not answer, he swore viciously.

A naked, roly-poly six-year-old at that moment ran up to the half-caste's mules, brandishing his toy weapon and shouting gleefully. The mules took fright and backed the

Cape Cart on to the side of a large ant hill nearby, where it threatened to capsize.

With much cursing and capable handling of his long whip, the half-caste quickly gained control over his mules and righted the wagon. Then, leaping to the ground, *sjambok* in hand, he lumbered toward the innocent cause of the disturbance.

As the Cape Carts were between the child and the people waiting for the train the half-caste was unobserved by anyone save the youngster—who, firmly clutching his little *knobkerrie,* bravely stood his ground. He watched the lanky man's menacing advance—and Jim.

Even Jim did not at once realize the half-caste's full intention, thinking that it was all in fun, so the cutting lash of the huge *sjambok,* rose and fell once, leaving a bloody line on the naked little body—but extracting no whimper of pain—before Jim, with a bellow of rage, leaped from the Cape Cart. He caught the half-caste's upraised hand before he could strike another blow.

The two men wrestled furiously, the half-caste muttering white man's blasphemies and the lurid curses of his mother's people. Jim was silent, confident, not troubling to exert the full force of his superior strength. Slowly, but surely, he bent the half-caste's arm—the one which held the *sjambok*—back and back until, with a scream of pain, his adversary dropped to the ground, moaning, tenderly fingering his arm.

Now the child would have rushed in and struck the groveling man again and again with his *knobkerrie,* but Jim, laughing, caught him and lifted him up in his arms.

"Not so, little warrior," he said.

"You fought well for a dog of a Hottentot," the boy said gravely. "But it is not finished. He must die."

Jim chuckled. "Do you fear him, then, Great One?" he asked.

The boy's eyes flashed. "That dog! No!"

"Then let him live. It is only good to kill what we fear. He—"

"Give the boy to me."

Jim turned at the deep, booming voice.

"He has a lion heart," he said as he surrendered the child to the speaker, a tall, mightily-muscled warrior. "Some day he will be a big chief."

"He is the son of a fighter; in his veins flows the blood of Chaka. It is pure, unmixed with bastard blood," the warrior said with dignity, and walked swiftly away, taking the child with him.

Jim gazed after him wonderingly for a moment, then directed his attention to the half-caste, and examined his arm.

"You're a pig," he said contemptuously. "You cry out in pain before you're hurt. Not a bone is broken! The child is a better man than you. Get to your place and look to your mules, for soon the ter-rain will come. Should it frighten them you will, doubtless, attempt to beat *it* with a *sjambok*."

As the half-caste rose to his feet and sullenly climbed into his Cape Cart, Reamy rejoined Jim and heard the story of the fracas.

"Hans is a *schelm*, Jim, and his baas is a worse one," Reamy said. "You must look out for them. What was the name of the warrior?"

"I do not know, Baas Reamy, but he said that the child was of Chaka's line."

"Tchat!" exclaimed Reamy. "Then you've made a good friend as well as a bad enemy—that is if Magato remembers."

"It is no matter, Baas Reamy. Friend or enemy, it is all one to the Mahjah, and I, I am his servant."

"You think he is the rising and the setting of the sun, don't you, Jim?"

The Hottentot's eyes opened wide in astonishment. "And why not, Baas Reamy? He is—"

But just then the train arrived, with much blowing of whistle, panting and screeching of brakes, putting an end to Jim's panegyric of praise.

Jim watched the excited throng and waited patiently for his baas—the tall, sun-helmeted man in white ducks—to join him.

But first came a lean, sallow-faced man—the same one who had greeted Smith so boisterously in the dining saloon the previous day. He was not drunk now, but he made his way quickly through the crowd, obsequious to the white men and women, thrusting the natives roughly out of his path.

Coming to the Cape Cart next to Jim's he hailed the half-caste jovially and did not resent that man's insolent familiarity, but when he heard Hans's whining account of the fight he turned truculently toward Jim.

"You black devil!" he bellowed. "I'll—I'll—"

"You'll what, old man?" drawled the Major who, having been warned by Reamy, had come up unobserved.

Sam Miggs collapsed suddenly—and yet it was not from fear. The Major was sure of that.

"I didn't know he was your nigger, Major," he said lamely, "and I sort of lost my temper when I heard he'd

been manhandling Hans here. But that's all right. Us white
men ain't goin' to have no words about a niggers' quarrel."

Then he lowered his voice and added confidentially,
"I saw you chinning in the dining saloon yesterday with
Whip Smith—great pals you and he are, eh? Whip told
me afterward that you weren't in on this deal we're going to
pull off. He's a downy bird, is Smith. He's afraid I'll talk too
much, so I let on I believed him. But," he winked broadly—
"you'll be on hand, all right, when it comes to splitting up."

"I shouldn't be at all surprised, Mr.—er—"

"Miggs; Sam Miggs is my name," supplemented the
other.

"Thank you, Mr. Sam Miggs. No, I shouldn't be at all
surprised if I happened to be somewhere close at hand at
that delightful occasion."

Then, turning away, he sought Reamy. "Who's that
blighter, Reamy, old top?"

"That? Oh, that's Sam Miggs—transport rider for the
Ophir Mine. He's a good transport man but outside of
that he's a—damned skunk. Got two or three nigger wives.
Why?"

"Oh, nothing," said the Major thoughtfully.

"HE IS coming, Baas!"

Jim was excited, and his eyes shone with the joy of the
hunt.

The Major, whose khaki trousers and shirt with thick
spine-pad blended in so well with the veld as to make him
almost invisible—even at short range—lighted a cigarette
and puffed contentedly before answering with a half-stifled
yawn, "When will he get to the ford, Jim?"

"By sundown, Baas! See, there he is." He pointed to a
thin cloud of dust which spiraled lazily upward.

The Major looked at it—no need now for a monocle to aid his vision—estimated its distance, and groaned.

"One more hour to wait. And perhaps I'm on a wild goose chase, after all. What do you think, Jim?"

"Wild goose chase," repeated Jim, stumbling over the English words, "damme no."

"No? 'Pon my soul I believe you're right, Jim." Then he added in the vernacular, "The ground is hard, Jim, and my bones stiff; also the sun is very hot."

"The baas would not let me bring blankets for him to lie oh or build a shade," Jim said in an "I-told-you-so," tone.

The Major rolled over on his back and stared up into the brilliant blue of the sky. Then he shut his eyes, unable to conquer for the moment the sensation that he would fall off the earth and plunge into the limitless depths of space.

The *thud thud—thud, thud,* of the stamps of the mill at the distant mine sounded clearly, and so still, so rare, was the atmosphere that the thud of the stamps added to rather than detracted from the silence. To Jim's ears came other sounds, sounds which failed to register on the Major's eardrums; the lowing of cattle in distant *kraals,* the barking of dogs and nearer, much nearer and louder, the rattle of wheels and the cracking of a whip.

"I'm going to sleep again," said the Major. "Wake me when he gets to the ford."

"Yah, Baas," said Jim and resumed his watch.

His eyes hardly ever strayed from the dusty road which led arrow-straight across the veld. It was the road which the transport driver of the Ophir Mine traversed twice a month: to Two Tanks siding with the month's output of gold, and back to the mine with provisions.

Jim and the Major had taken up their position on the top of the steep bank which bordered the road where it sloped down to the river's ford. Here they could command a wide sweep of the country, yet, if they desired, remain unseen. In a nearby thicket, well hidden, the mules were standing, hitched to the Cape Cart, ready for a hurried getaway should unforeseen circumstances demand it.

A herd of impala buck, leaping gracefully, passed by on their way to the pool at the ford. It was nearing the end of the dry season and for miles the river was only a dried-up watercourse—a white, dazzling scar across the thirsty veld.

After the impala came a herd of zebra, the striped fools of the veld. They came up quite close to the two humans and eyed them with imbecile curiosity. They did not move on until Jim flung a chunk of rock at the leader, hitting him on the nose. Then, snorting in alarmed indignation, they galloped off.

Close behind the zebra faced a pack of wild dogs, their jaws slobbering with the hunger lust, hoping that a fat zebra calf would fall to their lot. Only the knowledge of the fearful execution of which the hard, horny hoofs were capable kept the dogs from attacking the herd.

Far away, so far as to appear like dead, limbless trees— trees which moved—were three giraffes.

From the steep, rock-strewn *kopje* across the river baboons descended, the "old men" barking warning to the others to avoid the cave mouth where a thing of splotched sunshine and shadows, with hungry green eyes, crouched in waiting. When the leopard leaped at a straying female the "barks" became sharp, imperative and the male baboons turned *en masse* and advanced threateningly, so that the leopard lost its nerve, released its victim and sped swiftly away.

But all this, and more: the gathering of vultures above some distant spot where a beast of prey had made its kill;

the tree python which let three-quarters of its great length fall upon and coil itself about a tiny duiker; the futile struggle and plaintive beat which was quickly stilled; the weird dance of the secretary birds—all this Jim sensed rather than saw.

The constant struggle for survival among the wild was commonplace to him. He and his people were involved in it, and the beasts of the veld only interested him if he were hungry and desired to eat—or if they were hungry and he desired to live. Jim never stopped to admire the grace of a buck before killing it—neither does a lion.

The spiral of dust which held Jim's attention soon resolved itself into a Cape Cart drawn by six mules traveling at a leisurely trot.

A white man was handling the whip; the leader, the man with the reins, was the half-caste, Hans.

"He comes, Baas," Jim, said after a while, the Cape Cart having come to the place where the road sloped down to the ford.

The Major sat up, instantly alert.

"They are outspanning, Baas," Jim continued. "What is the game we play?"

"I don't know, Jim. Perhaps it will play itself."

In silence they watched the newcomers turn off the road, come to a halt and proceed to make camp almost directly opposite the place where Jim and the Major were sitting.

"We will now go and visit them, Jim," said the Major.

Rising to his feet, rifle in hand, he led the way down the steep bank, crossed the road and clambered up the other bank.

They made no attempt at concealment, but the new arrivals were so busily engaged making camp that they were unconscious of their presence until the Major drawled, "You're damnably late, Miggs."

The lean man almost dropped the bottle from which he was in the act of drinking, his hand leaped to his revolver and he turned on his heels with cat-like swiftness.

Then his face broke into a leering smile of recognition and he held out his hand.

"Oh, it's you and your nigger, it is, Major? You put the wind up me for a minute."

Miggs seated himself on some cushions which he took from his Cape Cart and motioned to the Major to do the same.

"Where's your camp?" Miggs asked.

"I haven't outspanned. Don't know this bloomin' country—or the natives. I was afraid a party of warriors might be out on the warpath and so—" the Major looked embarrassed—"I decided to have all ready so that I could bolt if I had to."

Miggs laughed patronizingly. "You send your nigger for your outfit; Hans, here, will help him, and outspan right close to me. No nigger'll touch you while I'm around. I'm one of 'em, been taken into the tribe. That's why I was able to ride transport all through the rebellion. And my women tell me the warriors won't go on the warpath again—not before the rains at any rate."

The Major's laugh was one of great relief.

"Hans," continued Miggs to the half-caste who was glowering murderously at Jim, "you take this baas's nigger and help him to outspan over here."

Jim looked inquiringly at the Major as Hans said in the vernacular, "Come on, dog," and when the Major nodded, reluctantly followed the half-caste.

As they passed out of sight, Miggs turned to the Major and said in aggrieved tones, "I knew that Whip Smith was lying—you can't fool Sam Miggs—though I don't see why you should have a share in the rake-off. You don't take no risks."

"No," replied the Major absently. "And neither does Smith."

Miggs thoughtfully considered this for a moment. He was painfully slow-witted and the Major had no difficulty in anticipating his thought processes. He now drank deeply from the bottle and, first rubbing his dirty sleeve across the top of it, offered it to the Major.

"Never drink before sundown—and rarely after," said the Major, waving the bottle aside.

Miggs stared at him incredulously. "It's good stuff," he urged. "Not Cape Smoke."

"No, thanks!"

"Well, all the more for me!" He drank again, smacking his lips in appreciation.

"That's right, what you were saying—about Smith, I mean. He don't take no risks, does he?"

"No. None at all!"

"He couldn't pull this off as easy if it wasn't for me."

"You're a clever chap, Sam—deucedly clever."

Miggs drank again. "An' I don't see why Smith should horn in and claim most of the stuff. He's a greedy devil, ain't he?"

The Major nodded his head in agreement.

Miggs looked around cautiously, as if afraid of being overheard, and placed a dirty, talon-like hand on the Major's arm.

"Tell you what," he said hoarsely. "Let's do old Smith one in the eye."

The Major looked interested. "How?"

"How? That's easy! Here's you and here's me, and the gold's in there—" He nodded toward his Cape Cart. "An' where's Smithy? Tell me that. Why, Smithy's over there at Lion Head Kop, a-waiting for us."

He waved his hand in the general direction of a long, low-lying *kopje* some ten miles distant, which, silhouetted against the setting sun, vaguely resembled a crouching lion.

"Sure! He's waitin' over there to hold me up so's I can go back to the mine—afoot—an' tell 'em I've been held up by a bunch of Portuguese half-castes." He chuckled. "Smithy's got brains, at that. He's made up a good story for me to tell them at the Ophir. They'll never suspect me, nor him fer the matter of that. An' I'll still hold my job as transport rider an' we can do the job again. But, an' don't forget this, there ain't nobody else but me as could pull this job off fer him, an' I don't like seeing him get the hog's share. Suppose we leave him waiting there and beat our way for the Portuguese border—we can do it easily—there's no one can extradite us there, an' no Smith."

The Major shook his head.

"An' why not?" Miggs asked fiercely.

"Well—er—the country's unsettled and the natives—"

"I tell you that I can manage the niggers. I'd take a chance on doing the trip alone, but it'll be easier for two. And a man like you can get rid of the stuff better than I can."

"And further," continued the Major slowly, "you forget that Smith has men everywhere; you can't go where they're not. And it 'ud be easy for him to bribe the Portuguese officials to put you away for a long, long time. A chap like Smith doesn't need extradition warrants."

Miggs shivered. "I'd forgotten that. I know them dirty dago officials. They ain't a honest one among them. And I know their prisons, too. They're lousy holes where they treat white men like you and me worse nor niggers.

"An' speaking of niggers, where's them two of ourn? They ought to have been here with your outfit long before this."

As he spoke, the sound of voices raised in angry argument, followed by dull thuds sounded in the thicket across the road and, leaping to their feet, the Major and Miggs ran quickly to the place where Jim and the half-caste were rolling over and over upon the ground.

Hans held a broad-bladed knife in his right hand; Jim, bleeding from a wound in his thigh, was endeavoring to get in a blow with his *knobkerrie,* while the four mules attached to the Cape Cart regarded them with sleepy, mildly curious eyes.

"Jim, stop!"

"Hans, you devil! What's all this about?"

As the two men deafly ignored their baas' cries, the Major took hold of Jim by the scruff of the neck while Miggs held Hans—and so the two were separated.

Hans was sullenly silent and refused to answer his baas's questions concerning the affair, but Jim was voluble in his explanations.

"He called me many names, Baas," he said, breathing heavily, "but that was nothing—though I wished to beat him as I did at the place of the train two weeks ago, but there is no pleasure in beating such a puny fool. And then he spoke evilly of you, Baas, and my tongue in answering was even bitterer than his. And that angered him so that he sprang at me from behind and struck me with his knife. The rest you saw, only—only I wish you had delayed coming a little longer. Then you would have found him dead."

"We ought to *sjambok* them both," Miggs said roughly. "You can beat my nigger and I'll beat Jim. That'll make sure both of them get it good and proper." His dull eyes gleamed for a moment in cruel anticipation.

"There'll be no flogging," the Major said curtly. "Come, it'll be dark in half an hour and I'm beastly hungry."

He climbed into the Cape Cart, followed by Jim, and drove around to where the other had outspanned. Miggs and Hans walked back—talking angrily.

The evening meal was a very silent one—Jim preparing the Major's food and Hans attending to the wants of Miggs who drank frequently. The latter burst into occasional peals of laughter when the Major, apparently in a deadly funk, started to his feet at the cracking of twigs, the crunch of padded paws on the sand of the river bed and the cry of some night creature.

"An' I'd always heard you was a crack veld man," he said, wagging his head with drunken gravity. "What'd come of you if I wasn't here to take care of you, I dunno. As a matter of fac'," he went on, "I think I shall go on to meet Smith without you. Tell him you didn't show up—didn't expect yer anyway—and there'll be a bigger share for me."

"No," began the Major in alarm, but Miggs lurched to his feet.

"You shut up," he said and continued suspiciously, his little eyes blinking piggishly. "As, a matter of fac', how do I know you're in with us on this deal. Smith told me that you and him were at outs."

He looked at the Major thoughtfully for a moment, then, coming to a decision, said firmly, "Yes; I'm goin' to leave you behind. Ain't goin' to take no chances. First though—" he climbed into the Major's Cape Cart—"I'm going to look over your stuff. You won't need it where I'm going to send you.

"Um!" His voice sounded hollow within the canvas-covered cart. "Nothin' much here except a lady's fal-de-lals—" he had discovered the Major's very complete toilet set—"and some sacks of grain. Why do—?"

At that moment Jim leaped at the half-caste, fetching him to the ground. As they pummeled each other, cursing loudly, Miggs descended hastily from the Cape Cart, declaring that he would flay the hide off that nigger, Jim.

But he was still several feet from them when he was brought to an abrupt halt by the Major's curt, "Hands up, Miggs!"

Obeying, Miggs stared in ludicrous amazement at the graceful lounging figure and at the revolver, which glinted so menacingly in the flickering firelight, and which the Major held leveled at him.

"What all this about, Major?" he blustered.

"You'll see in a little while, Miggsy. I don't quite trust you; not, mind you, that I'd object very strenuously to you leaving me here an' goin' off alone to meet Smith—that 'ud be quite all right—but I'm afraid you'd never get to Smith. As you remarked a little while ago, the Portuguese border isn't very far away and I think you mean to cheat our mutual friend Smith out of his lawful share of the proceeds."

"So you're his dirty spy, are you?" Miggs exclaimed.

The Major laughed—not a pleasant laugh—and Miggs continued, his voice expressing alarm. "Don't tell him, mister. You know I was only joking. You know I wouldn't go fer to do Smith one in the eye; he's got too much on me;

he's got too much influence. Why, he's got all the big men out here eating out of his hand. You won't tell him, mister?"

"We'll see," the Major promised. "It all depends how you behave." Then he called, "Make an end quickly, Jim. It grows late and I'm very tired."

"Yah, Baas," Jim grunted joyfully and, getting a punishing hold on the half-caste with his muscular legs, pinned him to the ground. Then he proceeded to bind him hand and foot.

"There, Baas," he said complacently as he deftly inserted a gag in Hans's mouth, stopping a lurid stream of invective, "I have repaid him for the knife thrust and the names he called us. It was in order to punish him that I delayed the end."

The Major nodded. "I know. That is why I planned it this way—that you might punish him a little."

"What next, Baas?"

"Bind the white man and gag him, too."

"What?" bellowed Miggs. "You'd let that nigger bind me—a white man?"

"Are you white, Miggsy? I wonder." Then apologetically, "I'm sorry! I'd do it myself and let Jim cover you with my revolver, but it can't be done. Jim's very nervous about fire-arms and he'd probably plug you. So you see!"

Miggs was drunk, but not so drunk that he could not realize that he was helpless and resistance would be foolish. So his struggles against being tied by Jim were futile and spasmodic, although accompanied by much cursing. Thus, he fondly imagined, he was preserving the white man's superiority over the black, a superiority which he himself had betrayed many times. Indeed, his whole career in Africa had been such as to make him infinitely lower than the race he affected to despise.

"And what next, Baas?" Jim asked with a chuckle.

"Now we'll sit and rest for a while," said the Major and sat down beside the fire, Jim squatting on his haunches nearby. Miggs and Hans were lying helpless near them.

For a time the eyes of the two men glared at them balefully, unwinkingly. Then, after a while, the need of sleep proved stronger than hate, and the eyes closed—opened—closed again, and then minutes later both men were snoring lustily.

And still for a time the Major did not move, but when the moon appeared above the distant *kopjes* he rose to his feet, tiptoed noiselessly to his Cape Cart and taking out two light blankets spread them over the two sleepers.

"They'll be cold, Jim," he whispered to Jim.

"Yah, Baas," replied Jim. "Also the moon will shine in their eyes and awaken them." And he pulled the blankets carefully over their heads. "No matter now if they do awake," he added.

The Major nodded approval.

Then he and Jim found much work to do, work which required a small lantern, a screw-driver and much passing back and forth between the two Cape Carts.

WHEN MIGGS awakened early next morning, stiff and blear-eyed, his hands and feet were free, the gag removed from his mouth.

He sat up and, seeing Hans and Jim inspanning his mules, while the Major was sitting by the fire finishing his breakfast, began to wonder if the events of yesternight were a dream or the figments of a drink-sodden imagination.

But his jaw, still aching from the gag, his swollen wrists and numbed ankles were very strong proofs that he had not dreamed.

He answered the Major's cheery, "Good morning, Miggsy," with a surly, "Go to hell!"

"Oh, come now, Miggsy, old dear. Let's forget all that. You'd have done the same had you been in my place, you know. I couldn't take the risk of having you depart like a thief in the night, as it were. You know what Smithy is; you know what he would have done to me had I been obliged to show up without you, and you know that, sooner or later, he would have got you, too—" He drew his hand suggestively across his throat

"All right," Miggs said sullenly. "I'm willing to forget what happened last night if you are."

"That's a nice forgiving spirit, Miggsy. Now come and have skoff; we ought to be trekking very soon."

Miggs walked stiffly to the fire and poured himself a cupful of steaming black coffee.

"Don't want nothing to eat," he said. "Never do in the morning."

He looked about him uneasily.

"I'm ready to go if you are. Tell yer the truth, Major, I'll be glad when I'm through with this affair; don't half like it. The police are pretty slim devils and once they get after a chap he might as well give up the ghost. Besides, the niggers are acting ugly."

"Oh, no. Jim and Hans are quite chummy this morning."

"Them! I don't mean them—I mean the others."

"But you said last night they wouldn't go on the warpath," the Major interposed mildly. "You said your women told you they wouldn't."

"Suppose I did say that? What about it? What I said last night ain't what I know this morning. And I know niggers. Any man who trusts one is a bleedin' fool. They ought to have wiped them out last rebellion instead of giving in to them, talking pretty and promising them all sorts of things if they acted good. The only talk a nigger understands is a *sjambok* used hard and frequent.

"Come on!" He walked toward the Cape Cart, the Major close behind him. "Tell your nigger to inspan an' we'll get away. I'll feel safer when I've handed the stuff over to Smith."

"I'm going to leave my outfit here with Jim," the Major explained and climbed into Miggs's Cape Cart.

Miggs looked at him suspiciously, then, climbing into the driver's seat, looked around as if to satisfy himself that the contents of the cart were intact.

"What's them doing here?" he growled, pointing to some blankets carefully arranged as a cushion on top of a large box.

"They're mine," explained the Major. "I'm planning to have a nap on the way to meet Smith, and you wouldn't expect me to sleep on the dirty floor surely."

"You mean you're going to stick close to the stuff, don't yer?" Miggs sneered. "All right. Get in, Hans."

The half-caste jumped beside Miggs, sticking out his tongue at Jim, and, responding to the lash of the whip, the mules swung round and cantered down the road.

Jim ran after them; watched them cross the river bed, make the steep bank on the opposite side and gallop full tilt across the veld in the direction of Lion's Head Kop; watched until the Cape Cart was only a cloud of dust floating lazily upward. Then, hanging his head despondently, he returned to the camp, frightening a flock of birds which had swooped down to feed upon the grain which littered the ground about the Major's Cape Cart.

He sat down dejectedly on a boulder, cursing himself for having permitted his baas to play the game alone—whatever game it was his baas would play. And so engrossed was he with his self-condemning thoughts, that he did not notice a party oil warriors creeping stealthily upon him.

When he did observe them it was too late.

WHEN MIGGS pulled his mules to a halt close to the base of Lion's Head Kop, the Major was apparently fast asleep, although a few minutes previously he had been peering cautiously ahead and had been able to get a very good idea of the lay of the land. Also he had seen Whispering Smith seated on a rock talking to a big, red-bearded man. Their horses, hobbled, were grazing nearby.

"You're late, Miggs," Smith said irritably. "You ought to have been here two hours ago. What delayed you?"

"That's a hell of a way to talk to a man what's taken all the risks to make you rich," Miggs grumbled.

"Answer my question," Smith snapped.

Miggs flushed. He was not drunk now and he resented the tone of Smith's voice, resented, too, his own lack of self-assertion.

"If you must know," he said very slowly, childishly withholding the information as long as he could, "I met a friend of yourn."

"A friend of mine," Smith exclaimed apprehensively. "Who?"

"Sssh!" Miggs put his finger warningly to his lips. "You'll wake the little darling. He's in there," he indicated the interior of the Cape Cart with a jerk of his thumb, "asleep."

"Who is it, you fool?"

"Why, the Major, of course."

"The Major! You blasted fool! What did you bring him here for? Deemster, watch—"

The big Dutchman was tugging at his revolver which had in some way caught in the holster, and Smith turned to run for shelter as the Major rose to his feet, a revolver in each hand, his monocle firmly in place.

There was no need of his drawled command; Miggs and Hans tumbled from the wagon in their eagerness to get farther away from the revolvers. Deemster, knowing the Major's skill with any kind of firearms, immediately forgot his own revolver in his anxiety to follow the example of Hans and Miggs and reach high. Smith stood as if petrified, trembling violently, almost nauseated by the threat of firearms.

"Sit down, all of you," said the Major.

They obeyed him, sitting in a row, facing him.

"You. Deemster! Unbuckle your revolver and throw it here. Careful, dear man. My right trigger finger seems to have the palsy and I don't think you can afford to lose much blood. Ah, thanks! Now yours, Miggs. Strangely my left trigger finger has the same complaint as the other, so you will— Ah, thanks, again. Your knife, Hans, and be very careful how you throw. Give you five quid if you can throw it so that it'll stick in the hub of the wheel."

Hardly seeming to take aim, Hans threw his knife with an under-arm jerking motion. It sped swiftly to its mark and hung quivering.

"I don't think I'd like to have you for an enemy, Hans," the Major said, "so I'll pay my debt. Help yourself to a fiver from Mr. Smith's pockets—he is the rat-faced, black-suited gentleman. He owes me two hundred and fifty pounds, so that's all right."

Grinning, Hans rose and, indifferent to Smith's blasphemies and threats, went through that man's pockets, helping himself to five gold pieces. Smith gazed as if hypnotized at the Major's guns and seemed powerless to stop him.

Hans returned to his place in the line. The Major got down from the Cape Cart, careful to keep the men covered all the time.

"I don't want to crow, Smithy, old horse," he drawled, "but, 'fess up, now, you have lost your bet, haven't you?"

"Blast you, yes. But what's your little game? Better join me."

"Still got that old refrain running through your bean? Well, I'll tell you what my little game is. I'm going to tie you all up in one nice bundle and deliver you to Trooper Reamy at Two Tanks."

"Hell of a lot of good that'll do," Smith sneered. "You can't prove anything; you don't know anything, as a matter of fact, you only suspect."

The Major sighed. "I know—but, you'll pardon me, I know a hell of a lot and, somehow, I think that Sammy Miggs, here, will turn Crown evidence any day to save his own skin. Wouldn't you, Sam?"

"Me split on a pal!" Miggs said indignantly, but his eyes glinted hopefully. "I'd hang first."

"I think he protests too much, don't you, Smithy?" the Major said dryly. "You know, Smithy—I wish you wouldn't wear so many diamond rings, deuced bad form, pardon the digression—as I was saying, Smithy, or about to say, your great weakness is choosing such idiotic confederates. Why, they're all absolutely hopeless. Look at old Deemster there; ferocious to look at, I grant you, but then, so are Chinese dragons. Miggs here is another prize. Trouble with Miggs is he thinks he's clever.

"What's that, Smithy? Don't whisper to Deemster— terribly rude of you, really. Speak up, dear lad."

"I was saying," Smith said, endeavoring to take his eyes from the revolvers and failing, "that the sooner you take us into Two Tanks the better I'd like it. It's blasted hot here and the mosquitoes—"

He shook his head so violently that his helmet dropped off.

"You're acting deuced queer, Smithy, Must be delirious; no mosquitoes here. However, perhaps I'd better not take you to Two Tanks after all, as you're so eager to go. Think I'll escort you all to Portuguese Territory. It'ud be a merry jape and doubtless I could find an official *you* couldn't bribe to take charge of you. Yes, I think I'll do that."

"I don't think you will, Major."

"No? Why?"

"If you'll look closely at the rock to your right, at the marula tree over there and the clump of grass to your left—I won't ask you to turn your head to see what's behind you—you'll understand."

Much against his better judgment, but impelled to do so by the note of triumph in Smith's voice, the Major—with one eye, as it were, on his prisoners—looked at the rock, at the marula tree and at the clump of grass, and as he looked the monocle fell from his eye, and his jaw dropped. For he saw three rifles all leveled at him, he heard the ominous clicking of four bolts being closed.

"The fourth one's "directly behind you," Smith said maliciously.

"Jove!" the Major exclaimed admiringly. "You're clever, Smithy."

"Then we lower our hands and you raise yours?"

The Major hesitated. He thought for a moment of bluff-ing it out; by threatening to shoot Smith he could, perhaps, make that man order the others to surrender. But what then? Even if the bluff worked he couldn't handle eight men—four would be plenty. On the other hand, if Smith called his bluff, he couldn't shoot the man in cold blood. Even if he did, undoubtedly that would be his last act on earth; there would be no chance of all four missing him. Life was sweet, and so—

"All right," he said, threw down his revolvers on the ground and raised his hands above his head.

As he did so the four men came out from their places of concealment and closed in on him, holding their rifles at their hips. Two of them the Major had met before, the others were young, beardless Dutchmen with apparently, no great liking for the job.

"Bind him," ordered Smith.

"Let Hans do it," bellowed Miggs. "He had his nigger bind me last night. And Hans can tie a knot he nor nobody else can't untie."

Smith nodded and Hans, full of self-importance, quickly and expertly trussed the Major up.

"Get ready to trek," Smith ordered, "We'll start as soon after noon as possible."

The men scattered; some to get their horses which they had tethered out of sight on the other side of the kop, others preparing skoff, while Miggs, taking Deemster aside, questioned that man regarding the division of the spoils.

Smith stood over the Major, his heavily booted foot upraised, feinting to stamp on the bound man's face.

He started to say something to his captive, then, notic-ing that Hans, who had retrieved his knife, was standing nearby, addressed him. "I'll give you all the Major has if you can hit his helmet with your sticker."

Hans laughed, showing broken, discolored teeth. This was his day of easy pickings. Again the knife sped to its mark and the Major's helmet, pierced by the weapon, leaped from his head, the knife just grazing his skull.

Quickly Hans emptied the Major's pockets then ran, laughing exultantly, to help one of the men whose horse had broken loose from its hobbles.

"You're damnably clever, Smithy."

"You think so, eh?" Smith's tone was a husky whisper, his eyes blazed triumphantly. "But do you realize just how clever I am? I think not. But I'll tell you; it's my turn to talk now. I've outguessed you from the start. I gave you credit for possessing brains—and you have some. I told that mouthy fool, Miggs, just enough, knowing that he would jump to conclusions and talk to you. Miggs thought he was being damned clever, but he only did just what I thought he would do when I hit on this scheme to get even with you. And so you put two and two together and made—five.

"First you saw me talking with Miggs on the train—although I told you the pleasant lie that I did not know him—then I said, casually, that I had a little business to attend to in this district. That alone would have been sufficient, for you were sure to discover that Miggs was the Ophir Mine transport rider, but Miggs, thinking you were in with us, talks some more and what was simply conjecture became a certainty. So you camp at the ford and wait for Miggs to come along."

"If I hadn't come here with Miggsy," the Major remarked pleasantly, "you would have been in the soup."

Smith rubbed his hands together gleefully. "That's where I showed superior brains. Until he had crossed the ford, swung off the road and headed this way, Miggs was a law-abiding man. You didn't have a thing on him. You knew that—and so did I. I knew, too, that you couldn't resist playing a little joke and gambled that you would come along with Miggs, under cover, just as you did.

"And so I let you hold me up—just for the pleasure of seeing your expression when my men held you up. I don't, think you appreciate my cleverness, Major, but you should. It's your own brand."

"But I do, I assure you," the Major said earnestly. "And now you've got me, what are you going to do?"

"A favorite trick with the niggers," Smith said maliciously, "is to strip a man naked and leave him bound on the top of an ant-hill with a piece of honey on his chest."

The Major shuddered; he did not doubt that Smith would do just that if the whim took him. Then he said, contemptuously, "I always suspected that you had native blood in you, Smith. That explains a lot of things."

Smith's face was contorted with rage, but he said in a calm, quiet voice, "That's a damned lie, Major, and you know it—also you shall pay for it."

The Major was sincerely apologetic when he said, "I'm sorry, Smithy. That was a caddish thing to say, but you shouldn't threaten such fearful things, really."

Then he began to laugh loudly. "Dear me," he gasped. "I'd almost forgotten. You've been deucedly clever, but you've overlooked one thing—a very important thing, too."

Smith looked at him suspiciously. "What's that?"

"Ask Miggs—oh, this is too funny—ask Miggs where Jim, my Hottentot servant, you know, is."

Smith turned with a snarl. "Miggs," he shouted angrily. "Come here."

But Miggs was in deep conference with the other men and did not hear.

"Miggs, you fool!" screamed Smith. "Come here, I say."

Ana now Miggs, his face convulsed with anger, came slowly forward, the others crowding close behind.

"What d'yer want, Smith?" he asked sullenly.

"Where in hell is the Major's servant?"

"We left him at the ford with the Major's Cape Cart and stuff. Why?"

"Why!" Smith nearly choked with rage. "Why didn't you tell me?"

"You never asked me and I didn't think to tell you. What about it?"

"What about it? Why, you damned fool, he's probably at the mine by this time with a letter from the Major. The monocled dude," the Major bowed mockingly, "is always writing letters to someone. First thing you know there'll be a posse from the mine after us. You damned fool."

"Oh, stow your gab, Smithy." Miggs turned to the others.

"That settles it, don't it?" he asked.

They nodded agreement, the big man, Deemster, exclaiming, *"Allehmatig,* yes. Let's go!"

Without further word, ignoring Smith, Miggs and Hans climbed into the Cape Cart and drove off. The others, all except Deemster who came close up to Smith, mounted their horses and waited expectantly.

"Bring my horse, you big oaf," Smith ordered. "We'll leave this crook here, and I'll make Miggs pay for his sauce later." Then, as the Dutchman did not move, "Well, why in hell are you standing there for? Bring my horse here."

"Not so, Boss," Deemster said slowly. "Here you stay, too."

"What?" Smith took a step forward, and struck Deemster full in the face with his clenched fist.

The Dutchman took the blow stolidly, but when Smith would have struck again he caught the man's wrists in a grip of iron and, apparently unconscious of Smith's kicking struggles, bound them loosely together with a piece of rein.

Then, picking him up as easily as he would have a child, Deemster placed Smith on the ground beside the Major and lashed the two men's feet together.

"So!" he grunted in satisfaction. "Too long you have treated me like a dog, Smith. In your saloon you were boss, but here—you are only a *verdoemte roinek*. For once we others are boss and perhaps, if the niggers or the hyenas come this way before you can get loose, we will always be boss. And we will be rich, yes. For there," he nodded in the direction taken by Miggs with the Cape Cart, "is much gold, and your share is—nothing.

"There is the half-caste's knife—you can reach it, not? With it you can cut yourself free. The Major's revolvers I also leave you. When you are free, you can shoot him or knife him—it is all one to us. But take care—it may be that he will knife you."

Then Deemster mounted his horse and, leading Smith's, galloped swiftly away with the other men.

For fully five minutes Smith shouted curses and pleas, threats and promises of great rewards after the departing riders; his voice was accompanied by an almost continuous peal of laughter from the Major.

Finally, exhausted, they were both obliged to desist, and the Major said quietly, "You'd better try to free yourself. We can't afford to waste any time; hyenas are always hungry. You ought to be able to slip your hands out easily."

As Smith struggled violently, he continued, "This is funny, isn't it? Damon and Pythias, David and Absalom weren't bound together as closely as we!"

"I can't get loose," Smith panted, great beads of perspiration sticking out on his forehead.

"Then we'll hitch over to my helmet so you can get the knife."

Laboriously, painfully, they did this, and after many fruitless attempts Smith managed to get the knife held firmly between his knees. The rest was easy and in a few moments he stood up, a free man.

He stood for a moment trying to decide what course to pursue. He looked at the Major and ran his thumb down the keen edge of Hans's knife.

Then, coming to a sudden decision, he stooped quickly and cut the Major's ankles loose.

"Stand up," he snarled. "I'm going to take you in with me to Two Tanks."

As the Major obeyed, stretching himself lazily, he said with a chuckle, "I hope you're a good walker, Smithy, and can do without grub for at least twenty-four hours. There's a long trek ahead of us, but we ought to be able to make the ford by sundown—at least we can drink there. And I'm curious to know what you expect to do with me—going to try to frame a charge of murder or arson or something?"

"Never mind that—walk," growled Smith, prodding the Major with the point of the knife.

The Major's eyes gleamed.

"If you do that again, Smithy," he said quietly, "I'll leave you. Somehow I don't think you can run very fast or far.

I rather think that I could manage to get my hands free after a while."

"I won't do that again, Major," Smith exclaimed in alarm. He was a city man and the veld and its people were a mysterious menace to him.

Seeing this the Major was quick to seize his advantage. "Suppose you cut my hands free," he said, and when Smith commenced to threaten, sat down and said stubbornly, "I won't move a step until you do."

Smith hesitated.

"After all," went on the Major, "this seems to be stalemate, old horse, doesn't it? There's nothing you can do to me now that you haven't done; and there's nothing I can do to you. I'll promise to stick by you until we're out of this mess. And anyway," seeing that Smith was wavering, "suppose we run across some lions, or other objectional insects—or they run across us! We'd be in a nice pickle, wouldn't we? That is, unless you have got over your fear of firearms. And you haven't, have you?"

"No," Smith admitted, "I haven't. All right, Major. I can't get out of this mess without you; the gold's gone and neither of us'll see it again. But Deemster and Co. will see me, blast 'em. So we'll call this a draw and keep a truce until we hit the *dorps* again."

"Agreed," said the Major. "My word upon it. But don't expect me to be chummy with you, Smithy."

Smith did not answer, but silently cut the rope with which Hans had secured the Major's wrists.

The Major massaged his arms for a few minutes, then, picking up his revolvers, dusted them carefully with his handkerchief and thrust them in their holsters.

"Come on," he said finally and led the way toward the ford.

He had only gone a few hundred feet when he stopped with an exclamation of annoyance.

"What now?" Smith asked irritably.

"I forgot my bloomin' monocle. Wait a half a mo'."

He ran back and, finding his monocle after much searching in the dust, fixed it in his eye and hurriedly rejoined Smith, his face beaming with contentment.

SMITH WAS in poor condition. The sedentary life to which he was accustomed was not good training for a forced march over the veld in the blazing heat of the sun. He was very hungry and thirsty; his feet hurt him, and he constantly stubbed his toes.

So the trip to the ford took them much longer than the Major had estimated and it was nearly sundown when they came to the river. Here Smith, with one last spurt, ran eagerly to the pool; nor would he wait until the Major had dug a hole in the sand close by so that the water could filter through. Brushing the surface scum away with his hand, he plunged in his head and drank the stagnant, tepid water until the Major forcibly restrained him from drinking more.

After he had slowly drunk his fill the Major climbed up to where he had camped with Miggs the previous night, expecting to find Jim sleeping peacefully.

But the Cape Cart, the mules, Jim were gone!

There was plenty of evidence to show why they had gone. Trampled grass, broken bushes, naked footprints, a broken *assegai,* the plumed headdress of a warrior—all told the story only too plainly. And the spoor of the Cape Cart led straight toward the setting sun.

"Smith!" the Major called, his face drawn with anxiety. "Come here, quick."

"What's the matter?" Smith asked him suspiciously.

"There's been a party of warriors here—they've taken Jim."

Smith looked about apprehensively. "Do you think," he whispered fearfully, "there's any around here now?"

The Major shook his head impatiently. "No! They're far away by this time. I'm going after them."

Smith clutched at his arm. "No, you're not. You're going to keep to the agreement we made back there. We stick together until we're out of this mess."

The Major's face lighted. "You mean you'll come with me? That's bully of you, Smith."

"No. Like bleedin' hell I'm not coming with you. If the niggers have gone that way—we're going this. Come on."

"No, Smith. I'm going after Jim. You're safe now. Follow the road and you'll be at Two Tanks siding before moon-rise. Here—take this revolver."

Smith waved it aside in alarm. "You've got to come with me," he said doggedly.

"I can't, man. Don't you see—?"

"I see that you think more of a bloody nigger than you do of a white man."

The Major shrugged his shoulders. "Have it that way if you like. As a matter of fact, I do—when the nigger's Jim, and the white man, you."

He turned away abruptly and followed the track of the Cape Cart at a quick gait.

Smith looked after him, then afraid to go on alone, afraid to stay where he was, he took the only course possible and ran after the Major.

They went on and on in silence, the Major constantly having to slacken his speed in order that Smith might keep up with him.

After nearly an hour's painful trekking the sun set and the Major, knowing that very soon the veld would be in darkness, had almost decided to go on alone when, topping a slight rise, they came in full sight of a small party of warriors.

"Do as I do, Smith," the Major said quickly and, calmly kneeling down, tightened his shoes laces. Then rising, and feigning to see the oncoming warriors for the first time, he half-turned and, waving his arms, shouted as if to a large force concealed in the bush growth behind him.

The warriors halted as one man, then turned and fled.

The Major laughed boyishly; he laughed again, bitterly, as Smith rose slowly, trembling to his feet.

"You haven't any guts at all, have you, Smith?"

Then he held up his hand, silencing Smith's hot retort, as the thudding of hoofs and the rattle of wheels sounded above the yells of the retreating warriors.

A moment later his Cape Cart came into view! Jim was driving it and, sitting beside him, was an imposing warrior.

"Baas!" Jim cried exultantly. "I'm all right, Baas. It's me! Jim! Don't shoot."

He brought the mules to a halt and springing out of the Cape Cart, ran to the Major. "

"Come, Baas," he said excitedly. "This time I play a game. My friend Magato is in the Cape Cart. He is chief of all the black dogs in this country; he would speak with you. He wants you to be his mouthpiece and talk to the peace-maker for him. It is not his fault that some few of his young men went on the warpath. A white man—that white man whose servant I beat yesterday—gave them much gin. That is all! Tomorrow they will have sick bellies and be greatly afraid. Some of them captured me and took me to Magato. It was his son who was beaten by the half-caste, Hans, and he remembered—I must tell Baas Reamy that. He ordered them to let me go. Also he called them fools. And all this day, Baas, we have been driving from one *kraal* to another, calling drunken warriors fools. I, too, am a peacemaker," Jim continued breathlessly.

"A peacemaker, indeed, Jim," the Major agreed solemnly.

"Well!" It was the sneering voice of Smith. "What's your nigger gabbing about? Do I have to stay here while the conceited ape—?"

"If it hadn't been for Jim," the Major began curtly, but broke off and said, "What's the use of talking to a man like you?"

NEXT NOON the Major's Cape Cart drew up outside the quarters of the mounted policeman at Two Tanks. Jim and the Major jumped down and joyfully greeted Reamy who had come to the door of his hut. Then they all turned and watched Smith painfully climb down. Whip seemed broken, but the Major knew that the man's unnatural silence and apparent acceptance of a situation distasteful to him were only on the surface. A puff adder is not harmless until it is dead!

"Is the Southbound train in yet, Reamy?"

"No, Major. It's due any minute—ought to have been in and gone three hours ago."

"And have you the power to deport an undesirable?"

"Yes, why?"

"Will you take my word that this fellow, Smith, is an undesirable?"

Reamy smiled. "I know he is—I don't need, your word for it."

"And you'll deport him?"

"I'll take a chance if you advise it."

The Major sighed with relief. "Fine! I was wondering how he'd get back to Kimberley, but if he's deported the Government pays his fare, doesn't it?"

Just then a whistle sounded up the line.

"There she is," exclaimed Reamy. "Come along, Smith."

"Wait a minute," interposed the Major. "I want to show him something. I shouldn't, really, but I don't want to be hard-hearted, and he'll enjoy his trip to Kimberley much more. I'll tell you all about it later, Reamy."

He nodded to Jim who went to the Cape Cart and lifted to the ground, one after another, six sacks of grain.

"Watch, Smith," said the Major. "This is a sort of grab bag—nothing up my sleeve, you see."

He opened up one of the sacks and plunging his hand into it brought out a gold ingot. On it was stamped in large letters:

GOLD FROM OPHIR

From each of the other bags the Major produced a similar bar and piled the six neatly against the wall of Reamy's hut.

Smith's eyes shone maliciously. "Do you mean," he whispered, "that you took that stuff from Miggs, and he doesn't know it?"

The Major nodded.

"In the dark watches of the night, so to speak, and with my own little hands the deed was done."

"The fools!" Smith swore. "Inside a week they'll come crawling to me for money and they'll get—"

"Take him away, Reamy," the Major said wearily.

And as the policeman, having had dealings with the Major before, hurried off with Smith, anxious to get him safely on the train, so that he could return and hear the story, the Major called, "And, Smithy, I'd call this check, wouldn't you? And don't forget you owe me two hundred and fifty quid. I'll be down to collect it before long!"

THE HEEL
OF ACHILLES

WHISPERING **SMITH** chuckled with malicious joy. And that was strange, for he had little or nothing to laugh at in these days.

Smith was no fool, save in the sense that every man was a fool who defies man- and God-made laws. No fool could have held the whip hand over the countless number of rogues who flocked to South Africa in the early days of the gold fields and diamond mines. Indeed, far from being a fool, Smith was one of the cleverest men in the Dark Continent and, had he chosen other paths than those of blackmail and murder, corruption and bestial debauchery, it is quite possible that he might have become prominent in the country's politics and a respected leader of a young nation's government.

But there was some perverted mental twist in his make-up which led him to turn his natural attainments, his highly developed executive ability and genius for organization, into crooked channels; instead of the plaudits of honest men and women, he preferred the sycophantic flattery and servile homage of South Africa's most undesirable citizens—most of them fugitives from the police courts of their own countries.

Here, in the little office at the back of his Kimberley saloon, Smith had books filled with clippings from the newspapers of the world which would be sufficient to cause the arrest and conviction of at least ninety per cent. of the "Wanted" men and women of South Africa. Some few of these were now leading exemplary lives—were paying Smith blackmail for that privilege—and were endeavoring to wipe out and make an atonement for past misdeeds. But the majority were ably carrying out their earlier promise and, fostered by the loose morality of the country, were giving free rein to their particular criminal attainments.

And all paid toll to Smith, giving him a large percentage of their dishonest earnings. Punishment came swiftly to the man who dared to hold out. All looked to him for advice, took their plans to him for his final O.K. and blindly obeyed his commands. At least that had been the case until the past few months. Now he was conscious of a feeling of unrest among his henchmen; the spirit of rebellion was strong among them; they were deserting him as rats are said to desert a doomed ship.

He did not give way to panic, but acted swiftly. Some men he rewarded liberally, others were arrested and sentenced to long terms of imprisonment as a result of information given by Smith; still others died suddenly, violently and mysteriously.

And so for a time Smith's organization was saved, but— it has been said that he was no fool—he sensed that it could not last much longer and concentrated all his efforts on making his own position impregnable to all legal attacks and to revenging himself on the Major, the monocled dude, who had been responsible for his, Smith's, present precarious position.

Now it came to him that success was in sight and he lost no time in reviling himself for the fact that he had overlooked the obvious line of attack for so long. In the beginning he had made the mistake, as so many other men had done, of underestimating the Major's ability. He had thought that that man's continued success, first as an I.D.B., then as his antagonist, was due purely to luck and not to the Major's cleverness. But it did not take Smith long to discover that his first estimation of the seemingly lazy, brainless Major was altogether wrong and he had immediately changed his tactics. But he had not gone far enough.

Always in the past he had sent men to get the Major

who were, to say the least, not gentlemen; not men of refinement and culture; not men whom the Major could accept as his social equals. In each case Smith's tools had been men of apparent uncouthness; some had possessed a superficial culture, it is true, but, for the most part they were cunning degenerates, that was all. Able and willing to kill, yes, but quite incapable of meeting the Major on his own ground, on equal terms; they had been men whose appearance and conversation shouted "criminal."

What Smith wanted—the man who could settle the Major—was one who could play a Roland to the Major's

Oliver, who was sort and equally able to disguise his real intentions by a bland, inane exterior.

And that man had, at last, been found.

Smith rose and opening the door leading to the large barroom, stood looking intently at the couple seated at a table in a far corner of the room.

Presently the girl, raising her head, saw Smith and winked broadly, then patting her companion lovingly on the cheek, she whispered something in his ear, laughingly eluded his attempt to grab her, and joined Smith. The man rose and with a set face, and a dignity which some drunken men affect in an attempt to prove to themselves and others that they are not drunk, followed her.

"Don't you, know," he said gravely, addressing Smith, choosing his words with care, "that you are guilty of a great impertinence? My word on it. How dare you steal my, my—er—girl?"

He twirled the long, well-waxed ends of his black mustache and, swaying slightly, frowned.

Smith frowned.

"Come in," he said, jerking his head to indicate his office, "and we'll talk it over, man to man, you know. I have some stuff in there that's worth drinking. Not the rot I keep for fools who have to drink out here."

The man's frown vanished.

"Lead on, brave heart!" he cried. "I'm with you. Good-by, little one. It's most ungalland of me, of course, but when it comes to a choice between good whisky and a lady—why, lead on, Ganymede!"

The girl tossed her head indignantly but suppressed the hot retort which came to her lips. They would have been unheard had she uttered them, for Smith and her late companion had entered the office and Smith had closed the door with a bang.

Telling the stranger to seat himself in the only chair the office boasted, Smith produced glasses and a bottle of whisky. Extracting the cork, he poured out two drinks.

"Here's how!" said Smith.

"Cheerio," said the stranger and, drinking, wiped his lips daintily with a handkerchief.

Several more drinks quickly followed the first, but Smith poured the drinks and his glass was a trick one, inasmuch as, when full, it contained no more than a thimbleful.

They drank in silence, save for the brief toasts, and in between whiles Smith scrutinized the stranger carefully.

"Le's have another," the stranger said thickly after the sixth drink had gone the way of the first. "I'm—hic—bloomin' dry."

Smith laughed harshly.

"Blast it, no!" he said in his deadly quiet voice.

The other looked at him wonderingly.

"Oh, you're one of those—hic—quar—qua-el—angry drunks, are you," he exclaimed in deep disgust.

"No! I'm not drunk, neither are you."

"Of course I'm not drunk," the other expostulated. "I'm as shober—sober—as a—hic—judge. Then w'y won't you le's 'ave another drink. Come on! Le's have another. Two good fellows drinking together, but not getting drunk. What could be fairer than that? Come on!"

Smith shook his head, a gleam of amusement in his eyes.

"Why not?"

"I've poured out six drinks for you, and it's expensive stuff. And what have you done with it?"

The other patted his stomach.

"No," contradicted Smith in answer to the pantomime. "Of the six drinks you've had I should say that at least half of them you spat out into that large handkerchief of yours and you spilled most of the other three on the floor."

The other straightened up with a smile and, taking a large handkerchief from his pocket, rolled it into a ball and tossed it into the waste-paper basket.

"What a discerning chap you are," he murmured. "But I'm not quite blind. I've seen glasses like yours before, you know. And now what?"

"That's what I would like to know, Mr. Frank Slaughter."

The other started slightly.

"You know my name?"

"I know quite a lot about you. I know, for instance, that you were born in this country—your mother was Dutch—and you lived here until you were seventeen; then you went to England. I know that you held a commission in the —th Lancers and were cashiered for conduct unbecoming a gentleman. Cheating at cards, wasn't it? I know that you've tried your hand at blackmailing and professional gambling—and failed. I know that you came to Africa three months ago, expecting to make easy money; and so far you've failed."

"You know quite a lot about me, Mr. Smith, don't you? And it's all true. 'Specially the bit about making easy money out here, and failing. All right, proceed."

"There's one thing I don't know—" Smith hesitated.

"Astounding!" bantered Slaughter. "What is it? As you know so much, I might just as well tell you the rest."

"No one—" Smith watched Slaughter very closely—"put you up to spy on me? You are not in the pay of the police, are you?"

Slaughter's merriment was obviously unfeigned.

"My God, no!" he gasped.

"Then why did you come to my place with Martha and pretend to be drunk?"

Slaughter laughed again.

"Well, Martha's a pretty little filly, but rather obvious, don't you think? I met her quite by chance, don't you know—only I don't think it was chance on her part—and she seemed so very anxious for me to come to your place and plied me very prettily with questions and drinks. So I was very much on my guard. I spilled quite a lot of liquor on the floor near our table. And then you came on the scene—and you, too, were quite obvious—and so I remained on guard. That's all."

Smith looked relieved.

"You've heard of me?" he asked.

"Quite a lot, and not much to your credit. You must have been quite a chappy in your day. But your day, they say, was yesterday."

"Who says that?" Smith snarled the question.

"Everybody. I was talking to a chap in Jo'burg, name's Spencer, 'Brick' Spencer. Heard of him?"

Smith had. Spencer was a professional gambler who never lost except when players seemed to be suspicious of his phenomenal good luck.

"Well," continued Slaughter, "Brick told me that your days were over. He said you'd be serving a long sentence on the Breakwater before the year was up."

"He did, did he?"

"Yes. I was glad of the information. You see I had thought of offering you my valuable services. I thought we could get together for our mutual advantage. But now—" Slaughter shook his head doubtfully. "I think I'll have to join forces with the Major instead."

"The Major!" Smith managed to convey a world of contempt in his voice. "That damned fool! Look here, Slaughter, I can use you—and against the Major. You think my days are numbered because a few rats get the wind up them. Look here!" He tossed several bank books, which he had taken from a nearby file, on the table.

"But they mean nothing," Slaughter said slowly, almost disguising his amazement at the amounts he saw credited to Smith's account. "Money's all right, of course, but you can't spend it at the Breakwater."

Smith unlocked his ponderous safe and took from it a large book. It was labeled "Black Sheep." Opening it, he showed Slaughter the dossiers of many of Kimberley's prominent men—every walk of life was represented there; magistrates and police officials, doctors and clergymen, mine owners and politicians—and they were all paying tribute to Smith.

"You see," he said with a chuckle, "if I go to the Breakwater, they'll all go, too. And they don't want to go; so they'll leave me alone."

"Yes." Slaughter agreed. "You're safe until someone takes it into his head to burgle this office of yours and destroy this evidence. I've half a mind—"

"To do it yourself?" queried Smith. "Don't be a fool, Slaughter. These are only duplicates. The originals are in a place known only to myself and one other who has been instructed to make them public should anything happen to me. They'd have killed me long ago if it hadn't been for that. But, now, if you want to make money, easy money and lots of it, I've got a little job for you; and it won't get you in wrong with the police, either."

"What is it?"

"Get the Major," Smith said tersely.

"You mean kill him."

Smith waved his slender white hands impatiently.

"That's too easy. Kill him if you can't do anything else, yes. But I want him sent to the Breakwater, so that he'll spend the rest of his life wishing himself dead and cursing me."

Slaughter winced at the vindictiveness om Smith's voice.

"You don't like this Major chappy, do you?"

"Like him! But never mind about that. Will you do it?"

"What's it worth?" Slaughter countered promptly.

"If you can carry out my plan successfully and frame him so that he'll be sentenced to a long term, I'll give you ten thousand pounds. If you find that you have to kill him, five thousand. And I'll give you a thousand down, as soon as you agree, for expenses."

Slaughter whistled softly.

"The Major comes high, doesn't he?" he said. "All right, I'm your man."

"Good. Then let's have a real drink to bind the bargain."

He got himself another glass and poured out two drinks.

"Here's how!" said Smith.

"A pleasant trip for the Major!" Slaughter said mockingly. "And now, suppose you tell me your plan."

"According to the last reports which have come to me," Smith began, "the Major's on a hunting or trading trip in Matabeleland. He may be doing most anything. But the most important fact is that he's up there; and they're having trouble with the natives, expect a rebellion to break any day. All right! I'm going to send you up there on a hunting trip. You can shoot, I suppose?"

"Of course this is only a revolver, but I—"

Smith cowered at the sight of the revolver which Slaughter had produced, it seemed, from the air, so quick was his draw.

"Put it away!" he screamed hoarsely. "I hate the sight of the damned things."

Slaughter laughed, tossed the weapon carelessly from one hand to the other, then returned it to its holster which was strapped under his armpit.

"I was going to show you how well I can shoot," he said, "but now you'll have to take my word for it."

"I'm prepared to," Smith said nervously.

Smith looked at him curiously. "Why, man, you're as white as a sheet. I should have thought that a chap in your line of business would have found a lot of use for a gun. It'ud be easy work holding you up. Wonder no one's ever done it. Well, they say every man has a weak spot."

"You see that the Major doesn't find yours," Smith growled. "That's all you have to worry about. Now—"

"BAAS," SAID Jim the Hottentot, "I do not like this country."

"No, Jim?"

"No, Baas." Jim looked apprehensively at a crowd of natives who were lined up in front of the thorn stockade which encircled their *kraal,* watching with hostile eyes the white man and his servant outspan the sixteen oxen which drew the cumbersome wagon.

"No, Baas," Jim repeated emphatically. "It comes to me now that this is a foolish thing we do. Is there no way out?"

"There is no way out, Jim. Who can recall a word after it has been spoken? Who can recall an *assegai* after it has left the hand?"

"No man wishes to recall a word, Baas, unless it is a fighting word, and then it can be softened or, if needs be, a spear thrust will add point to it. And who cares to recall the thrown *assegai*—if it hits the mark?"

The Major laughed shortly and Jim, fill of his grievances, continued mournfully.

"Truly, Baas, each day that we travel away from the white man's fort at Victoria, brings us nearer to death. *Tchat!* That I should live to see my Baas playing the part of a missionary; telling these Matabele warriors to cease fighting the Mashona dogs. Does not the baas know that the Matabele are a fighting race? Blood of the Zulus flows in their veins. By fighting they live, by fighting they will die. I tell you, the only way to bring peace to this land is for the white man to wipe out all the Matabele, leaving not one man child alive; aye, it would be well, too, to kill all the women lest one of them give birth to a man child who, in the years to come, will become a thorn in the white man's foot."

"You're a bloodthirsty villain, Jim," chuckled the Major, "and perhaps you're right. Yet, I have undertaken this task and I will not turn back. But I would not keep you. Take one of the horses—take both, using mine as a pack—take all the provisions you desire, and go. I will not think less of you; neither will I remember it against you when we meet again."

"*Tchat!* The Baas speaks folly. How could Jim, the Hottentot, live in this country of the Matabele, alone? Could I get back to the fort? I think not. Too many warriors with spears stand between me and it. Besides," he added, "who would take care of my Baas, if I went?"

As he talked Jim had been very busy, and, now that all the oxen were unyoked and turned loose to graze with the two hobbled horses, he lighted a fire and with a nonchalant air commenced preparing his baas's evening meal.

Soon coffee was put on to boil and brickvelds were baking in the red embers of the fire.

But for all his pose of unconcern Jim was very uneasy and he kept close to the Major, who was seated on the *disselboom* of the wagon, smoking lazily.

And still the natives of the *kraal* did not move, did not speak. Once, when the Major took out his monocle and polished it with a bright, red silk handkerchief, one of the men uttered an astonished *"Au-a, baba!"* then giggled nervously as the others looked at him disapprovingly.

"Baas," whispered Jim presently, "have you noticed that these men all carry *assegais* and some have guns? Have you noticed that no children or womenfolk are to be seen?"

"I am not blind, Jim," the Major said curtly, "and it would be well if you did not watch them too closely."

"I try not to look, Baas, but I feel their eyes upon me and my body turns toward them."

"You're not afraid of them, Jim?" the Major said banteringly.

"Afraid of them, no, Baas. I'm only afraid of one of them."

"Which one, Jim?"

"I don't know, Baas. But one of them has an *assegai* which he plans to stick in me. It's that one I'm afraid of."

The Major laughed, knocked the ashes from his pipe and refilling it asked Jim to bring him a brand from the fire.

Quickly Jim obeyed and, as he was holding the blazing brand to the Major's pipe, something—an *assegai*—flashed between them and stuck quivering in the *disselboom*.

Jim stood as if transfixed; his face changed to a greenish-gray color and the pupils of his eyes dilated as he looked at his baas.

Then he relaxed and grinned slightly as the Major said quietly, "The coffee is boiling, Jim; the veld-bricks should be baked by now. Take the *assegai;* it will serve to rake them out of the embers."

Watched intently by the warriors, Jim released the *assegai* with a slight tug and raked the veld-bricks out of the ashes with it. As he did so the warriors burst into roars of uncontrollable laughter, aimed apparently at the man who had thrown the *assegai.* Somewhat of the tired look dropped from the Major's face, his jaw muscles relaxed and his face assumed an almost inane, vacuous appearance. And then the thrower of the spear, a sub-chief judging by his well-polished head-ring, walked with mincing step to the wagon; the warriors followed close behind him.

They were all splendidly proportioned men, nearly all standing six feet, with broad shoulders, mightily muscled arms and shoulders and slender waists. Jim looked almost a pigmy in comparison but, judges of man-flesh as they were, the warriors all looked at him something akin to respect. They knew that there was great strength in Jim's squat, ungainly frame, his long, gorilla-like arms and barrel chest.

"*Sauka bona, umlungu*—good day to you, white man," the chief said insolently. "But a little while ago death passed very close to you and your black dog."

The Major looked up at him, looked full into his eyes for several minutes. The warriors shifted uneasily from one foot to another.

"So?" questioned the Major at last. "But it passed me by. I do not forget that."

He took his long hunting knife from its sheath and toyed with it absently tossing it from one hand to another. Once he sent it spinning up into the air, turning over and over, and when it came down he caught the blade between his strong, white teeth.

"What are you doing here, white man?" the chief asked.

"Who asks?"

"This is Kawiti's *kraal.* I am Kawiti."

"Does Kawiti question a guest before he has eaten?"

"You are not a guest. No one asked you here. The road is before you. Go!"

He pointed to the narrow trail which wound its snake-like way across the veld.

"If I go," the Major said slowly, "how will Kawiti hear the things I have to say to him? Maybe I have word for him from Lobenguella, the king, may his fat ever increase."

The chief looked undecided. He knew, or at least was fairly certain, that the white man could have no message for him from the king. That dreaded autocrat was many miles beyond Kawiti's *kraal.* And yet—

"There is the road," he repeated. "Go!" But his voice had lost much of its self-assurance.

The Major rose to his feet and stretched himself lazily. The warriors looked at him in surprise. They had thought him a small man and soft with fat. But now they saw that he was as tall as the tallest one among them. And the fatness—truly the clothing of white men deceives the eye! And the Major inflated his chest they stared in open admiration.

"It is getting late, Jim," the Major said, "but this chief, this Kawiti, has stopped up his ears; he will not listen to the words I have to say to him. Therefore we will go on until we come to the next *kraal*. Perhaps there we will find this one's overlord; perhaps there we will find a man who is not altogether a fool. Inspan, Jim."

"Wait, white man," Kawiti said hurriedly. "The next *kraal* is a full day's trek from here. Stay here. I will listen to what you have to say."

"You hear, Jim," said the Major wearily. "Kawiti is kind; Kawiti is wise. He says we may stay here." Then to the chief, he said, "When I have eaten I will talk to you."

With that he climbed up into the wagon and sitting down on the seat ate the veld-bricks and drank the coffee which Jim brought to him.

When he was finished, Jim ate, noisily and with great gusto. The Hottentot had no fears now. For a time he had doubted his baas's ability to cope with these proud, warlike Matabele, knowing that their king was ready to make a stand against the encroachments of the white men; knowing that they were each day advancing farther into the heart of a strange and hostile country. But now, his absolute confidence in the Major, his baas, the man who could do no wrong, restored, Jim acted something like a spoiled child showing off before his less talented playmates.

Presently the Major got down from the wagon seat, rifle in hand, and sitting in a campchair which he ordered Jim to get out of the wagon, he motioned to the warriors to come nearer to him.

They obeyed, somewhat unwillingly, crowding behind Kawiti.

"The thing I have to say to you, Kawiti, and to you people of Kawiti, is a thing quickly told; it is a thing that I have told at many *kraals* in this land. I am the mouthpiece of the man who would see you dwelling at peace with the whites. You have heard of him?"

"Who has not?" said Kawiti. "What is his word?"

"He bids you walk softly, lest evil come."

Kawiti laughed.

"The white men are few," he replied. "The warriors of Lobenguella shake the earth with their tread. What evil, then, for us?"

"One white man—armed with this—" the Major patted his rifle—"can kill many warriors from afar, and no evil can come to him."

"*Tchat!* We, too, have the fire-sticks."

"That is true," the Major said softly. "But give me an *assegai.*"

One of the warriors handed him a long throwing-spear and, taking it, the Major rose and threw it with all his might at the stump of a nearby tree. It stuck into it, hung for a moment and then fell to the ground.

"Was it not a good throw, Kawiti?" he asked.

"A stripling could do better, white man," the chief said scornfully.

"What? Am I not stronger than a stripling, stronger, even, than many of you?"

"It is not by strength that skill with the *assegai* comes, white man. It is our weapon. It is to us as is our hand."

"True," assented the Major. "Now think of this."

He picked up his rifle and looked around for a mark. Some three hundred yards away were four calabashes, each about as big as a man's head. They made poor marks in the fading light and against the red dust of the veldt. Swiftly the Major brought his rifle up to his shoulder and fired four times in rapid succession, and each of the calabashes jumped a little at the impact of the bullets.

"*Au-a!*" the warriors murmured.

"And as quickly," commented the Major dryly, "four warriors would die. Could your warriors do that with guns?"

Kawiti did not answer and the Major continued, "No! But the warriors of the white men could do that—and better. The gun is to them as is their hand. Also they have the gun of many voices (the Maxim). Have you heard of that?"

"Aye."

"Then you know the folly of 'going out' against the white men. That way is death. Then here is the rest of my word to you: Give me your guns; I will give trade goods for them, as a token of peace between us."

"Have the white men none of their own that they seek to buy ours? Or is it that you fear the evil that will come to you?"

"Not so. We have no need of them, but in your hands they are a menace—to you and not to us."

"I have known white men to lie," Kawiti commented skeptically.

"True. But I do not lie. See! Each gun you give me in trade I will break before your eyes so that it will be of no use to any man. What say you?"

Kawiti turned to his warriors and they discussed the proposals in excited whispers.

Then the chief turned to the Major.

"It comes to us, white man, that you have a cunning tongue. Show us then what you will give for a gun."

At the Major's commands Jim handed from the wagon a quantity of trade goods which the Major arranged in little heaps, each heap containing a few yards of gaily colored cloth, a hunting-knife, a coil of brass wire, colored beads and a mouth organ.

"For each gun," he said, "all this." He indicated one of the heaps.

"Who is there to stop us from taking all that you have, white man, and yet keep our guns?"

"I would have something to say; a few warriors would die before I died. And you would be the first, Kawiti. Also Lobenguella would hear of it and, I think, he would be angry with the people of Kawiti for striking before he gave the word. Certainly the man whose mouthpiece I am would be angry. But such talk is folly. What say you? For a gun—all this."

It was the mouth organ which proved the deciding factor for, after hearing Jim blow a succession of discordant chords, every warrior present was anxious to become the owner of one.

Kawiti was the first one to make the trade, salving his conscience and fears as he landed the Major his gun, an old muzzle-loader, by saying, "You speak true words, white man. These things are of no use to us. They make a noise, true. But noise will not kill a man. Now an *assegai*, or this knife! *Au-a!* We can serve Lobenguella well with such."

And he stepped back, playing his mouth organ, to make way for the next man.

As each gun was passed over to the Major, he took it by the barrel and brought down the stock with all his force on a large rock, completely ruining it. Soon all the guns had been traded and the air was full of strange melody as the warriors, enveloped in colored cloth, danced their way to the huts, leaving the Major and Jim alone.

"It was well done, Baas," said Jim, indicating the heap of broken guns.

"True, Jim. Their fangs are drawn, but they still have their claws. And the country is big, the people many. I am the only one and—"

"Yah," Jim assented glibly, "and I am your servant. Let us sleep now, Baas. We have trekked far, today."

"Yah. Sleep, Jim. Presently I will sleep, too. I am very tired."

In a few minutes Jim was fast asleep, coiled up in his blankets near to the fire.

The sun set, darkness came. At the *kraal* all was revelry; the weird cadences of mouth organs with the sharp, insistent *pom pom* of drums, the shrill voices of children and the melodious contraltos of women, the loud, drunken laughter of men, the lowing of cattle and the bleating of goats. In the distance a hyena screamed weirdly and was answered by the furious yapping of the dogs at the *kraal;* the Major's horse whinnied fretfully; Jim tormented by a nightmare, cried out once his sleep.

The fire died down, flared up again when the Major threw on a fresh log.

The darkness began to lift. The moon rose above the horizon flooding the veld with light, throwing its glamor upon everything, making the squalid *kraal* a city of enchantment. The moon rose higher, the shadows shortened. At the *kraal* all was still, quiet was everywhere. And the Major, feeling inexpressibly lonely, could not sleep, but paced back and forth between the fire and the wagon, despondent, self-condemning.

"I've been a damned fool," was the burden of his thoughts. "I've wasted years playing the giddy Robin Hood, and, save for Jim, the dear old fraud, I've been alone all the time, chased from one bloomin' place to another. First the police, then Smith and the police; and now natives, Smith and the police." Then, "Bah! I'm talking like a bally two-year-old. I've had a rippin' time, take it by and large. And this job's a big one; the Big Man himself gave it to me, asked me to do it. And, if I come through, my little I.D.B. affairs will be forgotten. He didn't say so. He's too clever a man to try to drive that sort of bargain. Perhaps he'll make me a Native Commissioner. That would be rippin'. But I can't ward off this uprising. No man can. Jim's right. The Matabele are fighters. I've been a damned fool."

And so back again to the beginning.

In those long hours of the night he lived over his many adventures with the police, laughed at some of them, regretted others. And his regrets were always concerned with memories of man he had thought his friends, who had double-crossed him. When he thought of Whispering Smith, his jaw set. He regretted nothing that he had done to Smith, save that he had not hit the man hard enough. He had taken some of Smith's wealth, had been responsible for the breaking up of Smith's infamous organization. But that was not enough. Smith still lived; he was still a power for evil. He, the Major, had let slip many opportunities of breaking the man, solely in order to indulge in his fondness for practical jokes. That was all he had done to Smith, he thought bitterly; played practical jokes on him.

Again and again the thought of his loneliness came to him, and his desire for the companionship for his own kind.

The moon passed on. The morning star glowed brightly, faded, then in the east the sky glowed, a golden light.

The *kraal* awoke. Women passed by the wagon, on their way to the water hole. Cattle and goats scrambled through the narrow gateway in the stockade, followed by shouting, naked herdboys and yapping dogs. Coils of smoke floated lazily in the still morning air above the rooftops.

The eastern sky was a pallette on which a painter had cunningly mixed his colors. Jim awoke just as the sun shot up over the horizon, a ball of blazing brass; all other colors vanished, burned into nothingness.

"We trek at once, Jim," the Major ordered curtly.

Jim looked at him in amazement, surprised at his haggard appearance and the harsh tone of his voice. Ordinarily the Major was exceedingly fastidious about his personal appearance. Clean shaven, his nails well manicured, his clothing in good condition, the Major was very much the dandy, and indeed, many men, on first seeing him, called him a monocled dude, and believed their judgment of him correct when they heard him speak. He generally looked like a man specially turned out by a Bond Street tailor.

Even when on a hunting trip, campaigning on the veld, matching his wits and courage against beasts and men, the Major never relaxed, never allowed himself to get careless of dress and habits. But now his eyes were ringed with dark circles, his hair tousled, his face covered with a stubbled growth. His riding boots were lusterless, his shirt and riding breeches badly rumpled and soiled. His monocle was not in evidence.

"The Baas is ill," Jim muttered. Then aloud, "Will not the Baas eat before we trek?"

"No. We eat when we come to the river. I wash before I eat, and so do you."

He uttered this last with some of his old spirit and Jim, forgetting his fears of the moment, whistled gaily as he inspanned the oxen and tied the horses to the tailboard of the wagon. Soon all was ready. The Major climbed into the wagon and threw himself down on some blankets at the back, under the canvas cover, and in a few moments— even before Jim with much shouting and cracking of his long whip had got the oxen under way—had fallen asleep.

When he awoke some hours later it was with a feeling of alarm, for the wagon was not moving and there was no sound. Still heavy with sleep he made his way to the front of the wagon and silently took in his surroundings. The horses were grazing contently nearby; most of the oxen were down, chewing the cud.

Jim had outspanned on the bank of a wide, swiftly flowing river and, sitting on a boulder, not ten yards away, his hands held up on a level with his ears, was a white man. Just behind him sat Jim, holding one of the Major's guns gingerly in his hands, resting the muzzle of it in the small of the white man's back.

And, somehow, at that moment, the Major's fit of despondency vanished.

"What's the *indaba*, Jim," he called out cheerfully.

Jim and the white man looked up with a sigh of relief.

"You slept long, Baas. There is no trouble, save that this man does not understand my talk, nor I his. I told him that you were asleep and when he tried to climb into the wagon, making much noise, I took the Baas's gun and made him sit down where he now is. Now you are awake, I can put this down."

Jim crossed to the wagon, holding the rifle at arm's length, and put it down on the wagon seat as if he were afraid it might go off.

"I say," said the stranger, "do I have to sit here much longer with my hands up in this fool fashion?"

"No, old chap." The Major chuckled and fumbled for his eyeglass. "But, pardon me, you really looked awfully funny."

"Maybe it seemed funny to you; but it was not funny for me, I assure you. My arms feel quite dead, and my nerves are quite upset. That ugly old native was trembling so that I was afraid he'd squeeze the trigger and then Slaughter would have been slaughtered, as it were."

"Oh, no, Mr. Slaughter—I take it that's your name; mine is St. John, at your service, sir. No, the gun wouldn't have gone off. You see, it's not loaded."

Slaughter looked rather sheepish, removed his helmet and thoughtfully stroked the back of his head.

"Most astounding," he murmured. "To think that I should be bilked by such a trick."

He was a good-looking chap, eyes set a little too close together, perhaps; the mouth loose-lipped with a suggestion of feline cruelty about it. But the Major, looking on the man as a heaven-sent companion, saw no flaw in him. Slaughter, slim, of medium height, fair skinned (the kind that never burns or tans), his black hair parted exactly in the middle and his mustache well waxed and magnificently curled, was so absolutely his own sort; always possessed of an admirable sangfroid, equally at home on the hunting field or at social functions, and always playing the game for all it was worth, accepting victory or defeat with the same splendid indifference.

The Major, exuberant from the despondency of the past night, felt that with Slaughter for a companion he could subdue the whole country, that his task of persuading the Matabele to keep the peace was a childishly simple one.

He beamed joyfully as Slaughter came up to him, his right hand outstretched in greeting.

"You know, St. John," that man said, "I'm jolly well glad you woke up at last."

The two shook hands with formal solemnity and self-conscious embarrassment.

"What are you doing here?"

"I'm lost, dear chap. I came up here thinking to do a little trading and hunting, mostly hunting. Of course I don't know anything about the bally natives, or the country either, for the matter of that. But one learns. And no one told me that the natives were getting out of hand, so to speak. Anyway, I brought two natives with me, one to act as general help, don't you know, the other to be my interpreter. And this morning they got the wind up them, said they were afraid of the Matabele, and bolted, taking my wagon and mules with them. I tried to get on the track of the blighters, but the first thing I knew I was lost—went round in two pretty circles. Damned nuisance, the whole affair. At least I didn't pay the beggars their wages; some small comfort in that. But it's rather hard on you, old chap. Of course, if I'll be in your way, or anything, I'll go on. I'll catch up to those two Johnnies, sometime. And when I do—"

He laughed cheerfully.

"I'm not going on any hunting trip," the Major said gravely. "I'm just going from *kraal* to *kraal,* trying to persuade these black beauties to give up their guns. You see this is a new country, the whites are thinly scattered, and if the natives ever take it into their heads to rise there'd be blood murder and sudden death and all that sort of thing. Terrible situation, really. It'ud be bad enough if they were only armed with spears, but if they had guns— And they have! I'd like to quarter the rotter who sold guns to them! Why, it'ud be the deuce and all of a job to stop them. It's a risky game, but rather sport, and I'd like awfully to have you with me. Each *kraal* is a gamble. So far I've won, but at the next, or the next, maybe they won't listen to me and will put a period to my chat-chat with an *assegai.*

"Back there—" he indicated the country through which he had passed—"it's fairly safe. I've destroyed most of their guns and put the fear of God into them. If you want to go back to the fort in Victoria, it's only a three days' trek; you can take my horse and Jim for a guide. You ought to be able to make Victoria safely. Only," he hesitated, "only, you know, I rather hope you won't go."

Slaughter held up his hand.

"Go!" Of course I won't go," he said. "I came up here to hunt, and I'm going to. While you are talking to the native beggars I'll snoop around with my gun. Maybe I'll be able to hit something."

"That's rippin'," the Major exclaimed and then, over-come with confusion, said hastily, "But what a rotten host I am. You're hungry?"

"Ravenously so."

"Then Jim shall get skoff while I shave and so forth, what."

TWO WEEKS later the Major, Slaughter and Jim again camped on the banks of the river, a four hours' trek from the *kraal* of Kawiti.

They were on the return trip, heading for the Settlement at Victoria. The Major was in high spirits, for his mission had been more successful than he had dared hope even in his most optimistic moments, and he attributed not a little of his success to Slaughter's presence.

"Your moral support, old chap," he had insisted when Slaughter laughingly waved aside praise, "won the game. I had lost my vim until you came on the scene, felt the job was too big for me, and you bucked me up no end.

Besides," he added, "even if you can't shoot for little apples, you looked awfully impressive, don't you know, standing on guard by my chair."

And now Slaughter was swimming in the river, stemming the swift current with lazy, effortless, yet powerful strokes.

The Major and Jim were seated on a boulder watching him.

"Baas," said Jim suddenly, "that one is no fool. In some things he is like you."

"Yes, Jim?" The Major was not interested.

"Yah, Baas. Like you, he pretends to be what he is not."

"Yes?" The Major tossed a pebble at the swimmer. It hit the water near to Slaughter's face and he looked up at the Major, his white teeth flashing in a friendly grin.

"Yah," Jim continued. "He is no fool; but he is evil!"

"*Tula,* Jim. Hold your tongue."

"It is true, Baas. You say he does not understand my speech, yet, whenever the Baas talks to me, he listens. Aye, and he understands, too."

Something came into view, midway between the two banks, floating on the surface of the river. Jim pointed to it and the Major was about to shout a warning of, "Crocodile!" to Slaughter when he saw what Jim had already seen, that it was only a waterlogged trunk of a tree.

"Now watch, Baas," Jim said, and raising his voice he shouted in the vernacular, and fear was in his voice, "O-he, Baas Slaughter! Come out—quick! A crocodile! A crocodile!"

Slaughter looked up as one might who hears shouting and wonders what it is all about. Then he turned and swam farther out into the stream, in the direction of the drifting log. This he suddenly saw, and taking it for a crocodile, turned, and with a mighty splashing made for the shore at great speed.

Not until he heard the Major's laughing shout, "It's only a log, Slaughter, take your time," did he slacken his speed and gasp, "What a do! I thought it was a bloomin' croc."

"There, Jim," the Major turned to the Hottentot, "are you satisfied?"

"No, Baas." Jim shook his head. "A man can hide many things, he can pretend to be what he is not. But his eyes, Baas, they tell true things."

But the Major did not hear him.

After the midday meal they trekked again, the Major and Slaughter riding the horses at the side of the wagon, Jim walking near to the two wheel oxen, flourishing his long whip, muttering to himself, cursing the oxen and occasionally turning to scowl ferociously at Slaughter.

"That Jim of yours doesn't like me," Slaughter remarked. "I wonder why?"

The Major laughed.

"He's been with me a long time and we've been through hell together. I—er—think he's—er—jealous."

They rode on. The shadows lengthened. The pace of the oxen was slow but sure and the miles fell behind. After a while, when the sun as low, they saw the huts of Kawiti's *kraal* outlined against the sky. It was then that the Major, riding carelessly, was hit full in the face by a mapani branch which knocked his monocle off into the brush.

Reining in quickly he dismounted; he could see his monocle gleaming in the grass. He stooped to pick it up and as he did so felt a spatter of moisture in both eyes. It was repeated. It was as if someone were blowing a fine spray of water into them. Only water wouldn't hurt, while this—

He uttered an involuntary cry at the intense pain, rubbed his eyes and then looked about him. The veld seemed dim and shadowy.

He groped for his horse, clambered into the saddle and trotted after the wagon. By the time he had reached Slaughter's side again he was totally blind.

"What is it?" Slaughter asked, looking curiously at the Major's contorted face. "What is the matter?"

"I'm blind," the Major replied softly through set teeth. "Back there, when I stooped for my monocle, a cobra spat poison into my eyes. A damned nuisance! Can't see a bally thing. And they burn—my eyes burn."

Slaughter bent over into his saddle toward the Major and looked into his eyes, waved a hand in front of them and then whistled softly. An expression of disappointment, of annoyance passed over his face.

"Isn't there anything you can do? Surely the pain will pass away. The blindness is not permanent?"

"I'll bathe my eyes with milk when we get to the *kraal.* That'll cure them. It'll only mean wearing a bandage for a week, that's all. Are we near the *kraal,* now?" he added anxiously.

"Very near," Slaughter replied absently.

Just then Jim turned and noting the Major's condition, rushed back and lashed at Slaughter with his whip, crying, "What have you done to my Baas? You have—"

"Peace, Jim!" It was the Major's voice. "It was a cobra that did it, a spitting snake."

Jim lowered his whip doubtfully and his face contorted with anger as he detected, he thought, a sneer on Slaughter's face. Then, realizing that speed was all important, he returned to his oxen and urged them on with lash and voice.

A hundred yards from the *kraal* they were brought to a halt. Across their path the warriors of the *kraal* had aligned themselves. They were all, apparently, fighting drunk. Many of them had guns; all carried *assegais*.

They showered the two white men and Jim with stones, bidding them depart quickly. They refused to listen to Jim, and the Major they shouted down in derision, immediately realizing his impotency.

Then Slaughter tried to make himself heard and he spoke the vernacular as well as if it were his native tongue.

At the first sound of Slaughter's voice, remembering what Jim had said earlier in the day—that Slaughter was "no fool, but evil," and that he pretended to be what he was not—the Major stiffened and his hand leaped to his revolver. Then, sighing slightly, he relaxed, his hand falling aimlessly to his side. He was helpless, and he knew it. He was angry at the deceit Slaughter had practiced on him. But sorrow at confidence misplaced overruled his anger and he could not, even now, believe that Slaughter was evil.

And now he had something else to think about.

For a little while the natives listened to Slaughter, laughing at his jokes, and the Major was silently admiring the man's thorough knowledge of native psychology, counting it to his credit, believing that Slaughter's clever talk would end in a peaceful settling of the situation.

"Good man!" he murmured, ready, as always, to give praise, believing that at the proper time Slaughter would be able to explain satisfactorily his duplicity.

And then Slaughter struck a wrong note; he presumed too far and the natives rushed forward with fierce yells.

A cunningly thrown *knobkerrie* hit the Major's horse on the nose and the beast reared and, swinging round, galloped madly across the veld. A less able rider than the Major would have been thrown; even he lost his stirrups at the first mad plunge and was unable to check his mount until several hundred yards distant from the *kraal.* The Major waited, sitting motionless, soothing his horse with gentle taps and a low, tuneful whistle.

Again a feeling of helplessness took hold of him; he was like a blind man in a sea of fog. He did not know what to do. He could go back, guided by the fierce yells. But to what? Or he could go on. And then? He was alone in the world, deserted by the man to whom he had given his friendship; only Jim was left! Jim! Good old Jim! But Jim would not be able to get away from the warriors back at the *kraal;* and even if he did, there was still Slaughter.

"I'm behaving like a bally infant," he said loudly. "There's only one thing for me to do."

He turned his horse, intending to ride back to the *kraal.* His hand again sought the butt of his revolver.

He heard the sound of someone coming toward him on horseback. A moment later Slaughter rode up to him. Their knees brushed. Leaning over, Slaughter took the Major's bridle reins.

"We're goin' to camp on the veld," he said briefly. "Jim's just behind us. I don't think we have anything to fear from the niggers. Come on!"

He tried to turn the Major's horse, but the Major kept a tight hand on the reins. He was listening intently for the sound of the wagon wheels. Presently he heard them.

"O-he!" he called. "Is that you, Jim?"

"Yah, Baas," came the Hottentot's voice. "Go with the white man."

"All right now, Slaughter," said the Major. "Lead the way."

They made camp on a slight rise of ground about a quarter of a mile from the *kraal*. It was a clearing in the mapani bush which encircled the *kraal* and in some nearby rocks was water, stagnant, but still water, left from recent rains.

"When the sun has set, Baas," Jim said, "I will go to the *kraal* and get milk."

"No, Jim," the Major protested. "They will kill you."

"I am going," Jim repeated flatly, "And you—" he turned to Slaughter—"you will take care of my Baas. If anything happens to him while I am gone, death will not come easy to you."

Slaughter did not answer but looked curiously at the Major who sat motionless on the wagon seat, his lips firmly compressed to stifle the moans of pain which sought utterance.

The sun set. Still the men sat in silence. Darkness came.

"I go now, Baas," Jim said. "When I return you will hear the signal we have used at other times. Answer it, Baas." And then to Slaughter, "Remember!"

He tethered the horses to the tailboard of the wagon, threw fresh twigs on the fire and the flames sprang up, making weird, grotesque silhouettes of the three men. Then, taking a canvas water bucket, Jim vanished into the night's shadows.

"Jim has gone, Slaughter?" the Major asked softly.

"Yes."

"Then perhaps you will explain."

"Explain what?" impatiently.

"Why—er—you pretended to be what you are not. Why you posed as being ignorant of natives. You speak the language as well as I do, you know."

"Yes—I know."

"And—er—probably you can shoot?"

"I shot my first lion when I was fourteen; there are not many better target shots than I am," Slaughter said compacently.

"Ah! Then doubtless all the rest of your story was a lie."

"Most of it, yes."

The Major winced. Then his lips set hard, his jaw set in grim lines. For a little while he did not speak. Then, "But I don't see why, unless it was that you were having a game with me. It was that, wasn't it?" There was a wistful note of entreaty in his voice. "Of course you were just spoofin' me." He chuckled. "Oh, it was a regular do! 'Pon my soul, yes!"

"I spoofed you all right, Major, but it wasn't for fun."

"No?" The Major's voice hardened. "Then why?"

Slaughter hesitated a moment, then answered in a clear, cold voice.

"I am in the pay of Whispering Smith."

"Ah!" There was pain and incredulity in the Major's voice.

"You see," Slaughter continued swiftly, with a curious tenseness in his voice, "he offered me ten thousand pounds if I could frame a charge of gun selling to the natives on you. So I came up here, knowing that you were somewhere in this country. It wasn't hard to get track of you. You are quite famous, you know. I planned to meet you quite accidentally, with my Cape Cart and the stuff it contained—guns and a small quantity of ammunition. It doesn't matter how I intended to frame you. I couldn't have succeeded anyway, you being in the Big Man's confidence and doing his work. When my boys deserted me—that part of the story is true; only I didn't get lost—I still had a chance of earning some of Smith's money."

"Yes?" The Major sounded very weary. "You're rather a cad, you know—but—I'm interested. Go on."

"He offered me five thousand pounds if I killed you. It's a big price."

"And very easily earned—now."

"It'll be damned hard!" Slaughter's tone was bitter.

"But why did you wait so long? Why go to all the bother of gaining my confidence and run the risk of being—being found out. Jim suspected you from the first; but I—I was a fool. I accepted you as— Oh, never mind. Why did you wait? Out there there are plenty of rocks and bushes for you to have hidden behind. And you're a good shot. Of course you're a good shot; you fooled me about that, too, just as you did about not knowing the vernacular. You only had to fire twice, one shot for me, one for Jim. Why did you wait? Why do you wait now? There's no risk. I—I can't see."

The Major stiffened. Then, as Slaughter began to talk again, he relaxed.

"It amused me to wait—" Slaughter's voice dropped to a whisper—"to play with you. It was easy to fool you. You so wanted the companionship of the man you thought I was, the man I used to be, long ago, that you never questioned me. But that wasn't the only reason. I was afraid of this country. I knew that the natives were getting out of hand; I knew that, alone, I could never get out of their country alive. They don't like me. A day's trek from Victoria would, I thought, be soon enough to earn Smith's money—soon enough for you and Jim. But now—"

"Yes—now?"

"I wait until Jim comes back."

They did not speak again, but sat in silence, Slaughter staring fixedly into the fire, occasionally turning to look at the Major who sat rocking back and forth, his hands over his eyes.

Several times Slaughter started to speak, then, shaking his head, shut his jaws with a snap.

After a long time, hours long it seemed, they heard fierce yells wafted to them on the night's breeze, coming from the *kraal.*

"I'm afraid they got Jim," the Major said slowly. "I'll wait a little longer. And then, if he does not come, you will guide me to the *kraal,* Slaughter. Jim has never failed me, and I—"

His voice trailed off into silence.

Slaughter rose and busied himself with the horses.

"What are you doing?" the Major called.

"Saddling the mounts."

"Ah! Getting ready to make your departure, eh? That's wise."

A bell-bird *tonked* dismally nearby.

"That's Jim," the Major announced. "If I don't answer his signal he'll think that you've done for me—and it's dark, it must be dark, I can feel it. And Jim has the eyes of a cat— and a knife. You can't see him, Slaughter. He can see you. He'll creep up on you and—" The Major laughed softly. "If I lose, you lose, too, Slaughter."

The other man did not answer but left the horses and came back to the fire. The yells they had heard before sounded again, seeming nearer, louder.

"I can't lose," the Major said suddenly, firmly, and he gave the cry of the "Go-away" bird.

And Jim stepped out into the firelight. Blood was streaming from a flesh wound in his chest, he gasped for breath, but in his hands he carefully carried the canvas bucket within which a liquid gurgled musically. Ignoring Slaughter, he crossed swiftly to the side of the Major, took that man's handkerchief and bathed the Major's eyes.

"Good boy, Jim!" the Major said in relieved tones. "Some of the pain has gone already."

"More pain is coming, Baas," Jim said grimly. "I crept into the cattle *kraal* and wasted much time before I found a cow unmilked, and the warriors saw me, Baas, as I was leaving. The blood lust is on them; they are coming here. They are many and have guns. We are but three, and one of the three is a man of evil."

The yells were close at hand now. The fire burned low.

Vivid streaks of flame cut through the darkness, crisp reports of rifles echoed through the night's stillness, a bullet struck a boulder nearby and its *whee-e-ang* was a menacing portent of the evil to come.

Acting quickly, Slaughter took a tarpaulin from the wagon and with it covered the fire, dousing it with water.

One of the oxen rushed by at a mad, lumbering gallop; a chance bullet had hit it and it bellowed with the pain.

"It is time for us to make a getaway," Slaughter said coolly. "Soon they'll have us surrounded and it'll be too late. The boys who deserted me must have come this way. It's rather funny, Major, come to think of it, that I should be shot at from the guns I have planned to plant on you. At least I didn't have much ammunition. That's why they're not firing, I suppose."

He fired several times into the darkness and was answered by menacing yells. Then silence again.

"They're creeping up on us. Soon they'll rush. Get the horses, Jim."

"Obey him, Jim," the Major said, silencing the Hottentot's heated expostulations.

He finished the task Slaughter had commenced and brought the horses up to where the Major was sitting.

Slaughter made a pad of his handkerchief which, after he had soaked it in milk, he bound over the Major's eyes. "Come on," he said. "Mount! We've stayed too long as it is."

They guided the Major to his horse and helped him to mount.

"I'll ride the other," Slaughter announced. "I'll double up with Jim. Up you get." He boosted Jim into the saddle and gave him the Major's bridle reins.

Jim still clutched the canvas bag.

"Now go," Slaughter whispered so that only Jim could her him. "And take good care of your Baas. He is a man."

"It is well done, Baas," Jim whispered back. "Maybe I was mistaken."

Then, aloud, Slaughter said, "Hold tight, Major! We're off."

He slapped Jim's horse on the flank and stepped back as the Major and the Hottentot rode off.

He listened intently and soon the thudding of horses' hooves told him that Jim and the Major had reached the hard, dusty road and were galloping to safety.

"He won't know I stayed behind," he muttered, "until it's too late to come back. And then, perhaps, he'll understand—and forgive."

The sound of the galloping hoofbeats died away. Slaughter was conscious now of whispering all about him in the bush. For a moment he was panic-stricken and regretted the thing he had done. It would have been so easy for him to have earned Smith's pay—and his hands would have been clean. He had only to have ridden away himself.

Then, as suddenly as it had come, fear left him. He felt as if he had, in some part, wiped out the ugly blots on his record; that he had, at least, not entirely forfeited the regard of the Major. That thought, he found, was very comforting.

But there was still much to do. Because of his crime, part of the Major's mission had been rendered fruitless; he had been responsible for the arming of these natives, and before death came to him—as it surely would, though torture would come first—he meant to see that little or no ammunition was left them.

With great speed he fired all the chambers of his revolver into the darkness and was answered by yells and much shooting. He reloaded and fired again and again. And each time he was answered by a ragged volley.

His ammunition all gone, he climbed up into the wagon, intent on firing off the Major's store, and destroying the rifles. But there was little time for that. The circle of warriors was closing about him. Soon they would rush. And then—

Acting on a sudden impulse, he collected a pile of combustible stuff, saturated it with the oil the Major—comfort-loving dude that he was—carried for his lamp, and set fire to it.

The flames spread quickly, licking hungrily at the dried wood and the canvas top.

He jumped to the ground and reached the shelter of the bush before the startled natives could open fire.

He laughed happily, sure that the fire was beyond control and that the rifles and ammunition it contained would not fall into the warriors' hands.

Then, dropping to hands and knees, using all the veld-craft he possessed, he crept stealthily through the bush. He knew that escape was impossible, but he was determined to postpone capture—and death—until morning and the rising sun!

WITH ONE STONE

YESTERDAY, WHISPERING Smith had come to the conclusion that he had run his course, that the time had come for him to get away from Kimberley—secretly and in great haste—before it was too late. He knew what "too late" meant. For him the words were fraught with terrifying and most uncomfortable complications, handcuffs on his wrists, a long, painful trial—if he escaped lynching—followed by dreary years of dreary labor, hard labor, strictly regulated hours and no luxuries save a smoke on Sundays and holidays.

This conclusion of Smith's was not hastily arrived at; it was not the fruit of momentary panic or a nightmare fancy bred of an uneasy conscience. Smith did not jump to conclusions—he was too methodical and weighed every move. He was not given to panic except, perhaps, at the sight of a revolver; and he most certainly was not troubled by conscience. He did not have one—otherwise he would have died of remorse many years ago.

Neither was Smith a fool; egotist though he was, he at no time credited himself with more power than he actually had. He never endeavored to deceive himself, even if he made a practice of deceiving others.

So he was cognizant of the diminution of his powers, had been for a month past, and had fought with a cunning and courage worthy of a far better cause, to stop the constant lessening of his prestige.

In the little back room off his saloon at Kimberley he had sat day after day, consulting his famous books, his records of nearly every criminal operating in South Africa; pulling strings here and there; summoning this man and that to reason with him, and, when reason failed, to threaten; giving information to the police which inevitably led to the arrest of this man or that in the hope that he could frighten the rest of his tools into line again.

But the strings broke; after a while men refused to obey his summons and the police neglected to act on the information given them.

The word had been passed around among the under-world that the Big Man of South Africa, the man whose dreams concerned the creation of empires, the man who was the Diamond Mining Syndicate, was out to get Smith. Like rats sensing that disaster is about to overtake a ship, the men and women who hitherto had obeyed Whispering Smith in all things, laughed at the whiplash of his whispering voice. They knew that they could no longer look to him for protection and—this was even more important—that his power to punish was diminishing day by day. They knew, too, that eventually Smith would be compelled to seek safety from arrest in flight.

But Smith knew all this, too, and had planned well and wisely for his getaway. He meant to go in a blaze of glory—of a sort. This, being interpreted, meant that he was going to cause a lot of uneasiness among certain officials who were so unfortunate as to have their names in his books. He intended to broadcast all the information he had concerning the past misdeeds of these unfortunates; he was going to publish all the evidence he had which had made it possible for him to levy blackmail on men and women who were seeking to forget the mistakes of youth and were seeking to make amends by being good citizens.

Thinking of all the misery he was going to cause, the disgrace of public officials, the wreckage of many happy marriages, in some part reconciled Smith to his impending flight. Then, too, he was going to leave the Colony a rich man—a very rich man. Actually he was well content to go.

There was only one fly in his ointment—the Major, the monocled dude, was still alive and flourishing. Yet it was the Major who had been the cause of his downfall; it was the Major who had spoiled his plans time and time again, showing Smith that his organization was not omnipotent. It was the Major who had been responsible for the Big Man taking an active interest in Smith's activities.

Smith had sent man after man out with the order "to get the Major." He had gone after the man in person, but had only succeeded in making a laughing stock of himself. And so, although Smith had plenty of money to keep him in the life of voluptuous luxury his peculiar soul required; although the coast was still clear for him to depart well equipped to pursue his nefarious profession in some other country, Smith felt that he had failed.

His desire to get the Major had become an obsession with him, an obsession which unbalanced him and caused him to lose all sense of proportion.

But that was yesterday. Today, this morning, his papers and mail brought him most cheering news.

First: Rinderpest had broken out up north and the natives, blaming the deadly cattle plague on the white men, were on the point of open rebellion. A strong hand was needed to deal with the situation and the Big Man, with his ablest lieutenants, had gone north. That meant that Smith was given a new lease on crime. In the face of the calamity that would follow a rebellion, Smith was small fry; they would leave him alone. And so, relieved of the Big Man's personal attention, Smith could build up his shattered organization and, if the rebellion broke—he meant to do all in his power to insure that it did—he would have time to entrench himself more firmly than ever.

The other item of news Smith found even more cheering. It was in the form of a letter from one of his henchmen, a man who kept a native trading store up north. It read:

> *Dear Smith:*
>
> *The niggers are getting bloody cocky up here. Yesterday a big buck bumped into Captain Grey and swore at him. But nothing happened. The police daren't do anything. They've had orders to treat the niggers gently. The damned fools! However, that's neither here nor there. All I know is I'm going to leave this country. You don't catch me staying just to give a nigger the pleasure of sticking an assegai into my belly. And if I don't get out quick, they'll be yelling for volunteers to protect the women and kids. Hell! I've got enough to do to protect Sam Quinn.*
>
> *But here's something that'll interest you. The Major's here. He's as blind as a bat. It seems that a cobra what didn't have any manners*

spat in his eyes, and when he got to a kraal the niggers wouldn't let him get any milk—which is the only treatment for that—and by the time he got here it was too late. Knowing cobra poison as I do I'm betting that he'll never see again. His Hottentot nigger, Jim, leads him around. Hell! It's funny to watch 'em....

Oh, and here's something else. I heard say that a bloke named Slaughter rescued the Major from the niggers and got killed himself. Ain't Slaughter the chap you sent to get the Major?

Hope it's all right with you, boss—about me leaving here, I mean. Anyway I'm coming. As I said before, no nigger's going to use my belly for a pincushion.

Obediently yours,
Sam Quinn.

Smith chuckled, rubbed his long thin hands gleefully, and again read the part of Quinn's letter which dealt with the Major.

"Blast him," he muttered. "That's better than killing him or having him framed and sent to the Breakwater. I can get him any time I want him now. I'll have him working in the bar for me before I'm done with him; I'll have him emptying suds; I'll—"

Leaning back in his chair, Smith indulged in pleasant day dreams of the sport he would have with his enemy *now that he was blind.* He did not question the truth of Quinn's report. That man had proved his reliability too many times and, fortunately for Smith, was too far away from Kimberley to know how things were with the man he called boss.

After a little while Smith sat up to his desk again and idly examined a package addressed to him in unfamiliar handwriting, endeavoring to guess the identity of the sender. Failing, he cut the string and removed the paper wrapping, disclosing a wooden box with a sliding lid. On the top of the box was a letter. Picking it up he opened it and read:

> *Dear Mr. Smith:*
>
> *Because a very nice little girl is writing this letter for me—I can't see, you know—I can't call you all the names I'd like to. In fact I can't call you any names at all—she tells me that wouldn't be polite. Bally nuisance, what? However, I imagine that you have a very good idea of all the things I'd say if I could. I'm coming down to Kimberley very soon and the first thing I'll do is to instruct Jim to lead me by the hand to your famous resort. And I'm going to have a long, long talk with you. If you're wise, you won't wait for my arrival. But in case you decide to stay, I'm sending you a little present. Better find out how to use it. You'll hear from me again—whenever the spirit moves me.*
>
>

The Major.

Below the signature was written:

> *Mr. Smith, I am only ten. Don't you think I write well? I think you ought to do what Mr. Major says. Isn't it sad that he can't see? I heard my daddy say this morning that Mr. Major always got whatever he went after and that he'd hate to have him for an enemy even if he is blind. With love,*
>
>

Helen Parson.

Smith laughed softly as he came to the end of the letter. The Major's threats had no terror for him, they were amusing. Yesterday, perhaps, he might have quailed at the mere mention of the Major; would have looked for some hidden message in the letter; would probably have made arrangements to leave town at once. But today, knowing what he knew— Bah!…

"I wonder what the fool's sent me," he said.

He removed the lid from the box and collapsed with a frightened gasp, shrinking back in his chair away from the desk. And there he sat, his face ashen gray, staring fixedly at the thing the box contained. It seemed to have an hypnotic effect on him, paralyzing his muscles, making him incapable of movement.

He sat thus for a long time, and then with a sickly smile he reached out a shaking hand and opened one of the drawers of his desk. With his other hand he swept the box and its contents into the drawer which he shut violently.

"God!" he muttered, and rising to his feet walked nervously up and down his office.

Sweat rolled off his lean, hawk-like face, his slate-gray eyes were dilated, his nostrils twitched. He had the appearance of a man who had been subjected to great mental stress, yet the box had contained only a small toy revolver.

Presently a knock sounded at the door.

With an effort Smith regained control of himself, quietly seated himself at his desk and shouted harshly, "Come in!"

The door opened slowly and two men entered, shutting the door carefully behind them.

One was slim, wiry and evidently accustomed to life on the veld. He had the face of a hunter, a cruel, ruthless hunter. His sun-browned face was criss-crossed by many wrinkles, and he moved noiselessly with a cat-like tread. His sandy hair was cropped exceedingly close and his enormous ragged mustache hung over, but failed to conceal, a mouth that was set in a contemptuous leer. He wore the nondescript costume of a prospector, khaki slacks—patched with a weird assortment of cloth, a piece of flour sacking being the most conspicuous—gray flannel shirt, a black, clerical-looking, felt hat and stout hobnailed boots.

The other man was of an entirely different breed. His black, beady eyes were almost hidden from sight by rolls of fat; his long black hair was plastered down with some strong-smelling pomade; his mustache was wonderfully waxed and curved belligerently upward—he twirled it continually with his fat, pudgy fingers. From his chin downward he billowed out, the billows reaching their peak at the waist line which was unbelievably large. It was physically impossible for him to see his own feet, and he gave one the impression that he was leaning back at an angle of forty-five degrees in order to balance the load of his enormous stomach. His clothes were wonderful to behold; Solomon in all his glory might have outshone him, but that is a debatable point.

Smith eyed them both for a time, a mocking smile on his face.

"You sent for me, boss," the lean man said at length.

"Yes," Smith snarled. "I sent for you three weeks ago. Why didn't you come then, Gibson?"

"I was way up country, on the Portuguese border, and I didn't get back until yesterday, boss. So—"

"Don't lie," Smith interposed harshly. "You've been in the *dorp* here for the last ten days. You didn't come because you'd heard that Smith was at the top of a greasy pole with the Breakwater at Cape Town waiting for him when he slipped. You thought that what I said didn't matter any longer; you thought that my jig was up and that you could thumb your nose at me and my orders."

Gibson moved uneasily, shifting his weight from one foot to the other.

"There's no need to get mad, boss," he said placatingly. "I'm here now."

"Yes—you're here now," Smith was very contemptuous, "and pretty soon all the other rats'll be crawling around to lick my boots. You've heard that I'm not a back number yet, not by a long chalk, and you want to get in on the easy money as usual. You want me to plan deals for you, not having the brains to think for yourself. Bah! I've a good mind to tell you to get to hell out of here and shift for yourself."

"Now see here, boss," Gibson's tone was slightly aggrieved, "you're barking up a wrong tree. It may be that I didn't come as soon as I heard you wanted me because the rumor was going around that you were on the skids. That's as may be.

"Just the same there's no reason why I should put my head into trouble; that wouldn't have helped you. But when it comes to planning deals, don't forget that I've put you on to more than one or two myself. Yes; and after I've done all the dirty work you've taken the lion's share of the takings."

"And why not? Can you tell me of one deal you could have brought off without my help?"

Gibson was silent.

"No! Of course you can't," Smith continued excitedly. "If it hadn't have been for me, you—and a hundred like you—would be begging from farm to farm for your day's grub; either that or working for a living."

"All right, let that go," Gibson said impatiently. "I know you're a little God Almighty—you never give us a chance to forget it. The point is, I'm here now and I've got hold of a good thing for you."

"Is that it?" Smith indicated the fat man with a contemptuous jerk of his thumb.

"In a manner of speaking—yes."

The fat man who had hitherto been silent whispered something to Gibson, then waited expectantly, fingering the enormous diamond stickpin in his flaming red tie.

"This," said Gibson, "is *Senhor* José Alvaro, Mr. Smith."

"Charmed," Smith murmured sardonically,

"The honor, it is all mine, *Senhor* Smith"; the man's voice was a piping falsetto, "we shall do pleasant business together."

With a grandiloquent air he took off his sun-helmet—its pugaree was a brilliant green—and made a sweeping bow. Then, straightening up, red in the face and wheezing from his exertion, he continued, "If the *senhor* would permit me to sit, we could talk better."

Smith laughed. "I'm not sure that I want to talk with you and, unfortunately, I am sitting in the only chair."

Senhor José Alvarez looked around the place. Save for the desk, some filing cabinets, a pot-bellied stove and the chair in which Smith was sitting, the office was devoid of furniture. He sighed.

"That is to be regretted," he murmured. "I can not talk standing up and—er—and I have many things of utmost importance to say."

"So?"

"So. But since you are so lacking in the little courtesies one gentleman expects from another, I will go. Come, *Senhor* Gibson."

He turned ponderously and waddled toward the door.

"Wait a minute," Gibson exclaimed hastily. "*Senhor* Smith does not know who you are."

The fat man halted and turned, a smug smile of self-assurance on his face.

"Ah," he purred, "I had forgotten. That explains many things. Tell him, *Senhor* Gibson."

"*Senhor* José," Gibson said hurriedly to Smith, "represents a certain official of Portuguese Territory. He has a proposition to make to you."

"Oh!" exclaimed Smith thoughtfully, looking at the fat man with renewed curiosity.

"Yess-s-s!" said *Senhor* José, nodding his head violently.

Smith turned on Gibson with a snarl. "Why the hell didn't you tell me this at first? Get a chair for the *senhor*—quick."

Like a reproved schoolboy Gibson hastened to obey Smith's order, and returning a moment later with a chair placed it close to Smith's desk.

"That is better!" *Senhor* José lowered himself into the chair with a sigh of relief. He hitched up his trousers so that their immaculate crease would not be spoiled, then, placing his fat hands upon his knees, he looked admiringly at his gaily patterned socks.

At a sign from Smith, Gibson took three glasses and a bottle of whiskey from one of the drawers of the desk.

"You are thirsty perhaps, *senhor?*"

"Truly." The big man took the glass Smith handed him and eyed its amber colored contents appreciatively. "Your very good health, *senhors.*" He drank the whisky at a gulp and looked suggestively at the bottle. "It has the smoothness of honey and—ah, thanks, *senhor.* Again your very good health."

"You have a proposition to make to me, *Senhor* José?" Smith said softly.

"Truly—but it is good to drink. It is hot and talking is very fatiguing."

"It is possible to talk and drink." Smith filled the glasses again.

"You Anglo-Saxons are an energetic race—no wonder you inhabit the earth. But—ah!—do you enjoy life? Now we Latins wait, believing that all things will come to us.

And if they don't come, what matter? At least we have enjoyed life."

Smith moved impatiently.

"A morning spent thus," continued *Senhor* José drowsily, "with charming companions—" he bowed to Smith and Gibson—"and such refreshment as this for the inner man… is worth more than much wealth or—" he closed his eyes—"or the acquisition of more territory for one's country."

Smith started slightly; he had the feeling that *Senhor* José's eyes were open and that, from behind their fatty ambush, they were watching him intently.

"Is it of that you wished to speak to me, *Senhor* José?"

"Perhaps—yes. It is a pity you are so direct, because I must be direct, too. But then your countrymen are direct. They go into a district unasked and without consulting the inhabitants thereof add thousands of square miles of territory to your so great empire. That is all right. A black man has no rights—of course not. But other nations have—my nation has." *Senhor* José's eyes were wide open now and fixed unwinkingly on Smith.

"You mean?"

"I mean that when they annexed the district up north—your Big Man was responsible for that—they trespassed on our ground. But what could we do but wait?"

Smith looked impatiently at Gibson, but when that man raised a warning finger, he changed his mind and did not give vent to the anger he felt.

"Sometimes," the fat man's voice droned on, "direct methods recoil on the heads of those who use them. It is so up north. The blacks are considering taking back by force what your people took from them by force. And then—and then we who wait will come into our own."

"Maybe," Smith said tersely. "But the rebellion may never get under way, or, if it does, will be put down by quick and very direct methods."

"True," sighed *Senhor* José. "That is why I have come to see you."

"Yes?"

"Truly. If, after I have talked with you, you agree to do certain things, I shall give you five thousand pounds for—for a bottle of whisky, say. It is very good whisky and of that value. But it must be understood that I—*Senhor* José Alvarez—give you that money. No official would countenance such a thing—officially. You understand that, of course?"

"Of course," Smith agreed." Then—?"

Senhor José closed his eyes again, he leaned back in his chair and clasped his hands across his stomach.

"The rebellion must break."

Smith nodded. That was in line with his own plans.

"And it must succeed—at least to the point of making your people evacuate the country."

"That is a big order."

"And the price," *Senhor* José countered swiftly, "is not that big? And if the blacks had rifles and plenty of ammunition, is it not possible that they would be victorious? They outnumber your people—ten, twenty, maybe thirty, to one. Under those conditions it is not possible that they would fail."

"Quite true," Smith agreed softly. But he knew that it was not numbers alone, or numbers well armed, that determined the course of such things. Neither did he point out to *Senhor* José that, should the rebellion be successful, the existence of such a large force of armed, victory-drunk warriors would be a very dangerous problem for the rulers of Portuguese territory to solve. He was not concerned with that. All he wanted was a breathing spell, a chance to rehabilitate himself before the return of the Big Man and his lieutenants. And now he saw his way to do that—and he was to be well paid for it.

"Of course," *Senhor* José continued hastily, mistaking Smith's silence for disapproval, "we shall give you all the assistance and men you require. The real officials who are back of it must not appear, however. The Government would not countenance it. But I have been very cautious. Indeed I am acting entirely on my own initiative. Should things go wrong, the blame will all be mine. But, should we succeed, then will I notify my superiors and—who knows?—great honors will be mine. And yours, too," he added as an afterthought. "You'll do it?"

"Not so fast. Where is the money?"

"Here," *Senhor* José took an envelope from his vest pocket, "here is a check for the full amount, we trust you, you see. And here is a bill of sale which you will sign. You will see that it is simply a record of the fact that you have sold me a gold claim for five thousand pounds. Of course, I was only joking when I said I would give you that much for a bottle of whisky. You sign this—" he waved the bill of sale in one hand—"and then I give you this." He flourished the check.

"Give it to me," said Smith and signed.

"That is good, *senhor.*" The fat man carefully folded the signed bill of sale and put it in his pocket. "Now here is the check."

Smith laughed harshly.

"If I were not an honest man, I needn't do a damned thing and still keep your money, *Senhor* José."

"Ah! But you are honest, I hope, *Senhor* Smith. And if you are not— I have known men to die. It is very easy! Yes, very easy to kill a man. With a knife, now, or a revolver. Better a knife, perhaps. A revolver is so direct—but we should not talk like this, no. We are good friends. You are honest, of course. Is it permitted that I should know your plans?"

"Not now," Smith said shortly. "Not until I have deposited this."

"Ah, cautious man. Then tonight?"

Smith nodded.

Senhor José Alvarez rose to his feet. "Until tonight, then, *Senhor* Smith," he said and left the room.

"Well, boss," Gibson exclaimed exultantly, "isn't that steering easy money your way? Do you split fifty-fifty with me?"

"No, you fool!"

Gibson looked dejected.

"At least you'll give me a ten per cent. rake-off?"

"I don't give you a penny—unless you earn it."

"Why, boss, I have earned it, haven't I? Didn't I steer the greasy pig to you? I might have collared that check myself. The fool would have given it to anyone who claimed to be you."

Smith sneered. "You think so, do you? Well, let me tell you that *Senhor* José Alvarez has a damned sight more brains than you have. He's no one's fool."

Gibson was unconvinced.

"At any rate he gave it to you quick enough; and any fool would have known that you don't intend to do anything to earn the money. You couldn't if you tried."

"That's where you make a mistake, Gibson. That money is going to be earned."

Gibson's eyes opened wide with astonishment.

"But how, boss? You can't do anything like that. Do you know what'll happen if the niggers do go on the warpath? Bloody murders and torture—and there's women and kids up there. But you're only fooling, boss."

"I don't fool, Gibson. You ought to know that by this time. What Alvarez wants me to do, I was going to do anyway—for my own sake. I want the Big Man and his crowd out of the way for a time—and that's the best way I can think of to work it."

"But it's treason, boss. We'd get shot if we're caught!"

Smith winced. "You won't get caught. Or if you do it'll be your own damned fault. How many men can you lay your hands on right away—by tonight?"

"City or veld men, boss?"

"Veld."

Gibson thought a moment. "Ten, boss."

"So many?"

"Yah! A bunch came in yesterday from a labor recruiting trip."

"Oh!" Smith's face brightened. "Did they have any luck?"

"No. They tried to go up north, but the Big Man had given orders to keep them out."

Smith nodded.

"Fine! Have them here tonight at eight sharp. Tell them to get ready for a long trip."

"They may balk at the job, boss. I don't like it much myself."

"You wouldn't," Smith snarled. "But you'll do as I tell you—and so will they."

"Shall I tell them what you want them for?"

"No. Not now—or at any time. You can tell them that I've planned a labor recruiting trip for them. And I have. I believe in killing two birds with one stone." Smith smiled and silenced the questions Gibson was eager to ask with a wave of his hands. "And to make them feel better," he continued, "you can tell them that I don't want to cut in on their takings. Or, if you like, you needn't tell them that. You can keep my share for yourself."

Gibson whistled softly. A successful labor recruiting trip meant big money. The mines sometimes paid as much as ten pounds a head.

"I don't know what your plan is, boss," he said, "but I'll put it through for you."

"I knew you would," Smith said softly. "You'd cut your mother's throat for a shilling. Now get to hell out of here."

As the door closed behind the departing Gibson, Smith opened the drawer of his desk in which he had put the Major's present and, averting his face, took hold of the toy revolver. As his fingers closed on it, he trembled violently. Then, with a supreme effort of will, he forced himself to look at it and toyed with it, tossing it from one hand to the other. Presently he laughed nervously, threw the revolver into a wastepaper basket and poured himself out a stiff drink.

"Blast the Major!" he muttered as he sat the empty glass down on the desk. "I'll make him pay for that, too."

"BAAS," SAID Jim the Hottentot, "I do not like this country."

He flourished his long whip and urged the eight mules drawing the Cape Cart to a better speed.

His baas, the Major, glanced sidewise at him and smiled.

"I suppose," he said slowly, "that presently you will say that you are afraid?"

"Damme, yes!" In the two words Jim almost exhausted his English vocabulary, then he went on in the vernacular, "Yah, baas, and why not? Strange things happen up here. Think of it. First the baas goes to many *kraals*, obeying the order of the big white chief, preaching peace. The baas makes many friends among this people whose one delight is war. Aye, they listen willingly to his talk of peace. And then, as we return again to the white man's *dorp* at Victoria, a snake spits its poison in the baas's eyes. That would have been nothing, save that when we went to a *kraal* to get milk that the eyes might be made well, the warriors there set upon us. And all because a white man—whom the baas thought his friend—had put guns into their hands and thoughts of war into their heads. *Au-a!* An evil man, that. May he—"

"Don't forget, Jim, that he died—and I live."

"I have not forgotten, baas." Jim's eyes glowed. "He in some part made amends. But the evil was done. My baas's eyes are still sick: he has to hide them from the brightness of the sun."

The Major took off the smoked glasses he wore, but quickly replaced them.

"They are getting better, Jim," he announced cheerfully—the veld ahead had been but a blur to his vision. "In two or three days—"

"The baas has said that for many days past," Jim grumbled.

"If you are tired of being my eyes, Jim—"

"*Au-a*, baas!" Jim exclaimed reproachfully. "Just the same it would have been better had we stayed at Victoria. There were white men who are fighters and who know the baas and—"

"And white men who are not fighters and think your baas is a fool," the Major interrupted softly.

"True, baas. Yet, as I have said, there we were safe, well fed and sleeping on soft beds. Here," Jim indicated the monotonous sea of bush veld with a disconsolate sweep of his whip, "death is everywhere."

"That is why we are here, Jim. There are white men, with their women and children, living in this district who do not know how near death is to them. They must be warned. And better that I who am as one blind should ride to warn them, than one who is able to see and fight."

Jim grunted his disgust and murmured softly, "My baas is worth a hundred women, and the child is not yet born— be it woman child or man child—that is worth his little finger. But he is my baas and what he orders—"

"There is no question of orders between us two, Jim."

Jim nodded sagely. "That is what the hunter said to his favorite dog, baas. That is why I obey."

He grinned, cracked the whip, and with well chosen curses abused the off-lead mule for its laziness.

They trekked for a while in silence; the Major occupied with his thoughts; the mules—they were a new team and not yet broken to Jim's driving—demanding all of the Hottentot's attention.

Jim kept them going at a hand-canter, cleverly swinging them around thick clumps of bush, his keen eyes straining to pick out the course ahead; the trail was unbroken and he had to use caution. But no matter how many times he turned to the right or to the left—and once he made a sweeping, half-mile detour to avoid a patch of ground which was covered with gigantic termite heaps, and honeycombed by ant-bear holes—he always came back to his original course, heading for a thin, almost invisible thread of smoke on the horizon. To a white man, even a veld-wise man, that column of smoke would have been wholly invisible.

"We will be there by sundown, baas!"

"Good, Jim. Can you see any *kraals?*"

"No, baas. But there are *kopjes* to the right and to the left of us, before and behind. Doubtless there are many *kraals* in those hills; and in each *kraal* there are warriors who would like to give their *assegais* our blood to drink."

"Our task is an easy one, Jim. We have only to keep our blood to ourselves."

"As easy, baas, as to dam a flooding river with the fingers of your hand."

The Major laughed. "Where is the sun, Jim?"

"If I stood facing the west, baas, my shadow would fall behind me and be no bigger than myself."

"Ah!"

"Take the reins, baas, the course is even for a little while and the mules will not turn. I think they smell water. I will get the milk for the baas's eyes."

He handed the reins to the Major and climbing into the back of the Cape Cart busied himself there a while.

Presently he came to the driver's seat again, carrying a white enamel bowl, half-full of milk, and some clean linen rags.

The bowl he placed on the Major's knees, handed him the rags and took the reins from him.

"Thanks, Jim," said the Major and, taking off his glasses, bathed his eyes with the milk. "It is very soothing, Jim." He shaded his eyes and looked at the Hottentot. "It takes the film away. I can see you, you damned old heathen."

Jim turned toward his baas and looked intently into his eyes, then taking off his old, battered felt hat, he passed it slowly back and forth before the Major's face.

The Major did not blink.

"What is that, Jim?" he asked.

"What, baas?"

"Something passed between my face and the sun."

Jim sighed. "It was a cloud, baas," he said sadly.

"Ah yes, of course," the Major agreed confusedly and with feverish haste commenced to bathe his eyes again.

"But my eyes are better, just the same," he drawled in English. "Jim's a bally old pessimist. I did see him distinctly just for a moment. He looked thin and very tired. No wonder! I must be a bally nuisance; he's waited on me hand and foot; fed me, even."

The Major was not looking very fit himself; his cheeks were hollow, the corners of his mouth sagged, his shoulders were bowed. But his clothing was as immaculate as usual, his face clean-shaven, his hair neatly brushed and parted, his hands white and the nails well trimmed. He was still the dude, the man who often dressed for dinner when alone on the veld, miles away from civilization. Only one thing was lacking, and that his monocle.

It was strange how that piece of glass could completely change the Major's appearance. It was his stalking horse. Wearing it, he deceived wise men into thinking him a fool, a dandified fool. When he was not wearing it, men doubted their first judgment of him—based on his affected drawl and foppish clothes—and walked very warily when dealing with him.

But now—his eyes inflamed and bloodshot—he looked like a man who lacked self-restraint and was suffering from an over-indulgence in whisky.

They rode on for a time in silence and then Jim, his keen eyes having discovered something which demanded a closer investigation some distance to the right of the course they were taking, swerved his mules sharply toward it with a loud shout.

"What is it, Jim?" the Major asked. He was almost jolted from his seat by the sudden change of direction.

"I do not know, baas," Jim replied gravely, "but I think it is death."

"And we run away from it?" The Major's tone was slightly caustic.

"No, baas. Like fools, we go toward it."

Five minutes later Jim pulled up the mules beside a huddled shapeless object, putting to flight three vultures which had been perching on nearby rocks.

"What is it, Jim?" the Major asked again.

"It is death, baas," Jim answered grimly. He was closely scrutinizing the adjacent bush as if suspicious of lurking foes; yet, at the same time, he was confident that there was no one anywhere near. Had there been anyone in hiding, the vultures would not have been there.

"Is it a white man, Jim?"

"I think so, baas. I go to make sure. You stay here."

He climbed down from the Cape Cart.

"Yes, baas," he announced. "It is a white man. No, not a man, but a boy not old enough to grow a beard."

The Major's face was very stern, his body was tensed.

"How did he die, Jim?" he asked quietly.

"An *assegai* is sticking through him, baas, but—" Jim shook his head doubtfully—"I do not think it was the *assegai* which killed him."

"He was lost, perhaps, Jim, and died of thirst. Then a warrior found him and—"

"No, baas," Jim interrupted. "He was killed by a bullet which made a hole as big as my fist in his head."

The Major swore softly and, clumsily descending from the Cape Cart, made his way with shuffling step and hands outstretched before him to where Jim was standing.

Jim went to meet him and guided him toward the body. The Major knelt down beside it and, removing his glasses, endeavored to see with his own eyes the things Jim had told him.

Failing, discerning only a blurred outline, he cursed again.

"I'm as helpless as a new-born babe, Jim," he confessed.

"It will pass, baas, the blindness," Jim said reassuringly, "And there is nothing here that you could see that I haven't seen."

"True, Jim. If you were as blind as I am, and could I see as well as I ever saw, things would still be plain to you that are hidden from me. But tell me—is there no spoor of the men who did this evil?"

"None, baas. I first looked for that. But the deed was done yesterday and last night there was a heavy rain."

"I had forgotten," the Major murmured. "But feel in his pockets, Jim. He may have a talking-paper, something to tell us who he is."

Jim quickly obeyed. "There is nothing, baas. His pockets are empty."

"Ah, well. But a talking-paper would not have helped us. We could not have read it. And he has no knife, no gun—or—?"

"Nothing, baas."

"And he is very young, you say. Ah!" The Major sighed. "Get the shovel, Jim. We must protect him from the vultures and wild dogs."

And Jim, not telling his baas that that precaution was too late, got a prospector's shovel from the Cape Cart and swiftly dug a shallow grave in which they gently placed the murdered boy's body.

"Poor little devil. I hope he died unafraid," murmured the Major and, somehow, what he said sounded like a prayer.

On the top of the mound they piled stones and then, climbing up into the Cape Cart, resumed their trek, both very silent. The Major was afraid that their errand was a fruitless one; Jim was pessimistically sure of failure.

It was a little after sundown when they came to their day's destination—a group of well built huts which were the living quarters of an old Dutch settler and his family.

Oom Jan du Plessis came to the door of the largest hut, an old muzzle-loading elephant gun in his hand.

"Who are you?" he demanded truculently in the Taal.

"We're from the fort at Victoria," the Major announced. "I've come to tell you that you must go into the fort with your family. You have been warned twice before. This is the last warning. After this it will be too late. The natives are going to rise and—"

"*Allemagtig!*" Oom Jan exclaimed. "Am I then a fool? That is known to me already this long time past."

He watched the Major curiously as that man descended from the Cape Cart and, led by Jim, walked toward him.

"*Stilte!*" he roared presently. "Is it that no men are left that they have to send a blind man with a Hottentot dog to warn the burghers?"

The Major laughed harshly.

"That is all I can do, Oom Jan. I can not fight, but I can talk and, perhaps, make an old fool like you see reason."

"And is it reason that I should leave my farm and my cattle? What I have here," he indicated the cultivated acres surrounding the homestead, "represents the work of many years. If I leave it the dogs of Matabele will make my work a vain thing. They will burn my huts and—"

"But at least you will be alive, while if you stay here, you, and your *vrouw* and the *kinder* will die."

Oom Jan spat in disgust. "Why does not the government send men to protect me and mine? That is its duty. Instead of which—"

"My baas is tired," Jim interposed roughly. "You keep him here talking when we have trekked far and must trek still farther on the morrow. Let him eat. Afterward, when his belly is full, you may talk."

"Jim—" the Major began reprovingly, but Oom Jan chuckled with good humored appreciation of Jim's thought for his baas.

"*Ach sis!*" the farmer exclaimed, twisting his long, bush beard around his huge, gnarled hand. "Let him be. He is right. You must be a good man, mynheer, or the Hottentot would not have spoken so. 'My baas,' he said, as if you were the good God. Outspan, black one. I will feed your baas and food shall be brought you. Come, mynheer."

He took the Major by the arm and led him into the hut.

"Sit there," he said, pushing the Major gently onto a stool. "Oh, *vrouw, kinder,* an Englisher eats with us tonight."

From an inside room there sounded a confused, excited babel of voices; a woman's, sharp and shrewish, boys' voices, hovering between the soprano of adolescence and the deep bass of manhood, the soft tones of girls.

Presently the Major was conscious of a sudden crowding in the room as Jan du Plessis ushered in his brood—his tall, angular wife and seventeen children.

One by one he introduced them to the Major, accompanying the introduction with an anecdote which aptly hit off the particular child being presented; details attending the birth of each child were also added.

It was a long performance and the Major sighed with relief when Oom Jan announced, "And that is all—save my oldest son who is not here. Now let us eat. Katje, you sit by the Englisher and take care of his plate."

The meal was a very frugal one and called for a healthy appetite. The noise was deafening. Oom Jan's offspring quarreled constantly, were continually on the point of coming to blows, and always paying momentary obedience to their father's insistence on quiet and order.

Katie, a pretty, dark-haired girl who boasted of two years at a school in Jo'burg, cut the Major's meat for him and attempted—very obviously and clumsily—to flirt with him.

The Major was very glad when, the meal over, Oom Jan dismissed the children. He felt, however, that even should he be killed by native warriors before he got to the next homestead, his mission had not altogether failed. The new country needed pioneers of the du Plessis breed and his children were decided assets.

And so, without any preamble or mincing of words, the Major put the facts of the situation before the shrewd old Dutchman and his stolid, phlegmatic wife.

"I do not understand," Oom Jan said when the Major had finished. "You say that the Matabele are going on the warpath and that the Mashonas are coming out, too. So the white men have all gone in *laager*. And yet, only yesterday morning, a troop of police called here and said there was no danger, that the chiefs who were to have led the rebellion have all been captured and are now prisoners of the government."

"What? Police here?" the Major exclaimed incredulously.

Oom Jan nodded emphatically. *"Ja!* Twelve of them, no less. They took all my laborers—and I had only five because I am very poor and have many sons. They said that the government needed them to build roads."

"But," the Major said slowly, "you must be mistaken, Oom Jan. All the police are in *laager* at Victoria."

"Stilte!" Oom Jan exploded. "Am I then as blind as you? I saw them, I tell you, and I talked with them. And so did the good *vrouw. Hein?"*

He turned to her and she nodded in confirmation.

"You may have seen twelve men as you say, Oom Jan," the Major said in puzzled tones, "but they were not police."

"What?" Oom Jan leaned forward, his eyes trying to bore into the Major's. *"Allemagtig!* Take off your glasses so that I can tell whether you are a true man or not."

Without a word the Major took off his smoked glasses and looked toward the Dutchman.

"Stilte!" Oom Jan turned to his wife, deep concern on his face. "See, *vrouw;* he is not suffering from a blindness sent by the good God to punish him for his sins. It was the poison of a spitting cobra. Not?"

The Major nodded.

The woman rose from her chair and crossing over to the Major held a lighted candle before his eyes.

"You see a light?" she asked.

"Yes—I can see a little."

"And have you been like this long?"

"A month—thirty days or more."

"And you have done nothing?"

"I bathed my eyes with milk, that is all."

"That is good; sometimes it is enough, but not always. Did not the doctor at Victoria do anything?"

"He said that there was nothing he could do. Maybe, he said, the film will go away suddenly and I shall see again. Maybe not. He did not know."

The Dutchman and his wife exchanged triumphant, meaning smiles.

"*Ach sis*, man," Oom Jan shouted. "We know better than that. My *vrouw*, she knows many medicines not known to doctor fools who talk big words to hide their ignorance. Yes; many charms are known to us Boer folk. How else could we have lived in the early days?"

"You just wait a little while. *Vrouw*, you can make his eyes well, not?"

"*Ja*," she replied simply and, placing the candle on the table, took a small jar from a wall shelf. She poured some of the thick, viscous liquid it contained into a large spoon and heated it over the candle flame.

"It will be very painful," she said slowly. "It will feel like burning fire. Are you afraid?"

"Will it cure?" the Major asked quietly.

"It has never failed," Oom Jan said stoutly and the Major believed him. He knew that the Boers were well versed in many simple remedies which cured seemingly fatal diseases.

"Very well, then. I am ready."

"Good."

The Major moved restlessly and inwardly reviled himself for allowing these good, but ignorant and superstitious people to try their concoctions on his eyes. And yet—

To hide his nervousness he turned to other topics.

"Tell me more about these men who said they were policemen, Oom Jan," he said.

The Dutchman laid a forefinger along his nose.

"*Ach!* I am no fool. I suspected those *verdoemte schelm,* but I did not let them see I suspected. *Ja,*'I said when they desired 'yes' for an answer. '*Nein,*'I said when they wanted 'no.' Oh, I am very *slim.* I let them think that I believed all that they had said. But when they had gone— Is all ready now, *vrouw?*"

"*Ja.* Put back your head, mynheer, and open your eyes wide."

He obeyed and she bathed them gently with a rag dipped in milk.

"So," continued Oom Jan, "when they had gone little Katje wrote a letter. In English she wrote what I told her to say— Open your eyes wide, mynheer. My *vrouw* is ready. It will hurt! *Allemagtig* how it will hurt! But by sunrise tomorrow you will see. I, Jan du Plessis, swear to it— But about the letter. I sent it with my boy Piet to the captain at Victoria. Yesterday I sent him, after they had left."

The Major started violently. He had forgotten all about the body he and Jim had buried way back on the veld.

"You—" he began, then stopped short. He could not tell them so brutally.

The woman was watching him closely. She came forward now. The heat of the candle flame had turned the viscous stuff to a milky-colored fluid of watery consistency.

"Hold his head back, Jan," she said. "And you, mynheer, open your eyes wide. Drop by drop I am going to pour this into them; and they will burn. But you must not move; it must stay there."

Oom Jan took the Major's head in his two powerful hands and tilted it back; the Major opened his eyes and stared upward. The woman stood over him and two drops of the liquid splashed into the Major's eyes, and seemed to congeal there instantly. It burned as if red-hot needles had pierced his eyeballs, but the Major did not move. And, except for an involuntary groan, he was silent.

"Do not rub your eyes," she warned him as the Major raised his hands to his head.

He let them drop to his side again.

"You were going to say something," the woman went on, speaking in a low voice, widely spacing her words. "Something about Piet. Go on—talk. Tell us about it. Talking will help you forget the pain."

She let two more drops fall and the pain was intensified.

"I have forgotten," he said lamely.

"No, you have not forgotten," her voice was hard. "Tell. You were going to say something about Piet. You saw him, perhaps?"

The Major did not answer, and Oom Jan said with a laugh, "Twenty-one *kinder* she has had. Eighteen are still alive, but Piet was her first-born son. So tell her, man. It is hard to keep anything from my *vrouw*; about Piet it is impossible to keep anything. Answer her."

"Yes—I saw Piet.

"And he was all right—tired after trekking, maybe, but all right.

"It was late yesterday afternoon, the sun was sinking fast, we were in a hurry to get here. We did not stop—"

She let two more drops fall. There was very little of the liquid left.

"Yesterday afternoon!" she said in surprised tones. "That must have been not very far from here. Yet he should have been far away. Was his horse lame, or he had been thrown? Answer me—and speak truly."

"You will not see Piet again," the Major said slowly. "He is dead."

There was silence for a little while, broken only by the woman's sharp hissing intake of breath and a muttered, *"Allemagtig!"* from Oom Jan.

But the woman's hand as she allowed the last of the liquid to drop into the Major's eyes trembled slightly; Oom Jan's grip on the Major's head tightened slightly.

The woman held the candle again before the Major's eyes.

"Can you see anything?" she asked in a low, toneless voice.

"Nothing. It is as though a thick cloth had been placed over my eyes."

"That is good," and she made a bandage and fixed it in place. "Tomorrow morning take the bandage off and wash your eyes. You will see then."

Oom Jan loosed his hold on the Major's head and slumped down in a chair close to the table, tugged nervously at his beard and stared fixedly at a crack in the floor of the hut.

As if she were handling liquid gold the woman put her precious jar of ointment back on the shelf. She stood there for a moment, her back turned to the two men.

Facing about suddenly, she asked fiercely, "What killed our boy, Piet?"

"A bullet."

"*Ach!* Then it was not the Matabele?"

The Major shook his head. "No." And he told them in short, simple sentences of Jim's discovery of the body and of the little grave in which they had buried it.

When he had finished the woman bade him good night and went into the other room of the hut. Presently they heard her scolding one of the children, then silence for a little while. This silence was broken at length by the sound of weeping.

Oom Jan cursed violently.

"He was her first man child," he said as if in explanation. Then, "Who killed Piet?"

"The men who called themselves police, I think, Oom Jan."

"*Ja.*" He nodded agreement. "That is what I thought. But why?"

"They probably wanted to keep word of their doings from the police at Victoria as long as possible. Tell me more about them. They wore police uniforms you say, and they were English?"

"They wore the police uniform, *ja*. But not all were English. Some were Boers; two looked like Portuguese. And they had blacks with them who, they said, they were taking to work for the government. They got the natives from the nearby *kraals*."

"Were the natives free? Did they go because they wanted to go?"

"Ach sis, no. What fool talk. Who ever heard of a black happy to go to work? No. They were roped together."

"And where do you think those white men are now?"

"Who shall say? What do you think?"

"I think they are heading for Portuguese Territory. Perhaps they left one or two men to watch here and they followed Piet and killed him and then joined the others."

Oom Jan jumped to his feet. "Then why do we stay here?" he cried. "The Good Book says an eye for an eye—"

"And where will you go?" the Major asked quietly. "And what could you do even if you found them—one against so many?"

Oom Jan returned to his chair. "It is true," he muttered.

"Besides," the Major continued, "you have to think of your wife and children. If you go, who is left to take care of them? Tomorrow you and they must go into Victoria."

"I am not afraid of the blacks—we can hold them off. I have never had trouble with them. I have always been friends with them."

"When a Matabele goes on the warpath, he has no friends. You know that. Then, too, the white men might come back."

"True, I had forgotten that. In the morning, then, we will go. But—" his eyes blazed fiercely—"we will come back. This place is mine. I made it with my own hands. I will not give it up. As for those men who killed my son— But you will come with us?"

"No. I must get word to Kaffir Jones. He's the nearest, and then to as many others as possible. Perhaps he will help me."

"Ach! That *schelm!* He will not help you. Let him go."

Kaffir Jones was a settler of unenviable reputation. A man who had forgotten his race and, mired by South Africa's blackness, had lived like a native with several native wives.

"No, Oom Jan. I must warn him. He must have his chance. I may have time to get all the others in, too, with his help. The natives won't go out until after the full moon. That's ten days more."

Oom Jan grunted. "You are a fool," he said, "but you are a man, too. Give me your hand and I will take you to the place where you are to sleep. Then I must go to my *vrouw. Allemagtig!* She will be lonely!"

EARLY NEXT morning the Major was awakened by much shouting and the lowing of cattle. For a moment or two he was bewildered, not knowing where he was. Then he sat up and called softly for Jim.

The Hottentot came running in answer to the call, bearing a basin of clean warm water.

"Your eyes, baas," he said excitedly.

"I had forgotten, Jim." The Major was now as excited as the Hottentot, and his fingers trembled so that he had difficulty in loosening the knots in the bandage. In the past few days the Major had practically reconciled himself to permanent blindness and he half-feared to remove the bandage feeling that, should the Boer remedy prove a failure, he would cave in.

Jim's next words gave him courage. "The baas du Plessis said the medicine was sure, baas. And I remember now having seen a cure. Fool that I did not remember. Make haste, baas."

"Cut the bandage with your knife, Jim. My fingers are clumsy."

"There, baas. Now bathe your eyes."

There was silence for a little while, broken only by the trickle of water as it rolled from the Major's face back into the basin.

"I can't open my eyes, Jim," the Major said softly.

"Do not stop bathing them yet," Jim urged.

"All right, Jim?"

"Yah, baas."

"What is all that noise outside?"

"The baas du Plessis is making ready to leave. They have inspanned eighteen oxen to a big wagon and in the wagon they are loading everything!"

"I had forgotten."

The Major laughed softly, and as he laughed, the leaden weights which seemed to be pressing down on his eyelids dropped off. He opened his eyes and looked about the hut, sighed, then recommenced to bathe them.

He gasped, looked up again, blinked, screwed his eyes up tightly, slowly opened them again.

"Jim," he cried excitedly, "I can see. I can see."

"Truly, baas?"

"Truly. All things are misty—a yellow mist—it is gradually going."

Jim beamed with happiness.

"Baas du Plessis told me that it would be like that."

The Major rose quickly, shaved and washed, then, feeling in his pocket for a monocle, fixed it in place and strode buoyantly from the hut. He blinked owlishly in the brilliant sunlight.

Mrs. du Plessis greeted him with a wan smile, apparently deaf to his expressions of gratitude, turning quickly away to discipline one of the excited children who crowded about the Major, staring at him wonderingly.

The Major went to Oom Jan who asked, "Are not both eyes well that you must wear a glass in one?"

"Yes. I see with both, Oom Jan. The glass I have always worn. It is my custom."

"These English are a queer race," Oom Jan muttered under his breath. Then aloud, "We are all ready now. We only waited to say good-by to you. The *vrouw* would not let me waken you."

They walked toward the wagon into which the younger children and Mrs. du Plessis now climbed.

All of them were armed; the youngest boy, a sturdy eight-year-old, carried an old muzzle-loader slung across his back, and a much younger girl tightly clutched a cross-bow.

"We can give a good account of ourselves," Oom Jan said gravely as he picked up his long whip. "Good-by, Englisher. If I don't see you, s'long, hullow!"

He cracked the whip and the well-trained oxen moved slowly off, two young du Plessis, rifles slung across their backs, riding ahead on bony mules as advance guard.

The Major watched them until they passed out of sight, wondering at their stoicism, at their ability to pull up stakes with such little fuss or display of emotion. Then, remembering that he had work to do, he turned and went to the Cape Cart, ready to tackle, with a keener appetite than he had known for some time, the meal Jim had prepared for him.

Half an hour later Jim was inspanning the mules, preparing for the trek to the place of Kaffir Jones—four hours distant.

"All ready, baas," he said finally, climbing into the seat beside the Major.

And then a man staggered into view, a white man, nearly naked, hatless and barefooted. He waved his hand wildly when he saw them.

They jumped down from the Cape Cart and ran to meet him.

"The niggers are out," he croaked hoarsely and then collapsed in a huddled heap on the ground.

They carried him back to the Cape Cart and placed him gently on some blankets left behind by the du Plessis.

"He has been stabbed, baas," Jim said.

The Major nodded and ripped off the man's dirty, blood-stained shirt. There was a deep wound in his side; blood still oozed gently from it.

"He will not live very long, baas."

"No, Jim. The wonder is that he lived at all after that wound. Bring whisky."

Jim got a bottle from the Cape Cart and the Major, gently raising the man's head, poured some whisky into him.

He gagged slightly, then opened his eyes.

"Thanks," he whispered. "But don't waste your time on me. The blighters have done for me and—I'm damned glad."

"We'll soon have you fixed up," the Major began cheerfully.

The other laughed. "There isn't any blood left in me. Give me another drink."

The Major silently handed him the bottle and, while he drank, gently fingered the wound, endeavoring to close it.

"You're a good scout," the other whispered. "But perhaps you don't know who I am—I'm Kaffir Jones." He spoke as one who expects criticism and is prepared to resent it.

The Major nodded. "I guessed so. I was coming to see you."

Jones's eyes opened wide. "To see me? What for?"

"To warn you to get into *laager* at Victoria before it was too late."

Jones sniggered. "That's funny—sending a man all the way out here to warn me. Why man, the niggers wouldn't hurt me. I'm one of them."

"Yet they did this."

Jones's eyes clouded.

"Yes, the beasts." Then he sat up with a suddenness which started him coughing violently.

"Where's du Plessis and the kids?" he said when he had recovered.

"Gone to Victoria. They went nearly an hour ago."

Jones sank back with a sigh.

"Perhaps they'll be all right," he muttered. "The niggers'll come here first, looking for them. They won't be here; but we will and we'll give the black devils a warm time."

"No. We won't be here. We're going on to warn the other whites."

"You'll have to go a long way then. They're—all—dead. I warned them a month ago to get away. But they laughed at me. Called me a white kaffir. I am, maybe, but that's my affair, and I knew what I was talking about—and they're dead and I soon will be."

He drank again and continued, his voice fainter.

"You see, my nigger women used to tell me all the talk of the *kraals*—secret plans—and when I heard yesterday that they were going out right away I rode to the other homesteads. But it was too late. The niggers got there first."

"You're sure of that?" the Major asked softly. "You're not lying?"

"Why should I lie," Jones said simply, "now?"

The Major was all contrition, "I'm sorry, old man. I—"

"That's all right. So I turned my horse and rode here, thinking they'd leave du Plessis and his kids for the last. Hasn't his old *vrouw* mothered a quiverful? But they got me and my horse. He's back there a mile or more. Carried on as long as he could and then foundered. I couldn't shoot him—I had no cartridges left. And they are coming here after me. Take me into the hut. Tell your nigger to inspan. They'll come here and if we make it hot for them for a while, they won't think du Plessis has gone. That'll give him and his *vrouw* and his kids a chance."

He closed his eyes and did not move or speak again.

For a long time the Major sat by the dead man, pondering on the strangeness of things, marveling at the spirit which had been alive in Kaffir Jones although he had endeavored to kill it. Living, Jones had betrayed his race, but when the supreme test had come he had been ready to meet it and, by the manner of his death, had proved himself, had kept faith with his own people.

The Major was aroused from his reveries by a shout, half-strangled, from Jim.

With his hand on his revolver butt the Major went to the door of the hut in time to see six horsemen, wearing police uniforms, ride up and encircle the Cape Cart.

Unobserved the Major watched them dismount; their horses, he noted, were done up—black with sweat and looked at the point of total exhaustion. Indeed, two of them collapsed suddenly and pawed frantically at the ground. Two of the white men—the others had surrounded Jim—examined the horses, brutally kicking them. Then, as the two that were down made no effort to rise, they turned away and began talking in excited tones.

The Major hesitated a moment, then took up a stick, put on his smoked glasses and tapped his way slowly forward, calling, "Jim! Jim!" in a high, querulous voice.

The men turned quickly and one who was holding a revolver to Jim's head whispered harshly, "Answer him. Say you called out because you were afraid. Don't let him know we are here."

"I'm here, baas," Jim cried, his voice trembling with excitement. He knew that his baas was playing a game. "Something moved in the bush, I thought it was a lion."

"*Au-a!* Fool." The Major came slowly forward, feeling his way with his stick. The men whispered together.

"Who's with you?" the Major called sharply.

"No one, baas."

The Major halted, raised his head and gazed uncertainly about him—he was like a blind man endeavoring to judge his distance by sound. He noted with satisfaction that the men had drawn away from the Cape Cart and were huddled together, leaving the mules—Jim had not yet out-spanned, he had been busy unloading the rifles and ammunition—and their horses unguarded.

Then he moved slowly forward again, passing so close to the men that by putting out his hand he could have touched them.

He came to the Cape Cart, felt his way along it until he came to the whip, the long driving whip, which was leaning against it.

Then he became galvanized into action.

Picking up the whip he lashed the mules hard and fast, yelling. Half-maddened they galloped away at breakneck speed, followed by three of the horses.

The Major laughed and throwing the whip and his smoked glasses to the ground turned round to face the astonished men.

They sprang forward, then back at the sight of the revolver in his hand which menaced them.

"You damned fool," one of them cried. "The niggers are out; they're after us. And now we can't get away."

"Splendid!" exclaimed the Major. "That's fine. Now you can stay here and help me."

Cautiously he fished in his pocket and, producing his monocle, fixed it in his eye.

"Hell! Then you weren't blind, after all? I thought—"

"Shouldn't think, Gibson, my dear fellow. You should be sure. Suppose you let Jim go—I can't talk sanely when I see you manhandling him that way. Oh, and you had all better keep your hands away from your revolvers. I'm a bally good shot, if I do say so myself."

Gibson released his hold of Jim and put up his revolver.

"What's your game, Major?" he growled.

"I might ask what's yours? But you asked first. So here goes. You see, you chappies are particularly unpleasant people. First of all you are in the pay of Whispering Smith who is, I imagine, in the pay at certain unsavory Portuguese officials acting outside the government for the moment. Is that it?"

Gibson and the others were silent. They did not seem to be listening to what the Major was saying, but on the alert, rather, for signs of evil approaching from the bush.

"So you came up here and, by pretending to be police, roused the anger of the natives against the whites. I don't know just what your game was; that doesn't matter. What does matter is this: you murdered Oom Jan Plessis's youngster, you were the cause of the natives going out and killing the settlers, you were responsible for the death of Kaffir Jones who was a better man than any one of you."

Gibson moved a step or two from the rest of his companions.

"Silence gives consent, eh? Well, well. Now see how things work out. You find that your little plan acts as a sort of boomerang, as it were. First thing you know the—er—natives are after you. And you have to run for it, and you come here, your horses all tuckered out, thinking that you'd help yourself to my mules and Cape Cart. And that wouldn't do, really. You see, I want you here. Soon the natives'll come, and if there's no one here to keep them—er—amused, why they'll go after poor old Jan du Plessis. And that old chap has all the troubles in the world. And, of course, you wouldn't want his children—quite a lot of them, aren't there?—tortured by the natives, would you? Of course not. So you're going to stay and help me fight a rearguard action as it were. And to make sure you'd stay I sent the mules and horses off—putting temptation out of your way, as it were."

At this moment Gibson ran swiftly to the remaining horse, jumped on its back and spurred the jaded beast away.

As one man the other five reached for their revolvers, but let their hands drop empty to their sides as the Major said, "Let him go. He won't get far on that nag."

"The dirty swine," said one of the men fiercely. "He's the cause of all the trouble. If it hadn't been for him— What's that!"

From the hush sounded fierce yells, revolver shots, the despairing cry of a white man—then silence.

"That," said the Major gravely, "is death. The natives have put an end to Gibson's dirty work. Now what do you say? You've caused a lot of trouble, and you're damned rotters. Are you going to help me, and, in part, make amends for everything; or do I have to strap you all up?"

"You couldn't do that, Major," answered one. "We're too many for you to handle that way. We've been quiet so far because you caught us by surprise, and we didn't know what your game was. But now! All right; I'm with you. We'll keep the blacks from getting the du Plessis crowd."

"Fine. How about the rest of you?"

"It's the only thing we can do," grumbled one. "Sure; we're with you."

The Major was not entirely satisfied, but he was forced to accept what they offered. They would fight, he thought, for their own skins and that was sufficient for his purpose.

Under his direction they hastily threw up a barrier round one of the huts, got buckets of water filled and close to hand, knocked down the other flimsy buildings.

Then they took stock of their rifles and ammunition. They were safe there, at least. They had plenty and to spare.

The hours passed; although they kept a keen lookout they did not see any natives, though they sensed that the bush around was teeming with them. Occasionally an *assegai* head would reflect the gleam of the sun."

For the most part the men were silent, but Evans—the man who had first promised to throw in his lot with the Major—talked a great deal to the Major.

"It was a dirty game from the start," he said. "But, once in Smith's books, there's not much chance of getting out. I don't understand the rights of the affair. But the idea was, I think, to make sure the rebellion would break. That was to give certain crooked Portuguese officials a chance to step in. We'd have done it all right, maybe, but Smith was greedy. He wanted to kill two birds with one stone. So we dressed up as police and commandeered natives— we knew that would do the trick—and planned to run the natives out, through the Portuguese Territory, down to the Transvaal."

"Labor recruiting, eh?"

Evans nodded.

"What was the hitch, then?"

"That was that swine Gibson's fault. To make sure that the rebellion would be a halfway success, we brought with us a lot of rifles which we sold to the niggers. But back there the niggers discovered that the rifles were no good. One exploded and killed the buck who was using it. So the niggers got mad. They cut six of us off and wiped 'em out. Then they chased us here, other *kraals* joining in as we came along."

"I see. You're right, it's a damned dirty business." The Major rose to his feet and stretched himself lazily. "There's one thing to be thankful for—we've nothing to fear from the native rifles. I take it that Gibson bought a condemned lot cheap and pocketed the extra money himself."

Evans nodded,

"Something like that," he agreed.

The Major was watching Jim who was signalling excitedly.

"Get your rifles ready," the Major called out. "I fancy we're going to have some visitors."

As he spoke, the bush beyond the cleared space about the homestead echoed with the shouts of many warriors and, a moment later, a large force of warriors advanced slowly toward the huts.

They were met by a withering volley of shots. Six men fell. Another volley, and they turned tail and ran.

"That attack was only a bluff," the Major said calmly, "Next time they'll be more cautious. They've discovered how strong we are."

The white men waited, smoking nervously.

The next attack came very soon. This time the natives rushed headlong, shouting, leaping, brandishing their *assegais* and shields. Some carried lighted torches which they flung at the hut. But they all fell short, and the attack was beaten back before the warriors could get to close range.

"It's a good job they don't know anything about fighting in open formation," the Major remarked.

"Yes," Evans agreed. "But why the hell don't they attack us from all sides? Why only a frontal attack?"

"They'll come to that, before they're through," the Major said heavily.

Time passed, the sun set, darkness came and the natives did not attack again.

"They've sent for reinforcements," suggested one of the men. "Let's make a getaway."

Evans looked at the Major. "What do you say?" he asked.

The Major nodded. "I think we've given Oom Jan a good start. He ought to be safe now. I suggest, though, that we go separately—no chance of us going through in a bunch. We'll draw lots to see who goes first."

The others agreed, drawing straws from the Major's hand, the one who pulled the longest one being the first to try his luck.

It was Evans. "Good-by," he said to the Major, and vanished into the blackness. He made no attempt at concealment, but whistled and sang loudly as he walked.

"The damned fool!" muttered one of the men.

There was fierce yelling in the bush, and then silence.

One after another the other men left, and each one's departure was followed by the yells of the natives, testifying that their attempts to escape had failed.

Only the Major and Jim were left.

"Now we go, Jim," said the Major. "But first we will plan a little."

Quickly he and Jim collected the rifles the other men had left, loaded and cocked them. Then to the trigger of each he tied a tin can and fixing the water buckets above them, pierced holes in them so that the water would run slowly out into the cans. His idea was that when the cans were full enough their weight would be sufficient to discharge the rifles. He put stones into some of the cans, thus making sure that all the rifles would not go off at once.

"That's that," he murmured when all was arranged to his liking. "It may not work, but, by Jove, it should. It's a brilliant thought of mine. Very." Then to Jim, "In a minute we will leave."

He fired several rounds into the bush before him and then, with Jim, crept stealthily away in the opposite direction.

They were barely two hundred yards from the hut when a report sounded. Five minutes later another. Then another.

"It's working, Jim," the Major whispered in the Hottentot's ear. "It's working. It'll keep them too busy to look for us."

WHISPERING SMITH was in an evil temper.

First word had been brought to him that morning that the rebellion up north had petered out. A few settlers in isolated districts had been wiped out—but that was all!

Also, he had received a long letter from the Major. The monocled dude had spread himself very well and, having written the letter himself, had not hesitated to call Smith all the things he thought him.

With the letter had come another present in the shape of a toy revolver and the concluding words read, *"Shortly after you read this I shall be with you. And I shall carry a real revolver, and it will be loaded."*

Just then a knock sounded at the door and before he could move the door opened and closed again.

"Good morning, Smith." It was the Major.

Smith turned with a snarl and then dropped back in his chair,

"I'm glad you are alone, because there are many things I want to say to you. Of course, you understand, we've got all the proofs necessary to convict you of inciting the natives to rebel up north. Of course there are other counts against you, too. But that will do to start."

Smith attempted to bluster.

"Get out of here before I have you thrown out."

The Major smiled. "No. I don't think you will. You see, you're finished."

He patted his revolver meaningly.

Smith wanted to curse, to threaten, to execute the threat; he leaned forward in his chair, his hand clawing the air before him; he seemed like an evil beast of prey ready to spring—a cowardly beast, cornered and made to fight.

When his eyes saw the revolver in the other's hand he slumped back in his chair again, twitching nervously.

"What do you want, Major?" he asked in a hoarse, husky whisper.

The Major laughed.

"What do I want? Oh, quite a lot, quite a lot, I assure you. Just now I'm gloating. But I don't think I'll gloat for long! You're such a nasty cur that there's no pleasure in it. And you're coming to such a beastly end that perhaps it is not quite sportin' to gloat."

Smith sunk back still farther in his chair; seemed to shrivel up; shifted to the right and to the left in his fruitless endeavor to get away from the revolver's aim.

The Major considered him coolly, almost impersonally, then returned his revolver to its holster.

"I've a lot to do, Smithy," he said, "and I can't stay to have the little chat with you that I would like. So I'll just tell you that your career is at an end—oh, abso-bloomin'-lutely."

"Don't talk like a damned fool, Major."

Now the revolver was out of sight, Smith's nerve returned to him.

"Oh, but I'm tellin' you the truth, the whole truth, and all that, you know. All your friends and so forth, at least nearly all of them, are under lock and key. In a little while they'll be on their way to *trunk* and there they will finish out their careers, some making little stones out of big ones, some picking oakum and all will scrub the floors of their bedrooms, if you know what I mean. Perhaps they'll be made to listen to Holy Joe preach! Can you imagine anything more terrible?"

Smith turned round to his desk. "If that's all you have to say, Major—"

"But that's not all! Don't be so impetuous. Look!"

He opened the door and Smith, looking in spite of his desire not to look, saw that the barroom was filled with men. Many of them were his creatures, the others were uniformed policemen. Looking still closer Smith saw that the men in civilians were handcuffed to each other.

Then the Major closed the door.

"Quite a haul, eh?" the Major said pleasantly. "And I planned it. I'm devilishly clever, don't you think?"

Smith did not answer. He had much to think about.

"They're coming in to handcuff you in a moment," the Major continued. "You'd be surprised, you will be surprised, at the number of crimes you are going to be tried for. So many of your—er—friends have, to put it crudely, gabbed."

"They can't touch me," Smith said uneasily. "They've got no proof. I'll be out free again in a few days and then I'll make the skunks pay!" His eyes wandered to the drawers where he kept his files.

The Major smiled.

"I wouldn't count on those famous books of yours, Smithy. The Big Man, he's a great friend of mine, realized that we couldn't do anything with you while those books were in existence. So I assured him that, really, you weren't a bad fellow at heart and that, of course, as soon as the matter was put up to you in the right way you would destroy them. And you will, won't you?"

"I'll see you in hell first." Smith laughed harshly. "You must think I'm a fool, Major. Why, nearly every big bug in town is mentioned in that book in some way or other, even the magistrate who'll not—"

"Yes!" the Major interrupted. "I do think you're a—pardon me—fool, Smithy. Of course we've been fools, too. We should have collared those books long ago. Ah, well! It's never too late to mend, what? So we'll burn them now. Can't take any chances at all."

He took the lid off the pot-bellied stove.

"Now," he ordered, and the drawl left his voice; he spoke as one accustomed to getting instant obedience. "Put your filthy books in here. Quick, it's chilly. I want to have a fire."

Smith did not move until the Major took him by the coat collar and lifted him to his feet.

"Quick!" repeated the Major and as he spoke his revolver leaped from the holster.

And then Smith moved.

Under the Major's keen eye he took his books from the drawers and tearing out the pages stuffed them in the stove.

The Major applied a match and the papers blazed furiously. Drawer after drawer was emptied and its contents, after being subjected to a swift scrutiny by the Major, added to the pyre. The room was soon stripped bare and Smith's pockets were turned inside out.

The stove glowed a dull red; heat waves shimmered above it. The room was filled with the scent of scorched wood, the heat was suffocating. Sweat rolled down the faces of both men, but they stuck grimly to their task; one inspired by the righteous joy of destroying an evil thing, of a task well accomplished, the other driven by the fear of death.

At length the fire died down, became only a red, glowing mass, became only a gray, feathery heap of ashes.

"I'd have given you half, Major," Smith croaked. "We could have run this country to please ourselves if you'd come in with me."

The Major shrugged his shoulders.

"Your 'if' was too big a handicap. And now it's finished." He looked at his watch. "They'll come in to arrest you in five minutes and you're harmless; as harmless as a fangless snake."

He turned to leave, hesitated a moment at the door, then came back and placed his revolver on the desk, close to Smith's hand.

"I shouldn't do this," he murmured, "but then, I was always too soft-hearted."

He turned to leave again. As he did so Smith's hand closed convulsively on the revolver. He tried to pick it up and aim at the Major, but his nerveless fingers were not equal to the task and before he could steady himself the door closed behind the monocled man with a bang.

Smith sat for a few minutes, then slowly he turned the revolver on himself, guiding it with trembling hands to his temple. He held it there, pressed it hard against his skin, and closed his eyes. For a full minute he sat thus and then, with a dry sob, he opened his hand and the revolver fell with a clatter to the floor.

When the police entered two minutes later he rose, as one in a stupor, and held out his hands to be handcuffed.

The sergeant who made the arrest was very clumsy—he was looking at the angry red circle on Smith's right temple—and pinched Smith's flesh in the hinge of the handcuffs.

But Smith made no outcry; he was defeated, broken, and had eyes for nothing but the revolver on the floor.

THE HAT TRICK

OF COURSE the Major should have known better. He did know better. Long experience in the diamond fields of South Africa had made him fully cognisant of the laws regulating the buying and selling of diamonds; and he knew, no one better, the penalties a person found guilty of illicit traffic in the precious stones would have to suffer—if caught.

So, in this case, it wasn't ignorance of the law which made him a criminal; neither was it a trap into which he unwittingly had stumbled. The Major thrived on traps! So many men had essayed to earn their salaries as private detectives of the diamond mining syndicate, by slipping diamonds in his pockets when he wasn't looking—or, rather, when they thought he wasn't looking—only to find, when they later arrested and searched him, that the diamonds had disappeared mysteriously!

Other traps, very complicated and most ingenious, had proved just as worthless as far as results for the detectives were concerned—and quite as profitable to the amused Major. Consequently the word was passed around eventually that it was a waste of time trying to trap the man with the monocle; and the Major, thereby, lost one of his chief sources of revenue—the sale of diamonds planted on him by detectives.

But diamonds gravitated to him just the same—although he never mined them; he had no license—and the police knew it and tried their utmost to catch him with the goods, but in vain. The Major justly was called the *slimest* I.D.B. in the country. He always was under suspicion, but that was all!

Then, after years of careful evasion of the many pitfalls which await the steps of an I.D.B. he did a thing that a new-chum just out from trustful London would have hesitated about doing; he accepted a package from a perfect stranger, knowing that that package contained diamonds! Worse yet, the transfer of the package from the stranger to the Major was made in broad daylight—and before witnesses!

The party of the second part was a woman, a very beautiful woman who called herself Lola de Sousa—and the Major never could refuse a woman anything. He treated them all with the utmost chivalry and deference until faced with undeniable proof that they were deserving of neither. After that he treated them as he treated men of like quality.

He was seated on the *stoep* of Kimberley's most popular hotel, waiting impatiently for the arrival of the mail, when it happened. He was expecting a draft from a diamond dealer in Cape Town who did not inquire too closely into the origin of stones offered to him for sale, and who had learned by experience that the big blobs of sealing-wax which adorned certain packages mailed him from the North were deserving of a very close investigation.

The fact that this draft was several weeks overdue may have had something to do with the Major's carelessness. He did not like being forced to stay so long at the *dorp;* the petty social conventions of town irritated him. He rarely entered the place except on his own peculiar business, the registering of his protest against the harsh, unjust I.D.B. laws by breaking them.

He had planned a wonderful hunting trip with Jim, his Hottentot servant. A native whom he had befriended had told him of an enormous cache of elephant tusks—his for the taking—in Portuguese territory near the Swaziland border. He waited only for the draft that he might outfit properly for the expedition. The Major was too old and seasoned a campaigner not to travel in as great a luxury as

possible. He could trek harder and faster than any other man in South Africa if he had to, but preferred, however, to do his trekking in style, and to organize this expedition in style meant the expenditure of real money.

So he waited, riding in every day to the hotel from his camp on the veld just outside the township in time for the distribution of the mail. Each day impatience grew, boredom became more marked.

Today he had reached the limit. Draft or no draft, he resolved that this should be the last day among the flesh pots of a young and very crude township. Tomorrow he would trek, he and Jim, and let the clean sweet air of the veld blow the dust of civilization from his lungs.

"Bah Jove," he murmured half-aloud, *"that's* really living, you know! This—"

He glanced around at the other loungers on the *stoep*. They all were huddled together at the far end, near to the door leading to the dining room; they would lose no time getting to seats when the dinner gong sounded. Most of them were women, dowdily attired in dresses five years out of date, but still fashionable in Kimberley. The women looked burned out and very tired; their mouths drooped at the corners; they appeared discontented, shrewish. Pioneer life in Africa is hard on complexions and dispositions alike.

Suddenly there was a stir. The women looked at each other meaningly and pulled their voluminous skirts close as if to avoid contact and contamination with filth. All conversation ceased; every one of the women looked fixedly across the street. Yet they were just as conscious of the movements of the newcomer as were the men who stared with unfeigned admiration.

The Major, too, turned toward the door leading in to the hotel. His monocle fell from his eye socket to the floor and shattered into small pieces. That marked the depth of the Major's admiration, for his monocle was part of himself; and his indifference to its destruction was far from explained by the fact that he nearly always carried several replacements with him.

One of these he now fished absently from his pocket, affixed it in his eye, and stared until, suddenly becoming conscious that he *was* staring, he grew very red in the face, and turned away in confusion.

The girl who had been standing in the doorway laughed scornfully, stepped on to the *stoep* and walked slowly up and down. She glanced at the men with eyes that were at once provocatively inviting and insulting. One man slipped forward as if he intended to join her in her promenade and then, as she turned the battery of her scorn upon him, shrank back, a ludicrous expression of mortification on his face.

She was clad in a black dress which, on almost any other woman, would have looked very sedate, ultra-conventional; but as she wore it, somehow it was daring, *wicked!* The flaming red poinsettia pinned at her waist accentuated that hint of wickedness. She had no hat; her only head-dress was a black jet comb stuck with careless grace into abundant blue-black hair which was coiled simply about a well-shaped head. Her face was ivory white, unrelieved by any hint of color save for the red splash of her full, sensuous lips.

Up and down she walked, each turn bringing her a little nearer to the corner where the Major was lounging in a canvas-backed deckchair. She looked full at the Major, levelling a questioning glance; and at one turn her lips moved. "I'm in great trouble," she said softly. "May I sit down and talk to you?" Then she looked about her, as if fearful of being overheard, and with an expression of alarm turned and walked down to the other end of the long *stoep*.

Returning, she intently watched the Major. He nodded; and with a little sigh of relief she sat down in a nearby chair. Casually, as if she were moving it to get a better view of the street, she edged it close to the Major. Some of the women saw through the maneuver and laughed at the expression on the Major's face; it was very much like that of a man, a woman hater, who finds himself in a trap from which there is no escape.

"The designing minx," one of the women sniffed indignantly. She took no care to lower her speech, so that the Major heard every word. "Look at her! But you'd think she'd know better than try to flirt with the Major. He's no game for *that* kind!"

"Bless you, dearie," another answered with catty sweetness. "Don't be jealous. You can't compete with her. Her sort of woman thinks she only has to hold up her little finger to have every Tom, Dick and Harry, doing tricks. As for the Major, you'll notice he's not trying very hard to get away from her."

Meanwhile the girl had settled herself comfortably in her chair and was fanning herself with the huge, black ostrich-feather fan she carried. Her eyes were half closed and she seemed to be thinking of things far remote. A subtle odor of jasmine enveloped her; its sweetness was cloying.

The Major casually took a cigarette from a heavy, neatly-monogrammed case, tapped it tentatively on the back of his hand, then lighted it and puffed in lazy contentment, apparently without a thought beyond the blowing of intricate smoke-rings, breaking into soft exclamations of annoyance when the rings failed to hold the integrity of their shapes.

Presently the girl spoke in a soft, rich contralto. "It was good of you to offer to help me." Her speech was distinct in spite of a foreign accent and the fact that her lips barely moved.

"Not at all—charmed—really," the Major murmured, gazing speculatively at the glowing end of his cigarette.

"Ah, but it is," she insisted. "You see—you don't know me, but I *do* know you! Oh, very well indeed. So it is that I take advantage of you."

The Major stole a sidewise glance, and noted her firm chin, the aquiline, predatory curve of her nose, her full lips. A beautiful woman, he conceded cheerfully, and then wondered at the hard, calculating gleam in her eyes.

"You are very clever," she went on, "You understand that we must talk low so that they"—she gestured with her fan toward the other end of the *stoep*—"will not hear us. But you must not look at me hard, no."

The Major quickly glanced away.

"I am in great trouble," the soft, even voice purred. "Oh, this so terrible town. I was most foolish to come here."

"Yes," assented the Major on general principles, not knowing what else to say. "Then why did you come?"

"Ah, you men! You are so direct. I came, *Senhor* Major, because I needed money."

"Ah!"

"But you don't understand. You must not think of me as those—" she shrugged her shoulders "—old cats think. They are afraid I would steal their men from them. They whisper bad things because I sit, oh, so close to you. They are jealous! Is it my fault that I am beautiful and that men are fools?"

The Major murmured something to the effect that his thoughts of her were highly complimentary.

"It is no matter," she interposed hurriedly. "It is no matter what you think, if you will only help. We talk much, too much—the time is short. At any moment—" She hesitated; glanced around; apparently was relieved to find that the little group at the other end of the *stoep* was enjoying a wordy warfare between a West Indian fruit seller and a Chinese laundryman.

"You see, *Senhor* Major," she went on swiftly, "we, my brother and I, found a diamond pipe in our territory. I am Portuguese, you know that, of course. We tried to sell the stones in Lourenço Marques, but the price the dealers offered was too small. We went to all the dealers, and always the price was the same, so my brother he would not sell. After a while bad men got to know that we had those diamonds, and they tried to steal them from us. My brother they stabbed." Her voice quavered and the Major, looking at her quickly, saw that there *were* tears in her dark, expressive eyes! "They hurt him very badly so that he was unable to travel. He wanted me then to give up the diamonds. But I wouldn't. So I left him in Lourenço Marques and tried to sell the diamonds myself."

The Major murmured an expression of sympathy for the brother's misfortune and of admiration of the girl's courage.

She was silent for a little while, watching two policemen and a stout, dumpy woman who were walking leisurely up the dusty street. Her eyes hardened as she continued: "So I left my brother and went to Cape Town, thence to Johannesburg, but no one would buy; they were afraid the diamonds were—what do you say?—I.D.B. And those same bad men followed me. Yes, they followed me to this town of diamonds where, a dealer in Johannesburg told me, I would get good money for my stones. How was I to know that dealer lied, that he was a friend of those so wicked men who followed me? And how can I sell here? It is like—what you say?—carrying coals to the Newcastle.

"Three days I have been here and three times those men have searched my room, when I was not there, looking for the stones. Once they caught me and would have searched me—and then they would have found what they sought—but they were afraid. I always carry a revolver; my brother said I must."

The policemen and their companion were very near to the hotel now but their attention was engaged by the quarreling fruit-seller and laundryman.

"And now," went on the girl, "they have informed the police that I am an I.D.B., that I have stolen the stones from them! How can I prove that they lie? What is it that I can do? Of course the police will find the stones and I will be sent to the Breakwater. Ah, I have heard of that so terrible place. And my brother! What will he think? That I have not kept faith with him, and he will die. What can I do? They are coming now to search me. That pair and woman—" She clasped her hands tightly together; there was bitter anguish in her eyes.

"You have the diamonds on you?" the Major asked curtly.

"Of course. Where else could I hide them?"

"Give them to me."

She looked at him hopefully. "Oh, that is so good of you. You will take them to my brother in Lourenço Marques. The name, the place where he is, is on the package I will give you. We will travel together unless the police—what you say?—frame me. Ah! I am afraid of the police."

"We will travel together," the Major assured her and taking off his helmet placed it on his knees, crown downward. "But are you sure you can trust me?"

"Quite sure. The *Senhor* Major's fame has traveled far. We know of him in Lourenço Marques and admire him, oh, so greatly. Quick then, turn your head. They come."

As the Major tilted back his head and gazed upward at a vulture which hovered high above the town, the girl bent down swiftly and lifting her skirt took from a pocket cunningly concealed in its lining a small, brown paper wrapped package.

Rising with languid grace she fluttered her fan, then sauntered slowly toward the hotel entrance just as the policemen and their companion, having put an end to the international argument, climbed the long flight of steps leading on to the *stoep*.

Accosting the girl they spoke to her in low, urgent tones. She drew herself up haughtily and would have passed on but one man caught her arm in an iron grip.

"None of that, ducky," he said coarsely. "You'll go with Mrs. Simson, here, and let her search you nicely or we'll put the 'cuffs on you and come along and *help* her search! How'd you like that?"

"Pig!" she retorted, and then added quietly, "I will let this woman search me, but afterward—"

The other officer led her away and laughed as they entered the hotel with the searcher at her elbow. His laugh was echoed by subdued, malicious titterings from the women on the *stoep*.

The Major who had been watching very closely, now took a large handkerchief from his pocket and mopped his forehead. The arrest was vulgarly done, but it really was too infernally hot to stickle over as small a thing as chivalry.

One of the women rose and whispered in the policeman's ear. He nodded and then wheeled suddenly. "Why, hullo, Major," he said cheerfully. "You here still?"

"So it would seem, dear lad, so it would seem. It's deucedly hot, isn't it?" The Major gave his forehead one last mop then rolled his handkerchief—it was a fine, white silk—into a tight ball and tossed it negligently into his helmet which he had placed on the chair the girl just had vacated. The handkerchief opened out as if worked by springs.

The policeman walked over to the Major. "What are you doing here?" he asked.

The Major laughed fatuously; he seemed such a silly ass. "Watching the world go by," he drawled, "and listening to a police chappy insult a lady."

"She's no lady!"

The Major held up his hand in reproof. "Tut, tut! Let's not discuss it, old bean. It's too hot for argument and you couldn't, I'm sure, appreciate the niceties of the—er—subject under discussion."

The policeman glared and fingered the stiff collar of his tunic, undecided what to do or say. "Sit down, do, and let's have a chin," the Major continued, a gleam of amusement in his eyes. "You look deucedly uncomfortable standing there. Such a bally idiotic uniform you laddies have to wear; all right for the arctic regions, perhaps. I think I'll write a letter to the papers about it. Oh, sit down. It makes me hot just to look at you."

Taking his helmet and placing it on the ground beside him, he patted the chair beside him invitingly. "This is my friend's seat," he chanted.

With a grunt the policeman sat and they talked for a time of this and that; of big finds on the diamond fields; of rich men ruined, and paupers made wealthy over night; of native labor problems and the ways of I.D.B.s.

Presently the policeman said abruptly, "What do you know of Lola de Sousa, Major?"

"Who?"

"The 'lady,'" the policeman's voice was thick with sarcasm, "who just has gone upstairs with my assistant."

"Oh! Is *that* her name? I don't know the lady, and most surely I know nothing about her. Why do you ask, old bean?"

"Never mind," the policeman said slowly. "Only, I thought perhaps you being here had something to do with

Lola: you were chinning with her just before we came up, weren't you?"

"Why, yes, now you recall it, we did exchange a few pleasantries. Oh, yes, and she told me about her brother. A very sad case. But you don't seem to be interested."

"I'm not, I've heard all of Lola's sad stories before. She's getting a reputation to almost as big as yours in the I.D.B. game."

"Oh, come now," the Major expostulated. "If you bally police Johnnies are to be believed, I'm the biggest villain unhung."

"Maybe you are," the policeman conceded slowly. "But—damn it all, I'm going to take a chance and do it."

"Do what, old bean?" the Major asked in alarm.

"Search you."

"Search *me?* And for what?"

"Ivory tusks, of course!" The policeman did not excel at repartee. "Come on!"

The Major thrust his hands hurriedly into his trouser pockets. "I won't come," he said positively. "Why should I?"

"Don't see how you can get out of it, Major. We've got the right to search anybody at any time. You know that."

The Major sighed. "Yes. I know that. But why do you want to search me now? It's positively ridiculous."

"Maybe, maybe not. You see, Major, you've got a reputation, and Lola, she's getting one. We received information this morning that she's carrying diamonds about with her, so she's under suspicion. You and her were talking together; that puts you under suspicion. See?"

"Yes, I see. But you're not going to search me, just the same."

"I am." The policeman's hand rested lightly on his revolver butt. "And you'll keep your hands in your pockets. Come on, we'll go to one of the rooms in the hotel. I'll search you there, then, if it happens that you've got no diamonds on you, you'll be spared the trouble of walking down to the station in this blasted heat."

"Kind of you, old soul. But you mean, don't you, that you're taking care not to make a fool of yourself before your heroic comrades on the force. Isn't that it?"

"Never mind that, and don't forget what I said about not taking your hands from your pockets." He rose from his chair and stood waiting expectantly. "And don't think you can make a getaway," he went on as the Major looked longingly at his horse, the black stallion, Satan, which was tethered to the hitch rack which stood in the shade in front of the hotel. "The first break you make, I'll plug your horse. Get that?"

"How do I know you won't frame me?" he expostulated.

"You don't," the policeman snapped. "But I've got a reputation for square dealing."

"Yes, you have, and, 'pon my soul, I believe you deserve it. Pardon my doubt. All right, let's go! But, I warn you, you're going to be most frightfully disappointed."

"Maybe," he policeman admitted with a wry grin. "Come on."

"Can't I pick up my helmet? Some one might steal it."

"No, you can't. Keep your hands in your pockets, see? You don't need a helmet. Plenty of shade in the hotel; more than you'll get at the Breakwater."

"I wish you'd let me take it," the Major murmured. "If it is stolen, I'll sue you for a new one."

With an air of hopeless resignation, his broad shoulders sagging, the Major rose wearily. "All right, forward,

MacDuff," he said and slouched toward the door, the policeman close behind him.

FIFTEEN MINUTES later, just after the dinner gong had sounded and the *stoep* was deserted, the Major emerged from the hotel followed by the policeman who looked extremely sheepish. The Major, however, was beaming with satisfaction; his whole bearing was one of virtue triumphant.

"Well," he said cheerfully. "I hope you're satisfied, old dear."

"Well, I'm not," the other snapped.

"But surely you searched me very carefully. I found it most embarrassing. And you've quite ruined my boots, you know." He looked regretfully at his highly-polished, brown riding boots. The heels of them had been pried off. "Aren't you satisfied yet that I'm not carrying diamonds around with me? Even supposing I was an I.D.B.—and I'm not, you know; wouldn't break the jolly old laws for anything—I wouldn't be such a fool as to carry diamonds about with me."

The policeman shook his head doubtfully. "It's a fact you haven't any sparklers on you, Major. I've searched you damned hard. No; you're not carrying diamonds on you, I'll take oath on that, and I can't hold you. But, if you'll take my tip, you'll steer clear of Lola. She's dangerous."

"Thanks for the warning, old top. But I wonder how your assistant is getting on with her little searching party?"

"Whether she finds anything or not, it's all one to me," the policeman growled, "I've got a warrant for her arrest. She forget to pay her board bill at Jo'burg."

"Ah, I see. That's too bad. Life's full of little sorrows, isn't it? But there are compensations. For instance, I'll have a lot of fun telling the chappies about how you held me up and searched me, with absolutely nothing to go on save the fact that I had exchanged a few words with a very charming lady."

The policeman moved uneasily. "You won't blab, Major?" he blurted appealingly.

"What? You'd rather I didn't? Why, then, of course I won't. It shall be just a little secret between us, as it were. Only, just one little word of warning. I don't like to preach, but even supposing Miss Lola to be an I.D.B., the fact that I talked with her doesn't make me one. You seem to be too easily misled by that jolly foolish proverb, 'You can't touch pitch'—whatever that is—'without getting dirty.' For example, think of the number of criminals you police laddies have to consort with. And yet, who ever heard of a dishonest bobby?"

The policeman snorted in disgust.

"Well, toodle-oo, old chap. I must away and begone. Jim—you know Jim don't you? He's priceless!—will be wondering what's keeping me."

The Major slowly descended the *stoep* steps. He was halfway down when he stopped, clapped his hand on his head and—

"My hat!" he exclaimed in tones of annoyance. "I'd forgotten my helmet." He ran back up the steps and to the place where he had left his helmet. Picking it up he took from it his handkerchief which he put carefully in his tunic pocket, fixing it so that a white peak of handkerchief showed artistically against the khaki tunic. Then, using the shaded window of the hotel as a mirror, he preened himself; patted his pocket to smooth out the bulge made by the handkerchief; smoothed back his hair and, with many weird facial contortions, fixed his monocle in his eye.

"You do more primping than a woman, Major," the policeman growled contemptuously.

"You think so," the Major drawled. "But then appearances do count, old bean, and the quickness of the hand does deceive the eye. For instance—but never mind that. You wouldn't understand. You're a bally good searcher—give you a most glowing testimonial any day; be charmed to—but you can't find much, can you?"

The policeman took an angry step toward the Major who, in mock alarm, jammed his helmet on his head, vaulted over the *stoep* rail, landing lightly on all fours, unhitched his horse, mounted and with a parting, mocking "Toodle-oo," rode swiftly away.

The policeman watched until only a dust cloud marked his progress, watched until the Major had passed entirely from sight. And as he watched the policeman's forehead became wrinkled by deep lines of puzzled wonder.

"I wonder," he exclaimed suddenly, but did not finish his wonder, realizing that his opportunity, if opportunity it really had been, had passed from his grasp. It was too late to do anything now. The Major was out of reach, and on guard.

And then a window opened above his head. "She's got no stones on her," Mrs. Simson called. "Did you have any better luck with the Major?"

"No. He didn't have a thing on him we could hold him for. Hell! I'd like to get hold of the party who sent us off on this fool chase. Never mind. Bring Lola down and we'll *hamba* toward the police station. Perhaps we can make her talk when we get her there."

IT WAS after sunset when the Major reached his camp on the veld. By the time he had off-saddled and had given Satan a rubdown—Jim was busy preparing skoff—it was quite dark.

"Skoff will be ready in a little while," the Hottentot announced. He was dressed, as always when preparing or serving his baas's meals, in a suit of white duck as spotless and well creased as any the Major ever wore. The trousers, however, were much too long for him; he had turned them tip seven or eight inches at the bottom. The coat fitted too snugly across his shoulders. Jim's chest measurement was abnormally large; he had the strength of a gorilla in those long, muscle knotted arms.

"The baas stayed too long at the *dorp*," he said chidingly.

"No, Jim," the Major contradicted. "I stayed just long enough."

Jim caught the note of triumph in his master's voice. "Then the money has come, baas? Tomorrow we trek?"

The Major laughed. He was washing himself at the canvas basin Jim had placed in the firelight at the door of the bell-tent. He was stripped to the waist and his torso showed great muscular development. The Major's physical strength was as well concealed by his clothes as his keen brain was masked by the monocle he wore.

"No, Jim," he said. "I haven't the money; I forgot all about it. But tomorrow we trek."

Jim's eyes gleamed. "We play a game, baas?" he asked eagerly.

"We play a game, but it's a new one, I think. The towel, Jim?"

"It is at your hand, baas."

There was silence for a little while as the Major briskly dried himself. Then he retired into the tent which was lighted by an oil lamp fixed in a bracket on the center pole, and a few minutes later was ready for skoff—as ready as any member of a big city's social whirl, and equally as well-dressed. It was one of the Major's little idiosyncrasies to dress for dinner whenever possible. No one who mattered, or who was deemed deserving of an answer, ever had questioned his motive; if they had, he probably would have given some foolish and absolutely irrelevant answer. Actually, it was a way of keeping faith with his caste. This little gesture of attachment to a conventional custom in some measure counteracted the effect of voluntary exile from his own kind; it helped him to combat the insidious snares of Africa; it continually held before him the fact that he was white and must not betray his race. The defeat of so many white men in Africa's dark places is marked first by an indifference to personal appearance; after that, the moral let-down is sudden and complete.

The Major pulled his chair up to the table on which Jim had spread a snow-white cloth set with gleaming silverware, and ate with unfeigned enjoyment the well prepared food the Hottentot set before him.

When he came to the coffee, the Major lighted a cigarette and took from his pocket the small package Lola de Sousa had dropped into his helmet under cover of her fluttering fan.

He turned the package between his long, capable fingers, and scrutinized it carefully. He read aloud the name and address written in a bold, flowing hand, and committed it to memory. Then he broke the flimsy string and opening the package spread its contents—twenty uncut, unpolished diamonds all nearly as large as grapes—on the table before him. As he handled each one he gauged its weight, quality, and value with a practiced certainty which could only have come from much experience.

"My word!" he exclaimed softly. "What a haul! But I wonder just where Miss Lola obtained these. You know, Jim—" the Hottentot was seated near the flap of the tent, mixing dough; he realized that he would have little time for baking in the morning—"You know, Jim, I don't *quite* believe that young lady's tale. It was tall, quite tall, if you know what I mean. Somehow I don't believe she has a brother. But, on the other hand—Oh, I say, Jim, you don't mind me speaking to you in English, do you? But of course you don't. I've done it so often. You see, you grinning old heathen, talking aloud helps me to put two and two together. And I like to pretend that I'm talking to you and that you understand me. I'm glad you can't because, if you could, you'd be sure to have some half-baked theory about two and two making four and that would throw me off my balance, as it were. On the other hand, it is so much better than talking aloud to myself. That's a symptom of insanity, you know. Eh, what, Jim?"

The Hottentot looked up with a grin.

" 'San'ty. Go'blessme, yes. My word, are you?" he said with parrot-like intonation.

The Major laughed.

"That's the question, old bean. But to return to the subject of Lola. I wonder what is her little game? I think the police chappy was absolutely on the square and, of course, Miss Lola may have been on the square too. Ah, well! There's only one thing for us to do, and that's to go to Lourenço Marques and find out. So we will trek very early in the morning, Jim, and we will trek very fast. 'Pon my soul, I'd be in a deuce of a pickle if the bally police took, it into their silly heads to search me, Yes, a deuce of a pickle. Trouble is, I can't get rid of these stones in an emergency. I've got to hold on to them. Bally nuisance, but what would you?"

There was silence for a little while. The darkness deepened. The firelight died down. Night birds called to each other. The whining yelps of mongrel dogs at some distant *kraal* sounded faintly. The air was filled with fragrant earth smells; the smoke from the wood fire blended pungently with the yeasty smell of the dough Jim was kneading.

"It is very dark, baas," Jim said suddenly and began to hum, very softly, a hunting song of his people. Presently he put words to the tune—but they were not the words of the song. Instead, he improvised,

"Darkness hides evil which comes quickly. Ho, warrior! Keep watch!"

Twice he repeated this, softly, so that to any one over twenty feet away the worlds would not have been audible at all. Then he called loudly:

"O-he, baas! Have you finished skoff? It is in my mind, if the baas pleases, to wash the dishes before I cook; and the dough is ready for the baking."

"Yes, Jim," the Major said absently—yet he knew well that the Hottentot had cleared away the dirty dishes before he had brought into the tent the Major's coffee. "Take away the cloth and be sure that you leave the crumbs for the birds."

Jim jumped to his feet and entering the tent, carefully took up the table cloth by its four corners.

"Don't let the crumbs fall in here, Jim," the Major continued. He was leaning back in his chair, his monocle gleaming in his eye, sipping his coffee with evident enjoyment.

Then his jaw sagged, his monocle fell from his eye and splashed into his coffee, he let his chair come down to all fours with a sudden jerk. "My word," he exclaimed peevishly. "How you frightened me!"

Jim turned with a start to face a policeman who had entered the tent softly behind him. It was the same policeman who had searched the Major that afternoon at the hotel. Jim looked at the revolver in the policeman's hand, an expression of fear on his homely, goodnatured face. For a moment all three men were motionless, as if they were actors in a tableau. Then Jim made a move as if to leave the tent but the policeman interposed his bulk between the Hottentot and the opening.

Jim looked to the Major for instructions. "Tell your boy," the policeman said slowly, "to be good. He can sit where he was sitting before, just outside the flap of the tent. But if he makes any move I don't like it'll be all the worse for you. See? Tell him now, what I say. And, mind. I'm watching you both all the time."

"You're a clever chappy," murmured the Major. "But I'm very much afraid that you'll get cockeyed if you try to look two ways at once." Then, turning to Jim, the Major quickly translated the policeman's instructions.

"If the baas, orders," Jim said sullenly. "I will kill this pig."

"Oh, no you won't, dog," the policeman said in the vernacular.

Jim looked very sheepish. "Pardon, *inkosi*," he said. "How was I to know that you could understand my talk?" He shuffled slowly outside, the tablecloth still held carefully in his hand. A moment or two later, he was squatting on his haunches, giving some final pats to his bread dough, shaping it before putting it to bake in the red ashes of the fire.

The policeman turned to the Major who was shaking with silent laughter. "What are you giggling at," he asked suspiciously.

"Why, er, at the merry jape you played on dear old Jim. He makes believe he's a terrible fire-eater, you know, but really, he's as harmless as a cooing dove. Oh, quite! And when you talked to him in his own language, the expression on his face was too, too funny." The Major laughed loudly and the policeman grinned in spite of his endeavor to keep a straight face and look very official. The Major's laugh was contagious; it had that unrestrained, jubilant ring of the Eternal Boy in it.

Presently the Major sobered, however. "But, I say, old chap, why are you here, if the question is not too bally personal? And don't you think I ought to know your name? After our intimate session of this afternoon, names, perhaps, are rather superfluous. Still—"

"Name's Higgins, Sergeant-detective Higgins," the other said sourly.

"Ah, thanks. Now won't you let me give you a cup of coffee? I'll call Jim and tell him—"

"Don't want no coffee—and don't talk to your nigger. I want to have a little chin with you."

"Charmed," murmured the Major,

"Perhaps I'll hold another little searching party."

"Not so charming," the Major said hastily. "But good God, man, it's getting to be an obsession with you; I think you must be a little mad! How else can one explain this beastly epidemic of searching fever? Are you quite sure the old bean's working properly?"

"It is now. It wasn't this afternoon."

The Major nodded sagely and commented to himself. "Yes, poor chap. Undoubtedly suffers from delusions. Must be the heat, aggravated by that tom-fool uniform he has to wear." In a louder voice he said soothingly, "I assure you, dear Sergeant-detective Higgins, that you searched me most thoroughly this afternoon. You have no cause to reproach yourself."

"I flatter myself I did a pretty good job, Major," Higgins said complacently. "But I overlooked one thing. You see, when you made such a show of putting your hands in your pockets and then insisting that you be allowed to take them out in order to pick up your helmet, you threw me off my guard. I thought you had some diamonds in your pocket—that's where your hands went, you know, as soon as I said I was going to search you—and I thought you were looking for a chance to bring your hands out again, full of diamonds which you had found a chance to get rid of somehow."

The Major looked at the sergeant admiringly. "Now that's bally clever of you," he said generously. "I'd never thought of doing anything like that."

"Not so clever, Major," Higgins said ruefully. "You see I forgot all about your helmet. I didn't search it, and I'm willing to bet now that the diamonds handed on to you—yes, she told us she'd given them to you—were in that helmet all the time."

"My hat!" exclaimed the Major. "And you're only a sergeant! I don't believe it!"

The sergeant sat down on the edge of the camp-bed so that the Major and Jim were both in his line of vision. "Laugh away, Major," he growled. "Maybe I'll laugh before the night's through."

"Yes?"

"Yes."

The Major looked at him thoughtfully, at the revolver the sergeant held in his hand. Then he looked at one of his own revolvers hanging in its holster on the tent-pole, near to the lamp bracket. He sighed. "You *are* a bally nuisance, you know," he said wearily, "and I don't know why I put up with you at all. But I suppose you are duty-driven. There's my helmet over there. Search it just as hard as you wish, old dear."

The other laughed scornfully. "You don't think I came out here and crawled on my belly three hundred yards or more, so as to take you by surprise, just to have a look in your helmet, did you? What do you think I am? A bloody fool?"

"Well," the Major temporized, "I don't think I'd go so far as to say that—"

"No," the sergeant blundered on, "I'm not such a fool as to think that the stones are there now. I'm going to search you again. See?"

The good-humored smile left the Major's face; his lips set firm; the vacuous, almost inane, expression entirely left his face. "I'm damned if you are," he said tersely.

The sergeant laughed. "Don't see how you can help it," he said. "There's your gun," he nodded toward the revolver on the center-pole. "Here's mine, ready for use. You can't do a thing."

The Major smiled. "Oh, I don't know," he drawled. "You mustn't be misled by externals. The hidden, unknown danger is always more to be feared, you know, than the obvious one. In other words, the revolver up there is, admittedly, harmless, but this one—"

His right hand darted with the speed of a striking snake underneath the table and up again, grasping a revolver which pointed unwaveringly at the pit of Higgins' stomach.

"This one," he concluded with a smile, "is a form of sudden death!"

The sergeant flinched, then rose slowly and walked toward the Major. "That was pretty work, Major," he said, "but I must have been asleep or I'd never have let you do it. All right, we start even now. Go ahead, shoot if you like, but as for me—" he returned his revolver to its holster— "I'm going to search you."

The Major looked fixedly at him for a moment and then, with an exclamation of disgust, threw his revolver down on the table.

"All right," he said wearily. "Search your fool head off. But the lord only knows why I don't blow it off; because I'm too bally squeamish, I suppose."

Higgins really was dumbfounded. Not desiring to chance an exchange of shot with the Major—at such a close range it would have been a combination of murder and suicide—he was quite prepared to give up the search party. He had not expected any bluff to work and had been prepared to throw up his hands at the first intimation from the Major that the latter intended to shoot. He did not know the Major very well, having been transferred quite recently to the Kimberley troop; did not know that the monocled dude never had fired a shot at a policeman who was endeavoring honestly to do his duty. For that matter, the Major at all times had aided the police rather than obstructed them, save in such little matters as his own ventures in the I.D.B. game.

The sergeant did not allow his astonishment to show too plainly; neither was he slow to take advantage of the situation. Grabbing up the Major's revolver he said triumphantly. "I thought you'd see reason, Major, and because you're being sensible, I'll show you that I'm ready to meet you half way. Give me your word that you haven't the diamonds on you and I won't search you." The sergeant, had heard enough of the Major, at least, to know that his word was his bond.

"Of course I haven't," the Major said. "Give you my word of honor. So let me give you a cup of coffee, then we'll say nighty-night. I'm bally tired."

"Not so fast, Major. I'm taking your word about not having any diamonds on you, and I won't search you. But I didn't say anything about not searching your stuff here." He glanced toward the large, steel uniform-case at the foot and the bed. "And in your Cape Cart."

The Major groaned. "I wish you weren't such a persistent chap. But, look here. Before you start your task, let's have some fresh coffee made. Jim!"

"Yah, baas?" The Hottentot was busily engaged in raking his bread from the embers and knocking the ashes off it with a stick.

"Make fresh coffee, Jim," the Major ordered, "and throw this stuff away. It's cold." The Major placed his coffee cup—he had been holding it in his left hand all this time— on the table. The Hottentot rose slowly to his feet.

"Sit down," the sergeant shouted angrily in the vernacular. "Your baas does not want coffee; neither do I. Sit down."

"Yes: You'd better sit down, Jim," the Major echoed mildly. And Jim sat.

"This is how I look at it," the sergeant said. "I'm going on the theory that having been searched once today you figured that you were safe; that there was no danger of being searched again. Correct me if I'm wrong."

"I said once before that you are a bally clever fellow."

"I'm no fool," Higgins agreed placidly. "Well then, it's my bet that you haven't taken the trouble to hide the stones— there were twenty of them, Lola said. Perhaps you just put them in the top of your uniform case or"—he looked keenly at the Major, "—perhaps you were looking at them just before I came on the scene." He stopped and grabbed up the Major's coffee cup with a quick pounce and slowly poured the lukewarm liquid over the palm of his hand.

The Major watched him, a mocking smile on his face, until his monocle slipped out into the sergeant's hand. "Bah, Jove," he then exclaimed. "I'd forgotten all about that. Give it to me, old dear."

The sergeant handed it to him, a sour expression on his face as he watched the Major dry and polish the glass carefully and fix it in his eye.

"You should wear one, sergeant dear," the Major said with a beaming smile. "It might—one can never tell—help you to become a much better searcher."

"Oh, hell," exploded the sergeant and he flung the coffee cup angrily to the ground where it shattered into small pieces.

"Oh, tut-tut," admonished the Major. "You shouldn't lose your temper."

The sergeant turned irritably to the uniform case and throwing back the lid with a vicious yank, turned out its contents, piling them into a disordered heap on the floor, ignoring the Major's complaints that he was soiling the white linen and spoiling the perfect creases Jim had pressed in the white duck trousers. For all his anger the sergeant's search was thorough. He was well convinced by the time the case was empty, that the Major had not cached the diamonds there.

The fact that the sergeant was conscious that his actions were a source of great mirth to the Major did not improve the sergeant's temper. When he turned his attention to the cot-bed, he was absolutely without consideration, throwing the bedding on the floor, slitting the pillow and covering the ground with feathers. He was about to serve the mattress in the same way when the Major drawled:

"I want to sleep there tonight, Higgy—or is it Piggy?—Will you accept my word that I've nothing hidden there?"

Higgins looked rather shamefaced at the ruined pillow. "All right," he said gruffly. "And listen, Major. Instead of telling me where the diamonds ain't, suppose you tell me where they are."

"Oh, but no, dear old horse. Deprive myself of the pleasure of watching you search? Not for the worlds. Go on, old bean. Don't let me stop you. The night's young yet."

The sergeant sat down on the edge of the bed and gnawed thoughtfully at his mustache. He was beginning to doubt the wisdom of his course. It would have been better, he thought now, to confess himself beaten. He was, he knew, carrying things a bit too far. Of course if he succeeded in finding the diamonds, everything would be all right. Otherwise, there was every chance that he would be put on the "peg" by his superior officer. The Major had a lot of friends on the force. He was, as one trooper put it, such a damned good sport.

The sergeant did not relish the task of going through the equipment, and he winced when he thought of the way his comrades would pull his leg when they heard. Surely the victim would tell them of his attempt to catch the Major with the goods. Why hadn't he placed more credence in the stories told of the Major's *slimness?* Why, he reproached himself, hadn't he left the Major alone?

It came to the sergeant now that the Major already had got rid of the diamonds, probably on his way out from town. How else explain the man's ready surrender, his half-hearted refusal to be searched? He had heard enough of the Major to know he was no coward. If only the damned man wouldn't grin at him so!

The sergeant was quite sure that Lola had given the Major some diamonds that afternoon; Lola was getting quite well known as an I.D.B., and the sergeant did not doubt that the Major was her accomplice. If he only had searched the Major's helmet! He would have found the diamonds, and the Major then and there would have been started on the long journey to the Cape Town Breakwater while he, the sergeant, would have been in line for quick promotion.

Damn the man! Damn his grin and his silly ass way!

The sergeant came to a sudden resolution, born of anger at his own impotent stupidity and vindictiveness toward the Major who had made such a fool of him. He was beaten, he admitted, but he intended to make things uncomfortable for the Major; he'd do something that would make the monocled dude think twice before he told any one of how he had made a fool out of Sergeant-detective Higgins.

The Major stiffened slightly as he sensed the change in the sergeant's mental attitude. "Well?" he asked quietly. "What now?"

"What now?" the sergeant repeated with an oath. "Why now I'm going to search your Cape Cart. Here!" He unhooked a pair of handcuffs from his belt and tossed them to the Major. "Put them on," he ordered. "Quick!"

The Major obeyed, laughing softly as he did so.

"Jim! Come here," the sergeant snapped.

Jim came quickly and was silent as he read the message in the Major's eyes. With the straps used to secure the uniform trunk, the sergeant bound Jim's hands firmly to the Major's feet, and strapped the Major's arms to his sides, allowing a little play so that by many painful contortions it was possible for the Major to reach the strap which bound Jim's hand to him.

"I'm very much afraid that you'll have to suffer all sorts of unpleasant experiences, old top," the Major said sweetly. "This sort of thing isn't done, you know. Can't say that I admire your methods, but I would like to know what you intend to do next."

"I've already told you I'm going to search your Cape Cart," the sergeant growled, "and I'll feel safe now I know that you two can't get up to mischief while I'm gone. I'll be back in a little while." He threw the Major's revolver down on the pile of clothes, and taking the oil lamp from its bracket, he left the tent.

He had no intention of returning. First he would make a show at searching the Cape Cart, taking care to disarrange things as much as possible. That done, he would go back to the town. And if his conscience troubled him at all about the way he was treating the Major, he pacified it with thought of the many stories he had heard of the practical jokes the Major had played on members of the force at one time or other. He was sure that the Major would succeed in freeing himself from Jim; but it would be infinitely harder, he thought, for the Major to get out of the handcuffs. The sergeant thought it quite possible, that the Major would have to ride into the *dorp*, perhaps to the police station, in order to have the 'cuffs filed off him. Higgins meant to lose his key.

"Lucky I brought along that old pair of 'cuffs," he mused as he walked slowly toward the Cape Cart, feeling his way carefully through the darkness. "There's nothing about them to say they belong to me. And when the Major rides in tomorrow—won't he look a fool!—and tells his yarn, I'll deny every word of it. I'll—"

At that moment something hit Higgins on the head and he went down like a pole-axed bullock. The Major, anger, mirth, diamonds, everything was blotted out. Only a great, abysmal darkness remained and in that he wandered for a long time, alone.

AS SOON as Sergeant Higgins departed the tent, leaving the two men in pitch darkness, Jim said in a fierce whisper, "Baas! Why did you let that pig do this? Why didn't you kill him?"

"This is no cause for a killing, Jim," the Major answered with a low chuckle. "No harm comes to us. Let him go his way and play his game. Later, maybe, we will laugh. As soon as I get my hands free I—"

"Can the baas do that?" Jim asked incredulously.

"Truly, Jim. The handcuffs are old and I know a trick—end even if they were new and I knew no trick, to get free would be simple. The policeman was angry, also he was in great haste. So he did not look to see if the handcuffs were locked. And so, Jim, we will wait a little while until he is busy in the Cape Cart."

"If the baas wishes to be free," Jim said grimly, "he must work quickly."

"Why, Jim?" the Major asked and as he spoke he strained slightly at his wrists.

"Because, baas, other men are near."

"Friends, Jim?"

"Who knows, baas," Jim said cryptically. "Maybe they came quietly—I heard them while the policeman was talking to the baas—because they wished to take the policeman unawares, and so free the baas. But hyenas steal upon a camp at night and men do not call *them* friends."

At that moment there came the sound of a dull thud, followed by the *tinkle* of breaking glass.

"They are here, baas."

"Poor old Higgins," said the Major, "They must have broken my bally lamp."

"Never mind that, baas. Are your hands free yet? It is time we were up and doing."

"Quiet, Jim. We will remain as we are for a little while. If we are bound, and harmless, we may learn things."

"Aye," Jim commented dryly. "And we may suffer things."

The Major chuckled. "*Sssh!* They are coming."

Outside they could hear men talking—the voices came nearer, nearer. Two dark shadows blotted out the strip of star-strewn sky visible through the tent opening. Into the tent they came, walking slowly with heavy tread, muttering foreign curses, grunting under the burden they were carrying. Just inside the tent they dropped their load with a sigh of relief. There was silence for a little while, broken only by the labored breathing of the two newcomers.

Presently the Major said sharply, and there was a nervous inflection in his voice, "Here, I say! Who are you? Help! Untie me!" His voice trailed off into silence, the silence of a badly frightened man.

One of the newcomers laughed and, striking a match, lighted the lantern which the other carried, and placed it on the table. Then they both looked at the Major and Jim and laughed uproariously; there was something mean and vindictive in their laughter. The Major watched them narrowly. He noted their pasty, yellowish complexion, their short, dumpy figures, their ornate jewelry. They were much alike, brothers undoubtedly, possibly twins.

When they stopped laughing, the Major's expression changed instantly. The hard, calculating look vanished from his eyes, his jaw muscles sagged. He changed from a man of quick wit and action to a slew thinking, unenergetic dude. "I don't see what you are laughing at," he said pompously. "And I *do* wish you'd release me!"

"Presently, presently," answered one of the men in a soft, lisping voice. "First we must talk business. You know who we are?"

" 'Pon my soul, no. Unless—ah, yes. I have it. You are Tweedledum and Tweedledee. No."

Then men scowled and the Major continued thoughtfully, "Well, perhaps you're not. But you do look alike. Both have your long black tresses greased with—er—grease. It smells vilely! Fat faces— can't see your eyes—adorned with wondrous mustaches, beautifully curled. White duck suits, the trousers whereof are supported by gorgeous red cummerbunds. Well! If you aren't Dee and Dum, who *are* you?"

"My name is Manuel de Silva."

"And mine, Ricardo de Silva."

"Ah," murmured the Major. "I thought so. Brothers and—er—Goanese?" The last word was drawled in a contemptuous manner which added to the insult of the word itself. "Goanese" is the word applied to Portuguese half-castes.

Its effect on the two de Silvas was instantaneous and violent. Manuel hit the Major across the cheek with his open hand; Ricardo aimed a kick at his shins but missed because, in some mysterious way, Jim interposed his body. Both men cursed long and loudly in a mixture of Portuguese and English. "You swine!" gasped Ricardo when curses finally failed him. "You *dare* to call us Goanese!"

"We are Portuguese," shouted Manuel. "Our blood is unmixed."

The Major inclined his head maybe to hide the sparkle in his eyes. "Pardon," he said humbly. "I was mistaken.

But the light is poor and—er—and I did not think that nobles of Portugal would delay so long in setting a white man free."

"First business," said Ricardo coldly, "and then, who knows?" He looked at his brother who was busily engaged in twirling the waxed ends of his mustache.

Manuel nodded. "Then," he said, "we will set you free or—" His plump white hands fumbled with his cummerbund, exposing the handle of a dagger.

"Or this, eh?" Ricardo drew his finger across his throat.

Manuel nodded. "*Sí,*" he wheezed, and fussily rearranged his cummerbund.

"Splendid," murmured the Major admiringly. "You should be in a Drury Lane pantomime! I never have seen two better—er—villains. You deserve long and loud hisses. But tell me," and his voice hardened slightly, his eyes focussed on the inanimate object the two men had carried into the tent with them, "have you killed the sergeant?"

"No. He's not dead."

"But he hasn't moved or spoken since you brought him in. And that's strange. I've found him to be a man of many words."

"He's gagged and bound."

"Ah! I see. But why the hood over his head, old dears?"

"So that he can't see. We expect to stay and do business in Kimberley for a long time."

The Major nodded. "Think of everything, old dears, don't you? But I can see, you know. I'd know you again, and so would Jim."

Ricardo shrugged his shoulders.

"You don't count," Manuel said contemptuously. "You are not of the police."

"You're not very flattering. But suppose we get to business. I confess to same curiosity as to my ultimate fate. A natural curiosity, you will admit. Do I get stuck, or do I go free?"

"We want the diamonds Lola de Sousa gave you."

"Really!" The Major's eyebrows arched. "But suppose I answer that you're talking through your hat. I mean," he amended, "suppose I say I don't know what you're talking about—and I *don't*, you know!"

They laughed. Then, "We know you have them, *Senhor* Major. Lola told us all about it. That was funny the way you believed the story about her brother and the bad men. Lola is very beautiful and so very clever. And you are clever too. Where did you put the diamonds when the policeman first searched you?"

"In my helmet," the Major admitted.

"You are not very clever after all, *Senhor* Major," Ricardo said contemptuously. "Once more I ask. Where are the diamonds?"

"I'm hanged if I know, old dears. And even if I did, I couldn't give them to you."

"Why not?"

"Because the so charming and clever Miss Lola asked me to take them to her brother at Lourenço Marques. You wouldn't have me false to my trust, would you?"

"We tell you," Manuel said slowly, "that Lola is our partner. She asked you to take the stones because she knew that she was going to be searched. She has no brother. So, for the last time, will you give them to us."

"I don't know what to think," the Major said plaintively. Then, decidedly, "Look here, if you're so bally sure that I have the diamonds, why don't you go ahead and find them?"

"We will," said Ricardo. "We first wished to be kind to you. By telling us where they are you can save us much trouble and yourself much pain."

"I don't know where they are, my dear fool," the Major said wearily.

"Then we will search for them."

"But the policeman has already searched and could not find them," the Major exclaimed in alarm.

Manuel sneered. "Yes. We watched him. But he did not know how to search—we do. Just the same we are grateful to him for tieing you up. That saved us a lot of trouble."

Without further words, disdaining the Major's pleas, the two men searched and searched thoroughly. They did not miss a thing, but systematically, inch by inch, explored the tent and its contents.

At length they whispered together for a little while and then Ricardo, standing over Jim, took out his dagger and held the point of it on Jim's Adam's Apple.

"Tell us where are the diamonds, *Senhor* Major," he said thickly, "or—"

He pressed slightly on the knife, and Jim gulped loudly.

"Stop!" the Major shouted in alarm. "I will tell you! In the Cape Cart, in the flour bag under the driver's seat. You will find them there."

The two men looked at each other triumphantly. "We go there now to search," Ricardo said.

"But if you have lied," Manuel added, "we will soon return and then it will he too late to stop the knife from slitting the nigger's throat." They took up the lantern and hurriedly left the tent; Manuel cursed loudly as he stumbled and almost fell over a loaf of Jim's baking.

Left alone again in the tent the Major and Jim were silent for a little while until Jim asked irritably, "And do we wait here, baas, until they return and it is too late?"

"No, Jim. We go now." The Major strained his wrists apart once again and this time the handcuffs opened with a click. The rest was easy. In a very little while he had freed himself of the straps about his arms. To release Jim, then, was the work of a few minutes. They rubbed their stiffened muscles. Then the Major, taking his revolver from the holster which hung on the tent pole—the other one he could not find in the darkness—crept softly out of the tent and toward the Cape Cart.

As they neared it, Satan, the Major's horse, catching the scent of his master, whinnied softly and the whinny was immediately followed by the raucous braying of the mules. The Major and Jim froze in their tracks as Manuel came from under the hood of the Cape Cart, a lantern in hand which he shielded so that it threw its light on the veld about him. But the lantern light was very feeble and its only effect was to make Manuel and his brother who joined him two splendid targets.

"The fools," muttered the Major. "Shall I give them a scare, Jim?" He raised his revolver slowly, planning to shoot the lantern out of Manuel's hand.

"No, baas."

Jim put his hand on the Major's and before he could say anything else the two de Silvas, talking in loud, excited tones, went under the canvas hood and the Major's opportunity was lost.

"Why did you stop me, Jim?" he asked peevishly.

"When a man has cornered a poisonous snake, baas, so that it cannot escape, does he stick out his tongue at it and let it go? No. He kills it, or at least draws its fangs, making it harmless."

"Your point is well taken, Jim, old top. Deucedly well taken. Well, let's go and render them harmless."

They went slowly, silently forward again and coming to the rear of the Cape Cart could see Manuel and Ricardo slowly sifting the flour from the sack through their fingers.

Both men were engrossed with their task, yet each found opportunity to scrutinize closely the other's movements. Evidently the brothers did not trust each other.

The Major watched them in amused silence, and then, his eyes sparkling mischievously, he stooped down and groped about until his hand closed on a good-sized rock. This he gave to Jim. "Do you think you can throw it in the flour, Jim?" he whispered in the Hottentot's ear.

Jim nodded and threw the rock swiftly and with sure aim. It passed right between the heads of Manuel and Ricardo and landed *plop* in the midst of the flour, which squirted up into their faces, momentarily blinding them.

At the same moment the Major leaped into the Cape Cart, followed by Jim, yelling like warriors on the warpath.

The de Silvas danced around, screaming curses, rubbing their eyes, each blaming the other for the predicament in which they found themselves. At the Major's curt command, however, they immediately quieted, and after their offer to share on equal terms with the Major had been rejected, lapsed into sulky silence. Neither did they make any resistance when Jim bound them, although the Major was laughing so hard that he found it almost impossible to keep them covered.

"And now what, baas?" Jim asked. He had lashed the two men together, back to back, so tightly that they were unable to do much more than blink.

"We'll take them to the policeman. Perhaps he'd like to arrest them."

Jim grunted and, dragging the two de Silvas to the edge of the Cape Cart, jumped down and carried them on his shoulders as if they were bundles of sticks, to the tent, the Major walking before him, lantern in hand.

"Good, Jim," the Major exclaimed approvingly as the Hottentot placed his burden on the ground several feet away from the policeman. Then in English, he drawled: "The old boy's strength always amazes me. He's a bally Samson."

"Damme, yes, baas. Sammyson. Go'-blessme!"

The Major laughed. "Inspan, Jim," he said. "We'll trek at once."

"Yah, baas."

As Jim joyfully set about striking the tent and packing it and the equipment on the Cape Cart, working with efficiency and speed despite the darkness, the Major carefully examined the sergeant and then, convinced that he was all right, sat down on the veld. Holding the lantern on his knees he wrote swiftly on pages torn from his note book this letter.

> *Dear Higgy-Piggy,*
>
> *I hope you'll be able to free yourself; but even if you can't some one's sure to find you before long. It won't hurt you to breathe a little fresh air, you know. I think you'll admit that I'm treating you bally well, much better than you deserve. Of course I can't give you the diamonds; don't know where they are myself at this moment—word of honor! But I'm making you a present of two villains of the first water. They're the chappies who hit you on the boko. They were after the diamonds too. Most extraordinary. I think you'll know what to*

do with them, I believe they're a bad lot. Probably—wretched men! I.D.B.s.!

One other thing… Will you tell Miss Lola de Sousa that I'm on my way to Lourenço Marques with the message she gave me for her brother. Say, too, that I know the man who lives at the address on the package she gave me. He's quite well known as a dealer in stolen stones. I'm afraid Miss Lola doesn't keep good company.

Ta-ta, old man. I doff my helmet— Ha-ha!—to you.

The Major.

This letter the Major pinned on the sergeant's tunic. Then he helped Jim inspan.

In a very little while, when all was ready, he carefully loosened the sergeant's bandages so that it would be possible for the policeman to release himself if he exercised great patience. "All right, Jim," the Major cried and mounting Satan, rode swiftly through the darkness toward the East, where the paling sky announced the birth of a new day.

Jim called to the six mules harnessed to the Cape Cart, cursed them lovingly and then, cracking his long whip with rifle-like reports, wheeled them around and followed swiftly after his baas.

THE SUN was high when Sergeant Higgins succeeded in freeing himself. His head throbbed painfully, every muscle of his body ached, but he felt much better after he had read the Major's note. He lost no time in preparing the two de Silvas for their trip to the *dorp*.

About the same time the Major and Jim had halted for breakfast about twenty miles to the east. "I say, Jim," the Major said suddenly. "Where are the diamonds?"

"Diamonds, baas?" Jim repeated wonderingly. "What diamonds?"

"Why the ones you took out in the table cloth last night!" The Major stopped short and looked at Jim curiously. "Do you mean to say," he began slowly. Then he stopped again, whistled softly and, rising to his feet, yawned luxuriously. "You're a bally old fraud, Jim," he said. "Of course you don't know anything about the diamonds. No, of course not! But why are you making fresh bread. You baked last night."

"That bread is no good, baas. The men trod on it last night."

"But you brought it along with you. I saw you put it in the Cape Cart."

"True, baas." And Jim took from a dirty sack three or four loaves of bread. He gave one of them to the Major, and grinned happily.

The Major crumbled it between his hands. "Yes, Jim," he drawled. "You're a clever old blighter. Dear old Cleopatra hid her pearl in wine—and lost the jewel. But you—you hide diamonds in the staff of life and they are with us always, even unto the end."

Jim grinned: his baas was happy, therefore he was happy. "To the end," he echoed with a queer inflection. The words were quite meaningless to him. Then in the vernacular he asked, "Where do we go now, baas?"

"To Lourenço Marques, Jim."

"Do you play a game, baas?"

"Yes, Jim."

"What game, baas—diamonds?"

"Who knows?" The Major shrugged his shoulders. "Any game the friends of Lola may put before us."

ZULU PRIDE

"**I TELL** you, white man," the naked, grease-daubed native said tonelessly, "that I do not know where rubber is."

The white man whistled softly a few bars of a song at that time immensely popular in the London halls. Presently he stopped whistling and sang a bar or two of the chorus: "Ta-ra ra boom de ay!"

"And I have no ivory, white man." The native broke in on the song.

The white man looked quizzically at the native and then at the collection of squalid huts which formed the village over which the lanky, emaciated native was chief.

"I can well believe that," he said softly, and he spoke the vernacular as fluently as the native. "Yes, I can well believe that, M'Mandi."

The white man rose slowly to his feet and picking up the large handkerchief on which he had been sitting, shook it and put it in his pocket. Then he strolled unconcernedly about the *kraal*, wondering not a little at the fear in the eyes of the old women and at the strange absence of younger women; hurt because the children—they all had the distended stomach, the sunken eyes and pipe stem limbs of semi-starvation—ran screaming away at his approach.

He was puzzled, too, at the absence of menfolk. There were none save M'Mandi and a few graybeards so old that they could do nothing but sit in the sun and exchange mournful reminiscences of the days of their youth.

He stopped inadvertently before the grain store hut, all faculties concentrating on an attempt to discover the reason for the cloud of gloom which hung over the village.

"And I have no grain, white man," said a voice at his

elbow. The native who had followed the white man as he wandered aimlessly about the place, now was standing behind him.

The white man turned about quickly and, taking a monocle from the breast pocket of his white, silk shirt, toyed with it absently. "That, too, I can well believe, M'Mandi," he nodded slowly. "Never have I seen such hungry looking children! But why? You are of Zulu stock—"

"Truly," the man said proudly. "When Mzilikazi broke away from Chaka and came north, at that same time Manikos broke away also and traveled north, but not with Mzilikazi. Aye! He settled in this country and made himself a great chief. He drove the Portuguese dogs—" M'Mandi broke off suddenly and cringed as though expecting a blow. "Your pardon, white man," he said humbly.

"It is nothing," the white man denied slowly. "But still I do not understand how you came to this way of desolation. Manikos was strong, his warriors were many and powerful. Now Manikos is dead, true, but his son M'Zila is yet stronger. His people go up and down the land—and they do not look fearfully behind them, as you do."

"The white man knows many things. He should know, too, that a few among many are helpless. Long years ago Manikos left my father in this place with certain warriors and their women. My father's duty it was to guard the back of Manikos, who went on and forgot my father and the warriors left with him. But, because Manikos ordered, 'Stay and guard my back,' my father stayed behind and built this *kraal*. For a few years he ruled the country as if he were king, enslaving the M'Hlengwe people who lived in these parts, giving their maidens to his warriors. By and by, the jungle growth and jungle ways choked his warriors' strength and courage—we are not jungle people, we Zulu—and the M'Hlengwe ceased to fear us. A little later they became our masters, for they were many and we few. Also the Portuguese dogs—"

Again M'Mandi paused and cringed, looking in amazement at the white man when the expected blow did not fall. "And the Portuguese dogs," he repeated, brazenly this time, "also took toll of us. And so we became as we are."

"Yet M'Zila is alive and strong," the white man suggested. "He would not, perhaps, be deaf to a plea for help."

The native's eyes flashed, he drew himself erect with an imperious gesture. "Zulu blood is in my veins, white man. And a Zulu does not cry for help. Also," he added lamely, "M'Zila is deaf. Once we sent word to him and he did not answer."

"Perhaps the message never reached him."

"*Au-a!* But it did, white man. Our messenger returned to us after many moons and M'Zila had dealt harshly with him. His right eye had been put out, his right ear was gone and his right arm cut off at the shoulder. This was the answer M'Zila sent to us: "You are no true Zulu, so why should I help you? Too much M'Hlengwe blood flows in your veins; you are only half Zulu. That part which is mine, I will protect—as I protected this messenger dog. The part that is mine, I keep. So much I will do for any other of you to come to me."

"*Au-a!*" exclaimed the visitor. "A harsh man, M'Zila."

"True, white man, and just. But none other of my people ever desire to taste more of his justice." M'Mandi smiled bleakly, then added in a matter of fact voice, "As for the messenger, we killed him; for, after M'Zila's pruning, *he was all M'Hlengwe* and had no place among us!"

The white man nodded, fixed his monocle in his eye, took out his handkerchief again and, spreading it carefully on a large, upturned calabash, sat down. For a while he gazed reflectively at his well polished brown riding boots, the native standing expectantly before him. "Sit down, M'Mandi," he said presently and, when the native, surprised into a betraying ejaculation at this courtesy on the part of any white man, obeyed, took a bag of *gwai* (Boer tobacco) from his pocket and tossed it to the Zulu.

"*Au-a baba!*" M'Mandi exclaimed as he eagerly clutched the bag. "And it is all mine, white man?"

"Truly."

The white man rolled himself a cigarette, lighted it and puffed in lazy enjoyment. "I really shouldn't smoke," he murmured in English; "at least not until I'm sure of my ground. And I'm not; far, far from it. But there are so many beastly smells about this place. Old M'Mandi himself is no bloomin' violet; quite the opposite, in fact.

"Wish Jim 'ud come. 'Fraid the old bounder's having the deuce an' all of a time with the mules. Perhaps I should have stayed with him. But of course not. I had to come ahead, to spy out the land as it were.

"I believe old M'Mandi would like to be quite chummy—but he's afraid to be. Scared of the Portuguese, most likely. They're a messy lot. Don't know how to treat natives at all.

"Wonder what the old blighter's up to now?"

The native suddenly had jumped to his feet and had vanished into one of the huts. He no longer could keep the story of this so strange white man to himself.

Hitherto, in M'Mandi's experience, white men meant only unjust taxes, brutality, the burning of huts and the ravaging of women. Never before had he met a white man like this one; so tall and strong, so stern and yet so soft. Never before had he met a white man who gave him kind words, and presents.

He emerged from the hut again presently, carefully carrying in his two hands a small calabash. He knelt down before the white man and handed him the calabash. It contained beer, a thick, evil smelling brew.

The white man drank deeply, through closed teeth that he might strain from the beer the foreign matter which floated in it, conscious that the native was watching him closely. "That was good, M'Mandi," he said at length, handing the calabash back to the native. "If I die," he added in English, "I'll have only myself to blame. But the old blighter evidently thinks so highly of it that it 'ud never do to let him see that I thought it filth—oh, quite that!"

"The white man was saying?" M'Mandi asked curiously.

"That he had never drank better beer; it was a true Zulu brew."

M'Mandi bridled with pleasure. "Ah, white man. M'Zila was wrong. We are still more Zulu than M'Hlengwe. We have not forgotten the old ways." He peered into the calabash; it still was half full. "But has the white man had all he requires?" he added anxiously.

The other waved his hand airily. "Enough, M'Mandi. I was not thirsty; and the little I had, because of its great excellence, sufficed. You will finish it?"

"Truly!" And M'Mandi put the calabash to his mouth and with much smacking of lips registered great satisfaction. Presently he called an old graybeard to him and gave the man the calabash.

Although his attention appeared to be riveted elsewhere, the white man noticed that the calabash still contained as much beer as it had when he had handed it to M'Mandi. In other words, the chief only had pretended to drink. That was cause for much thought.

As if answering the unspoken doubts in the white man's mind M'Mandi said apologetically, "We are very poor, white man. This season the crops failed us and we have very little corn to spare for beer. So, what beer we have we save for men like you; for men who *are* men!"

"It is understood," answered the white man softly. "It was a man's courtesy, M'Mandi."

"By what name shall I call you, white man?"

The visitor laughed. "Among my people there are some who call me 'Major,' others, 'Aubrey St. John' and still others, 'the damned monocled dude!'"

"M'Mhahja—A'bree-sing—domedmon—" M'Mandi stumbled over each of the names. "And what mean they, white man?"

"They have no meaning. It is not our custom to name a man for what he is."

"A foolish custom, M'Mah— *Au-a!* Already the names have gone from me."

"My servant—he is a Hottentot—calls me 'Baas.'"

"Baas! Ah, that is easier. And what does that mean?"

"Master, M'Mandi."

M'Mandi shook his head. "It is a poor name, white man. Now I—I shall call you *Inkosi*, for surely you are a big lord among your people. And when I speak of you to others, your name will be *Mushla Ameyhloe*, for truly your eyes are straight and nothing is hidden from them."

They sat for a while in silence, each well satisfied with the other's mettle. The children having lost their fear, played happily in the dirt; women passed to and fro about their tasks, looking inquisitively at the white man. But still no young men or girls appeared. Apparently the *kraal* was inhabited only by the very old and the very young. And the man called the Major knew that this could not be; and was curious to know the explanation of the absence of the young men and maidens. Perhaps the young men were hunting, the maidens working in the corn patches; perhaps they had all gone to a beer drink at some distant *kraal.*

He wanted to ask M'Mandi all about it, but knew that if he showed too great an interest in the affairs of the *kraal,* he endangered the friendship just formed with M'Mandi.

Instead he said slowly, "I came here, M'Mandi, a stranger, seeking little, asking nothing. You said: 'I do not know where rubber is. I have no ivory. I have no grain.' Now, I had not asked for ivory or rubber or grain—and I shall not ask. Then why—"

"What then do you want of us, *Inkosi?*" M'Mandi interrupted. It was inconceivable to him that a white man should not have some wants; very expensive wants, generally.

"I wanted to buy, maybe, a little corn meal, at a good price. I wanted to arrange to leave my horse—" he pointed to a coal black stallion standing drowsily in the shade of a nearby hut, "and my mules with you. I wanted to hire young men to carry my baggage—at good pay—to Lourenço Marques."

M'Mandi's eyes opened very wide. "The *Inkosi* jests, surely. He wants to buy, to *hire?* He does not take without asking permission? What sort of white man are you?"

"Is it so strange, M'Mandi, that a white man should deal justly?" the Major asked softly.

"Truly!" M'Mandi looked at him closely before asking abruptly, "And if you leave your horse here—as indeed you must, for there is no way for it to travel beyond this place of mine, the jungle is thick, the flies many—how will you travel? Will you need men to carry you in a *machilla?*"

"I am no woman," the Major answered tersely. "I have feet. I can walk."

"*Wo-we!*" M'Mandi exclaimed. "What a fool I am. Now I know the truth. You are no woman; neither are you a Portuguese. That people always travel in a hammock as if they were indeed women. You are—" he hesitated. "You are of that race which—it was even so in my father's father's time—sends out its young men in ones and twos to conquer the far corners of the earth. I have heard of your people; much that is good, a little that is evil. And I, fool that I am, thought you were a Portuguese!"

"No! I am not a Portuguese. But yet I do not know why you told me, 'I do not know where rubber is. I have no ivory. I have no grain.'"

"I said that, *Inkosi*, because I thought you were a white man of that other race. Their foot is on our necks; we are their slaves. They always are seeking those three things, and evil always follows their search. They do not ask, they take. They do not pay, save with blows and abominations. So it was, that when word was brought us by a herder that a white man approached, I sent all my young men and all my young maidens—the comely ones—into the bush and came to meet you alone. For I am old, and these others, too, are old, It mattered not what happened to us, or to the children. But the young men and maidens, they are the heart of a race. They must live. *Aie!* I thought it strange when you came riding alone, unattended, for never have the white men whose dogs we are come to us that way. But I was cautious, fearing a trap."

"What is there to fear, M'Mandi? The country is at peace."

"And do you not yet understand? Come with me, *Inkosi*."

M'Mandi led the way to a narrow path leading out from the *kraal* into the steaming jungle growth. They walked along it a little way and came presently to a clearing. Under the vines and rank grasses which already were beginning to hide its nakedness, the Major could glimpse the charred embers of what once had been huts; here and there the skeletons of cattle gleamed white against the oily green of the verdure and blackened soil.

"Three moons ago," said M'Mandi sadly, "my son's *kraal* stood in this place and he, in some way that is not known to us, displeased the white men who are our overlords. That same day his *kraal* was put to fire, his cattle destroyed and burned. Aye! They would not permit us even to fill our bellies with the meat. His grain became smoke. And then, when it seemed that the fires of their wrath must needs be appeased, they fed to the flames old men, women and children!"

"And your son, you and your warriors permitted this evil?"

"My son and his warriors were in chains. As for me and my people, what could we do? We were held in check by the sticks whose voice is thunder and whose tongue is lightning. We could have died, but to what end? Would our dying have aided these others who already were dead?"

"True," the Major murmured. "And your son and his people? What happened to them?"

M'Mandi shrugged his shoulders and spread his hands expressively. "Who knows? They went from here; the jungle swallowed them up. It is not well to inquire too closely into the sharpness of a poisoned *assegai!*"

The two men slowly retraced their steps. Halting near to four old men, M'Mandi pointed out that each had only one arm; the other member evidently had been amputated clumsily at the elbow.

The Major took his monocle from his eye. His jaw set firm. The vacuous expression vanished from his face. "And you tell me, M'Mandi," he said slowly, "that a *white* man did these things?"

"A white man, or the half-caste dogs who bark for them," M'Mandi said bitterly. "It is enough that he did not call off the dogs."

Then he shrugged and laughed softly, casting aside thoughts of yesterday's evil; ready as are all Africa's black children to accept things as they come. They are incapable of dwelling too long on the past; indifferent to what the future might have in store; content with the present, if the present is good; happy in the sunlight though seeing only the darkness if the sky is overcast. Africa knows no twilight!

And so M'Mandi laughed softly. "My young people will believe that evil has befallen us," he said. "I keep them waiting too long." He crossed to a tree under which was the big signal drum which he struck sharply three times, a pause, then twice more.

Hardly had its deep booming note died away when the bush about the village echoed to the sound of joyful shouts and high pitched, girlish laughter. Presently the Major was conscious of a rustling all about the place. In ones and twos young natives, the men armed with spears and *knobker-ries*, materialized, it seemed, from nothingness. They had, thought the Major, been close at hand all the time. When he had walked up the path with M'Mandi, he doubtless had passed within arm's length of some of them. And he had been at their mercy had their intentions been evil.

He counted twenty men, a puny lot save for one or two who had pure Zulu characteristics and physique, and nearly twice that number of girls. They all looked at the white man with awed curiosity, then occupied themselves with various tasks. Some started to tan skins, others thatched the roof of a hut. Seven of the maidens, calabashes balanced on their heads, left the *kraal* by a broad, well defined path which led to the river.

Marveling at their graceful carriage, the Major watched them until the last one vanished from sight round a bend in the trail. Then he turned and surveyed the other occupants of the *kraal*. Something of the peace and tranquility of the life got hold of him For a little while he forgot this people's sorrows, their constant struggle for existence against the natural perils of the bush. He forgot their hopeless struggle against the white man's civilization which was throttling their lives just as much as the jungle growth threatened to overrun and choke their corn patches.

It all was very peaceful. The song of the girls on the way to the river had a lilting humored cadence; it harmonized with the songs the men were singing as they worked. Childish laughter, the soft, musical voices of the women, the deep voices of the old men, all accentuated the atmosphere of rest.

The Major chuckled softly as M'Mandi took a *knobkerrie* away from a little four year old who was in danger of braining himself as he made a brave attempt to flourish it after the manner of a warrior. It was a small incident, yet it brought home to the white man more strongly than anything else could have done, that the similarity of people goes further than the Colonel's lady and Judy O'Grady. He thought there was very little difference between the people of this small *kraal* and those of a village at home. Fundamentally they were the same; only the externals were different.

The Major leaned lazily against the side of a hut, M'Mandi close by, enjoying it all; conscious of nothing save a happy people playing in the sun. But then a memory of the destroyed *kraal* and the one-armed men came to him. The veil of happy contentment was brushed aside. And now the low drone of a myriad insects drowned all other noises. They had been there all the time but only just now he was conscious of them. The menacing voice of the jungle sounded blatantly.

A shriek, quickly stifled, brought all the men folk to their feet; the women looked at each other fearfully. M'Mandi moved a few paces nearer the white man.

"What was it?" the Major questioned, noting their alarm, his hand resting on the butt of his revolver.

"It was the voice of one of the maidens who went for water," M'Mandi answered slowly. "Perhaps a crocodile has taken her." He and the other men waited expectantly, tensed.

There followed a deep, pregnant silence. No one spoke, no one moved. Gradually the tension lessened. Men shamefacedly returned to their tasks. The women emerged from their huts into which they had fled. M'Mandi squatted on his haunches close by the Major, and struck playfully with his *knobkerrie* at a passing younster. "It is nothing to trouble us," he said in response to a questioning glance from the Major. "She was frightened, belike, without just cause. Maidens are like that, seeing danger where none is. They—"

And then with a startling suddenness a man, wearing a flamboyant, gold laced uniform, came into sight. Close behind him, reclining in a *machilla* carried by four uniformed natives, was a white man. Behind the *machilla* marched a detachment of native troops. In their midst were a number of prisoners—among them *six* of the seven maidens who had gone from the *kraal* to get water.

That was all the Major saw for, with a fierce yell of, "You've trapped us!" M'Mandi leaped to his feet and brought down his *knobkerrie* with great force on the visitor's head. The Major's knees sagged under him. He pitched face forward to the ground and lay there unconscious.

Meanwhile, at the first appearance of the strangers, the young men and women of the *kraal* had fled hither and yon panic stricken, intending to seek the shelter and safe hiding place of the jungle. But, to their alarm, they discovered the *kraal* surrounded by black soldiery, who roughly herded them back to the center of the *kraal*, prodding the laggards with their bayonets.

And now the gorgeously uniformed man spoke to the man in the *machilla* who nodded gravely and then rolled out—he was pig fat—and waddled toward the inert form of the Major. The newcomer was a ludicrous figure. Standing a little less than five feet six, clad in gaily patterned silk pajamas, his white pith helmet completely hid the top of his face. His bare feet were thrust into high heeled, womanish looking slippers. His mouth sagged open and he wheezed loudly, a black, walruslike mustache fluttering outward with each exhalation.

As he came to where the Major was lying supine, motionless, he prodded him with his foot and with some effort turned him over. Then he laughed softly and called the other man. "Do you know this one, Carlos?" he asked in Portuguese.

"No, *senhor*," the other replied harshly. There was queer inflection in his speech, a muddiness which matched his *café au lait* complexion; that went well with the soiled whites of his eyes and his short, crisp hair which showed a tendency to curl despite the grease with which he had plastered it. "Undoubtedly he is a trouble maker, like all the English. Perhaps he is the slaver we have been seeking for so long a "time," he concluded meaningly.

"So?" questioned the fat man in surprised tones. And then, with a chuckle. "You think fast, Carlos. I did not know what you meant, at first. But, of course! I take the man to Lourenço Marques and tell His Excellency, the Governor, that here is the slaver for whom we have so long been searching. His Excellency will reward me greatly, and will forget his so unjust suspicion that I am the slaver! So shall we be free to continue our so profitable—er— ventures. Ah, yes. So clever of you, Carlos!"

He rubbed his plump, white hands together. Then, taking off his helmet—the top of his head showed entirely bald, save for a long, well-greased black lock which was so arranged as to show to the best advantage—he mopped his red face. As he did so he looked with cold, calculating eyes at the *kraal's* inhabitants. Each of the latter endeavored to avoid his scrutiny.

He laughed again and returning leisurely to his *machilla,* seated himself. "Have the slave runner guarded," he ordered.

With evident enjoyment, the man called Carlos transmitted the order to two of the black soldiers, who expertly trussed up the Major, and, with fixed bayonets, stood guard over him.

"Bring M'Mandi here," the fat man next ordered. It was curious how quiet the *kraal* people were. Not one had moved, or talked above a whisper since the arrival of the Portuguese force. Now they watched breathlessly, with eyes which held hate as well as fear, as two of the soldiers dragged their chief up to the *machilla* and forced him to his knees.

One of the soldiers brought the butt of his rifle down with bone breaking force on M'Mandi's back, and a low moan—like that of a dangerous beast, wounded and at bay—burst from the men of the *kraal* and they pressed forward, against the bayonet points of their guards.

The fat man rolled his eyes apprehensively.

"Quiet, dogs," Carlos shouted, "or your chief dies!" He held his revolver to M'Mandi's head.

The murmuring ceased. The men relaxed, no longer straining to break through the barrier of steel; once again they became a cowed and subject people.

"It is all right, now, Don Pedro," Carlos said with a sneer. "The dogs have come to heel."

The color flowed back into Don Pedro's face. Sitting up with an assumption of dignity, he said to M'Mandi, in a soft, lisping voice. "I have heard many complaints of you and your people, M'Mandi. I did not believe them. It was not possible, I said, that a man should be so ungrateful to such a good friend as I have been to you."

"My son's *kraal* is no more; that is the proof of your friendship, white man," M'Mandi interrupted.

Don Pedro spread his hands expressively and laughed like a muted hyena. "Oh, that. Yes. Carlos told me about it. If a child is disobedient, a good parent punishes him; it is for the child's good. Your son was disobedient, and so he was punished. But what of you? *Senhor* Carlos tells me you give him much trouble; you are too stiff necked, I think."

"I do not know where rubber is," M'Mandi began, then stopped realizing the futility of it.

"I could not believe you were so evil," Don Pedro continued, "so I came here to see with my own eyes. And, alas! I saw that the reports of you were all too true. Before my eyes you dared to strike a white man. Perhaps you have killed him, who knows? For that there must be great punishment." He paused and looked up at Carlos triumphantly.

"Clever, Don Pedro," that man said in tones of sycophantic sweetness. "I never could have thought of that. It makes everything most just."

The little fat man smiled and made a purring, throaty noise. "Yes, there must be a punishment," he said complacently and folded pudgy hands over a rotund stomach. "You say you do not know where rubber is, M'Mandi. That is sad. But it is an old story. You also would have said that you had no ivory, no grain, no young men or maidens. That is sad. That means you cannot pay a fine and must be punished in some other way."

He turned to Carlos. "It is cold. No? Let us have a fire, just a very little fire to warm us."

Carlos, his eyes gleaming with a malicious light, shouted sharp staccato orders and some of the soldiers, flaming torches in their hands, ran from hut to hut, sowing the red seed of fire.

With a yell of dismay, M'Mandi broke from the hold of the men who were guarding him and, running to his hut, entered. He emerged immediately, bearing in his hands the calabash from which the Major had drunk. This he carried with faltering steps to Don Pedro and offered it to him as if it were some priceless treasure. "It is all we have, white man," he said. "It is yours. Be merciful."

Don Pedro took the calabash and raised it to his lips; then his nose wrinkled in disgust and he gagged violently. "You would poison me," he yelled, and threw the contents of the calabash full in M'Mandi's face.

As the chief staggered hack, half blinded, Carlos hit him on the head with the barrel of his revolver. The old man dropped like a log, moaned and was silent.

"It is time that we go, Don Pedro," Carlos said. "In a little while it will be too hot."

The fires which the soldiers had started had taken good hold and each hut was blazing fiercely. But, save for a scattered curse, the people of the *kraal* were silent; even the children accepted the disaster which had overtaken them with mute, stoical indifference. Satan, the Major's horse, moved away from the hut near which he had been standing and whinnied in alarm, calling the attention of Carlos to him. "May I have the horse, Don Pedro?" he asked.

The fat man nodded.

Carlos walked quickly over to the horse and taking hold of the bridle, endeavored to lead the spirited animal away.

But Satan reared and struck out viciously with his fore-feet, then swerved sharply, pulling the reins out of Carlos's hands, and galloped swiftly away.

"He seemed not to love you," Don Pedro said with a chuckle. "He is a white man's horse. But now let's go. It is very hot." He fanned himself gently with his helmet.

"The soldiers are thirsty for blood," Carlos rebelled in a sulky voice; he resented Don Pedro's gentle reminder that he was not a white man, "There are a lot of old men and women who are of no value," he continued. "Let us—"

Don Pedro shuddered delicately. "You are so savage, Carlos; and you are too lenient with your men. Some day you will regret having taught them the joy of killing. In any case we have no time to waste now in idle amusement. We will take all the people from this *kraal*, old men and young children. They all shall go. Doubtless we can turn them to some profit. Come! Let us start."

Carlos glowered. He looked as if he were about to remonstrate further with Don Pedro and then, thinking better of it—he knew from experience that the fat little man was dangerous to cross in spite of his soft exterior—he bowed agreement, turned and gave the necessary orders.

Quickly the soldiers lined up the people of the *kraal*, shackling them together, and marched them down the broad pathway leading to the river. Four of them picked up the Major, who still was unconscious, and placed him on a crude, roughly constructed litter.

Five minutes later the *kraal* was deserted save for M'Mandi, who had not moved from the place where he had fallen.

Twenty minutes later M'Mandi groaned and rolled over; the hut nearest him had been the last to burst into flames, but now the heat from it was intense.

Presently he sat up and groaned, opened his eyes and groaned again. With dull, uncomprehending eyes he watched, one after another, the huts cave in and collapse with a muffled roar, sending up a fountain of sparks.

The cur dogs of the *kraal,* yelping in fear, their tails between their legs, crept belly down out of the range of the heat; scrawny fowls clucked and crowed in dismay; snakes, so suddenly and violently deprived of their nests in the roofs of the huts, crawled peevishly away into the jungle.

M'Mandi rose slowly to his feet, and with hands outstretched before him staggered down the broad pathway, calling to his people. A little way he went, only a little way, and then his legs refused to support him any further. They crumpled, and he slumped heavily to the ground.

Ten minutes later the *kraal* was not; the fire had burnt itself out; only a mass of blackened, smoking ruins remained where once had been huts and the home of a tribe.

A dog timidly returned, sniffing eagerly, smelling, no doubt, the cooked carcass of a fowl which had been trapped in the fire. But the ashes still were hot, and he ran yelping away, creating a panic among the other dogs who were waiting in the jungle beyond. They fled with him.

A bold, but foolish rooster flew clumsily down from a tree on the outskirts of the *kraal.* He alighted on a jumble of smouldering calabashes, moving them slightly, creating a draft. They immediately burst into flame. The rooster squawked once and then was silent. The *kraal* was a place of death, deserted, desolate.

Hours passed. The ruins ceased to smoke. The sun dropped quickly toward the western horizon. Jungle gloom was triumphant.

And now M'Mandi moved again. He sat up, rubbing his eyes in bewilderment. He wondered, vaguely, why his head throbbed so painfully; what was the matter with his right shoulder and thigh.

Presently he remembered the coming of the first white man whom he had named, *Inkosi—Mushla Ameykloe.* He remembered the coming of those others—the white man, the black soldiers and the man who was neither white nor black—and of how he had struck down *Inkosi.* A foolish deed, that, he commented bitterly. He must hasten to make amends to *Inkosi,* beg his forgiveness.

He blinked and rubbed his eyes again. Other memories crowded upon him. He remembered everything now. The blow which caused his head to throb, the firing of the hots, the heat which had caused the skin to peel from his shoulder and thigh.

He rose to his feet and walked slowly back along the path, not sure what he would find; hoping that one or two of the huts would remain untouched by the fire, that some of his young people had escaped and would be on hand to greet him.

When he came to the place where the *kraal* had been, he made no outcry. "*Au-a!*" he said softly. That was all.

Then he wandered dismally from one blackened heap to the other, apparently oblivious to the still hot ashes which must have scorched the soles of his naked feet. Occasionally he raked among the embers, as if hoping to find something untouched by the fire. But this act was purely mechanical.

He came to the tree where the signal drum hung. The drum was untouched, though blackened by the fire. He tapped it tentatively. Then he struck it again, loudly, sending out the old return signal; three quick beats, a pause, two more beats.

But the drum's booming was a hollow mockery; there was no one to answer its call. M'Mandi waited for a few moments, listening, and then, his head bowed, walked slowly away. He turned presently into a path—not the one leading to the river—which wove its way through the jungle growth to some far distant *kraal*. After he had gone a few hundred paces he stopped and looked back. The path had made several abrupt turns, so his eyes met nothing but the green slime of the jungle. There was no indication that a people recently had enjoyed their life nearby; nothing to bear witness to a white man's brutal injustice. The material evidence of that crime was hidden from sight by the tangle of creepers and grasses; as completely hidden as knowledge of it would be kept from the governor of the Territory.

A few paces further on and M'Mandi halted again. His quick ears detected the approach of a newcomer along the path. He looked around quickly for something he could use as a weapon, picked up a stone about as large as his two fists and, stepping quietly off the path, hid himself behind a tree. Then, having taken stock of his surroundings, making sure that there was no obstacle in the way of a quick leap out to attack, if the situation so demanded, selecting a path of retreat for use should he be faced by superior force, he leaned against the tree-trunk. Partly relaxed yet every nerve tensed, he waited.

Presently the noise he heard resolved itself into the hoof-beats of two animals. One, he judged, was lame. A little later and his keen, sensitive ears detected a man's tread. Still he waited.

A voice sounded. It was a harsh, unmusical voice. A moment later two mules, one of them very lame, both in very poor condition, came into view around a bend in the trail. Close behind them walked a squat, powerfully built native. He wore a battered felt hat. Through a hole in the crown he had stuck an ostrich feather. A gaily colored shirt was tucked into a pair of tightly fitting riding breeches behind, but in front hung down, outside, reaching almost to his feet. In his right hand he carried a *knobkerrie* and two *assegais;* in his left, a pair of brown, pointed toed shoes. The base of his nose was abnormally wide even for one of Bantu stock; and his cheek bones were high and prominent.

Just before the mules came opposite to M'Mandi's hiding place, the squat man stopped. Lifting up his left foot he examined the sole carefully. Then he raised the other foot and from it extracted a large thorn.

M'Mandi straightened himself carefully, stood back a little from the tree and tightened his grip on the stone.

The mules had halted and were nibbling dispiritedly at the long, rank grass. One of them brayed mournfully. The stranger carefully placed his shoes on the ground, then straightening and shifting his *knobkerrie* and one of the *assegais* to his left hand, he called softly, "I come in peace. Why hide behind a tree? I am only one. What need to take me unawares?"

M'Mandi vouchsafed no answer, did not move from cover.

"If you desire my blood," the other continued, "come out and take it. Let us fight as men should, face to face."

M'Mandi hesitated a moment longer then stepped out on the path, still holding the stone poised ready to throw. "You have good eyes," he began.

The other chuckled. "My nose saw you," he said. "My ears saw you. My eyes were blind. I can not see through a tree. But the grease you use is strong. You breathe like a pig. Well? Are you thirsty for my blood?"

"Nay," M'Mandi answered decidedly. "I have seen enough of evil this day. If you come in peace, so be it. And if you seek my blood, why, so be that too." He threw the stone into the bush. "But what do men call you? What is your tribe?"

"I am of no tribe," the other said with a grin, his teeth showing pearly white against the blackness of his skin. "Though, truly, my baas always speaks of me as 'Jim, the Hottentot.'"

"From the south—"

" 'Baas'—'Jim, the Hottentot,' " M'Mandi cried. "I have heard somewhat of you!"

Jim grinned again. "Then you have seen my baas. Is he not a man? Perchance he sent you to guide me to him."

M'Mandi shook his head sorrowfully. "Aye! He is a man indeed. I called him *Mushla Ameyhloe.*"

"There you prove yourself to be no fool, old one," Jim exclaimed enthusiastically. "And discovered you also that he is the friend of all black ones?"

"Aye—and then thought my judgment false."

"Therein you were a fool!"

"True. But I discovered it too late."

"Too late?" Jim looked at M'Mandi closely and noted the blood which had flowed down his face from the scalp wound and had dried there. "What mean you by, 'Too late?' Where is my baas?"

"I do not know. He has gone on. Maybe he is dead."

"Dead? How? Did you—" Jim raised his *assegai* threateningly.

M'Mandi did not flinch. "No," he said. "I do not think I killed him though, it may be, through my folly he will die. Come with me."

He turned and led the way back to where the *kraal* had been, driving the mules before him.

"*Au-a!*" exclaimed Jim dispassionately as he viewed the ruins. "And whose hand was this?"

"Hear me to the end, O black one called Jim, and I will tell you. Judge not too hastily—and yet I judged hastily," he added in sorrow.

"Speak quickly," Jim bade irritably. "My baas will need me. I must go to him." The two men squatted on their haunches, side by side.

"Listen then!" And without further preamble M'Mandi told Jim of all that had happened. In an unemotional voice, he told of a village laid waste, of a people enslaved, as matter of factly as if he were telling of some remote, inconsequential event in which he had no interest.

"*Wo-we!*" Jim cried mournfully when M'Mandi had finished the recital. "You acted the part of a fool, M'Mandi. When you struck down my baas, causing the heavy sleep to fall upon him, it was as if you yourself had committed all the evil which followed. He could have saved you."

"He was only one," M'Mandi interrupted. "They were many. What could he have done?"

You do not know my baas. He is all wise, all powerful. He is the Mahjor and I—I am Jim, his servant." He jumped to his feet. "But why do I stay here?" he demanded excitedly. "I must go on and take my baas away from those wicked ones. And heed this, O fool named M'Mandi. For this little while I will forget the blow you gave my baas. But, if I find him dead, then—then I shall return, and death will not come easily to you!"

M'Mandi's eyes flashed, but he answered quietly, "It will be most just. I was beside myself."

Jim spat contemptuously and turned away.

"Wait!" M'Mandi cried.

Jim halted. "What is it, dog?"

"Wait until morning before you follow the trail. In a very little while now it will be dark, so dark that you can not see your hand before you. Rest now and eat, if you have food. Then, in the morning, we can follow the spoor quickly."

Jim looked at the sky and considered the matter thoughtfully.

"It might be well," he muttered. "In the darkness I am as a child in this country. Also I am hungry and very tired. I have trekked far since the rising of this morning's sun. The baas will understand." Aloud he said, "It is good counsel, M'Mandi. Here I will stay and eat and sleep. In the morning I—"

"Not you alone, black one. I will go with you. It may be that I am old, and a fool, and a dog—of that last I am not so sure. Zulu blood flows in my veins and, so my father told me, the Hottentots were always slaves of the Zulus."

"I am slave to no one," Jim retorted hotly, "save to my baas. And that is an honor too great for you to understand, dog."

"Let it pass. But this is true. I know this country as well as I know the palm of my hand. The man does not live who can follow spoor as well as I."

"A loud bark from a little dog," Jim commented dryly, and without further words unpacked the mules and hobbled them. A little later the two men were eating ravenously, huddled close up to the fire for, with the setting of the sun, a heavy dew had fallen and there was a chill in the air.

While they still were eating four natives from a distant *kraal* came to the place. These men had seen the flames, from the burning huts earlier in the day and had come to investigate. They listened sympathetically to M'Mandi's story, but balked at his request that they should join forces and help release M'Mandi's people.

"Nay," said one. "This is your bone. We will not chew it for you."

Jim, they regarded with suspicious interest. Was he not confessedly a white man's dog? Nevertheless they eagerly accepted the food and the trade stuff he gave them, promising, in return for the gifts, to care for the mules and the rest of the provisions.

They accepted this responsibility a little too readily to please Jim, but he was in no position to question their motives. So he was forced to content himself with making a charm over the mules and the equipment, telling the men that if they broke the *tabu*, death in the most painful form surely would follow.

They were greatly impressed and asked Jim to repeat the charm. He did so with portentous gravity, rolling his eyes fearfully, making mystic passes in the air—they were strangely like the flourishes the Major made when rolling and lighting a cigarette! "Gor bless-mi Dammeyes no. If I don' see you s'long, hullo," the charm ran, almost exhausting Jim's English vocabulary.

"Au-a, baba! A powerful charm, surely!" exclaimed one of the men.

"Great indeed," Jim agreed. "The evil spirits are now all around us—" He broke off suddenly. There was a snorting and a heavy crashing in the jungle just beyond the *kraal* clearing.

The men looked at each other, drew closer together. On their faces was an expression of fear, a dread of the supernatural. When they noted that the charm maker himself was alarmed, their teeth began to chatter like castanets.

Presently Jim's face lighted. "Have no fear," he said importantly. "It is only my baas's horse which the spirits have brought to you. Did not the charm put all my baas's possessions into your keeping? Sit still and watch."

He stood up and whistled a low, sweet note. He was answered by a soft whinny; a dark shadow emerged from the darkness of the jungle and moved with mincing steps to where Jim was standing. There entering the radius of light thrown by the fire flames, the shadow ceased to be a shadow and became a horse. It nuzzled Jim fondly as he took off the saddle.

"It is time that you go now," Jim said and, unhobbling the mules, helped the men load the equipment in the pack saddles. That done he gave Satan's bridle reins into the hands of one of the men. The horse snorted and hung back until Jim spoke softly to him; after that he followed the man meekly.

"Remember the charm," Jim called out, "and tend the beasts well. In a little while I will come to your *kraal* and hold you to a strict accounting."

"We will not forget, O charm maker," one of them shouted. Then the jungle blackness swallowed them up; but for a long time Jim and M'Mandi could hear the songs they sang to ward off the evil spirits.

Presently M'Mandi, having in mind the morrow's trek, turned over on his back and slept, snoring loudly.

The hours passed slowly; stars waxed and waned. Jim did not move, but sleep was far from him. He sat with his chin resting on his updrawn knees, gazing steadily into the glowing embers of the fire, planning how best to rescue his baas—his baas, who could do no wrong.

THE MAJOR grinned impudently into the face of Carlos the Goanese, the half caste, creature of the high born Don Pedro. "You're a filthy beast, you know," he drawled. "Glad you speak English. I can't *buk* Portuguese well enough to slang you as you ought to be slanged."

Carlos swore and kicked the Major in the ribs. "My blacks will have much sport with you by and by; they will make you come crawling to me and you'll be ready to lick the dust off my shoes—*anything* to get away from my niggers!"

"You—er—niggers have to stick together, eh, what?" the Major commented casually.

Carlos's eyes narrowed; his face flushed a queer, mottled crimson under his yellow, jaundiced skin. "I am no nigger, you swine," he yelled. "I am white, as white as you are."

"Really! I never would have thought it. You act and talk just like a—er—Goanese, you know. You're quite sure—"

Carlos did not allow the Major to finish his sentence, but yelled curses and threats at him.

"Well, 'pon my word," the Major drawled when Carlos was forced to pause for lack of breath. "That's very much like Goanese talk. If, on the other hand, you're a white man—why, then, you're the most abject rotter I've ever met; quite an out and outer, I should say." And then a memory of the things he had witnessed during the past three days overwhelmed the Major, broke down his icy barrier of reserve and a cold flood of vituperation and condemnation poured from his lips. His eyes flashed angrily. From a mild blue they changed to a hard, steel gray. At that moment the Major was a remorseless killer, and Carlos, sensing it, flinched visibly.

Then as suddenly as it had started, the Major's stream of condemnation ceased. He became on the instant a dude, a hopeless, ignorant seeming nincompoop. "No, I won't," the Major now said slowly, enunciating each word with great clarity. "I wouldn't be a partner of yours for all the ivory and niggers to carry it, in the world. Neither will I buy my freedom by murdering Don Pedro. How could I kill the dear man?" he chuckled softly. "Why I have never been introduced to him. Who is he?"

A shadow fell across the Major's body—a strange, distorted shadow. Carlos started back in dismay and the Major, turning his head slightly, saw a queer apparition. He stared hard, blinked, then burst into a peal of laughter. "Really!" he gasped admiringly. "That's positively tophole, Mr.—er—"

"I am Don Pedro," the apparition snapped pompously.

"Oh! The chappy this worm wanted me to murder, eh? I'm not sure that I blame him!"

"It's a lie, Don Pedro," Carlos shouted indignantly. "He is a liar. He—"

"That will do, Carlos. You may go. I will talk with this so wicked slave dealer alone."

"But," Carlos stammered. "He will tell you lies. And, if I am not here to deny them—how will you know that they are lies?"

"Go! I am no fool." Don Pedro pointed imperiously to the line of campfires about which the soldiers and their prisoners were squatting, eating the evening meal. "Go!" he repeated and Carlos slunk away, muttering angrily to himself.

"And now," Don Pedro said to the Major. "We will talk."

"That's nice of you, old dear, but—you'll pardon me, I'm sure—I do want to say how clever that getup of yours is. I must have one like it; oh, *positively*! Let me see how it's arranged, will you? Turn around, there's a good egg."

Solemnly Don Pedro turned himself about, and then snorted wrathfully because he had been so weak, so susceptible to flattery, as to expose himself to the Major's barbed shafts of satire.

"Ah, I see," continued the mocking drawl. "You have a wire hoop attached to your helmet, from which you suspend the mosquito netting. Around your waist you have another hoop—a much wider one—which keeps the netting from touching you. And then the bottom part of the netting is reinforced by—er—calico, is it?—and made into pajama trousers. Quite neat! 'Pon my soul, you should have it patented!"

Don Pedro nervously twirled the ends of his moustache and glared down fiercely at the Major. "You talk a lot," he said.

The Major sighed. "I'm afraid I do. So many people have told me the same, that it must be true. But that getup of yours absolutely demands eloquence, you know. Just fancy! It makes it impossible for any nasty insect to get at your precious hide and sting you. But—er—doesn't your bally conscience ever give you a sharp nip? Eh?"

"That's enough," Don Pedro interrupted sharply. "I will do the talking now. Who are you? What is your name? What are you doing in this territory?— Well, why don't you answer?"

"I thought you wanted to do the talking, old dear," the Major replied sweetly.

"Answer!"

"But first tell me who you are. What right have you to question me?"

"I—I am Don Pedro D'Andra. I am the Resident in charge of this district."

"The deuce, you say. That's splendid. You're the chappy I want to see. You must have that man, Carlos, you called him, didn't you? Well you must have him arrested at once. He has committed the most frightful crimes."

"So-a! You surprise me. I had always considered Carlos a very just and lenient man. But if he has been guilty of any crimes, he shall be punished, I assure you. What has he done?"

"Well, first of all, he knocked me out, nearly broke my skull."

"You're quite wrong there. M'Mandi did that."

"He did? Why, I thought he was a most friendly old soul," the Major exclaimed in surprise. "You are joking, perhaps?"

"I speak the truth. I do not joke!"

The Major was nonplussed, and not a little hurt at the thought of M'Mandi's treachery.

"At any rate," he continued, "Carlos has kept me a prisoner for three days, bound hand and foot—I must be most frightfully dirty—when I asked him why I was a prisoner, he treated me vilely. I must be all black and blue from his kicks. Deucedly uncomfortable, I assure you."

"That is to be regretted," Don Pedro said suavely. "But then, you are a so dangerous character, that our dear Carlos has to be a little stern with you. Is that the sum total of your complaints?"

"In respect to myself, yes. But I do not count. I have other, infinitely more terrible charges to bring against this fiend, Carlos." The Major's tone was very much that of a pigheaded, professional reformer with a real grievance to gloat over. "I understand from Carlos, in fact he boasts of it, that he killed M'Mandi, set fire to his *kraal* and brought all the people away, prisoners. And, you know," the Major lowered his voice to a whisper, "I believe Carlos is going to sell them for slaves."

"M'Mandi was killed because he—as we thought— had killed you; I know that he tried to poison me. And for that we punished him, burned his *kraal* to the ground and took his people prisoners. How else could we instill a proper respect for a white man in the minds of this so savage people? All that was done at M'Mandi's *kraal* was done at my orders. Yes?" He paused, waiting expectantly.

The Major breathed deeply, exhaling with a sharp hiss. "Ah, I see," he exclaimed presently. "You explain every- thing so charmingly. I am beginning to look upon Carlos as quite an angel of mercy—oh, quite. But how, I wonder, are you going to explain his murder of the old man—in cold blood, mind you—yesterday, the woman he shot this morning; how will you excuse the brutal way in which he flogs the prisoners with a *sjambok?*"

"I do not have to explain it," Don Pedro answered mildly. "But please, *senhor,* rest assured that Carlos does not exceed his authority. He would not dare to do that. You see, he is answerable to me for all that he does, and I—I am answer- able to no one."

"Not to His Excellency, the Governor?" the Major queried mildly.

Don Pedro shrugged his shoulders. "If he knew, then perhaps things would be unpleasant. But he would have to have definite proof. He dare not act on suspicion alone. I have friends, most powerful friends at—how do you say?—at court."

"I think, 'Dog' Pedro," the Major's tone and facial expres- sion were very insulting; even more insulting than his words, "you must be a Goanese, too."

With startling swiftness, Don Pedro produced a revolver from somewhere and aimed it at the Major's head. Then he replaced it with a sneering laugh and the Major noticed that he kept it in a holster slung under his armpit, inside his pajama coat.

"Glad you thought better of it," the Major drawled. "It 'ud be a pity to shoot a hole in your nice mosquito netting; and there are quite a swarm of the beastly pests abroad tonight."

"Yes. I'm glad, too, that I did not act on a hasty impulse," Don Pedro said softly. "You are much more valuable to me alive—for a little while longer at any rate."

"May I ask just what you intend to do with me? Of course, you understand, my government will take this affair up with your government. This sort of thing can't go on, you know. And I'm afraid things will go very hard for you."

Don Pedro laughed.

"Your government will never bother to inquire about you; they won't know what has happened. You see, you will be imprisoned in the jail at Lourenço Marques; and white men do not live there very long."

"So you're going to take me to Lourenço Marques, eh? How jolly. I was on my way to that delightful town. And what charge will I be tried on—I suppose you'll go through the formality of a trial?"

"You're a slave dealer," Don Pedro answered tersely. "At least that will be my evidence. I shall testify that I caught you *in flagrante delicto,* and my evidence will be all that is necessary."

"Seeking to divert suspicion from yourself, eh? Ah, well. I always say that if one means to be a rotter, one should be a thorough rotter. No sense in doing the thing in a half hearted fashion."

And now Don Pedro remembered that certain questions he had asked some time previously remained unanswered. He repeated them. "What is your name? What are you doing up here?"

"My name is Aubrey St. John and I came up here on a hunting expedition."

"Alone?"

"Of course not, my dear ass. But I got lost, separated from the rest of my party, don't you know, and wandered about—"

"You're a liar," Don Pedro interrupted.

"Yes, of course," the Major assented. "You did not expect the truth, surely?"

"I insist on the truth, you fool. Don't you see that I have you entirely at my mercy? And I allow nothing to stand in the way of what I want. A word of suggestion to Carlos and—" He drew a pudgy forefinger suggestively across his throat.

"Quite melodramatic, aren't you?" the Major murmured. "But I'm afraid you put too much faith in Carlos."

Don Pedro looked at him sharply. "Sometimes I look at you and think you're a fool. Then again there is something about you that makes me think that there's more than appears at first. I wonder which is the real you."

"Oh, I'm awfully clever, really. You must not think me a fool, except that I sometimes credit white men—some white men—with having more decency than they actually possess. Now, take for example my faith in you—"

"Have done," Don Pedro advised him sourly. "And now, having admitted that you lied a little while ago, suppose you tell me who you really are?"

"I wonder," the Major murmured, "if I ought to tell him." Then in a louder tone, he said, "I am the Major. You have heard of me, perhaps."

"The Major?" Don Pedro echoed. "Of course! I should have known." He had heard of the Major. There were few men south of the Zambezi—or north of that mighty river, for that matter—who had not heard of that dandified, monocled dude who, as a protest against the unjust laws regulating the diamond mining industry, had become an I.D.B., to the despair of all the police in the country. And his fame was not confined to illicit diamond buying. He was respected universally and admired by men who could see beyond his silly ass pose and dudish attire, and knew that he used the languor, the inanities of a fop, as a stalking horse behind which his active brain schemed and planned. Even the police admired him and took in good part the tricks he turned on them.

"The Major," Don Pedro said again. Then asked suspiciously, "And what's your little game?"

"No game at all, dear lad. I came up here on a strictly business venture. Oh yes, diamonds of course. You see, a very charming young friend of mine, Miss Lola de Sousa—"

Don Pedro started slightly.

"What?" exclaimed the Major, noticing the start, his eyes narrowing. "You know Miss Lola?"

Don Pedro nodded. He knew Lola very well; had, with her aid, put through quite a number of unsavory deals. He knew her to be a clever, unscrupulous and very beautiful woman. If the Major was a friend of Lola's, or better still, infatuated with her, then it would be well to consider very carefully before he carried out his original intention concerning his disposal of the monocled one.

"Well," continued the Major. "Miss Lola was in trouble and she gave me a little package of diamonds which she asked me to take for her to an address in Lourenço Marques. That was just before the police arrested her on suspicion of being an I.D.B. Fortunate for her—oh, very—that she had given me the stones. Otherwise she'd now be languishing at the Breakwater, or whatever the female equivalent for that dour place is, and be likely to languish for a long, long time. That would be sad, for she is so beautiful."

"And where are the diamonds now?" Don Pedro asked. He was willing to accept the Major's statement as true. It sounded so like Lola. The Major was not the first to discover her alluring charms irresistible. He, Don Pedro, had. "Where are the diamonds!" he repeated sharply.

The Major opened his eyes wide. "That's just it," he said wearily. "You chappies were so eager to burn down the *kraal* that I never got a chance to talk to you. I wanted to very much. But every time I asked Carlos for his master, he got quite angry and insisted that he would carry any message I had. But I didn't quite trust him, you know."

"The diamonds," Don Pedro insisted. "I am here now. Tell me where they are."

"Oh, but I couldn't do that. I can show you where they are though. You see, I expected to stay at M'Mandi's *kraal* for quite some time and not wishing to carry the stones about with me—I was afraid I'd lose them, don't you know; or that some one would search me when I was asleep—and so I hid them in a very cunning hiding place. No one would ever think of looking for them in the place I put them."

Don Pedro swore. "Are you lying?" he demanded.

"My dear fellow! Why should I?"

Don Pedro considered this. Then, "It would be very fool-ish of you to lie," he said softly.

"Of course! So, I suggest this. That we depart secretly in the night from this place and return to M'Mandi's *kraal*. It can't be a very long trek, as we've been circling about a good deal, I imagine. Then, once we've got the diamonds, we'll make for Lourenço Marques—alone. I've told you before that I don't trust Carlos. And I think we ought to start tonight before Carlos gets up sufficient courage to stick a knife into you."

"You suggest that I travel with you, alone, through the bush in the darkness—"

"Why not, old bean? I'm no murderer. But what's that?" A loud, harsh cry sounded from the jungle. "Oh—foolish of me!—it's only a Goaway bird."

At that moment the crisp report of a rifle thudded against their ear drums; a bullet ricocheted near Don Pedro's head with a vicious *pee-whang;* and around the fires, silhouetted against the setting sun, men were strug-gling in a confused mill.

Another report sounded and one of the black soldiers crumpled up. Carlos's voice could be heard above the din. He was swearing, threatening, pleading. He broke from amidst a group, revolver in hand, and crouching, backed away slowly; and at each backward step he took, his revolver spat fire.

With a curse, Don Pedro tore the mosquito veil which shrouded his form and ran, with surprising agility for so fat a man, toward the scene of the combat, drawing his revolver and firing into the air as he ran.

With an effort the Major sat erect and watched; chuck-ling happily when Don Pedro gave Carlos a backhanded blow as he passed him.

"Down, baas. Down and roll this way!" a voice whispered hoarsely from the bushes to the Major's left.

The Major wasted no time in obeying the summons. "Good old Jim," he murmured as he rolled. "I knew he'd find a way."

Three times he rolled completely over, finally coming to a rest, almost touching the stalks of the bush from which the voice came. A long, muscular arm protruded through the leaves and a knife gleamed in the hand. Quickly it severed the bonds on the Major's feet and hands. Then the arm was withdrawn.

"Rub my ankles, Jim," the Major whispered, "and keep good watch."

"Nay, baas. Come now. They will never find us in the jungle."

"No, Jim. There's a game yet to be played."

"It is a game with death, baas," Jim grumbled; but his two hands came out of the bushes and he gently and expertly massaged the Major's ankles.

"That is good, Jim. What are the fighters doing now?"

"It is all over, baas, or nearly. The fat man is clever. They listened to him when they would not listen to the man who is neither white nor black."

"Ah!" the Major raised his head slightly and saw that order of a sort had been restored and that Don Pedro was in hot argument with Carlos.

"Did you bring a gun, Jim?"

"*Tchat!* I had nearly forgotten, baas. Here." He thrust a revolver into the Major's hand. The latter, as he took it, saw with dismay that it was not loaded. But he did not let Jim know that. It would almost break the faithful Hottentot's heart if he knew that he had failed so badly. The lack of ammunition called for a new plan of operation. He was tempted for a moment to take Jim's counsel and seek safety in flight.

Then he said quietly, "Make it look as if I am still bound, Jim."

Unquestioning, Jim obeyed. When he had finished, the Major rolled carefully back to his original position. "What game do we play, baas? Is there to be a killing?"

"Maybe many killings, Jim," the Major said seriously. "But we play the game carefully, hoping that there will be no need for bloodshed. Wait for my word always. You have an *assegai*?"

"Two, baas; a knife and a *knobkerrie* also."

"Good. Now talk for a little while, until the fat man, or the other one, comes this way."

"And if they come together, baas?"

The Major sighed. "If they come together, Jim, there will have to be a killing. But what of yourself, Jim? For these past two days I have known you were near. The Goaway bird cried many times, and once I thought I saw you peering out of the jungle grass as we passed."

A low chuckle came from the bushes.

"When I came to the *kraal* of M'Mandi, baas, and that fool told me of what had happened—"

"Then he is not dead, Jim?"

"Nay, baas. But he nearly died at my hand when he told me he had struck you down."

"Why did he do that, Jim?"

"Because he thought you had betrayed him and his people to the evil white men."

"I see," the Major muttered in English. "The poor devil." Then, in the vernacular, "Go on, Jim."

"There is little to tell, baas. I gave the baas's horse and the mules and all the provisions into the keeping of men of another *kraal*—but first I made a charm so that they would deal honorably with the things—and in the morning M'Mandi and I followed the spoor of the men who had carried you away.

"It was easy to follow, baas, and we two, traveling light, traveled quickly. Soon we caught up with you and ever since have been circling around you—now in front, now behind; to the right and to the left. And—*au-a*, baas!—that M'Mandi is a *schlimm* one. Time and again he put the fear into the hearts of the black soldiers. Aye, he worked on their fear of the evil spirits. He put signs for them to see everywhere: A pile of stones here; there a broken bough placed just so; here an empty gourd, upturned, directly in the path he knew they would take! there a bunch of feathers hanging from the limb of a tree under which he knew they must pass. At night he made strange noises—"

"I heard them, Jim, and thought evil spirits were about."

Jim chuckled. "I was nearer to him than I am to you when he made those noises, baas, and I, even I, trembled and looked over my shoulder. Aye, a man is M'Mandi. I have forgiven him somewhat for the blow he, in his ignorance, gave you. But had I found you greatly harmed, M'Mandi would have died. He granted me that right.

"Last night M'Mandi made his way past the sentries and talked with some of his people. They told him many things. How that there was an enmity between the fat man and that other; how some of the soldiers were losing stomach for the things they had to do, The signs of evil M'Mandi had placed in their way were working on them.

"So, when they made camp tonight, M'Mandi again went to his people, openly this time, and by cunning talk caused trouble between the soldiers—setting the men of this tribe against the men of that—and encouraged his people to show fight. That was to give me a chance to come to you and— But quiet, baas. They are coming this way; the fat man and that other."

The Major cursed softly. "They've stopped again," Jim continued in a lower tone. "The fat man is angry. He is sending the other back to the soldiers. He comes on alone."

"Good!" the Major breathed in relief. "Be ready, Jim."

"Ready, baas. All the time while we rested, M'Mandi and I, I put edges to my *assegais*. They are very sharp."

For a moment the Major could hear nothing but the confused murmur of voices about the fires; then he heard the footsteps of Don Pedro and his labored breathing.

Presently Don Pedro was standing over him. "And there are more crimes for you to report," he said suavely. "That is, if you live to report them. Carlos was very hasty. He killed four of our soldiers, and that is to be regretted. He also killed two prisoners, but they were only old women so that does not matter."

"What was it all about?" the Major asked wearily, as if he realized the hopelessness of his situation.

Don Pedro shrugged his shoulders. "Does it matter? The soldiers have been very high strung the past few days, the superstitious fools! And Carlos was a little harsh with them. To make matters worse, the prisoners got a little out of hand—the guards have been too easy with them—and *phau!* Like a match touched to dry tinder, the trouble blazed up. It took fire—" he patted the bulge under his pajama coat meaningly—"to put it out. I'm afraid you'll have to report my atrocities too."

The Major groaned. "You're a bloodthirsty devil, Don Pedro. Is there no decency in you? No feeling, no pity?"

"None at all, Major. Remember that."

"Yes, I'll remember that," the Major said tonelessly. "But how about my proposal. Do we go to M'Mandi's *kraal* for the diamonds? If we do, we ought to start tonight in about an hour's time. Shortly after sundown. And if we're going, I wish you'd cut me loose. I want to get a little circulation in my arms and legs, they're bally stiff and I won't be able to walk."

"You are very funny, Major. Almost I believed your story about the diamonds you hid at M'Mandi's. But before I do anything so foolish, I'm going to search you very, very carefully."

He laughed as he saw the look of chagrin on the Major's face. "I'll go halves with you," the Major offered despairingly.

"You are in no position to bargain," Don Pedro reminded him. "I take all."

"But you'll spare my life?"

"Who knows. Where are the diamonds?"

"In my right hand tunic pocket."

Don Pedro stooped, and finding that too much of an effort, got down on his knees, his eyes shining with greedy anticipation. Then his mouth sagged wide open, his eyes bulged alarmingly.

"It must be rather disconcerting," the Major said with a chuckle, "to find the man you're going to rob—thinking him bound and helpless—quite able to take care of himself. And I assure you that I am and this *really* is a revolver and I'm quite a good shot, awfully good. But no doubt you have heard that?"

Don Pedro had, and remembering what he had heard made no attempt to reach for his own weapon.

"And now you'll do exactly as I tell you," the Major stated coldly, all the fun gone from his voice. "Of course you may have heard that I've never killed a man in cold blood. But then, *you're* not a man! Stand up! Keep your hands down."

Don Pedro obeyed, rising ponderously from his knees.

"Now back slowly toward that bush. That's right; back further. That's enough. Jim!"

"Yah, baas!"

"Take his revolver from him and throw it here. It is under his arm, beneath his coat."

Jim's arm came out from the bush and explored, with no gentleness, Don Pedro's chest.

Finding the revolver he took it from its holster and tossed it to the Major.

"Has he any more weapons on him, Jim?"

"No, baas," Jim said, and the Major broke the one he had. Satisfied that it was loaded in all chambers, he threw his own revolver at Don Pedro, hitting him in the stomach, so that he sat down suddenly with a gasp like the wind soughing from a big bellows.

But his wits were all about him. He was sitting on the revolver the Major had thrown at him. Presently he planned to maneuver so that he could get it into his hand. And then—

"It's not loaded," the Major said sarcastically. "Stand up! I've got a lot to do."

And Don Pedro stood up.

"Hold your *assegai* firmly against his back, where the flesh is soft, Jim. If he moves, drive it in."

"Yah, baas. I hope he moves."

Don Pedro flinched as he felt the prick of the *assegai*.

"Vindictive devil, Jim; isn't he?" the Major remarked pleasantly. "And he has a strong arm. I've seen him kill bulls with one spear thrust. Now call Carlos. No quaver in your voice, mind; no little signals, unless you are very tired of life. Like you, sometimes I can be absolutely ruthless and conscienceless."

"Carlos!" called Don Pedro. "Come here." And despite the Major's warning he could not keep a quaver out of his voice.

The half caste sprang up from his place near to one of the fires and walked swiftly toward the Major. Some of the soldiers started to follow him but shrank back to the fires at a shouted order from him.

"What is it?" he asked in a sneering voice as he neared. "Have you thought better of it and decided to let my black dogs have this swine to play with?" Then he halted, came on a few steps further—very slowly—his eyes darting from the prostrate form of the Major, to that of Don Pedro cringing against the bush. His suspicions were aroused. His beady black eyes darted from one to the other. He saw something in the Major's right hand, and then the meaning of it all came to him. Don Pedro had hired the Major to kill him! There could be no other explanation. Then, before the Major could make a move, Carlos's hand leaped to his revolver, drew it and fired, shouting, "You swine! And that is how you would get rid of me!"

Don Pedro doubled up, his hands pressed to his stomach, then sat down heavily, as a man sits in a chair which is not there. On his face was an expression of hurt surprise, like that of a child who is having some digestive trouble resulting from an unwise meal of stolen green apples. His hands were still clasped across his stomach; between the fingers blood oozed slowly.

Before Carlos could fire again, the Major's revolver spoke. The half caste's weapon was jerked out of his hand as if pulled by some invisible string, and the man gazed mutely at his limp, useless hand.

At the same time the Major leaped to his feet, retrieved the other's revolver and ordered sharply, "Sit down close to Don Pedro, with your back to him. Quickly."

Carlos meekly obeyed. It seemed as if the wound—only a superficial wound—had taken all the spirit from him. Like many bullies raised to a position of authority, given the power to maim and kill, now that he saw that authority taken away from him Carlos became a cringing coward.

"Now tie their hands together, Jim."

"It is done, baas," Jim announced. "But I think there was no need to tie up the fat man."

"No, Jim?" the Major said absently. He was anxiously watching some of the black soldiers who were approaching to investigate the shooting. "Why not?"

"Because he is dead, baas."

"Dead!" the Major exclaimed. He was conscious of a feeling of regret, of irritation. Don Pedro was not deserving of such a clean, easy death. "Halt," he cried to the advancing soldiers.

They came on steadily, relentlessly. He jumped back, putting the bodies of Carlos and Don Pedro between him and the soldiers. Jim joined him, his *assegais* gleaming red in the rays of the sinking sun.

"Tell them to halt, Carlos," he ordered and thrust his revolver against the half caste's ribs.

"Halt," Carlos cried in a piping, tremulous voice.

The soldiers wavered and halted. One of them came forward alone. He was a big, powerful native.

"Don't let him come near me," Carlos said, his teeth chattering. "He hates me. It was only because that he was afraid of Don Pedro that he did not kill me long ago. And now Don Pedro is dead—"

"You killed him," the Major said tersely. "But that is good," he laughed in great relief. "That is what I wanted to know. Guard the white man closely, Jim."

"My spear is over his heart, baas, and will be ready."

The Major nodded approval and went forward to meet the native.

"Your name?" he asked.

"Simba. Sergeant Simba"—the native said truculently, gazing intently at the Major. "Sir," he added after a pause.

"Then know, Simba, that I have been sent by the great white chief at Lourenço Marques because word of the evil these two men were causing you to perform had come to his ears."

"*Au-a!* We had fears that way. But what then? Does the great white chief send out only one against so many?"

"Is there any need of more? Don Pedro is dead, killed by Carlos—the man who is neither white nor black. And Carlos is my prisoner."

"True. But we are here, and we are many."

"And your death is here, should I need it," the Major countered. "And yet it is of no value to me—see." He very ostentatiously stuck his revolver in his waist band and, after fumbling for his monocle—frowning with annoyance when he discovered that it had been smashed into many small pieces—thrust his hands nonchalantly into his trousers pockets.

"You could kill me," he said. "You could kill my servant— but what could you do with all those others?" With a wave of his hand he indicated the jungle about them. Long, mysterious shadows, night shadows, moved there as the grasses bowed before a passing breeze.

Simba shifted uneasily. He had a lively remembrance of the portents which had crossed his path during the last two days. "What do you want of us, white man?"

"You must free the captives you have taken and acknowledge me as your commanding officer; giving obedience in all things."

"Is it permitted that I speak with those others?"

The Major hesitated.

"If their word is 'No,'" Simba added, "I will come back to this place and all shall be as it is now."

"It is good. You are a man, Simba."

The sergeant nodded, turned away and joining the other three, returned to the fires.

The Major waited impatiently, a little nervously; not quite sure what course to take should the decision of the soldiers be against him. The shadows lengthened; in a little while it would be dark. It was a weird setting for a tragedy, for death: The jungle noises, the flickering light from the campfires, the voices of the men raised now in angry protest, now in agreement.

The Major turned around and looked at Jim; he smiled as he noticed the shoes which Jim carried strung about his neck. Then his eyes fell on Carlos and the huddled, lifeless heap that had been Don Pedro.

Carlos looked at him. "You won't give me to Simba?" he pleaded.

"I don't see why I shouldn't," the Major answered curtly.

"They are coming, baas," Jim said quietly.

The Major whirled quickly, every muscle tensed. Then he relaxed, for in the half light he could see that Simba's face was one broad grin. "We are your men," he shouted, "if you promise to speak for us to the white chief at Lourenço Marques."

"That I promise you," the Major said quietly. "Now give orders that some dig a hole in which to bury Don Pedro. Others shall guard Carlos—and he is not to be harmed," he added quickly noticing the expression of grim satisfaction on Simba's face.

"It is an order," Simba said sorrowfully. "And what will you do, white man?"

"Why I," the Major spoke slowly, reveling in the luxury of anticipation, "I will shave and bathe and help myself to such of Don Pedro's clothing as will fit me. I will eat and then sleep."

That night, after he had dined sumptuously in the well-equipped tent which the luxury loving Don Pedro considered essential, the Major ordered M'Mandi to be brought before him.

"I was a fool," that man said dejectedly. "My life is yours."

"I give it back to you. The blow is forgotten. It is another matter I wish to speak to you about. What think you of this place for a *kraal*?"

"It is good, *Inkosi*. The ground is high, the water pure. The soil is fertile. Once the jungle growth is cleared—"

The Major waved his hand in dismissal and M'Mandi, somewhat puzzled, left the tent.

Early the next morning the Major addressed all the people, soldiers and their late prisoners. His remarks were forceful and quite to the point. As soon as he was finished, there commenced a great laboring; each one had his task allotted to him and work progressed apace so that, by nightfall, a large area of ground had been made clear; hut poles cut and trimmed and reeds for thatch cut.

Ten days later the work was finished. Where had been a jungle, now stood a *kraal* of many huts encircled by a stout pole *scherm*. M'Mandi and his people were very happy, if tired. They had worked hard, but the soldiers had worked harder, and the Goanese, Carlos the half caste, had worked hardest of all. The Major and Simba had seen to that.

Now the Major was ready to leave with the soldiers and Carlos, for Lourenço Marques. There the Major intended to report to his excellency the governor on the evil ways of the late Don Pedro and Carlos. He regretted that Don Pedro, the greater villain, had escaped his just punishment.

He had also some business in that seaport that had to do with diamonds which had been given to him by a certain Lola de Sousa.

"Yes," he said to Jim, as they left the place of Mushla Ameyhloc, for so M'Mandi insisted on calling his new *kraal*, "I'm glad they didn't search me."

From his pocket he pulled out a handful of diamonds. They were not beautiful, looking like pieces of common, dirty glass. But men have murdered for less.

"It's a great game, Jim."

"Yah, baas. The greatest in the world." And neither man had in mind the game of I.D.B.

THE CANDLE BID

"**BAAS, WE** have done many foolish things, we two, but all that has gone before is as the wisdom of gray beards compared to this folly you now plan."

The speaker, a squat, ungainly Hottentot, looked up with a scowl at the white man who sat his mount—a coal-black stallion—with the graceful ease of a man born to the saddle. But the scowl became a grin—a good-natured, mirth-provoking grin—as the white man he called baas hunched up his shoulders and cowered in his saddle as if to avoid a blow.

An elephant trumpeted loudly somewhere in the thick bush to the right of them and an excited babble of voices broke out along the trail behind them.

The Hottentot turned in his saddle.

"Silence," he commanded sharply. "Get in line."

The excited cried dies down to a vague whisper, became one of the mysterious noises of the bush, and the motley crowd of natives—old men and young boys—who straggled along the winding trail attempted to adopt some sort of military formation, carrying their weapons, an assortment of *assegais, knobkerries,* axes and hoes at something remotely resembling the "slope."

But even as he watched, they broke their formation and became a gesticulating, purposeless mob once again.

"*Tchat!*" The Hottentot exclaimed in disgust and turning away from them drummed his bare heels on the fat ribs of his mule, urging it to a better speed so that he could catch up with his baas.

"I said we were fools, baas," he said loudly.

"Yes, Jim. I heard you," the white man answered. "But I do not see this with your eyes. It is not the work of fools to save a people from great evil."

"What are you to them, or they to you?" Jim asked. "They are born to die. What matter then if they die today or tomorrow?"

The white man ignored this.

"If you saw a man drowning, Jim, you would fetch him out?"

"Not if there were crocodiles in the river, baas!"

"I have known you to do even that, Jim," the white man said softly.

"*Au-a!* That was the bark of another dog, baas!" Jim expostulated. "Was I to stand by and see my baas drown? Besides, I knew how to deal with those *schelm* of the river. There was no danger."

"And I know how to deal with these *schelm* of the bush, Jim—and there is no danger."

The white man spurred his horse a little ahead, then looked back at the Hottentot, a half-mocking, half-affectionate smile on his face. The rays of the sun caused his monocle to gleam like a ball of molten gold.

Cursing softly, Jim urged his mule on again, groaning at the beast's awkward gait.

"Not so fast, baas!" he pleaded, then, as the mule resumed its normal pace, he went on in grieved tones:

"I said we are fools, baas. We go to our death, but hurrying to it does not make us any the less fools. *Au-a!* We see it before us, yet we rush into it. *Au-a!* Walking is not fast enough; you needs must make me ride this misbegotten beast."

"It would not be seemly for the captain of an *impi* to walk, O Grumbler," remarked the Major.

Jim was silent for a moment.

"Just the same, baas," he went on as a memory of the happenings of the past few months came to his mind, "we have played the part of fools from the beginning."

"You mean that I have been a fool, Jim? You have always been wise, is it not so?"

"Truly, baas. But I have fasted with you and feasted with you; we have faced death together many times; your kill has always been my kill—and so now, your folly is my folly. *Au-a!* I say that we were fools from the time the baas met

Later they saw that white man striding down the street, carrying in his arms a black man, who hung limply, as one dead.

the white woman at the city of diamonds, for that woman's eyes made my baas forget that he was the Major, the man who trod only in a path of his own making. Yet that of itself was nothing. A man cannot always escape the snares of women. The folly began when the baas took the diamonds she gave him so that the *Nonquai*—the mounted policemen—who was coming to search her would not find them. And then, when those two men who called themselves Portuguese tried to steal the diamonds from the baas, he was content to play a trick on them; content to laugh at them and let them go."

"And what should I have done, Jim?" the white man interposed.

"Killed them, baas. Dead snakes are harmless. Yet that is not the end of the folly. The baas needs must remember that he promised to take the woman's diamonds, the ones she had stolen, to Lourenço Marquez and we trekked for that place. It has been a long trek and a hard one. And not yet are we done with this cursed place."

Jim hit out viciously with his *sjambok* at a tangle of vines which looped themselves and fell like dangling nooses above the trail.

"But I had given my word, Jim! I couldn't steal the diamonds!"

"Truly, baas," Jim agreed sarcastically. "The Major has taken many stones, but he has never stolen—no!

"And so we leave the open veldt and come to this country where a man breathes with difficulty, where there is no air. And still the tale of folly is not all told. When we come to a *kraal* and the people there tell of an evil white man and a man who is neither white nor black, together with fifty black soldiers, who have carried off the young men and maidens to sell as calves, the baas must needs follow the spoor of those evil ones. He is resolved, he says, to punish them. And with those—" Jim jerked his thumb contemptuously over his shoulder—"weaklings—the men the slavers would not trouble to take with them—he intends to do great deeds. We are like fools who walk into an uncovered elephant pit."

The white man smiled and then began to sing softly.

"At least the spoor is easy to follow, Jim," he said presently.

"Truly, baas. But they are at least a day's trek ahead of us, and soon it will be night and we will have to camp again without fires for fear that we should be seen; so we will suffer the torments of insects and danger from the beasts of the bush. And I am hungry, baas. Between my belly and my back is nothing but a great emptiness. And to what end? Death at the hands of the Portuguese dogs—if we do not all die of fever first."

"What would you have me do, Jim?" the Major asked softly. "Turn back? And before you answer, think of the *kraals* these evil ones have burned down. Think, too, of the one-armed children back there and the bleeding backs of the old men and women. And be sure you remember the warrior, the man whose muscles were mightier even than yours, who blindly sat in the gray ashes that had been his *kraal,* a broken, helpless thing. Think—"

"*Au-a!* Baas," Jim interrupted quickly. "I do remember and am ashamed. We will go on, baas, we two—even if those others should turn back. What we will do is past my understanding. It may be that the baas, by holding up his hand, can dam a mighty river. I know not. But we will go on and if we must die—it is better to go now than to wait until old age and regrets come. As I have said, baas, we are fools!"

"Fools enjoy life, Jim. Wise men regret it—so be content."

A GRAY-BEARDED native, the ring of a petty chief on his head, naked save for a loin-cloth about his middle, stepped out of the bush directly in their path.

"What is it, Simba?" the Major asked sharply. "Why are you not with your scouts?"

"I hastened back to tell you, white man, that the evil ones we seek are camped only a little way ahead," he panted. "By sundown you will reach the place. The white man and the black soldiers talk loudly as men talk who are near to blows."

The Major smiled, then his eyes hardened, the lines about his strong jaw tightened.

"And what are the scouts doing, Simba?"

"They are watching the camp, white man. I have also ordered that they should try and get in touch with my people who are the prisoners of the evil ones; that should be easy, for no guard is set over them. What need of guards? They are leg-ironed and yoked together."

The Major nodded. Then:

"You are hurt, Simba."

The old chief's left arm hung helpless at his side.

"It is nothing," he said. "I am old and old bones break easily. So, when I fell into an elephant pit, my arm under me—" He broke off with a chuckle. "At least my right arm, my killing arm, is good. I can still fight to free my people."

The white man dismounted quickly and expertly strapped up Simba's broken arm. While he was thus occupied, the natives crowded around and watched him with curious eyes.

When the bandaging was finished, he gave them terse, explicit instructions of the part they were to play.

"Bwana," they chorused when he had made all clear to them. "In all things we will obey."

They raised their weapons in silent salutation and then the bush swallowed them up; they became black, flickering shadows in the African bush, and presently the shadows vanished, as shadows will when commanded to do so by the sun.

"They may be poor soldiers when it comes to drill," the Major drawled in English, "but, by Jove, they know how to lose themselves in the bush!"

"The *bwana* says?" the old chief questioned wonderingly.

"Hush, old one," Jim said sternly. "My baas makes a charm. He is a great man. He is the Major—and I, I am Jim, his servant. An' if I don't see you s'long hullo!" the Hottentot babbled in conclusion, greatly pleased at the effect his own little patter of English had on Simba.

"We tarry here too long," Simba said, and refusing to ride the horse or the mule went on along the trail.

The Major mounted and followed closely after him, with Jim riding at his side.

"Take heart, black one," he said to the Hottentot with a low chuckle. "Did you not hear the old chief say that he had fallen into an elephant pit? But he got out alive! It is an omen!"

But Jim refused to be cheered up.

"He broke his arm, baas," he said lugubriously. "An evil omen, surely!"

THEY TREKKED on in silence until, about half an hour later, Simba halted at a bend in the trail and held up his hand.

The Major and Jim reined in their mounts and listened.

A confused murmur of voices came to them—voices raised in hot dispute. A shot echoed weirdly through the bush; it was quickly followed by another, and then another.

Simba's eyes blazed exultantly.

"They fight amongst themselves," he cried. "Our work will be easier."

The Major nodded agreement.

"Go and join your men, Simba," he ordered. "Do not forget to wait for my signal—and there must be no killing, no bloodshed if that can be avoided. It is an order."

"It is an order, *bwana!*"

Simba left the trail and hurried swiftly through the thick bush. Here and there the tall grasses quivered at his passing, but he made no sound.

"Now we go on, Jim," the Major said cheerfully.

"Au-a!" the Hottentot replied with a grimace. "Now I know how feels a goat which is used as bait to snare a lion."

The Major laughed.

"If I did not know you very well, Jim, I should say you were afraid."

"The baas does not know me—I am."

They rode on and came presently to a large clearing in the center of which stood a cumbersome tent. About the tent swarmed some fifty excited natives dressed in the uniform of the Portuguese black soldiery.

Beyond, at the opposite side of the clearing, two or three hundred natives—men and women—huddled helplessly together. They wore leg-irons, their hands were tied behind their backs and yoked to each other by a short length of heavy chain.

At the tent opening stood two men. One, he was very tall and thin, wore gaudy colored pajamas and a large sun helmet, the other, a heavily built man with thick, pouting lips and broad-bridged nose, was dressed in a gorgeous uniform—the blue of the cloth of which it was made served only as something on which to hang medals and gold lace.

Both men were very drunk and frightened; they tried to bolster their courage by drinking from the bottles they held in their left hands and threatening the soldiers with their revolvers.

The Major and Jim halted just at the edge of the clearing and watched; apparently their presence was not known.

"The black soldiers will spring the trap," Jim murmured softly, "then we can walk in unafraid."

The Major nodded. His eyes were fixed on the thin white man at the tent opening and his half-caste companion.

"Perhaps it would be better," he mused, "to leave those two to the mercies of their own men. I think, before the night is over, they would be made to suffer enough pain to pay for the torture they have caused the natives hereabouts. The devils!" His eyes glinted coldly. "But no; we still have to think of the prisoners over there. The soldiers are a little drunk now; later, after they have killed their officers, they will get very drunk and then—"

He knew to what terrible extremes of brutality a savage will go when under the influence of white man's liquor—especially when that savage has been under the tutelage of degenerate whites.

One of the natives, a big fellow with a sergeant's chevrons on his sleeves—stepped forward from his companions. He held his hands above his head to show that he was unarmed.

"Let us talk this over," he said in a deep, bellowing voice. "Listen to our commands so that bloodshed may be avoided."

The thin man at the tent staggered a few paces forward.

"What mean you by 'commands,' dog?" he called in a piping falsetto voice. "Come crawling on your hands and knees, licking the dust from my shoes—beg for mercy. Then I will listen to you. It is enough, I have spoken. Only, think of this; you forget that behind me, Don Felix, is all the power of Portugal. Harm but the tip of my little finger and a thousand white men will come searching for your blood."

The Major nodded approvingly.

"He understands natives," he murmured, as the big sergeant turned sheepishly toward his companions. They crowded about him, talking rapidly, heatedly, and presently he turned once again to face his officer.

"Sir," he said humbly, "my brother there tells me to say this: We are tired of burning *kraals* and the killing and torturing of our own people. We will have no more of it. We are men—warriors—and that is not the work of men. Neither will we any longer be the dogs of Carlos—that man who is neither white nor black. He is beneath us; he is fit only to cook food and carry water. He is neither white nor black, but a sneaking bastard. Yet, because you have given him authority, we have daily bent our backs to the lash of his whip. Therefore, we demand—"

"Demand," screamed the white man in a frenzy of passion and fired.

"Ah! He does *not* understand natives," the Major corrected his first impression. "And now what?"

For a moment the soldiers stared dumbly at the sergeant—he had gone down with a bullet through his shoulder—and then at their commandante who stood there, a mocking smile on his face.

They then took a step forward—forty-nine of them moving as one man.

The white fired again and a soldier fell—his ankle snapped by the shot.

But the others did not halt. They came on, slowly, their bodies bent forward, their eyes gleaming. There was something terribly grim and implacable about their slow movement.

"Come!" said the Major shortly to the Hottentot. "It is time for us to take a hand."

He rode across the open space, Jim close behind him.

Three shots sounded in rapid succession; the thin man had fired twice—and missed. The third shot came from the half-caste's revolver—and did not miss.

With a strangled sob, a strange look of hurt surprise on his face, the thin man spun round and then pitched in a lifeless heap to the ground.

This halted the soldiers for a moment and the half-caste yelled,

"See! I am on your side. I have killed—"

Then he ran from the place, the soldiers, yielding fearful threats, close on his heels.

"Stop, warriors!" the Major's voice rang out commandingly, but it was startled surprise, rather than obedience to the order, which halted the soldiers.

THEY LOOKED up at the white man—and he was a man; they could see that—who had appeared so suddenly.

Carlos ran to the Major and clutched frantically at his stirrup.

"You're just in time," he panted. "They have killed the commandante and now they would kill me. The mutinous dogs."

"Give me your revolver," the Major said coldly.

"But, *senhor*—"

"Give it to me."

With a shrug of his shoulders, Carlos handed it to him.

"Now get behind my horse and keep your mouth closed."

"Give us that half-caste dog, stranger," a native cried, "and then you may go your way. We have no bone to pick with you."

"But I have one to pick with you," he answered. He took out his monocle and polished it carefully with his handkerchief.

They watched in awed amazement; never before had they seen a man who could take out his eye.

"You have forgotten that you are warriors and men," he said at length, sure now that he had their attention. "You have become like unclean beasts; you go up and down the land devouring your own kind."

"We acted not by ourselves," the sergeant shouted. He had risen slowly to his feet and made his way to the front of his men. Blood streamed down from the wound in his shoulder but he seemed indifferent to it. "We are soldiers of the Government—we only obeyed the order of the man in authority over us."

"And he is dead—he cannot give you the lie. He cannot say that the evil things you have done were done in defiance of his commands. You were wise to kill him before he could bear witness against you."

"We did not kill him; the half-caste did that."

"So? And if you kill Carlos—then what? Who will believe your story? No one. They will say that you rose up against your officers and killed them because they rebuked you for the evil you did. Every hand will be against you."

"*Au-a!* It is true, stranger. What then?"

"It is well for you that the Great White Overlord, having heard of the evil in this district, sent me to take you and your officers in chains to Lourenço Marquez; it is well that he sent me, I say, for all things are known to me. I know Carlos killed Don Felix and I know you had no stomach for the things you were ordered to do. Therefore I will speak to my friend who is the Great Overlord and undoubtedly he will deal gently with you. But Carlos I take in chains to Lourenço Marquez, and there you must go too that the governor may hear the full story and order such punishment as he may think best."

"If you promise to speak softly for us, stranger, we will go," the sergeant said stolidly after talking with his men. "But we will not go in chains. We are free men—you are alone save for that grinning ape of a Hottentot. Therefore, we tell you not to try us too far, lest we kill you and the half-caste, then lose ourselves in the bush."

"But I am not alone," the Major said. "Listen!" He put his fingers to his mouth and whistled shrilly.

Immediately, loud shouts sounded in the bush all about the clearing. Again, the Major whistled and the shouting ceased.

The soldiers whispered together uneasily.

"I am not sure that I will take you in chains," the Major continued. "If you obey my commands—"

"What are your commands, *bwana?*"

"Your name, sergeant?"

"M'Linda, *bwana.*"

"THEN LISTEN to my commands, Sergeant M'Linda. First the people who are bound yonder shall be returned to their *kraals.*"

"That is to our way of thinking. That we were prepared to do. Is that all?"

"Nay. You must help rebuild the *kraals* you have destroyed."

"That, too, we will do, *bwana,*" the sergeant said slowly and groaned. He saw ahead weeks of fatiguing labor. But it was just—most just.

"Does he speak for you all?" the Major asked.

"Truly, *bwana,*" the others replied in chorus. "He is our mouthpiece. To what he gives his word, we give our word."

"What then?" the sergeant asked.

"Then—" a smile flickered over the Major's face—"then when the fat of soft living has been sweated out of you, I will make you real soldiers."

"And you give your word to speak for us to the governor?"

"My word has been given."

The sergeant hesitated a moment, sighed and then—

"We are your dogs, *bwana!*"

"Then file before me and stack your rifles here."

They obeyed without hesitation.

"Now two of you take the half-caste and guard him closely. But he is not to be harmed. The rest of you, release the men—the women we will attend to later—you have taken prisoners, and bring them here to me. Make haste! Soon it will be dark and there is much work to be done."

Again his orders were obeyed without question.

"And now you shall see my army," the Major said slowly to the soldiers.

He whistled three times and in response to the call, natives broke from the cover of the bush all around and converged slowly on the tent.

The soldiers looked at them wonderingly—the wonder gave place to anger. These newcomers, the army of the white man, were composed of old men and beardless youths. They had no guns—they—

It was a mock of an army!

The soldiers turned wrathfully on the Major—they had been tricked—they would retract the promises they had made—

And then they saw that the men of the *kraals*—the prisoners they had just released—a hundred and fifty of them—encircled the white man in a ring three deep. And each one of the fifty in the front rank held a rifle in his hand.

They had been tricked—but it was no shame to be tricked by such a man.

"*Bwana!*" they cried happily. "We are your men!"

THERE WERE many curious spectators of the procession which wound its way along the dusty thoroughfare which was the main street of Lourenço Marquez—the fever-infested seaport of Portuguese East Africa. Before each ugly, whitewashed, square hut, made even more hideous by a broad band of vivid brown paint around the doorway and windows and along the outside edges of the buildings, sat a little group of men and women who watched with sleep-laden eyes this strange interruption of the noonday siesta.

Here and there, their appearance was greeted by a lazy ripple of applause; elsewhere, there were low mutterings. It occurred to many of the onlookers that these native soldiers formed the advance guard of an invading force from Rhodesia. That invasion had long been feared. Lourenço Marquez would be a most valuable asset to the new colony and several schemes had been instigated to annex the seaport by peaceful means. They had failed. Very well, then. Why not occupation by force of arms and then, possession being nine points of international law, how would it be possible to oust the British lion once he had ensconced himself?

Consequently, certain citizens—American, German, French and English traders—seeing an end to the present criminally lax administration, applauded, while others—officials of that administration, gambling hell proprietors and certain ladies—thinking of their imminent loss of revenue, sighed, cursed and covertly shook their fists.

The belief that this was an invading force was heightened by the fact that, following the detachment of police, slouched a Goanese—a half-caste—dressed in the tawdry remnants of what had once been a much gold-belaced, flamboyant uniform. He was weaponless and evidently a prisoner, for on either side of him marched two of the police.

"It is Carlos!" the whisper marked his passing. "They've captured Carlos!"

"I hope they string you up so high that your neck reaches to your heels," a red-headed, pug-nosed man yelled. "An' sure that's better than you deserve, and so it is."

The prisoner scowled and turning slightly swore venomously, ending with:

"My time's coming soon. You—"

One of his guards prodded him in the back with the butt of his rifle and he stumbled on.

"You bet your time's coming," the red-headed one yelled, "and I'll be on hand to see it, so I will."

After the prisoner and his guard came a rabble of natives carrying loads on their heads. They all gaped in astonishment at the white men, most of whom were barefooted and wore gaudy colored pajamas, and the *kraal* they had built for themselves. The women stared with a mixture of envy and dismay at the native women of the town who were dressed in gaudy cotton prints. Somehow the comparison between the women of the town and those of the bush greatly favored the latter, made their nakedness essentially modest. As for the men—*Shenzis*—the two natives shouted contemptuously—naked save for a loin-cloth, they were as gods compared to their mockers who had sold their heritage of splendid physique, a knowledge of Nature and all her ways, for a mess of pottage, for the sops and dregs of a white man's civilization.

"Fine lot of ivory those niggers are carrying," commented a lean, long-shanked American. He and his companion, a fat little Cockney, were seated at a table outside one of the saloons. "I'd like to get a chance to buy it without greasing a lot of palms."

"Well, yer won't," the Cockney replied in a low, cautious tone, looking around to make sure that he was not overheard by the proprietor of the saloon—a greasy-skinned, villainous looking Portuguese—who was hovering nearby, watching the procession with despair. "You ain't such a bloody fool as to think them coveys are part hof a Henglish force, surely? Can't yer see they're hall Portuguese niggers—an' I've recognized one or two of 'em. That big sergeant, there. 'Is name's M'Linda. No, Yank! There's somefing bloomin' funny abart all this, but it don't mean the Portuguese are going ter be kicked hout. You'll be payin' palm oil ter a lot of greasy Dagoes fer a long time ter come, I'm finkin'. But, blimne! Look wot's a-comin' now! Ain't 'e the darlingest pet? Ain't 'e too sweet fer words?"

"That's a mighty fine horse he's riding," the other said slowly, "an' he sits him as if he knew how a horse should be ridden. If I were you, Cockney, I wouldn't let him hear me call him names. He's no momma's pet. I'm willing to bet he's upward of six foot and weighs over two hundred—or I never won a soote at a county fair."

"Well, wot abart it, Yank? Two 'undred pounds an' six foot ain't nothin' at all if 'e ain't got guts. An' 'e ain't. 'E can't 'ave, else 'e wouldn't wear a monocle."

AT THAT moment the object of their conversation, an immaculately attired white man, reined in his horse, a coal-black Basutu stallion which had in him a strong leavening of Arab, close to the two men and drawled:

"I say, old chappies, can you tell me if the bally governor's in town?"

"In a manner of speakin"e is, Percy, dear boy." Cockney's drawl was very labored, and making a ring of the thumb and forefinger of his right hand he squinted through it while with the other hand he tenderly twirled an imaginary mustache. "And hin a manner'e ain't. Haw!" he concluded.

The rider turned to the American whose face was purple with poorly suppressed mirth—Cockney's burlesque of the monocled dude was very funny—and taking out his monocle polished it with a white silk handkerchief then, satisfied that it was clean, replaced the monocle with a flowery gesture, returned the handkerchief to the sleeve of his well-fitting tunic-coat.

"I say, old bean," he said, "I wish you'd elucidate the riddle propounded by your humorous friend—'e is, an' in a manner 'e ain't—if you know what I mean." His imitation of Cockney's nasal twang was perfect and the American chuckled.

"Sure! I know what you mean. But about the governor, Cockney was right. He is and he ain't. He died two weeks ago—black water fever they say. Poor devil."

"Dead, eh?" the other said gravely.

"Yep! An' they buried him at noon the same day. He didn't have a chance to live—"

"Who—er—is—in charge of things now?" the horseman interrupted.

"Ferdinand de Paulos. He—"

But the other did not stop to hear more and rode off after his charges, followed closely by a grizzled Hottentot who rode a mule and seemed to be mutely protesting that he should be forced to ride anything so immoral as the result of a donkey's mismating.

"Hi! What's all this about?" the American shouted.

"Can't stop now, old dear. See you later!"

"But wot's yer name, Percy, me love?" Cockney screamed.

"Aubrey St. John," the drawl floated back, "but most people call me Major."

"Oh, hell!" Cockney exclaimed lugubriously, and pulling out a red bandanna handkerchief he mopped his red face. "An' there I was a-flirtin' wiv death as hinnocent as a bloody baby lamb. Oh migawd!"

He pounded vigorously on the table. The rat-faced saloon keeper came running vigorously in answer to the noisy summons and filled up the two empty glasses.

"That is all right, *senhor*," he said hastily as Cockney put his hand in his pocket. "You will drink this one on Manuel, no? We must celebrate this day—this so great day. An' the *senhor* will not forget," he added with a leer, "to speak of my poor place when the white soldiers come. We must—what do you say?—stick together. No?"

He looked up and down the dusty street.

"Soon the army will be here, no? It must be a great many soldiers, eh, for see, they have captured the so great and cunning Carlos—"

"They'll be 'ere soon, Manuel," Cockney said solemnly. "Ten thousand of them—an' all thirsty. You'd better bring hus some more of yer stuff so we can sample hit. For, mind yer, if it ain't, they'll fill yer so full o' lead that it'll be heasy ter give yer a burial at sea."

"Por Dios! I will do it!" And Manuel, the saloon keeper, hurried away, yelling orders to his Goanese and native servants.

"Ain't it a treat to 'ear that yeller 'ound tork to a white man fer once as a white man ought ter be torked to? But won't 'e be wild when 'e finds it all ain't so? Course there ain't no harmy coming, and, also o' course, this is one of the Major's little games; he did it all on 'is little own. Lord love 'im! But wot we've got ter do, Yank, is drink fast afore Manuel 'ere finds out wot it's all about and then hook it. I've seen Manuel throw a knife, I 'ave, an' throw it bloody straight. But 'ell! Wot's the use of torkin' an' lookin' fer trouble? 'Ere we are drinkin' free booze—an' lots more ter come—an' all because o' the Major. Cheerio, Yank. Drink 'earty!"

"Down the hatch, Cockney. But say, ain't I heard of this Major chap somewhere before? Who is he? He's no monocled dude for all he looks like one."

Cockney chuckled softly.

"I shouldn't be a bit surprised if yer 'ad 'eard of 'im, Yank, not a bit surprised. But there, there ain't no call fer me ter be so cocky abart it, fer I've seen 'im afore an' torked wiv 'im—not saucy like I did a little while back—an' I didn't reckernize 'im! Made fun of 'im, I did. Lumme!" Cockney made a wry face at the memory of his impertinence. "But then—oo would 'ave thought ter see the Major in this 'ell 'ole? There ain't no diamonds 'ere."

The other frowned thoughtfully.

"The Major—diamonds," he muttered. Then aloud, "Oh, I remember. He's the illicit diamond buyer they talk so much about."

"They don't tork about anything else—at least the police don't—down Kimberly way. Why, say, Yank, that damned lazy lookin' dude is abart heverything wot he don't look ter be. 'E's got brains an' nerve, an' 'e's the best shot in this whole blamed country an' can ride anything. 'E's a real sport an' got more friends among the whites an' niggers—"

"But he's a crook," Yank interposed.

Cockney spat in derision.

"Crook, 'ell! All wot 'e does is buy a few diamonds for which 'e ain't got no license. There's a rumor that 'e got stung once—w'en 'e first came hout 'ere years ago—by the Syndicate. You knows wot the I.D.B. laws are."

Yank nodded.

"Don't see why you Limeys stand for them," he said briefly.

"Well then," Cockney said triumphantly, "that's all the crook the Major is. 'E won't stand fer them lousy laws, that's all."

MEANWHILE THE procession had passed on out of sight of the two men, and was now parading before a house, notorious even in a notorious section of a notorious town.

In the shade of an awning which had been improvised from a much patched piece of sail cloth sat a woman— her age was uncertain; somewhere between eighteen and thirty—and two men.

The woman was very beautiful; her large black eyes smoldered, ready to burst into flames of anger or passion; the color of her full, sensual lips made a vivid splash of scarlet against the ivory white pallor of her skin. She was a white woman—the only white woman in Lourenço Marquez— with all the outer shell of civilization, but primitive in her physical perfection and grace of carriage; primitive, too, in all her emotions. She languidly waved a dainty lace handkerchief, presumably to cheer on the procession, but as the handkerchief was drenched with jasmine perfume it served to disguise the stench of refuse which pervaded the atmosphere and which was one of the curses of the early days of Lourenço Marquez.

The two men, apparently whites and evidently twins, were vulgarly over-dressed. On their fat fingers flashed diamond rings. Both wore flowing, scarlet bow ties, and diamonds glistened in their billowing, not over-clean white shirts. They were both very short and their shortness was exaggerated by their full, rounded stomachs, about which they wore wide, crimson cummerbunds. Their upper lips were adorned by large mustaches, the ends of which were waxed and curled belligerently upward.

They viewed the procession with great alarm and turned angrily on the girl when she poked fun at their fears.

"You can laugh, yes, Lola," one of them snarled. "You're safe. You're a woman—and beautiful. But as for us—" he shrugged his shoulders—"we can't pay for safe conduct the way you can."

The girl's eyes flashed angrily and her hand closed about the butt of a small revolver which she carried tucked into her waistband.

"Have a care, Pedro," she retorted in a low, threatening voice. "You presume too far. And so do you, Ricardo—" she turned swiftly on the other and the sneering smile on his face vanished to be replaced by one of dog-like humility. "No man can talk to Lola de Sousa that way. No one!"

"Let us not quarrel," the man called Ricardo said suavely. "Pedro spoke foolishly—but take my word, he did not mean what he said. Is it not so, Pedro?" Pedro bowed grandiloquently.

"*Sí*. Of course, Lola. We are friends. I would not do nothing to harm you—you work your way and we work ours. But I was disturbed. This—"he waved a pudgy hand toward the passing soldiers—"is unsettling. I think we should get away from here before it is too late."

"That is my thought, too, Lola," the other added quickly.

The girl looked at them scornfully.

"Pish!" she exclaimed and throwing the black lace mantilla from her head, leaned forward in her chair, so that she might better see and be seen by the passers-by.

"That's a fine horse he's riding, an' he sits him as if he knew how a horse should be ridden."

The two men exchanged meaning glances, then tiptoed softly to the door of the house, intending to enter and make their getaway by the back door.

"You don't have to steal away like that," Lola said dreamily. "I would not try to stop you." They halted and looked at each other uncertainly. "But here comes Carlos," she went on. "First wait and see him."

They came back hastily, their faces beaming. If Carlos was with these strange soldiers—then everything was all right.

And then they saw Carlos and their jaws sagged, their bugle eyes threatened to burst from their sockets.

"He's a prisoner!" the two men gasped simultaneously.

"Why, yes—of course!" the girl said amusedly.

The man Pedro grasped her arm frantically.

"This is no time for fooling, Lola. Come. Let's go before it is too late. Carlos a prisoner can mean only one thing—"

"It can mean many things," she assured him calmly. "Maybe it is time for us to go—but at least let us wait until Carlos has come nearer so that we may ask him things."

With a poor grace, fidgeting uneasily, they waited. When Carlos was opposite, the girl called in a strong, clear voice:

"What is it, Carlos? Are the English going to take the town?"

He looked toward her quickly and a gleam of hope shone in his terrible dark, muddy eyes as he saw the two men who were with her.

"No," he snarled. "That devil they call the Major captured us. He caused the commandante to be killed and he takes me, he says, to the governor. Rescue—before it is too late."

"The Major!" the two men exclaimed and their hands leaped to their revolvers.

"The Major," the girl breathed softly, her hand to her heart.

"Rescue," Carlos pleaded forlornly—his guards held him by the arms now and were dragging him onward.

"No!" the girl cried imperiously. "There is no need for rescue, Carlos. The old governor is dead and Ferdinand de Paulos is acting in his place. Go on. Let them think you are beaten. Let the Major play his game—and then we will play ours."

The half-caste's face lightened up vindictively and he cursed his two guards, threatening them, predicting awful tortures, until they silenced him by jabbing him in the back with their rifle butts. He stumbled on, quite content to wait.

The girl turned to the two men and laughed merrily.

"You are so brave, my friends," she said scathingly. "You would run when none pursue and so miss many things."

"You are very clever, Lola. I'm glad we stayed. We have an account to settle with the *Senhor* Major, eh, Ricardo?"

"Yes. A big account, brother. And it will be settled—presently." He drew his forefinger across his throat.

"No, fools!" the girl cried sharply. "He is not to be harmed. Of what good is he to us dead? But alive—and on our side—"

The two frowned. Once the Major had affronted their personal honor. That was no light thing! That could not be forgotten just because a woman ordered it.

"Why so soft, Lola?" Ricardo asked. "It is nothing to you, surely, what we do with him. He made a fool of us, and has made a fool of you. He took the diamonds you entrusted to him—you are not in the habit of giving things up so easily."

"I'm not soft," Lola said patiently. "Also, I am no fool. I shall yet get my diamonds back, have no fear of that, and if not, it does not matter. The Major has the reputation of being honest. But listen, how long have we sighed for just such a man as the Major to help us? How many opportunities of making much wealth have we let go by because we had no one like him. Think of the Swaziland affair, and the black ivory waiting up north and—"

The two nodded eagerly.

"That is true, Lola, we had not thought of that."

"You wouldn't," she said contemptuously.

"But can you get him, Lola? Can you make him your man?"

"I shall get him," she replied arrogantly.

"And after you are through with him—he shall be ours, eh, to do with as we like? You will not interfere?" Again Ricardo passed his finger across his throat.

"When I am through with him," she said cryptically, "he shall be yours. Now hasten to the fort and warn Ferdinand that the Major is to be unharmed; say that I, Lola de Sousa, have so ordered it. And tell him that the Major has twenty diamonds in his pockets."

They looked at her wonderingly and were about to protest. They knew what would happen to those diamonds once Ferdinand de Paulos knew of their existence.

"Go!" she ordered, waving them away imperiously. "Say just what I have told you to say—no more, no less."

They departed quickly then, chuckling happily and congratulating themselves on their good fortune in having such a beautiful and clever partner in the many crimes to which they applied themselves with a zeal and courage worthy of far better things.

As the men departed, Lola drew her mantilla over her head so that it partly covered her face and pulled her chair back closer to the wall of the house.

The native carriers passed by and then, two or three minutes later, the Major cantered up the road, followed by the Hottentot on the mule.

Just before the Major drew level with Lola, she rolled her handkerchief into a tight little ball and tossed it into the roadway.

The Major could not have failed to have seen it—Satan, his horse, swerved a little to avoid it—but he rode on, looking straight ahead.

And so he did not see the Hottentot dismount and retrieve the handkerchief and inhale its perfume with a broad grin of ecstasy; neither did he see the beautiful, black garbed woman who rushed out from the shade of the house and, after threatening the Hottentot with a revolver, snatch the handkerchief....

"I THINK you must be a little mad, *Senhor* Major." The speaker was so fat that he was a monstrosity and when he leaned back in his chair, it creaked protestingly. "Yes, undoubtedly you must be mad and I—I confess it—I am afraid of you."

The Major smiled—he looked surprisingly cool in the white duck uniform he wore—and smoothed the green pugaree of his pith sun helmet which was resting on his knees.

"I am far from mad, Don Ferdinand," he drawled, speaking Portuguese with the faintest accent. "And you have nothing to fear from me. Unless—" He shrugged his shoulders.

The other's eyes narrowed, disappeared entirely behind rolls of fat.

"I do not like that 'unless,'" he said slowly. "It sounds as if you would threaten me—me, Don Ferdinand de Paulos, Acting Governor of Lourenço Marquez—"

"Soon, it is hoped," the Major interposed with elaborate sarcasm, "the so brave and so wise Don Ferdinand's appointment will be made permanent."

Don Ferdinand bowed.

"But I am afraid of you," he insisted. "You have the reputation of being a bold, bad man. And I am alone with you here in my so poverty-stricken office; you could so easily kill me. You are armed—"

"Yes. I could easily kill you—and I would not need my revolver. You would—" the Major scrutinized the other closely, shrewdly gauging his weaknesses. "I would only have to poke you with my forefinger there—" he indicated a point on the fat man's waistline—"and you would explode. You are only a rotten skin of bad wind. But why talk of killing? I am a peaceful soul. I ask very little of you, but—" the drawl left the Major's voice, his mild, blue eyes hardened, seemed on the instant to take on the quality of steel, his jaw muscles tightened—"but that little I ask you must give me."

Don Ferdinand coughed dryly.

"I have already said that the *Senhor* Major is a little mad; now, also, I say that he is very foolish. Yes. He comes here to the fort, to my office here, unannounced. He disturbs my siesta and puts to flight several ladies who were, ah— busily engaged in work of state, and he tells a wild tale of having evidence that a high official of my government and his assistant—one Carlos, a Goanese—was engaged in the so wicked practice of slave running. The *Senhor* Major tells me that he put an end to the slave raiding. Says that he saw Carlos kill his commandante, and has taken Carlos a prisoner. Then, to cap this colossal impertinence, he brings Carlos here, under guard of his own detachment of native soldiers, and asks that I punish Carlos—"

"I demand that," the Major murmured.

"Demands, then," Don Ferdinand amended, "that I punish Carlos by a public whipping and then hang him; demands that I promote certain of the native soldiers whom he incited to mutiny against their commanding officer and demands, also, that I, my government, compensate each of the many natives he has brought here to witness to the crimes of Carlos and the late, greatly lamented high official. Is that it, *Senhor* Major?"

"That is enough to start with, gracious Excellency. When you've done that, there may be a few other reforms I'd like to have you inaugurate."

Don Ferdinand scowled.

"Yes, you are mad, *Senhor* Major. Very mad. And suppose that I refuse to accede to your childish demands?"

The Major sighed.

"Ah, then, in that case, I would be compelled to take matters into my own hands. Yes, much as it would grieve me, I would become public executioner—and perhaps give you a taste of the lash too. Ah! You squirm. Well, well."

"You forget my government—"

"When the truth is known, Don Ferdinand, I do not think that your government will treat me harshly."

"It is easier to predict the flavor of an egg before the shell is broken than to guess the judgment of a government," Don Ferdinand said sententiously. "But, forgetting that, is it permitted to know how you intend to depose me and take the authority into your own hands? The *senhor* forgets, it would seem, that the fort is manned by a garrison of white and black soldiers. They did not oppose his entrance because it was the time of the noonday siesta—and of what use bloodshed? But when occasion arises the *senhor* will find them good fighters."

THE MAJOR smiled and thrusting his hands into his trousers pockets looked approvingly at his well-polished riding boots.

"It is permitted," he said at last. "In the courtyard of this so-called fort—which is but little better than a mud wall—fifty native police stand guard. They have been drilled very carefully for many days. I drilled them and I do not boast when I say that they are superb. Each one knows his rifle—

and how to use it—and, this is most important, Don Ferdinand, each one looks to me for orders. They have had their orders. Your own men—they were very drunk—are under careful guard and the fort is mine. So, my dear Don Ferdinand, should you be in any way mulish, or exhibit any trace of a hybrid degeneracy... why, a few commands to *my* soldiers and then where would *your* fort and you be?

"Why, most gracious Excellency—" the Major waxed enthusiastic—"I could conquer a kingdom with those fifty black fighting devils. They are afraid of nothing, hard as nails, and their knowledge of bush fighting is simply marvelous. Why even Jim—you should know Jim, he's my Hottentot servant—admits that, and he could play tag with a herd of elephants and the big beasts would not know he was there. By Jove! A happy thought comes to me. I will keep those fifty men and we'll go up and down the land seeking whom we may destroy—if you know what I mean. I think, perhaps, I might even win a kingdom for myself—yes, that has been done. It is worth thinking about. I know—" He broke off with a show of embarrassment. "Pardon me, dear Excellency! You are not interested in my dreams, are you? Of course not."

"No," Don Ferdinand exploded harshly. "I am only interested in what you will do with me if I agree to your so extraordinary demands. If I punish Carlos, as you insist, and reward the mutinous soldiers and pay compensation to the natives—what then?"

"Why then, dear old sausage," the Major cried gaily, "I will leave this fair town of Lourenço Marquez, I will leave this territory in great haste and, more than that, I will leave you to stew in—er—your own grease. After all, I cannot watch over you all the time. I fancy your government will take care of you in due course, and also, I imagine, there are some white men in the town who will see that you do not carry things too far."

A shrill whistle sounded.

Apparently, neither man heard it, but Don Ferdinand's tense attitude relaxed, his big bulk seemed to flow all over his chair. As for the Major, he quite casually toyed with the revolver that was lying on the deal table between them.

The whistle sounded again.

"It is a pity," the Major commented softly, "that this room is windowless—though it's cooler without one, no doubt—I would like to know who is whistling and why."

"You shall know presently, no doubt," Don Ferdinand answered, then very softly hummed the tune of a ribald song at that time very popular on the East Coast.

The Major absently polished his monocle and, fixing it carefully in his eye, became the complete, silly-ass dude; he looked incapable of saying a sensible word; his expression was one of vacuous inanity. More than that; it seemed as if he had become on the instant, a soft, spineless creature who was more at home in a lady's boudoir than in a place where men congregate. The steel-gray light vanished from his eyes; they were now a mild, questioning, baby blue.

"I have waited far too long for your answer," he said slowly.

"*Sí!* Far too long," Don Ferdinand agreed.

"So? Then you are ready to give it now?"

"Yes—quite ready." Don Ferdinand rose grunting to his feet.

"And it is—?"

"No."

The Major arched his eyebrows incredulously.

"You said, 'No'?"

"*Sí.*"

The Major rose languidly, yawned and stretched his hands high above his head.

"Oh, but this is magnificent," he drawled. "You have courage, you have—er—guts—nothing personal intended there, sweet Excellency. You intend to take the field, alone, against my so brave and well-trained black devils."

"I have already defeated your blacks, *senhor.*"

FOR A moment, the Major was nonplussed, then, with a chuckle,

"You are quite amusing, Don Ferdinand. By taking thought, as it were, you destroy fifty men. Pouf! Like that. And they are no more. Magnificent. But—pardon me!— you are a little mad, and also, I think, a fool!"

"Perhaps, yes!" Don Ferdinand said complacently, folding his hands across his enormous stomach as if it needed the support. "But no doubt the *Senhor* Major has heard of the Chief Mzila who said that he did not fear the white men because two omnipotent generals always fought on his side—General Bush and General Fever? The *Senhor* has heard of that saying, hasn't he?"

"Yes," the Major replied wonderingly. "Mzila was a crafty devil."

Don Ferdinand smiled triumphantly.

"I am a crafty devil too, *senhor.* I have an even greater general fighting for me. His name's—" He paused and leered provocatively.

"Go on," the Major said testily. "I am no good at guessing riddles. His name is—?"

"General Gin, *senhor.* You would like to see? Of course."

He waddled to the door and flung it open.

"After you, *senhor,*" he grunted with a mocking bow.

The Major hesitated, then snatching up his revolver hurried out of the room, followed by Don Ferdinand.

Passing along a dark passage they came presently to the courtyard.

For a moment, blinded by the fierce glare of the sun, the Major did not fully comprehend the meaning of it all. Then, as his eyes adjusted themselves to the brilliant light, he saw that the courtyard was dotted with the forms of his fifty soldiers—broken glass and the smell of gin was everywhere. Occasionally, one of the forms stirred fitfully; a voice was raised in a drunken song—its accompaniment was a volume of stertorous snores.

Sad faced, grieving deeply, the Major stooped over one and shook him. The man did not waken, and the Major, rising, turned on Don Ferdinand with a fierce oath of disgust and rage.

He looked into the revolver which that man was holding.

"Your revolver, *senhor*," Don Ferdinand said, suavely holding out his hand for it.

The Major hesitated a moment and then handed it over.

"Thank you, *senhor*. You were wise, I do not like bloodshed. And your soldiers—you must not blame them. They were very thirsty, they had marched far and the sun was hot. They will be much hotter and thirstier before they drink again."

The Major turned once more to the courtyard.

"Fall in!" he shouted in a stentorian voice.

But there was no response, save that here and there an arm waved drunkenly.

"The drink was very strong," Don Ferdinand murmured. "They do not hear you. And even if they did they would be helpless. You see, fearing that they would do each other mischief—when the wine is in, wits are out, eh?—I ordered that all their rifles and ammunition should be taken from them. Did you not notice that? Ah, well! Now I will give an order: Carlos!" he shouted in a high piping voice. "I would speak to you."

From a room on the opposite side of the courtyard, Carlos, the Goanese, emerged. He was dressed in a gaudy uniform, but his face was dirty, his feet bare and his hair, lacking the grease with which it was usually plastered smooth, curled about his bullet shaped head. He carried an enormous *sjambok* in his hand. Behind him marched ten white soldiers in filthy, misfitting uniforms; behind them came a detachment of the native soldiers attached to the fort.

Between two of the latter, handcuffed and leg-ironed, was Jim the Hottentot. Jim swayed as he walked, but not entirely from drunkenness. His shirt was torn and the Major could see that his back had been criss-crossed with the cutting lash of a *sjambok*. The Major swore.

"A guard here for this white fool, Carlos," Don Ferdinand ordered. "Then throw these pigs in the cells. In the morning, when they are sober—or dead—we will deal further with them."

Two villainous looking whites—undersized and diseased—came running over, bayonets fixed in their rifles, and halted a few paces from the Major.

"We will return to my office," Don Ferdinand suggested. "I have listened much to you—now it is your turn to listen to me."

With a gesture of hopeless resignation—the gesture of a beaten man, the failure of the men he had trained so carefully hit him hard—the Major turned and stumbled slowly down the passageway to Don Ferdinand's office. At the door he paused and his body stiffened as a wild scream followed the *thwack* of a descending *sjambok*. Then he entered the room and, as Don Ferdinand closed it behind them—having ordered the two soldiers to stand guard outside—slumped into a chair and moodily traced meaningless patterns with the toe of his boot on the dusty floor.

"It was all so easy," Don Ferdinand gloated. "I knew you were coming, so my men pretended to be much drunker than they were, and they had orders not to resist. That was very humane of me. I averted much bloodshed. You locked them up. There you were wise. But you locked the prepared gin up with them—and it was so easy to pass a bottle out of the window to the native you had left on guard; more bottles followed—How could those black mutinous dogs refuse so much liquor?"

"Yes, it was very easy," the Major said wearily. "I had overlooked that—I had forgotten that you—and white men like you—have always made a practice of enlisting General Gin on your side. You couldn't win even a minor engagement like this one without his help."

Don Ferdinand pursed his lips and was about to retort angrily, then he shook his head sadly and cat-footed to the door which he flung open suddenly, surprising one of the guards down on his knees—evidently he had been listening at the keyhole.

The fat man's wrath was terrifying, and as he cursed and upbraided the eavesdropper, his face became purple and his gross body quivered like jelly.

"Get ten paces from the door, you scum," he screamed in conclusion, "and if again I have occasion to reprimand you, I will have you beaten by Carlos."

He slammed the door violently and, mopping his brow agitatedly, returned to his chair opposite the Major. For a time no sound was heard save his labored breathing.

The Major looked at the fat man sitting opposite curiously, a little contemptuously.

"You are too fat to give way to anger, Don Ferdinand," he said presently. "You should get thin or cultivate a calm, placid disposition."

Don Ferdinand scowled; he was incapable of speech, breathing was all that he could manage.

"You see," continued the Major, "you have put yourself completely at my mercy. It would be very easy to kill you now—and everyone would say that you died of apoplexy. Your hands tremble so that you could not possibly use your revolver and you have no breath to call for help. I could—"

He rose and advanced menacingly toward the fat man.

"Don't be a fool," Don Ferdinand managed to gasp. "It would do you no good to kill me—you'd still have the others to face, and Carlos, I think, would be glad of the opportunity to do with you as he liked. He's a vindictive devil; sometimes I am afraid of him—he has so much power—too much power for a half-caste. Besides, I am not so helpless as you would imagine. See!" With an effort, he aimed his revolver at the Major who halted and endeavored to look into Don Ferdinand's eyes.

"I'm not sure," he mused. "I think I could get you—you can't hold the revolver still. But, there's a chance I couldn't, and, as you say, there'd still be the other to consider."

He returned to his chair and Don Ferdinand sighed with relief.

"Well!" the Major continued. "What is the offer you have on your mind?"

Don Ferdinand's eyes opened to their widest.

"How did you know—" he began.

"Oh," the Major waved his hand airily, "It's no witch-craft. You were afraid of eavesdroppers. What could the Acting Governor of Lourenço Marquez have to say to a prisoner that he does not want two of his soldiers to hear. Undoubtedly, the most gracious Excellency has a greasy itching palm, which—in some way totally inexplicable at this moment—he expects to be greased."

Don Ferdinand smiled. "The *Senhor* Major imagines vain things."

The Major shrugged his shoulders.

"Then let us forget that and return—er—as it were—to our sheep. You seem to have me at a disadvantage, Don Ferdinand. What do you intend to do with me?"

The other laughed softly.

"You are so direct, so impetuous. What am I going to do with you, you would ask? Let me see." He placed his pudgy finger tips together and frowned thoughtfully. "There are so many things," he continued smoothly. "You understand, of course, that here my power is absolute, I can have you hung, drawn and quartered—but that," he made a gesture of disdain, "is so barbaric. That does not please you? No? I am not enamored of it myself. Well then, life imprison-ment in one of our so comfortable cells—you have heard of them, yes? Of course, they are a little damp, and not exactly health resorts. But what would you? You are guilty of great crimes. Also, of course, in regard to the cells, once a man enters, he is as one dead—he ceases to be heard of. And that would go hard with a man like you, so prone to bask in the spotlight. And also, men do not live very long in our cells. That is their greatest drawback. You have heard that, no doubt. Fever, and pestilent reptiles and—yes, I've known of prisoners whose stomachs were too weak to eat the food we gave them and they starved to death. Most ungrateful. Of course, the food was a little coarse. But prisoners can't be choosers, can they? Yes, I think you would do our cells a great honor, *Senhor* Major. I think that that one a countryman of yours so lovingly named 'Black Hell,' is empty."

In spite of his belief that Don Ferdinand was only talking for effect and had no intention of carrying out his soft-voiced threats, the Major could not restrain an involuntary shudder. He knew that the "Black Hell" was well named. Men imprisoned in it went mad—if they lived.

Don Ferdinand, noticing the shudder, chuckled maliciously.

"I only talk of these unpleasant things," he said, "to show you to what I could sentence you and, knowing that, you will better appreciate my leniency. I am, you see, disposed to be merciful. I am going to release you."

The Major looked at him and laughed.

"And the conditions?"

"That you leave Lourenço Marquez within forty-eight hours and do not in that time attempt to incite another mutiny or proceed against me in any way. Also—" his eyes gleamed avariciously—"you must give me the twenty diamonds you have on your person."

The Major started.

"You know a great deal, Don Ferdinand. I suspected when you showed that you were afraid of being overheard that you had orders from someone higher up. Now I am going to make conditions."

"You are not in a position to make conditions, *senhor*. If you don't like mine—I keep you here and the diamonds too."

"Oh, no you can't," the Major exclaimed confidently. "If you could, you'd do it. But you daren't—dare you?" He looked sharply at the fat man and smiled when he saw that his conjecture had hit the mark. "Very well, then. I will give you ten diamonds—that's frightfully generous of me—and those I give you only on certain conditions."

Don Ferdinand started to bluster, then, silenced by the scornful contempt in the Major's eyes, he said:

"Name your conditions, *Senhor* Major."

"First, give me my revolver."

Don Ferdinand tossed it on the table and the Major's hand closed swiftly on it.

"I feel much better now," he said happily. "Less naked, if you know what I mean. And now for the conditions."

"You will not ask me to punish Carlos," Don Ferdinand interposed anxiously. "I am powerless to do that."

"No," the Major replied slowly. "I'll attend to that man later—in my own way. First, then, Jim the Hottentot shall be released at once. Order him to be brought here that he may leave with me."

Don Ferdinand nodded and waddling to the door opened it and wheezed an order to one of the guards.

"What else, *Senhor* Major?" he asked, returning to his chair.

"The native soldiers must not be punished."

"For discipline's sake they must be sent to a difficult district," Don Ferdinand expostulated. "Here they are a danger."

The Major nodded.

"YOU ARE no fool, Don Ferdinand. If you would only exercise a little bit and get the fat from your body and your soul, I believe you would be almost a man. Very well, I'll admit that. They deserve slight punishment. They—"

he smiled grimly—"got drunk. But no *sjambokings*—you understand?"

"*Sí, senhor.* I give you my word."

"Also, the native carriers shall be well paid for their trade goods, fed and returned to their *kraals*. That is all."

"It shall be done, *Senhor* Major," Don Ferdinand hastily assured him. "On my word of honor."

"I accept your word—but I shall watch closely to see that you keep it. If you fail—" he smiled significantly—"I know a way which will take many pounds of fat off your tub of a body—and the operation will not be a painless one."

Then, taking a small chamois leather bag from his hip pocket, he emptied into the palm of his hand twenty fair-sized uncut diamonds. Selecting the ten smallest, he dropped them one by one on the table and pushed them over toward Don Ferdinand.

"Graft makes up for the small pay you officials receive, doesn't it, Don Ferdinand?" he said as the fat man lovingly fingered the diamonds.

"A man must live, *Senhor* Major. He must have some compensations for being an exile and living in this hell hole."

"Ah, yes, of course. You don't feel like telling me, I suppose, who ordered my release? No? I thought not. Whoever it is—I am their servant forever, in a manner of speaking."

There was a scuffling sound in the passage way beyond the door, the sound of a man walking slowly, dragging himself along as if in great pain.

"That must be Jim," the Major said tersely, and a hard light came into his eyes. "I hope for Carlos's sake he has not been beaten very badly."

He jumped to his feet and running to the door opened it.

A loud exclamation of pity burst from his lips, followed by a string of curses uttered in a hard, metallic voice.

He went out into the passage way and a moment later returned, carrying the limp form of Jim, the Hottentot, in his arms.

He stood silently in the doorway for a moment, endeavoring to master his emotions, his face white with rage, his eyes hard, glittering.

"If you are a friend of Carlos," he said finally in a dry, harsh voice, "you will hang him."

Then he turned and strode swiftly from the place.

Coming to the saloon of Manuel, the Major engaged a room and tenderly cared for Jim's wounds, dressing them with clean linen and salve. At last Jim opened his eyes and smiled faintly.

"How did I come here, baas?" he muttered faintly, and tried to rise.

Briefly, the Major told him all that had happened.

"They have gone from my hand, Jim," he concluded sadly. "Great things were in their grasp but they bartered them for the sick bellies which come in bottles."

"I have known other men to do that, baas."

"True, Jim. But to place a muddy stone against a muddy stone does not make either stone clean. Now sleep."

He left the room and quietly closed the door behind him; but not before he heard Jim murmur, as he wearily closed his eyes:

"Mud can be washed from a stone, baas."

The Major found Manuel lounging against the wall in front of the saloon and, after giving directions for the care of the horse and mule, said, "You will see that everything is kept quiet."

"*Sí, senhor.*"

The Major looked at him amusedly.

"You'd like to say 'Go to the devil' wouldn't you? But never mind. Where is the little fat Englishman and the tall American who were drinking here this morning?"

"By the blood of Christ," Manuel swore angrily, "I wish they were here so that I could lay hands on them. They guzzled much of my wine, and now they have gone—leaving no money to pay for their drinking."

As the Major turned away, a lounger shouted, "You will find them at the wharves—they are always there."

The Major waved his hand in acknowledgement and strolled leisurely down the street.

Coming presently to the sea front he stood for a moment in silent admiration of one of the best natural harbors in the world; and then frowned as evidences came to his attention of the gross mismanagement which made Lourenço Marquez a byword up and down the Seven Seas.

THE WHARVES were heaped high with cargoes; a confused jumble of goods; cases of crockery and other fragile goods of a perishable, flimsy nature were hopelessly mixed with barrels of cement and heavy mining machinery. Most of the stuff had been there for a long time; most of it, due to rough handling and exposure to the elements, absolutely ruined. A man who imported through Lourenço Marquez in those days was a lucky man if he ever received his goods—still luckier if they arrived intact.

Seeing the chubby little Englishman, sitting on a broken crate, eating the contents of one of the cans it contained, the Major strolled up to him.

"Why, blimme, if it ain't the Major," the little man exclaimed, springing to his feet. "My name's 'Awkins, Major. 'Arry 'Awkins, though mostly I'm called Cockney. It's a fair knockout the names they'll give a cove hout 'ere, ain't it?"

"It is, Cockney," the Major admitted with a smile and took out his monocle. There was no need to pose now and he was content to let this man see him as he really was; not the silly-ass, monocled dude known to so many, or the cold, hard

The fat man fingered the diamonds. "A man must have some compensation," he said.

killer he had seemed to Don Ferdinand and Manuel— but just a splendidly developed, intensely likeable man. "Where's your American friend?"

" 'E's over there." Cockney pointed to the far end of the wharf where the tall, lanky American was wandering disconsolately from one heap to another. " 'E's lookin' fer 'is consignment," Cockney chuckled, "but 'e'll never find it. Yer see," he continued confidingly, "Yank's a big business man an' 'e imported four 'undred cases of taller candles— an' 'e can't find 'em. But I knows where they are. Yer see that 'eap over there—yas, that one that's covered wiv coal dust. Well, that's Yank's candles. Yer see, when the cases was landed, they left 'em houtside 'ere in the sun and the taller melted and ran hout o' the cases. And, when, later on, the Dagoes 'ad occasion ter move the cases, why the bottoms fell hout hand honly the wicks of the bleedin' candles was left. So they chucks the cases inter the bloomin' hocean and when Yank asks about 'is candles they shrug their shoulders and says they ain't seen them, an'—'Per'aps they ain't been shipped, yes, *Senhor,*' they says. But, blimme! I wouldn't fer the world let Yank know the truth of hit. He'd commit 'oly bloody murder, 'e would. Besides, 'e 'angs on 'ere, 'oping ter find 'em—an' I'd be bloody lonely wivout 'im."

The Major laughed.

"Let's go and have a talk with him, Cockney. There's something I'd like to say to you both."

Cockney jumped to his feet and a moment later the three men, having sized each other up as men can whose natures drive them into far corners of the earth, were talking and arguing furiously like old friends.

"I must get back to Jim," the Major said at length. The shadows had lengthened considerably. "But look here. First I'd like to ask a favor of you two. I'm after dangerous game—our Goanese friend, Carlos, to be specific—and something might happen to me. So, if I don't show up at the saloon in the morning I want you to take care of Jim for me. See that the old blighter gets down south in safety—you'll have to watch Manuel; he'd turn him out if he dared. Here—" he gave the little chamois leather bag to Yank—"there are ten diamonds in that; you ought to get a good price for them. Enough to buy Jim a few head of cattle and set him up like a small chief, and there'd still be enough to make a grub-stake for you two."

"Never mind that," Yank growled. "What I'm interested in is this—How about taking us into your game. I'm sick of hanging about this *dorp.* Only do it because Cockney here seems to like it. We're both good veldt-men—though you'd never think it to look at this blamed runt."

"Sure! Take hus along, Major," Cockney echoed. "I can fight, but, I'm tellin' yer, I can run a bloody sight better."

The Major laughed.

"You're two damned good sorts. As soon as I know how things are shaping—I'll get in touch with you."

He saluted them and walked swiftly away.

"Mi gord! We're rich," Cockney cried exultantly, and clumsily executed a few steps of a Lancashire clog. "Oh, blimme!" he said contritely, noting the look of disgust and contempt which passed over Yank's face. "I was honly jokin', Yank. I knows them diamonds ain't hour'n. But at least we can pay hour expenses, can't we?"

"Sure, Cockney. I guess the Major 'ud allow that—seeing as we both are as broke as hell."

On his way back to the saloon of Manuel, the Major was hailed from the doorway of one of the houses which lined the street by a woman's low, soft voice.

He halted and looked toward the house, shading his eyes with his hand.

"Won't you come in, Major! We have so many things to talk over."

A light of recognition passed over the Major's face to be instantly replaced by the expression of bland innocence which he used as a mask to hide his quick wit. He doffed his helmet and bowed courtier like.

"Why," he drawled, "it's the charming Miss Lola de Sousa!"

"You will come in please, Major?" Her English was made charming by a slight accent. "You will come in," she repeated, and it was not an invitation, but a demand.

"Charmed!" he said and followed her into the house.

She motioned him to a chair, seated herself, and—

"Now," she continued, holding out her hand, "my diamonds please, Major."

He looked at her in dismay, greatly embarrassed.

"But I haven't your diamonds, dear Miss Lola."

"It is foolish to lie, Major. And you are no fool."

"A pretty compliment, dear old thing. But still I am at sea. You ask for diamonds—"

"Is it necessary," she interrupted coldly, "to remind you of the diamonds I gave you for safe keeping at Kimberly several months ago?"

Her English was charming. "You will come in," she repeated.

THE MAJOR looked confused and toyed with his monocle.

"Oh, those," he stammered at length. "Those!"

"Yes—those," she echoed sarcastically. "Where are they?"

"Why, old thing, I'm frightfully sorry, really. You'll think I'm no end of a rotter, I know. But—er—the truth is, I just haven't them any longer. You see—" he stopped and looked at her shamefacedly.

"Go on," she demanded harshly. "Then, where are they?"

"You see, old fat Ferdinand made me a prisoner and threatened me with most awful tortures. And so—what would you?—I bribed him to set me free. I—" he watched her narrowly—"I gave him the diamonds—and he opened the gates wide and set me free."

She frowned.

"You gave him all the diamonds—twenty of them?"

The Major leaned back in his chair, apparently deeply concerned. Inwardly he commented:

"She is the one who ordered Ferdinand to set me free. Well, I'm most awfully obliged to her, but why, I wonder, did she do it? And she thinks I gave him twenty diamonds—and of course he told her I only gave him ten. I wonder if I answered her quite honestly? Oh, I think so. And I think she'll make things very unpleasant for his fat Excellency. Oh, very."

Aloud, he said,

"Oh, please, Miss Lola, don't cry. If there's anything I can do—"

She looked up swiftly and overwhelmed him with a fiery torrent of passionate abuse and reproach; but her eyes were dry—there were no tear stains on her cheeks.

"You gave away my diamonds, all I had in the world," she continued, "and then you tell me not to cry. And—and I trusted you. Everyone told me you were a man of honor—but you are only a thief. You buy your liberty with my diamonds."

He rose quickly.

"Where are you going?"

"Up to the fort to get the diamonds back. Perhaps if I tell Don Ferdinand that I have come to surrender myself he will return the diamonds."

She caught hold of his arm and held him.

"But no. They will kill you if you go there. You must not."

He looked at her genuinely bewildered.

"But what then? You cry for your diamonds; you call me many hard names—and not quite justified, if I may say so. After all, you stole the diamonds first, you know. But no matter—and now you will not let me get them back for you. What then can I do?"

She rubbed her cheek against his sleeve; it was cleverly done, almost as if by accident.

"You admit then, *senhor*," she said softly, "that you are greatly indebted to me?"

The Major bowed.

"I am greatly indebted to you. But for you I would now be languishing in the—er—pardon—Black Hell! Your diamonds purchased my freedom," he added in response to her sharp look of inquiry.

"I am afraid you know too much," she murmured. "But you admit your indebtedness and you have the reputation of being a man of honor. Therefore, you pay your debts, is it not so?"

"I always try to—all kinds—dear Miss Lola," he murmured.

"You can discharge this one very easily," she said softly and drew nearer to him.

"How?" he asked and edged nearer the door. The overpowering scent of jasmine almost sickened him.

She laughed harshly.

"Most men would not try to run away from me. But of that, no matter, save that I regret that you are—what do you say?—boorish. I had hoped for a pleasant journey with you. If you are going to be stiff, however—" she sighed.

"Journey?" The Major was mystified. "Did you say journey?"

She smiled at him.

"Yes. Tonight I start on a long trek into Swaziland—"

"It is not safe," he exclaimed.

"That is why you are coming with me."

The Major gasped.

"Alone, Miss Lola? Please consider. It's not done, you know!"

"We won't be alone, Major—unfortunately. The two de Silvas will be with us."

"Tweedledum and Tweedledee, eh?" the Major laughed in great relief.

"And there will be natives, of course," Lola added.

The Major nodded.

"I see. And this is, of course, purely a pleasure trip?"

"A little business and—" her eyes glowed—"maybe a lot of pleasure. That depends on how you behave."

"Oh, I'll be good," the Major assured her hastily.

"That would be sad," she sighed. "Then you will come?"

It was three months later, and night. The Major walked with Lola among the jumble of rocks which strewed the veldt at the base of a tall, precipitous *kopje*.

The moon was at the full and there was an atmosphere of mystery about the place. Vague, distorted shadows dotted the landscape; strange scents stung the nostrils and blood-quickening sounds impinged upon the ear-drums.

As if by some mutual agreement the two stopped and looked back.

"Can you see them?" the Major asked quietly.

"Yes," she said breathlessly. "I see them. They look like ants, don't they?"

"That's a good name for them—poor devils," the Major commented bitterly. "If everything goes as you plan they'll wish they'd never heard of a mine."

The girl looked at him, her lovely face made hideous for the moment by a contemptuous sneer.

"You are too soft, *Senhor* Major," she snapped, "sometimes I think you are more woman than man, and then—" her voice softened—"I remember how you thrashed that so big beast of a Boer; I remember the lion you shot when poor Lola missed and fell when she tried to run away. But those—" she indicated the distant black line—"they went free men."

"Their chiefs sent them, they were not free; they dared not disobey."

"Does it matter?" she said casually. "If they had stayed here they would doubtless be killed in battle—also at their chief's orders."

As she spoke, the black line shortened, vanished from sight as it was swallowed up by one of the deep depressions which corrugated the veldt.

"WON'T YOU go, Miss Lola?" he pleaded. "It is not safe for you here. There is still time. Mounted, you could catch up with them in one hour or so and—"

She shook her head.

"No. I'll stay to see the thing through. I planned it and I don't trust Pedro or Ricardo. They have been drinking too much. Also—" she hesitated.

"Also, you don't trust me, you would say?"

"Have it that way if you please—but I stay."

He caught her roughly by the shoulders.

"Look here," he said harshly, "I say that you must go."

She laughed in his face and murmured.

"You are so strong!"

He released his hold with a curse and walked abruptly away, turned and came back toward her.

"Now, really, Miss Lola," he drawled. Her lips closed firm, her body stiffened, her face was an expressionless mask and she closed her eyes so that he could not read the disappointment in them. "You are very clever, Miss Lola," he continued. "Most deucedly clever. I take off my hat to you. You can give any labor recruiting agent lessons at his own game. You come to Swaziland—an absolutely unexploited region, inhabited by the most bloodthirsty savages—and bag hundreds of natives for mine labor. And you've done it, as far as I can see, by the most uncanny methods—a few trade goods, much talk, and—er—gallons of jasmine scent. And paugh! How I hate the beastly stuff."

He appeared not to notice the handkerchief she crumpled up in her hands and let fall to the ground, but continued,

"Of course it does not matter about those natives you have sent off to the mines. They will be stopped at the border, you know—or perhaps you had overlooked that. This is a closed district, you know, and recruiting is forbidden."

"I knew that—but a little judicious bribing—" She did not finish the sentence but laughed mockingly.

He bowed and she did not see his smile.

"I have said you were clever. But this other affair—Ah, there, I'm afraid you have overreached yourself. You are playing with fire, dear Miss, and I'm afraid you'll get your pretty fingers burnt. And that would be a pity. That is why I once again suggest that you go."

"I shall stay, Major, unless—unless you go with me."

He considered this for a moment; then shook his head.

"No! Couldn't do that; couldn't leave old Tweedledee and Tweedledum in the lurch. Of course, they're most frightful villains—but they have their points. I mean to say that they are, at least, white and, by some strange ordering of—er—ethics, if you know what I mean, white men have to stick together. Rather asinine, but there it is—as fixed as the laws of the Medes and Persians."

A raucous scream disturbed the night's stillness. The Major jumped in alarm.

"My goodness! What was that?"

"Only a Go-a-way bird, Major. You're getting nervous."

"Yes, I confess it. I'm deucedly nervous. It's this affair of your planning, Miss Lola. It was clever of you to bring along a lot of defective rifles, guaranteed to burst at the third shot if not the first—and if they kill the users, that doesn't matter, does it?—and several cases of blank cartridges—the niggers'll never know the difference, will they? They can't shoot straight, anyway, and they'll be quite satisfied as long as they can make a noise. And it was quite clever of you to locate two hot tempered chiefs who are just aching to get at each other's throats. But, of course, your masterpiece was to play one off against the other—highest bidder gets the lethal weapons. Very, very clever, Miss Lola—but dangerous."

The girl laughed.

"There is nothing to fear, Major. If we were selling the stuff to only one bidder then we'd have to watch him very carefully. But two! They will watch each other while we run away with the loot."

"Have you never heard of the upper and nether millstones, dear lady?"

She looked blankly at him.

"Ah, I see you haven't. Then doesn't this make you think? Once I sold my wagon to a chief, but before I turned it over to him I unloaded my provisions. And, do you know, the greedy old blighter insisted that they were included in the sale. He said that if he sold a man a bullock he didn't first cut it open and take out its—er—inwards. Doesn't that mean anything to you?" He looked at her anxiously and sighed when she shook her head. "Ah, well. The moral's rather hard to point. But remember, dear Miss, the brain of the simple black is most frightfully complex."

"I can handle them," she said confidently.

SHE RAN gracefully away, skirting the base of the *kopje*, jumping the boulders which were in her path.

Just before she rounded the *kopje*, she paused and waved to him.

He made a pretence of giving chase to her, sprinted a few yards but stopped as soon as she ran on again and passed out of sight.

"Phew!" exclaimed the Major, as he sat down on a near-by boulder, vigorously fanned himself with his helmet—and that was strange, for the night was very cold. "She is a devil," he continued, "but a damned good pal in many ways, at that. At least she is when she forgets she's a woman…. But jasmine! Hell!"

At that moment, a vagrant breeze blew a fluttering white something to his feet. He stooped and picked it up.

"It's her handkerchief—and how the thing stinks!"

He shook from it the red dust of the veldt and put it in his pocket. Then he whistled a low, mournful tune, paused and listened intently.

"Strange," he muttered. "But, of course, it couldn't have been Jim."

"Go-a-way!" the noisy call of a gray lourie sounded from a deep donga nearby.

He rose slowly to his feet, stretched himself, and saun-tered over to the donga. Seating himself at the edge of it,

*"You are playing with fire, dear Miss," he said, "and I'm afraid
you'll get your pretty fingers burned. And that would be a pity."*

he picked up a handful of stones. He wrapped one of them in the pocket handkerchief and tossed it at a black boulder directly beneath him.

"That is folly, baas," growled Jim, the Hottentot, standing up and rubbing the small of his back. In his other hand he held the handkerchief. "And since when has the baas turned to womanish things?" He shook the handkerchief.

"I'm sorry, Jim," the Major said penitently. "I thought you were a Go-a-way bird."

It was typical that the Major did not show any surprise at meeting Jim again although he had every reason to believe that the Hottentot was hundreds of miles away. The Major had long ceased to be surprised at anything Jim did.

"I was a bird, baas," Jim answered. "But are you alone? Is it safe to talk?"

"I am talking, Jim," the Major replied. "But why come secretly? There is no evil here. No one would bid you keep away. I am a free man, I go where I please, I—"

"Undoubtedly the Major is all powerful," Jim said sarcastically. "Perhaps he knows too that an *impi* of the Rainmaker is on its way to wipe out this *kraal* and the two black bulls who seek greater honors and, also, the whites who sell them guns."

The Major started.

"No. I did not know that, Jim."

THE MAJOR sat down again—making it appear as if his rising had been only in order to find a more comfortable seat.

Jim laughed.

"The baas is clever—but I lied. There is no fear of any warrior seeing."

"Is the rest a lie, Jim?"

"No, baas, but—"

"Then I must get back to the *kraal*," the Major said hurriedly. "There is no time to lose. We must trek at once. I must warn the white woman and the two men who are with her. Later, I will hear the tale that is to be told."

"There is no hurry, baas," Jim said calmly. "The *impi* waits in the shadow of Two Tree Top—three hours' trek away. They will not attack until just before dawn. I have spoken," he concluded unctuously. Jim liked nothing better than to play a part before his baas, to appear all-wise, all-powerful. Sometimes he succeeded, sometimes—

The "boulder" moved and showed itself to be a man. "That is folly, baas," growled Jim the Hottentot, standing up.

"How do you know this, Jim?" the Major queried sharply.

"I captured the Rainmaker's scouts, baas."

"How many, Jim?"

"Twice the count of my two hands, baas. And after I had questioned them—a little harshly, it may be—they told me many things."

"And you captured them alone?" the Major asked incredulously.

"I did not say so, baas," Jim said, then added with a chuckle, "the baas is blind tonight. True, the shadows are dark here in the donga, but the baas has been known to see in even greater darkness."

Acting on the hint, the Major looked into the donga. At first he saw nothing but boulders—black boulders; then, as the boulders moved, he saw men. Twenty-five he counted—and there were other boulders he was not sure of.

"I said that boulders could be washed clean, baas!" Jim said gleefully.

The Major did not answer. He was watching a fat, rotund "boulder" which was moving closer to Jim; it seemed vaguely familiar. Suddenly it rose up and—

" 'Ellow, Major!" Cockney said in a hoarse whisper. "This is a fair knockout, ain't it? Lumme—Wot would my mother say hif she could see me now—naked as a bloomin' baby, halmost, an' painted black? That was Yank's idea. 'E said hour white skins 'ud show up too plain. Blast 'im! The paint itches. An' I ain't white anyway. I ain't washed for a week o' Sundays."

"And Yank's here too," murmured the Major, "This is too much. How did you get here? Tell me quickly. I must get back to the *kraal* before they send someone to look for me. Jim is so bloomin' cocky that I can't get a word out of him."

"An' good reason 'e 'as to be cocky, Major. 'E's a fool, that's wot 'e is. Listen: I'll tork quick, though there ain't no bleedin' 'urry as far as I can see, an' it's a yarn wot ought ter 'ave a book writ abart hit. Well, when yer didn't show hup that night, we went ter take care of Jim. Us sold the diamonds—Yank'll give yer an haccounting—an' went on a bleedin' spree, one at a time, so there was allus one of hus more or less sober ter sit wiv Jim. Two days later, Jim, 'ere, began to sit hup an' ask questions—lucky we can both

tork the bloomin' lingo—an' nothin''ud satisfy 'im as soon
as he 'eard you was gone but wot 'e must get hup an' try to
look fer you."

The Major fidgeted impatiently, but said nothing.

" 'Old yer 'orses," Cockney continued cheerfully. "I'm
a-comin' to the interestin' part. When Jim did get abart—
that was a week later—we makes inquiries for Carlos and
learns the yeller-skinned cuss left town the mornin' hafter
you torked wiv hus down at the wharf. A covey told hus
that he'd gone hup country wiv the niggers you'd licked
inter shape—them as yer tried to capture the fort wiv. This
covey said as the niggers marched like licked curs, 'e said
they walked as hif the bloomin' skin 'ad been flayed hoff
'em. Yer got to 'and it ter Carlos. 'E 'ad guts to go hof wiv
them niggers when 'e must 'ave known every mother's son
hof them 'ud be honly too glad ter stick a bayonet hinto
'im. Well! Jim 'ere would 'ave hit that you was on the trail of
Carlos so we houtfitted and went hon the trail, too. Carlos
'ad a big start and we travels a long way north afore we
catches hup wiv 'im. An' then we finds you ain't been seen.
An' wot does yer think Jim does then? 'E makes a speech to
them bloomin' nigger soldiers—tells 'em something abart
muddy boulders an' 'ow they ought ter wash themselves; I
couldn't see wot 'e was drivin' at, but Yank did. Clever lad,
that there Yank. Well, the hupshot hof hit all was—the
niggers deserted an' fer once in his life, Carlos looked like
a white man—I means 'is skin looked white; elseways 'e
showed dirty yeller. Of course, 'e couldn't say a word—Yank
an' me 'ad 'im covered. Then we torks gently to Carlos and
find hout you was in Swaziland with the Lola woman. That
made Jim as mad as 'ell because we'd wasted so much time
trekkin' the wrong way. 'E wanted ter kill Carlos hout hof
'and—so did the hother niggers. But Yank an' me wouldn't

stand fer that. Yer see, Carlos is 'arf white, and, besides, 'e was tied to a tree. Then Jim forms the soldiers in a line an' puts 'imself at the 'ead. 'E 'ad Carlos's *sjambok* in 'is 'and, a bleedin' big 'un hit was. Then 'e marches past the tree and lashes Carlos as 'e passes. 'E 'ands the *sjambok* to the next hin line an' the same thing 'appens—an' so it went hall down the line. Fifty-one lashes they gives the poor devil, an' 'e 'owled bloody murder. It make Yank fair sick, but 'e said as 'ow Carlos deserved it."

"HE DESERVED that and more," the Major assented, thinking of the brutal murders and torturing of natives—old men, women, and children—the half-caste had been guilty of.

Cockney nodded.

"Thought you'd say that. We cuts Carlos loose—'e ain't dead by a long shot—an' treks fer Swaziland. An' bleedin' 'ard goin' hit was. Four weeks we've been. Yer see us 'ad ter steer clear hof settlements and 'ad to loot our food on the way. But that Jim there, blast 'im, cussed an' halmost cried hevery time we stopped fer skoff or sleep. An' it seems as hif we came 'ere honly just in time. There'll be bloody blood a-flowin' 'ere when that *impi* gets in hits dirty work. Now then, ain't that a 'oly terror of a yarn?"

"It's more than that, Cockney," the Major said softly. "I can't tell you what it is just now. But, when we're out of this mess—" He stopped short, overcome by the magnificence of Jim's devotion, the loyalty of the two white men and the faith the fifty black soldiers had shown in him by deserting and making their wild rush across dangerous country ready to render him any assistance he needed.

"Where's Yank?" he asked suddenly.

" 'E's down the donga a ways wiv the rear guard. Lumme, Major, 'e's a fightin' fool."

A beating of drums, fierce yells and wild chanting suddenly sounded from behind the *kopje*.

"What's that?" Cockney asked, startled.

The Major rose quickly to his feet.

"They're drinking and dancing at the *kraal*—the bidding's begun again—I'll tell you about that later. I must get back. I'm goin' to try to get Miss Lola and the two men away without any trouble—but maybe I'll not be able to do it an' I'll need help. Get your men up close to the *kraal*, Cockney. Surround it! Don't let a man show himself. And do it quickly. Tell Jim to give the signal when you're in place. If I need help I'll fire my revolver."

"Hall right, Major," Cockney said resignedly. "Lumme! I 'ates ter fink hof comin' hall this way an' no scrap. But you're the bloomin' doctor."

"As soon as you get the signal, fire your rifles in the air and shout like hell."

"An' make 'em fink we're a thousand strong, eh, Major? Is that hit?"

A nod of understanding to Cockney, a few whispered words to Jim in the vernacular—words which made Jim puff out his chest; words which, he felt, amply repaid him for all the hardships of the long trek—and the Major hastened away.

And as he went it seemed as if the donga spoke, as if it was the mouth of Africa, and out of it came a mumbled salutation, a greeting to a white man who could do no wrong:

"Bayete!"

Once well away from the donga the Major quickened his speed and was presently skirting the base of the *kopje*.

Bounding a queer shaped spur he came into full view of the *kraal* which Lola had made her headquarters during her labor recruiting operations.

IT WAS a large *kraal* of some fifty beehive huts enclosed by a frail reed fence, before which stood the three wagons comprising Lola's outfit. Tethered to the *disselboom* of each wagon were sixteen mules.

None of Lola's native drivers were to be seen.

"They're probably in the *kraal*, drinking with the rest," the Major muttered.

He stopped long enough to get several bottles of whisky from one of the wagons and then went on up to the *kraal*.

He had almost reached the entrance in the fence before he was challenged; the challenge was immediately followed by a chuckle.

"At least, white man," a voice cried. "You can give witness that we do not sleep."

"No," the Major replied. "Your eyes are open, you are warriors. But may I pass?"

"Truly! We know you for a friend and a man—even though you are the friend of those others. But, as N'Gazi here says, not all the bulls of one herd are black. Pass in."

As the Major advanced two tall warriors showed themselves.

"How many of you keep watch?" the Major asked casually.

"Six, white man—but we were seven."

"*Au-a!* And you take no part in the drinking and feasting?"

The warriors laughed.

"In the early watches, one of us—the seventh—left his post to drain a pot of beer and the *N'Msan* saw him. That man is no more. So we others—we do not leave our posts."

"*Tchat!* And there is no one to bring beer to you? That is a pity for the night is cold. But see! I have here white man's drink—it will keep you warm."

"*Au-a!*" Eager hands took the bottles from him. "We will take care of it, eh, warrior?"

"Truly," said the other.

"And you will see to it that the other watches get their share?"

"Our word is given. We are brothers tonight. We share and share alike."

The Major passed on through the gate.

Inside the *kraal* a wild orgy was under way. But, as the Major pushed his way through the drunken, dancing warriors, he noticed that they were separated into two distinct groups—the men of the *kraal* forming one group, and the warriors who had accompanied the rival headman to bid for Lola's guns forming the other. The Major noted, too, that no women were to be seen. They gave him food for thought.

He paused for a moment before a large hut—then entered.

The smoke of a small wood fire made his eyes smart, the air was suffocating; a pungent odor, a mingling of whisky, tobacco, body sweat, and jasmine almost sickened him.

A tallow candle stuck on the top of a tin biscuit box supplemented the flickering light of the fire.

The girl, Lola, was seated on a camp stool opposite the doorway; the de Silvas sat on the floor, their backs against the wall—they were very drunk.

At the Major's left sat a thin, emaciated native; it was the local chief, Tekuba, and behind him stood his bodyguard of six stalwarts.

Opposite Tekuba sat a big powerful man, his face pitted with small-pox scars. And M'singa had his guards too.

All looked toward the Major as he entered and he fancied he saw a look of relief on Lola's face as she motioned to him to sit beside her.

He started to obey but Tekuba growled an order which was echoed by M'singa, and the Major remained where he was.

He was too wise to attempt to pass the barrier of spears the guards leveled at him.

The Major looked across at Lola.

"You must trek at once," he said in English. "A big regiment is on its way here to wipe out these Johnnies. Pedro! Ricardo! There is danger, do you hear?"

They looked at him and grinned fatuously—they were incapable of movement. Lola made a gesture of dismay.

"I've tried to bring this thing to an end—but I can't and—and they won't let me go. I'm afraid I've burnt my fingers, Major."

There was a quaver in her voice but her eyes met his steadily enough.

"It will be all right," he assured her. "I—"

But M'singa's booming voice interrupted him.

"Speak so that we understand, white man."

"It is an order, Earthshaker," the Major replied. "I was saying that Rainmaker has sent an *impi* to wipe us out. Therefore it is best to—"

A shout of laughter drowned the rest of his speech and he realized that the two chiefs were drunk; this news, which at any other time would have made them look to their defenses and prepare for flight, now only aroused their mirth.

"You lie, white man—or, if you do not lie, you shall help us wipe out this *impi* you speak of."

"At least let the woman depart—she has no part in the quarrel of warriors."

"You shall all go when the bidding is over," Tekuba said testily.

"That is true—I had forgotten that," M'singa agreed.

"HASTEN THEN," Lola cried. "You bid like timid maidens. 'Two hundred oxen,' says M'singa after many hours. 'Two hundred and one', says Tekuba. *Au'a.* See the candle; it has only a little way to burn. To the one who makes the highest bid while the flame is yet burning I will sell the guns."

"It is a good plan," M'singa cried. "The woman has wit."

"Truly!" Tekuba leered at her and she cowered back against the wall. "With such a woman to counsel him a man could go far."

"It is true," M'singa agreed. "But she is white—and what would my black heifers say if I took her to wife?"

"I did not say you should take her to wife, fool. Keep her in your *kraal*—let your women have charge of her and thus avoid jealousy—guard her well and seek her counsel whenever occasion arises."

"It is a good thought. I am beginning to forget my quarrel with you, Tekuba. I will act on your advice." He reached out a long, sinewy arm toward Lola.

The Major's muscles stiffened.

"Wait, fool!" Tekuba said harshly. "She is not yours yet. You must bid for her as you bid for the guns."

M'singa scowled.

"I remember our quarrel now," he said. "However it shall be as you say."

"It is all right, Lola," the Major said in English but got no further. It is hard for a man to speak with the point of a spear pressing against his Adam's apple.

Time passed.

The lips of the two chiefs moved constantly—they were counting their wealth, each getting ready to bid his all.

The candle burned lower—lower.

The Major was listening for Jim's signal, hoping that the candle would last until then—hoping to avoid the situation he would be called upon to face should the candle go out too soon. He knew that would be the signal for a bloody fight; the man who won would be in great haste to make use of his newly acquired weapons—but the man who lost would strike even quicker in order to prevent their use.

Neither chief spoke. It was as if each was saving his breath for one loud triumphant shouting bid when the time came.

A sudden gust of wind swirled inside the hut. The flame of the candle bowed to its power, the light dimmed, flickered—

"Five hundred head of cattle," M'singa yelled.

"Six hundred," Tekuba's bid followed like an echo.

"The flame still burns," the Major said gravely.

The two chiefs laughed sheepishly and then were silent.

One of the de Silvas opened his eyes and looked wonderingly about him. He started to speak and then, awed by the solemnity of the others, shook his brother into wakefulness.

The candle was completely burned down now, was only a short length of wick floating in a pool of grease.

Faintly, above the clamor outside of dancing and wild chants, the Major heard the Go-a-way signal. He drew his revolver.

"Six hundred and fifty oxen—"

"Seven—"

"An *impi*," yelled the Major and fired at the candle.

Spattered with grease the two chiefs jumped up with howls of rage, urging their guards to kill the insolent white man.

But not a warrior moved. They were not awed by the threat of the revolver—such a death would be easy—but by the bedlam of noise which sounded outside the *kraal;* the firing of many guns, fierce yells and threats of death.

They stood as if petrified and did not move until the Major said quietly,

"Brave men hide when the Rainmaker sends out his slayers. Run, warriors!"

With a yell they rushed from the hut, followed by the two chiefs, and joined the frantic crowd which was pouring out of the narrow gate in the fence at the rear of the *kraal.* They did not look back; they had only one thought and that to reach the comparative security of the hills where they could give a better account of themselves against the superior force of their King's *impi*—where they could die as men who had offended the King should die.

"They run and no one pursues," the Major chuckled. He and Lola and the two de Silvas were standing outside the hut, Lola holding to his arm, the men swaying back and forth, blinking owlishly, wondering what it was all about.

*The Major was listening for Jim's signal—hoping that the candle
would last until then—hoping to avoid the situation he would
be called upon to face should the candle go out too soon.*

"And here comes my *impi*," the Major continued proudly as Yank, Cockney and Jim at the head of fifty grinning natives, wearing the tattered remnants of Portuguese uniforms and carrying their well-cared-for rifles at the slope, entered the *kraal* and lined up in two-rank formation.

THE MAJOR ignored Lola's excited questions, shook off her restraining grip on his arm and went to join the others.

"How do, Yank?" he said and shook his hand. That was all—that was enough. They understood each other.

He talked a little with Jim and then passed down the line—Cockney, talking incessantly, escorting him. He had a word of praise for each soldier, calling him by name. They grinned at him affectionately.

"Have the mules inspanned, Jim," he ordered.

"It is already done, Major," Yank said, "and the drivers are in their seats."

"Good. Then let's get Miss Lola and these beauties on the way."

He escorted Lola out of the *kraal* and down to her wagon. She put out her arms to him and he lifted her up on to the seat.

"You are coming, too," she pleaded.

"Oh, no, dear Miss, positively no." His monocle appeared again. "You will be quite safe, I assure you. And I have work to do here."

"But you must come," she insisted. "You see—I am your property. Yours was the highest bid before the candle went out."

He frowned.

"And you see," she continued softly, "I am ready to stick to the bargain."

"Beastly awkward—what?" he muttered. Then, aloud, "Oh, but I'm sorry, dear Miss, really I am. I'm afraid I wasn't quite honorable. I may have bid an *impi*—my *impi*—for the useless rifles and your so beautiful self, but I never intended to close the deal. It was only a *ruse de guerre,* in a manner of speaking. I wouldn't pay Jim, and Yank and Cockney—not to speak of those fifty grinning devils—for—"

"Oh, go to hell, *Senhor* Major," she said wearily and then taking the long driving whip from the driver's hands she lashed the mules in a paroxysm of rage. They broke into a gallop and the driver cleverly turned them into the trail leading northward. The other two wagons quickly followed.

The Major watched them until they passed out of sight and then he returned slowly to where Yank, Cockney and Jim were waiting for him.

"And what now, Major?" Yank asked.

"I'm damned if I know, old dear. How about having a shot at trying to persuade that *impi* over there at Two Tree Kop to go home and be good. I hate bloodshed—it's so beastly messy,"

"We're game, eh Cockney?"

"Blimme, yes, Major. Hanything fer peace, I says. But, yer know, we thought yer was done fer?"

"Done for? How?"

"Why, we thought that Lola woman 'ad yer 'ooked!"

The Major laughed softly.

"She has, the dear lady. But she threw me down. I tried to *opsit* with her—you know the old Boer custom of sitting up by candlelight?—but she threw me down. In other words, Cockney—she refused to marry me. Ah, well! And Jim?"

"Yah, baas?"

"Mud can be washed from boulders."

"That is what I said, baas," Jim replied happily.

PESTLE AND MORTAR

IT WAS blazing hot. Not a cloud broke the fierce yellow-green light of the noonday sky; the sun had ceased to have form. It seemed to have melted under its great internal heat and spread like a molten, brazen flood above the thirst parched land. Heat waves danced grotesquely above the veld; distant hills changed shape constantly. Now they seemed near, now they vanished completely from the trekkers' bleared visions. Now they seemed substantial and unchangeable, now they shivered like a glutinous mass which threatened to dissolve into nothingness or, by some strange illusion of vision, they seemed to lose all contact with the earth and float in the air, towering over the veld like evil genii about to work vengeance on the puny mortals who were toiling painfully toward them.

There were thirty-four of these mortals. Three of them were white men, yellowed by the veld dust, ragged, unkempt, unshaven. The others were natives; they, too, were yellowed by the dust. One of them was Jim, a squat, powerfully built Hottentot who marched at the side of the white man who led the way. The others, marching in single file, their rifles slung across their shoulders, wore tattered remnants of what once had been ornate uniforms. The buttons which somehow held the scraps of cloth together were covered with grease and dirt which, nevertheless, failed to hide the Portuguese coat-of-arms embossed on them. But their rifles were clean; and cartridge belts sagged heavily about their loins.

The men moved slowly, apparently husbanding their strength, fearful of any unnecessary exertion which would sap that last vestige of strength which was needed to take them to the distant hills—rest, shade, and water.

They never looked up to the right or to the left, but with half closed downcast eyes were content to follow in the footsteps of their leader. They never questioned his veldcraft.

And he—his perfect proportions made him appear several inches shorter than his six foot odd—was clad in dirty white ducks, his face covered with a black, stubbled growth. He walked with a spring-less, slouching step, the stride of a jointless creature.

Occasionally he looked up for a moment to get his bearings; occasionally he glanced quickly at the Hottentot. At such times a whimsical, half tender light came into his eyes. Once the eyes of the two men, the white and the black, met.

"The baas is tired," the Hottentot said softly, mouthing the words rather than giving them utterance. "Better that we rest now."

The white man shook his head. "No, Jim. If we stop now some of those back there will never go on again. Besides, where shall we rest?"

"That is true, baas," the Hottentot agreed mournfully. "It is a torture to walk in this place; the soles of my feet—and there the skin is thickest; you know it?—are as tender as those of a new born child's. Yet, if you will not rest, baas, let me have your gun to carry. I need it. I want to show those black ones that I have no fear of the fire spitting stick."

The white man laughed and, screwing a monocle into his eye—it looked oddly incongruous at that moment—said banteringly in English, "You're a blamed old fraud, Jim. Of course you *are* afraid of guns and you don't need to carry mine in order to prove to the rest that you are a brave man. They know you—but not as well as I know you, you bloomin' old hypocrite. You think you're making it easier for me; but, of course, I won't stand for anything like that. No, of course not. I can carry my own gun, old top. Just the same, Jim, you're a most frightful old liar."

Jim the Hottentot—he had not understood a word the Major was saying—chuckled happily. "Me a fright-

ful liar, golly yes," he said with a parrotlike intonation. "If I don't see you s'long hullo!" And then, practically having exhausted his English vocabulary, he held out his hand, adding in the vernacular, "Then the baas will let me carry his gun?"

"No, Jim!" The white man's vernacular was as pure as the Hottentot's. "I am not a woman. I am not tired. Further, they," he indicated the straggling line of followers with a backward jerk of his head, "would think things if they saw you carrying my gun."

"What does it matter what they think, baas? They are not to be considered."

The white man laughed softly. "They are to be considered above all things, Jim. They are men."

"True, baas," Jim assented grudgingly. He now stepped a little aside from the trail and, halting, watched the rest of the party file past, his keen eyes closely scrutinizing each one, questioning, looking for some sign of endurance stretched to the breaking point. To some he spoke sharp, biting words—words which acted as a spur to flagging energies—while to others he spoke of the rest and food which awaited them at the distant hills.

One native, a big stalwart fellow, with a pair of pointed yellow boots slung about his neck, hobbled slightly as he walked and in response to Jim's look of inquiry pointed to the soles of his feet; they were bleeding.

"You thought you were a white man and wore shoes," Jim scoffed and, as he spoke, placed one of his naked feet on a round, black boulder. Even through thick soled boots a white man would have found the heat of that boulder unendurable; water poured upon it would have hissed and steamed. But Jim seemed indifferent to it.

"You do not hear me complain," the lamed man retorted tersely. "Neither do I step aside to rest, as you do. Shall I carry you, Hottentot?"

Jim grinned and clapped his hands together in recognition of the other's spirit.

THE COLUMN passed on but Jim waited until the two white men who walked far in the rear were opposite him. He joined them silently, listening in puzzled wonder to the never ceasing chatter of one of them.

They were a strange pair, these two white men. One was short, inclined to stoutness; and he rolled wearily in his gait, talking continually in a jovial, high pitched Cockney twang which jarred frightfully at first hearing but later became soothing because of its very monotony. The Major, whose stanch friend he had proved himself to be, called him simply, Cockney.

The other man, called by the little one, Yank, was tall and lean; he spoke rarely and when he did speak confined himself mainly to monosyllabic answers. Yet his nasal intoned, drawling yesses and noes contained more meat in them than Cockney's long winded periods. He walked easily, apparently unaffected by the day's long march and the terrific heat; he walked with the easy gait of the born trekker. Like the Major who marched in front, he had the faculty of submerging personality and making of himself a tireless automaton. The sun above, the scorching ground underfoot, the miles that had been covered, the miles yet to be traversed by the rescue expedition, the need of sleep, food and water had no apparent effect on him.

He carried the little man's rifle as well as his own and once, when Cockney reeled and almost pitched forward on his face, he put a supporting hand under the little man's elbow. "Better let me carry you, Cockney?" he suggested softly.

And at the same time Jim the Hottentot said, "Shall I carry the little baas?"

But Cockney summoned some reserve strength, straightened up, threw off the tall man's supporting grip and stepped out jauntily; he puckered his lips and attempted to whistle, but no sound came.

"Bli'me!" he exclaimed lugubriously. "I ain't got a tune in me. I ain't got no spit to wet me lips. Lumme! Me froat's bleedin' dry. It's 'ard to tork an' 'arder still not to. Funny though, ain't it? Hus a-goin' ter save a missionary, I mean. We're crusaders, that's wot we are. An' the way the Major 'as wiv niggers gets me. Look at them thirty ahead there. Wot are they followin' 'im fer? They won't get nothink out of it—except, maybe, *assegais* sticking through their ribs. But they don't care. If I was the devil an' saw the Major at the 'ead of them niggers a-comin' to my 'ouse, I'd run like 'ell!"

"These won't," glumly prophesied Yank.

"Eh wot? Wot *made* yer s'y that?" Cockney plainly showed that he had been startled, for he failed to rattle on in the half delirium of thirst and fatigue. Something had been in the back of his mind all the way—ever since the Major had enlisted the help of Yank and himself. Rescuing a fool missionary who somehow had incurred the wrath of the Swazis was all right enough in its way; but when it came as well to plugging along with a bunch of native troops freshly mutinied from the Portuguese standard, and with the scheming woman Lola de Sousa moving heaven and earth to be revenged upon the Major because he had flouted her—

Just how clearly these two saw the background of intrigue, and how each understood the mind of the other, was evidenced by Yank's terse reply. "I been wonderin'," he answered dryly, "if that there Lola de Sousa and Dom José—who's just lost these here sojers—couldn't of cooked up this missionary dodge, huh?"

Cockney's reddened eyes stared. "Bli'me!" he exploded. "Just to get the bloomin' Major by the nose, wot?" For a moment he looked ahead toward the Major striding along at the head of the column. It seemed as though Cockney was about to drag his sick, weakened frame forward. But then of a sudden the delirium returned.

"I used ter steal money from the missionary box w'en I was a nipper," Cockney started again with ominous suddenness. "Used ter put a penknife in the slot an' the pennies 'ud come out. I got a threepenny bit once, honly it was a bad un. An' now Hi'm payin' fer it by goin' ter save a blinkin' missionary. 'Ow! it's 'ot. Bli'me, Yank! I fink I'll sit down an' 'ave a little rest. Don't yer wait fer me, I'll catch up in 'arf an hour or so."

"No you don't, Cockney. I'm going to carry you. Here, Jim!" The tall man handed the rifles to the Hottentot.

Cockney giggled hysterically and swayed away from Yank's outstretched arms. "I fooled yer, didn't I? Yer thought Hi was all in, but Hi ain't—not by a long chalk," he said with a chuckle. Then his legs doubled up beneath him and he dropped unconscious to the ground.

Yank and Jim bent over him anxiously.

"Shall I tell the baas?" Jim asked, rising to his feet.

Yank shook his head. "Nope. He's all right. Only went to sleep on his feet, that's all. I've seen men do it before. It's the hunger and thirst sleep; the little chap's heart is too big for his body."

Jim nodded understanding. "Yah, Baas Yank, I know. So we will carry him, we two. And those black ones shall not know—otherwise he would feel we had put him to shame."

"They will not look 'round, Jim?"

"Nay, Baas Yank. Why should they? The hills are before them."

Yank rose easily, Cockney in his arms, and walked briskly on. There was no sound except the *sunch, sunch* of feet on the loose, sandy soil.

THE MOON was up when the party came to a narrow river which skirted the foot of the hills that had been their landmark through the two long days of thirsty, laborious trekking. A full hour or more before they actually had come in sight of the river the natives, their instincts infinitely more alert than those of the white men, had been aware of its proximity and their nostrils had quivered, animal like, in eager expectation. Their stride lengthened and the dull apathy into which they had fallen vanished; their eyes brightened. Some one among them commenced a weird, wailing chant which told of the hardships they had suffered and the deep throated, long drawn out *"A-ua,"* of the chorus intimated that all their troubles belonged to the past.

"Wot are they singing fer?" Cockney asked.

He had recovered from his breakdown and now, indignant with Yank and the Hottentot for having, as he bitterly phrased it, treated him like "a bleedin' baby," was walking with the Major at the head of the column.

"They smell water," the Major answered.

"Lumme! Where is it? Let me at it! Hi'm a-goin' ter waller in it!" He peered anxiously about like an inquisitive sparrow.

The Major pointed straight ahead where in the near distance the hills loomed up, appearing gargantuan, menacing, in the cold light of the moon. Far to the right a tiny point of light gleamed—a campfire.

"Bli'me!" Cockney groaned. "That's all you can do, point to them bleedin' 'ills. I'm beginnin' ter fink as hus'll never get there!"

"We'll be there in less than an hour," the Major encouraged.

"Honest to Gord? Will hus? Lumme! Come on! Yer walk too slow fer my way of finking." He broke into a shambling run.

"You'd better wait for us," the Major shouted after him. "There may be some warriors with spears waiting at the river."

"Hi don't care if all the warriors in Swaziland are between me an' the river, Major," Cockney responded. "Hi'd get a drink just the same." But, whimpering fretfully, he waited nevertheless until the Major caught up with him.

About a quarter of a mile from the river the Major halted his men in a deep hollow and after a whispered consultation went forward with Jim to spy out the land.

Yank had to use force to restrain Cockney from following.

Time passed. The Major's voice broke the silence. "The way's clear in front." He had returned as quietly as he had departed. Jim was nowhere to be seen.

As they took the trail again Yank asked, "Where's Jim, Major?"

"Wallerin' in water most likely," Cockney grumbled.

"Jim's gone to investigate the campfire up there," the Major replied curtly. "I doubt if he's been within a hundred yards of the river yet—and won't until he's finished his job."

To Yank the Major added, "I don't like that campfire at all. There's more to this tale than merely the threat to a bally missionary. I'm of the opinion that woman who wanted me to carry her diamonds that time to Lourenço Marquez and His Important Vengefulness, Dom José, have cooked up the whole notion, eh?"

Yank looked at Cockney and grinned; but he said nothing.

Arriving at the river they drank cautiously, slowly, as wise trekkers do after experiencing the great thirst. To do otherwise sometimes means death. And when they had drunk a little they plunged into the water, sat down on the sandy bed of the river—for sake of precaution holding their rifles and ammunition high above their heads—and absorbed moisture through the parched pores of their skins.

Ten minutes later, after a brief colloquy which concerned plans of action, the Major, Cockney and twenty of the native soldiers, moved swiftly away and were soon lost to sight in the hill shadows. Yank and the remaining ex-soldiers remained on the river bank.

Far down the river a hyena laughed fiendishly.

AN HOUR later the Major halted his men silently before the mission. It was a low, spreading building situated at the top of a gentle rise. Behind it, and flanking it on either side, *kopjes* towered. They looked starkly savage in the moon's brilliant, cold light. Although the hour was late, the windows of the mission were picked out by a soft yellow glow—lamplight softened and partly masked by coarse cotton window shades.

A little to the right of the main building, nestling close up against the walls of the rocky *kopje*, was a cluster of cone shaped huts. They looked like embryo *kopjes*. Recumbent, snoring forms cluttered the ground about the flickering fire which blazed near by.

The Major whispered a few commands to Cockney, and then quite ceremoniously fixed his monocle in his eye. It was polished clean now and, reflecting the moonlight, glowed like a live thing; queer, too, how it changed the Major's appearance; made him appear a pampered son of ease, a brainless incompetent. It was his stalking horse; it as effectively concealed the real man as the markings of a leopard's coat hides that crouching death where it lies motionless amongst the gay creepers and jungle flowers.

He rapped now on the mission door—a low, hesitating rap. He rapped again.

There was the sound of bars being withdrawn, a key turned in the lock and the door opened a little way. "Who's there, please?" a woman's voice asked.

"Two white men and—"

"Oh!" The door opened wide and the Major could see a slender, white clad girl; she held a lamp high above her head and its light, beating down, made her hair look like a golden halo.

The Major removed his helmet and bowed profoundly.

"Oh!" the girl said again, prettily confused. "Please come—"

"Who is it, Audrey?" A deep voice boomed from an inner room, interrupting the invitation.

"Two white strangers and their porters, father," she answered.

"Tell them I'll come and talk to them in a moment. Shut the door and come here."

She started to close the door. "I'm sorry—you heard?" Her attitude, the questioning raise of her eyebrows, her smile, was all one sweet gesture of apology.

The Major bowed again, thankful that he was in the shadows, uncomfortably conscious of his disreputable attire. "Of course, dear miss," he murmured.

They heard the bolts shot home, the *click-click* of the lock.

"Strike me pink," Cockney grumbled. "Wot do they take hus fer? 'Ere we marches through a bleedin' thirsty 'ell to save 'em an' they keeps hus a-waitin' at the door as if we was peddlers."

"Ah, well, Cockney," the Major said in light reproof, "they don't know what we are or what we're doin' here. They're wise to be cautious."

The voices of men in earnest discussion sounded from the mission. Footsteps echoed in the passageway. The key was turned, the bolts shot back and the door was opened again. An elderly man, gaunt and stooped, his face covered with a gray beard, stood on the threshold. In his right hand was an old, rust covered pistol; in his left a powerful acetylene lamp which he held so that its light was reflected outward. It pierced the dark shadows in which the Major's men waited.

He focussed it now on the Major and to held it relentlessly on him although the Major did his best to dodge its blinding glare, endeavoring to see the faces of the two who stood behind the man with the lamp.

"Well?" The man with the lamp half turned to those behind him.

Out of the indistinct murmur of voices which answered the Major caught the words, "Yes, without a doubt it is the man. But there should be another white man—he is, no doubt, in ambush. Close the door, *senhor*. It is not safe to parley with such a man, *Senhor* Sayre. Send them away."

"No," the gray bearded man replied. "I can't do that without first hearing what they have to say." He turned to the Major. "What do you want, sir?"

"Food, soap and razors, lodgings—but chiefly soap and razors!" the Major answered lightly.

"From where did you come?"

"Lobeni."

"When did you leave there?"

"Three days ago."

"Tut! That is impossible. It is a four days' trek at the best speed."

"We marched very fast, sir."

"And you came here 'chiefly for soap?' That is hard to believe."

"I did not say so, dear sir. That is what we want; we came for something infinitely more serious. We have it on good authority that a party of young Swazi warriors is planning to attack you!"

The other started. "But that is impossible. I have always lived with these people and they with me. They may not all"—his voice saddened—"have accepted my teachings but I have their respect and friendship."

"What I say is true, nevertheless," the Major said firmly.

"Preposterous," a voice said behind Sayre. "If the natives are on the warpath it is because he has insulted them. It may be that they are after him and his ruffianly crew and in fear for his life he comes here seeking sanctuary."

"And if that is true," Sayre said gravely, ignoring the Major's heated expostulations, "can I refuse him that sanctuary?"

"Without doubt," the same voice replied complacently. "Are you, *senhor*, to imperil your mission for the sake of this cutthroat adventurer? Are you going to throw away the work of a lifetime by letting your people see that you side with this so evil a man?"

"That is true," Sayre murmured. "I had not thought of that." He turned wrathfully on the Major. "And you would have me believe that you come here solely to protect me from an attack—you being what you are?"

"And what am I, reverend sir?"

"A white kaffir; a dangerous degenerate; a slaver; a man who, in addition to the evil traits of his own race, has adopted the worst ones of the natives! You are the pariah, the human leper whom others call the Major! Can you deny that you are the I.D.B. known as the Major? Can you deny that the natives with you are deserters from the Portuguese Government troops?"

"No, but—"

"But?" Sayre interrupted sternly. "Surely there is nothing else to say!" The door started to close.

"Wait!" the Major cried. "Have you made no native converts? Is none resident at the mission?"

"Yes," Sayre was surprised into answering. "Fifty have seen the light and stay at the mission."

"And you let them sleep on the ground there?" The Major pointed to the recumbent forms about the fire.

"No. They are the visitors' porters. My people—" he hesitated.

"Are not here, you would say? Of course not. They have gone—you probably haven't seen one since the day before yesterday. They knew all about the trouble that was coming and they have gone to their *kraals*. Perhaps some of them will be with the force that is coming to attack you!"

"No!" Sayre said decisively. "I don't believe a word you say. My people have gone to help with the harvests. They told me before they left. Even if I had not already been warned about you, I'd have believed my people's explanation of their departure rather than that offered by such a degraded looking object as yourself!" The door was slammed to, the bolts shot home, the key turned.

" 'Ell!" Cockney exclaimed. "Ain't he the cheerful old wogg? But wot did yer chew the rag about for such a long time, for? Why didn't yer state yer business sharp an' sudden like?"

"I'm not quite sure, Cockney. Partly because—oh, well! It was no use rushing things. The old boy's been told a lot of unpleasantly untruthful things about us, Cockney, and it was no good trying to force things. Then, too, I was trying to get a good look at the visitors. They were most unchristianlike, were they not?"

"Strewth, yes!" Cockney spat. "And did yer?"

"No," the Major answered thoughtfully. "But their voices sounded strangely familiar and I think—I *think*, mind you—I've seen 'em before. We'll just have to hang around. I'm afraid we'll have to help the old chappy and his charming daughter whether they like it or not."

Raising his voice a little he addressed his men. "There will be food in the morning," he said. "Now there is only sleep."

It was all they wanted. A low sigh of satisfaction came from their lips; then as one man they stretched themselves full length on the ground. In a little while they slept.

The Major paced moodily up and down for a little while, until the lights in the mission went out, then he sat down in the shadows, his back against the wall, his hands clasped about his drawn up knees. He seemed to sleep.

After a time the mission door cautiously opened and a man emerged, stealthily made his way to one of the sleepers about the fire, shook him into wakefulness and whispered a few intense commands. The native rose and silently departed into the night and the other returned to the mission, paused a moment before the Major's huddled figure and then went into the house. The door closed again.

"The more the merrier," the Major murmured with a low chuckle. "I only hope that messenger doesn't run into Yank or Jim."

And then he really slept.

IT WAS approaching the hour of sunrise when Jim the Hottentot came to the mission and stooped over his master.

Instantly the Major opened his eyes. "Well, Jim?" he asked quietly.

"It is not well, baas; it is evil. We must get from this place before the sun shows above the hills."

"Why, Jim?"

"The baas knows what happens to the grain when it comes between the pestle and the mortar? We are the grain."

"You have said a lot, Jim; but there is more?"

"Truly! But I have told you the juice of it. What need to tell how I crushed the meat in order to get the juice?"

"Yet I would hear—and speak softly, Jim. The strangers are beginning to waken."

Jim looked at the porters who were lazily stretching themselves. "We are like a lame man who poked a hornets' nest," he muttered, "and there is no way out for us. Listen, baas! I made my way to the campfire as you ordered and there saw three white men; they were evil looking and undoubtedly Dom José's Portuguese. With them were many black dogs, at least three times the count of my two hands, who bore themselves as these men of ours bore themselves before your voice made them soldiers. I crept up close, baas. And that was easy, you know how it is done, for they kept no sort of watch. I listened for a long time to the talk of the black ones. A lot they spoke of beatings and death. They have come—these and other men for whom they wait—to look for us, to capture us and take us to Lourenço Marquez for punishment."

"Ah," said the Major to himself. "Lola collaborates with Dom José; how earnestly that woman does hate!"

"Yah, baas," Jim continued soberly. "And while I waited a messenger came from this place. All that he said I do not know, but it seemed to give the white men great joy; they march for this place in the morning. And so, baas, it would be well for us to go before it is too late. They are the pestle."

"It is too late, Jim. It always was too late."

"I forgot to say, baas," Jim added slowly, "that the very fat man, he who is the big chief at Lourenço Marquez, was in command of the men at the campfire and with him, sitting on his knee, was the woman you know of."

"Ah," said the Major again. "It is sometimes wise to run from a woman, Jim."

"It is always wise to do so, baas. 'Specially such a woman. Shall I give the order now?"

"No, Jim, it is too late. We have started on a task; it must be completed. Also," he smiled at the Hottentot, "the tale is not yet told. You spoke of a pestle and mortar."

"True, baas. There is more to dread. There were shadows, many shadows, moving through the bush last night, and when they left the shade the heads of their *assegais* twinkled hungrily. The shadows are climbing the hills now. They are encircling us and when that is done the shadows will advance and—there will be no more sun for us. These Swazi warriors are the mortar, baas. Let us go before it is too late."

"It is too late, Jim," the Major said for the third time. "And the tale is not yet all told."

Jim groaned aloud at that. "You are like *N'dhlovu* the elephant, baas. You plow your way forward giving no thought to the bamboo and thorn scrub which impedes lesser beasts. Know then that my ears were open last night! That messenger did not tell the white men this, but he spoke afterward to the other black dogs: He was stopped by a Swazi warrior, baas, who asked him where he was going and for what purpose. And he told that Swazi that he was on his way to summon his master's friends to the mission. Also—*au-a!* I was the darkest shadow that moved last night—I later heard some Swazi warriors talk. They will attack when the hyena screams once then once again. That will be, I think, when the sun is high for he will not scream until he has seen the Portuguese come to this place. And then"—the Hottentot gestured dramatically—"the tale will have been told indeed. There are three hundred of them, baas. And some have guns."

"You tell an evil tale, Jim; it is a tale of shadows. Is there no sun? Nothing at which a man can laugh?"

Jim grinned sheepishly. "Is nothing hidden from you, baas? Know then that the Swazi are afraid that word of the evil they intend has got to the ear of the king and that he will interfere—because the missionary is under his protection. For what happens *after* they have wiped us out they have no care; the witch doctor has promised them protection. But when I told all this to Baas Yank, he and his men left for the *kraal* of the king to tell him of the evil his warriors plan. And if *that* is food for laughter, baas, remembering that the *kraal* of the king is a day and a night's trek from here—why then, baas, laugh!"

And the Major laughed softly—very softly.

JIM LOOKED to the east where the sky was glowing with living colors; the hilltops were softened by a mist which was pink-flushed by the coming dawn. Somewhere a cock crowed. The mission cattle lowed and their hunger cry was echoed by the bleating of goats. The porters were fully aroused now. Some of them were crouching about the embers of the night's fire, others were preparing their frugal morning meal and all looked with wondering eyes at the Major's sleeping men.

Within the mission people were moving about; a woman's clear soprano sounded in joyful song. Everything seemed very peaceful; the mist clouds vanished from the *kopje* tops, and the peaks were gilded by the rising sun. But the shadows remained, darkening momentarily, becoming more sharply defined.

"Is it permitted that I sleep now for a little while, baas?" Jim asked.

The Major made a gesture of assent which was, at the same time, one of self reproach that he should have kept Jim from rest so long.

Jim sighed with satisfaction and seeking a place which would afford shade for several hours dropped limply to the ground, and slept.

The Major awakened Cockney now and swiftly gave him Jim's report.

"Good old Yank an' Jim," Cockney commented. "They're fair knockhouts, ain't they? An' now wot, Major?"

"Wake the men, Cockney. There's a lot to be done." He looked about him with a shrewd, calculating glance. "Those huts'll have to come down and a stockade be made of the poles. And that'll have to be cut." He pointed to about an acre of high green corn through which ran a road leading out of the circle of hills. "You'll have to work hard, Cockney. I can only let you have half the men; the others'll have to stand guard over the porters and the house."

Cockney grinned. This work of knocking down huts and cutting the corn appealed to him. He swiftly awakened the men. Ten lined up before the Major for orders, the others worked under Cockney. Five started to tear down the huts, the rest cut the corn with the scythes they discovered in the store hut.

The porters looked on at the demolition of the huts with wide eyed surprise and then, of a sudden, they made a break for the mission. They were stopped by the menacing attitude of the Major's ten men.

"Soldiers," said the Major, addressing them, and they looked at him wonderingly. How did he know they were not porters? "Soldiers, in a little while the Swazi will attack us. Answer now, truly. Will you, until that danger is over, forget the bone those who lead you have to pick with me? Will you obey my orders until the Swazi see that we are a nut they cannot crack? Or will you be so occupied in the noise of your own talk that you cannot hear the *ghee* of the spears of the warriors?"

The soldier-porters—and they were twenty strong—looked at each other uneasily, then glanced at their packs which contained their rifles and ammunition.

"We have no bone to pick with you," one said presently, "but how do we know you speak truly?"

"You have heard much of me from your own people. Has anyone heard me called a liar?"

"No." The answer came promptly. "Still, when the lion is caught in a trap, he cries out in fear like a stinking jackal. And, seeing that we outnumber your men—and there are others of us nearby—it may be that this talk of Swazi is but a jackal's cry."

"Your eyes are keen, soldiers. Look up into the hills and tell me what you see."

They obeyed him and, as first one and then another caught sight of a sudden gleam here and there amongst the rocks, they gave voice to low exclamations of uneasy surprise. "We have seen," their spokesman said soberly. "The sun shines on the spears of warriors, of warriors who hide—and a hiding warrior is a killing warrior. But what then? It may be that it is your blood for which they thirst—and why should we help you pick your bone?"

"I do not lie," the Major said calmly. "Hear me! Soon, when the sun is high, other white men—friends of those who lead you—will come to this place with thirty more soldiers. A hyena will laugh twice, and then the *assegais* of the warriors will darken the sky. Now answer this. If the Swazi desired only my blood, would they wait for other white men to come here? Would they not attack at once while we are few?"

"He speaks truly," the men whispered together. "Unless it is all lies."

"This we will do, white man," decided the leader of the soldiers. "We will obey your orders—disobeying those of the men who lead us; and they are fools—until noon. If, by that time, the others you speak of have not arrived, or if, should they have come, the hyena should not laugh, then—" He paused significantly.

"Then," said the Major softly, "I shall still be here for you to do with me as you will. It is agreed?"

"It is agreed. What are your orders?"

He set them to work then, some assisting in the tearing down of huts, others building a stout stockade about the mission, still others preparing food for all, which he dealt out to them from the store hut.

The Major and his ten men stood guard outside the doors and windows of the mission. There was a great stir in the house; men's voices raised in anger—a running to and fro. A window opened and a man, his voice hoarse with rage, shouted orders to the soldier-porters and cursed viciously when his orders were ignored.

A moment later the door opened and two men rushed out, revolvers in their hands. But the Major, and the two men waiting with him beside the door, tripped them as they emerged and, when they would not listen to the Major's proposition of a truce until the present danger was past, bound and gagged them.

The missionary, the Reverend Sayre, came to the door and wailed aloud at the destruction of the huts and the cutting of the corn. He tried to speak but words failed him. He could only cry incoherently, "Wolves in sheep's clothing! The labor of years undone! Undone—all wasted!" He sat down on the doorstep and covered his face with his hands.

"What we have pulled down can be built again," the Major said softly. "The corn will grow again after another sowing, but if you die now this place will become a wilderness and your work will perish utterly. We only work to prevent that."

But the old man would not be comforted. He was very old, older than his sixty-five years. Forty years of Africa, of privation, of fever, of almost hourly danger had taken a heavy toll of his vitality. He shook as with the ague of fever.

The girl came to the door and, ignoring the Major's salute, led her father into the house. She returned again presently and beckoned him to enter. He followed her into the large, spotless kitchen.

"You asked for that," she said quietly, pointing to razor, soap and a large bowl of steaming water. "Call me when you have finished; I want to talk with you."

Whistling dolefully, the Major shaved and washed. He grinned at his reflection in the mirror. His black hair was brushed smoothly back from his high forehead; his smooth, clean shaven face glowed pink. In spite of the tattered rags which clothed his powerful frame, he was the Major, the "damned dude."

"Dear miss," he called softly, and fixed his monocle in his eye.

She entered immediately and there was a dancing light in her clear gray eyes as she regarded him closely.

"You do not look like a white kaffir," she said in her soft, musical voice.

"And do you think I am one?" It was amazing, the Major thought, how attractive was the cheap cotton dress she wore.

"Of course not," she answered hastily, flushing a little under his scrutiny. "Then it is all true—about the uprising, I mean?" She looked out of the window and viewed the warlike preparations.

"Quite true!" the Major assured her solemnly. "But there is no great cause for alarm, I think. None at all, dear miss. Before the attack begins there will be quite a lot of us on hand to repulse it. Bally fortunate that the Portuguese chappies happened to be on hand, isn't it?"

She frowned a little at that. "And is any of it true that they say about you?"

"I don't think we need to go into that, need we? You see it is a long story, and there's a lot to do."

She nodded. "Of course I don't believe anything they said." Strangely enough, a flood of color came to her cheeks. The Major looked away, smiling a little.

A silence followed. It was broken by Cockney calling, "Major. The corn's down, an' so's most of the 'uts. Can't these blighters eat now?"

The Major took up his helmet and moved hurriedly toward the door. "Comin', Cockney," he shouted. And to the girl, "Excuse me, dear miss."

She inclined her head. "Isn't there something I can do? It is terrible just to sit and wait. Oh, of course—" she was embarrassed with remorse "—you are hungry. When you have seen about the men you'll come in to breakfast?"

He nodded, and left humming a tune.

THE SUN was high in the sky, a molten, burning sun suspended in a sky of glaring, electric blue, when the Major made a last round of inspection of the defences and expressed himself well satisfied. "All we can do now, Cockney," he said, "is wait. It may be that when the warriors see how strong we are they'll decide not to attack. We haven't any too much ammunition, so I hope that'll be the case. If it isn't—well, I think we can hold them off until Yank comes."

Cockney grunted. "And supposin' as Yank don't come?"

"Oh, don't be a bally pessimist, Cockney; of course he'll come." But, in spite of his confident tone, the Major's face clouded. He knew that the tall, lanky American had a hard task before him. First he faced a long, difficult trek with men who were already tired, and then the problem of getting the indolent Swazi king to see the gravity of the situation and hasten back to reprove his subjects.

"Look, baas," Jim said suddenly, awakened from his short sleep. "The scouts are coming in."

As he spoke two of the Major's men crept through the opening which had been left in the pole stockade. "The Portuguese are coming," one of them panted.

The Major, followed by Cockney and the Hottentot, went outside the stockade. Looking down the road which led out of the hills they could see a man running swiftly toward them. It was another of the Major's scouts; one who had gone much farther down the road than he had been ordered, so great was his zealous desire to be the first to report the approach of the expected force. As he ran he leaped from side to side, now running erect, now stooping low.

The vicious crack of a rifle broke the silence. The running man staggered, then came on at a faster gait.

The Major, his face set and stern, started to meet him but was halted by Jim and Cockney tugging at his coat. "He is all right, baas. He pays a little—as is right—for disobeying orders. And if you go to help him, and meet death, what does that avail us?"

The runner came on; he shouted something and waved his arms.

"He wants us to go back, baas," Jim said.

A moment later the Portuguese force came in sight far down the ravine. As soon as they saw the Major and the stockade behind him, they halted long enough to fire a ragged volley and then came on at the double.

The scout reached the Major; blood was streaming from a wound in his arm, "Back!" he gasped. "The Swazi are closing down. They are hidden in the rocks beside the trail down there." He almost collapsed, but when Cockney and the Hottentot would have carried him into the stockade he pulled himself erect, and with a fine dignity of carriage walked in unaided.

Four hundred yards from the Major the Portuguese halted and, lying down, fired rapidly. But their shots all passed high overhead.

"They shoot like wimmen," Cockney scoffed.

The firing ceased. A pompous, fat little man stood up and advanced a few paces before his men. It was Dom José, governor of Lourenço Marquez.

"Do you surrender?" he cried through his cupped hands.

"I will agree to a truce," the. Major called back.

Dom José advanced cautiously; his men crept up slowly behind him. He advanced fifty yards before he spoke again. "I make no truce with you. Surrender unconditionally or—" He was advancing as he spoke.

"This is no time for quibbling," the Major said. "Come in quickly. The hills are full of Swazi warriors waiting to attack. Come up with your men and help us. Afterward we will talk over our differences."

José laughed at that.

"You are so-a very wise, *senhor.* But I am no fool. I do not walk into such a trap. No! Think you I am a child to be frightened by such bogey talk? Think! I have thirty soldiers here, besides three white officers: they all have you covered. Surrender or—"

"And I have two of your officers my prisoners within the mission," the Major replied. "Their men are fighting beside my men, and they all have you covered, Excellency."

Dom José dropped to the ground with a squeal, seeking what little cover was to be had. His stern bulked large, his head was hidden behind a tiny termite heap.

"Surrender!" he cried again, his voice muffled.

At that moment a hyena screamed once—and then again.

"Blood of Christ! What was that?" Dom José sprang to his feet and ran like a frightened rabbit back to his men. They, too, had risen and were now standing in a huddled group looking uneasily about them. In spite of their fore-knowledge of this, instinct warned them that the Swazis would not trouble to distinguish Portuguese from English.

Dark forms were descending the hills, leaping from rock to rock, yelling, brandishing *assegais.*

The deep bellow of muzzle loading guns split the air; the echoes were tossed back and forth between the hills. And then the Swazi rushed. *Assegais* flashed in the sun, rose and fell.

So sudden was the attack of these warriors they had believed to be allies, that the Portuguese force was over-whelmed. For a little while they resisted, and then ten of the native soldiers, with a woman urging them to haste, broke away and ran up the hill.

A moment's pause and then the warriors surged over the bodies of the others like a relentless tide and came on in fast pursuit. Behind them the ground was dotted with lifeless bodies.

The woman, Lola de Sousa, reached the Major. "Kill that pig José!" she gasped.

"There's been enough killing," the Major retorted sternly. "Get into the stockade."

She was about to protest, to use on him the wiles of her savage craft, but turning, she saw José staggering, his mouth agape, breathing hard, his eyes dilated with fear; saw the native soldiers running fast, passing the white men, deaf to his appeals for assistance; saw the pursuing warriors and the still forms behind them.

"Oh!" she gasped, her olive skin blanching with the fear of the death she had escaped, and went on into the stockade.

Dom José lagged far behind now; his pace was little faster than a walk. A warrior was hard on his heels.

Dropping to one knee, the Major fired, and the warrior spun around, then dropped to the ground. Yelling defiance, another warrior sprang to the front. As he ran, he drew back his *assegai,* poised it ready for the throw.

The Major fired again and the warrior pitched forward, recovered, and cast his *assegai* at José. But his strength had left him; the weapon clattered harmlessly on the rocks behind the panic stricken white man. The warrior fell headlong and did not move again.

The other warriors checked, scattered, sought shelter.

The fleeing soldiers sped past the Major and did not slacken speed until they were safely behind the stockade where, looking sheepish and very much ashamed, they endeavored to justify to the others who looked askance at them, the desertion of their officers.

The Major went to meet José and found Jim running by his side. "This is folly," the Hottentot snorted wrathfully as they caught hold of the reeling, fear blinded José. "But then, we are fools, we two. Let us carry the pig, baas. It will be quicker."

The Major nodded and between them they carried the portly governor of Lourenço Marquez back at a run to the stockade.

The warriors rushed to the attack again; but Cockney was ready for them and at his command the defenders fired rapidly, causing the warriors to seek cover once again.

Entering the stockade the Major and Jim unceremoniously dumped their burden down on the hard ground and left him to recover his breath and dignity as well as he might.

"Are the men all at their posts, Cockney?" the Major asked.

The little man nodded. "I've got 'em all 'round the blinkin' stockade, wiv reserves, like, be'ind 'em. The Swazi can't catch hus napping. Ho yes! Hi did as yer said, too. Hi got buckets full of water all abart the place an' arranged it so if the attack comes 'ard at one place, men'll go ter 'elp wivout leavin' the rest o' the stockade unprotected."

"Good man, Cockney. We ought to be safe."

"We'll be all right if the ammunition holds out."

Exultant yells sounded down the road.

"Bli'me! Wot's that?"

The Major and Cockney peered out through the poles of the stockade and saw warriors dancing about the dead bodies. The cause of their rejoicing was plainly evident. They had possessed themselves of the dead men's rifles and ammunition.

The Major looked worried. "Of course," he muttered. "I should have thought of that. And now, if they have the sense to get back up into the hills and pot at us from there, things'll be deucedly unpleasant."

"They won't 'ave the sense," Cockney said confidently. "An' if they did they won't know 'ow to fire the blinkin' things. They're new fangled guns—'ave yer seen 'em?—an' I don't properly know the rights of 'em meself. See! Wot did I tell yer?"

Three reports sounded; the dancing and yelling ceased. One of the warriors was squirming on the ground and the others were holding the rifles away from them as if afraid they would do further mischief.

"Let's put a volley into 'em, Major," Cockney pleaded, shuffling his feet excitedly. "We could blow them beggars hoff the map an' it 'ud discourage the others."

The Major shook his head. "No, Cockney. No shooting until I give the order. We've got everything to gain by not rushing our fences—if you know what I mean. I mean if we started things we'd have the whole bloomin' *impi* down on us. You've never seen the Swazi really fight, have you, Cockney? I have. We couldn't check 'em."

The warriors disappeared among the rocks, carrying their wounded with them. Everything seemed deceitfully still and peaceful. The Major made a tour of the stockade, pausing here and there to exchange jests with the men. He paused finally in front of the men who had fled before the Swazi onslaught and regarded them critically.

"Our shame is great," one of them said in a low voice. "Yet what honor would it have been to have died as those others died? It is no honor to die with white men whose voices always cursed and threatened, whose hands always held a *sjambok.*"

"Yet those other black men died with them."

The soldier laughed harshly. "They would have fled, too, had that been possible. It is because we all tried to run that the Swazi conquered us so easily. We had not stomach for fighting; all fighting had been beaten out of us by the lash of voice and whip. Also, white man, know this; we have heard of you and with you we had no bone to pick. Had we, you would have died when you stood outside the stockade that time."

"It comes to me that you tried to cause my death," the Major countered dryly. "A bullet took the helmet from my head."

"That was one of the white men," the soldier interrupted. "We black ones, we did not try to shoot straight. If we had! Listen, white man! I am by no means the best shot of us, but we are all picked men, And so—look!"

He pointed to a vulture which was soaring low over the dead bodies down in the ravine. For a moment he fumbled with the sights of his rifle, then put the gun to his shoulder, aimed and squeezed the trigger. The vulture flapped desperately then dropped, turning over and over, crashing lifelessly to the ground.

"You were a bigger mark than that vulture when you stood before the stockade," the marksman said meaningly.

"Ah!" The Major nodded thoughtfully. "At least you can shoot. But can you obey orders, also? Now I shall issue orders to you when necessary." He turned and passed on.

He halted at the sound of a woman's voice calling softly, "Major!"

He saw the woman, Lola, idling in a deck chair placed in the shade of the mission building. He frowned as he walked toward her.

"Come and sit here," she said indicating a stool by her side. Her manner was still that of Lola de Sousa, the imperious, voluptuously beautiful woman whose commands so many men jumped to obey—in Lourenço Marquez. Yet she was not the same, quite. She seemed older. In the brilliant light of the sun her complexion looked pasty; her lips, devoid of rouge, were not so full and her mouth drooped at the corners. Her eyes were still magnificent, but the hard lines about them detracted from their brilliance. Her hair was untidy and the khaki shirt and trousers she wore were ill fitting and unbecoming.

She flinched under the Major's cool, impersonal scrutiny. "Without my wardrobe, what would you?" she asked with an attempt at lightness. "Sit down, Major."

He stared as though he did not recognize her.

"Oh, yes," he said presently. "You are, of course, Miss Lola. I did not recognize you. But why are you here? No, thanks; I won't sit down."

"I came to look for you, Major," she said softly, leaning toward him. "I made that fat pig, José, send men to look for you; then I made him come and bring me with him. That was not hard, for the fool loves me."

"I should hate to have you call me a fool," the Major said with a courtly bow, albeit the slight edge of irony was apparent in his voice.

She smiled cryptically. A burning intensity lay behind the dark eyes, however—an intensity whether of love or hate for this clean, virile man probably Lola herself could not have said.

"You are so gallant, Major, but you will do as I say. You will pay attentions now to Lola, come with her back from this ugly jungle. Four other officers of Dom José are on their way to join us here. They will arrive—who knows? After the fighting is all over, I think; when your men are tired and you are short of ammunition. And they have soldiers with them who are brave fighters. Oh, yes! I think they will persuade you to come with me. If you don't, I don't think it would be very hard for me to persuade Dom José to hang you!"

"You are a strange woman, Lola," the Major answered. "But thanks for the warning; and don't forget that I hold Dom José and the other two as hostages. You also are my prisoner."

"For myself, I am quite content with that."

He bent low over the hand she held out to him in dismissal. And so he did not see the girl Audrey Sayre come to the door of the mission and stand looking at them scornfully, her fingers idly toying with the trigger of the revolver she held in her hands. Neither did he see Dom José, his face contorted with jealous wrath, draw his revolver and fire.

The bullet ploughed into the earth a little to the right of the Major, sending a shower of dust into his face, half blinding him. But before the fat little Portuguese could fire again Lola had leaped swiftly from her chair and stood between him and the Major. Swifter yet, Audrey Sayre fired and her bullet passed through the flesh of José's upper arm and he dropped his revolver, screaming with pain.

The Major, his eyes inflamed with dust, rose and turned swiftly, revolver in hand. "Bind the fool and gag him like the others," he said savagely to Cockney who came running with several soldiers. "Thank you, dear miss," he said to Audrey.

And then Lola slumped backward into his arms.

He picked her up and carrying her into the house put her down on the couch. "Did he wound her?" he asked anxiously of Audrey who had followed them into the house.

"No!" she replied and he wondered vaguely at the coldness of her tone, the contemptuous look in her eyes. "She has only fainted—if that. Look!"

Lola had opened her eyes and was gazing wonderingly at the Major. "José didn't kill you then," she said in a low, far away voice. "Then it doesn't matter about me, does it? I don't remember what happened after I jumped in front of you."

"You were very brave, Miss Lola. I—" He bent over her.

"Oh, go away," Audrey said tartly. "She's only imagining things. Get outside; the men need you. I'll attend to this woman."

Lola sat upright at that, her eyes blazing with wrath. "You cat!" she said to Audrey.

The Major walked hastily to the door, opened it and then asked, "Your father, dear miss, how is he?"

"He's locked up in his room. I locked him in because he wants to go out and give himself up as a sacrifice to the Swazi! Oh! I think all men are fools!"

The Major hesitated no longer after that but went out and shut the door firmly behind him. As he did so a low drumming noise filled the air, the noise of spear heads beating against bullock hide shields. The Swazi were mustering for attack.

THE MOON was high. At the mission all was quiet. Here and there a man moved briskly to and fro, for the night was cold, the fires and sleep very desirable. But these men could not lie down; their duty was to stand watch so that the others could sleep in safety.

Beyond the stockade the hills loomed large, yet seemed to lack solidity; they appeared like cardboard silhouettes. There was no depth to them, no thickness. In some manner they were like the fantastic scenery of a futuristic play. Here and there the light of campfires twinkled on their slopes. Drums sounded fitfully; snatches of song in barbaric, minor cadences floated weirdly out of the hills.

The Major made the rounds of the stockade, talking with those who were on sentry duty. His eyes turned continually toward the hills.

"They will not come again tonight, baas," one of the men said. "They mourn their dead."

He nodded. "True! But it is well to watch."

It had been a long day. Again and again the Swazi had rushed to the attack. Once they had come so close that their *assegais* had fallen into the stockade, wounding five of the defenders. That time the Major had, for his men's sake, given the order to shoot to kill. And the Swazi forces had lost heavily.

When they came later in an attempt to remove their dead, the Major had tried to parley with them, but failed. They would not listen to him save that they promised, in return for permission to remove their dead unhindered, they would pile rocks over the bodies of the Portuguese they had killed earlier in the day.

It was a bargain to which the Major gladly assented.

It had been a long day, but a longer night. With sunset and the darkness which followed before the rising of the moon, the Swazi had increased their activity. Three times they had succeeded in setting the mission on fire with lighted brands tied to the shafts of their *assegais* and men had been drawn from their posts at the stockade to fight the flames.

And through it all the native troops had worked like men possessed; no task was impossible. Was not the baas just? Did he ask others to do what he himself could not, or dared not do?

Once, when the warriors' attacks seemed likely to gain their objective, the Major led a small party of volunteers out of the stockade, Cockney and Jim grumbling loudly because they were not allowed to go, and attacked from the rear. When the Swazis turned to face this unexpected onslaught the Major retreated, drawing them away from the stockade, thus giving the defenders a breathing spell in which to repair the breach in the fence.

The Major dared not think of the morrow. Every shot fired then would have to be aimed to kill. Coming to that part of the stockade which faced the road he sat down on an upturned pail and stared moodily before him.

A shadow fell across his face. Looking up he saw Audrey Sayre. He sprang to his feet.

"You ought to be in bed, dear miss," he said reproachfully. "You have worked hard."

She silenced him with an impatient gesture. "I have done nothing compared to what you have done, and Cockney, and Jim and all the others. Besides, I couldn't sleep," she added lamely.

"Strain, nerves, and all that," the Major assented. "Of course!"

"No. But I've been thinking. I have come to the conclusion that father is right, So tomorrow we—he and I—will give ourselves up to the Swazi. It is our death they want and—after all—why should you and—" she gulped "—Miss de Sousa, and all of you die because of us?"

"Why indeed?" he answered absently, His eyes were fixed on the deep shadows far down the road.

"That's all," she said uncertainly, "Good-by."

"You are talking like a child," he said curtly ignoring her outstretched hand, "Has Miss de Sousa been talking to you?"

She did not answer.

"But of course she did," he continued, "I suppose she also told you that I was going to Lourenço Marquez with her when this affair's over?"

"And aren't you?" she asked breathlessly.

"I'm not."

"Oh!"

"Now suppose you get to bed and forget all this nonsense; of course I won't let your father and yourself leave the stockade! Go to bed and sleep. Everything will seem different in the morning and by tomorrow night our troubles will be over.

"And that's true," he muttered to himself, "if the cartridges give out."

At a faint *tot-a-tot, tot-a-tot* which sounded far down the road the Major sprang to his feet. "Stay here," he said roughly to Audrey and going inside the stockade gazed down the ravine. Audrey would have followed him but found her way barred by one of the native sentinels.

Presently a horseman emerged from, the chaos of shadows. "A trooper of the mounted," the Major said, "judging by his hat and the way he rides. I wonder—"

As he watched he saw the rider bend over his horse's neck, heard the beat of hoofs change from a walk to a trot, to a canter, to a full gallop. Yells sounded; black forms rose up beside the trail; others blocked the way between the horseman and the mission. He rode fast, firing as he came.

The sleepers in the stockade awakened and ran to their posts. Cockney and Jim joined the Major.

"Get back," he ordered curtly and they silently obeyed.

The horseman broke through the warriors who blocked his path; he was crouching in his seat, spurring madly.

Assegais flashed. The horse reeled, collapsed in a heap pitching its rider over its head. Warriors, yelling exultantly, rushed to make an end.

The men Cockney had summoned to the stockade opening fired a volley and the Swazis scattered, sought cover. They were well content to wait until darkness came again. The horseman did not move; his fall had stunned him.

"Keep 'em off, Cockney," the Major yelled. "I'm going to get him." He raced swiftly down the road to where the horseman lay prostrate fifty yards away.

Warriors rose to meet him but dropped to the shelter again before the covering fire of Cockney's sharpshooters.

The horse struggled to rise as the Major neared. An *assegai* hung from its neck, two others were sticking deep in its side.

Swiftly drawing his revolver the Major shot the tortured beast then stooped to take the policeman up in his arms. As he did so a *knobkerrie* whirled through the air and caught him on the side of his head, knocking him down; a flight of *assegais* followed. One stuck in his thigh but the throw was a weak one—the warriors were lying down behind cover.

He pulled out the *assegai,* then emptied his revolver at moving shadows. Again he bent over the policeman and picking him up, reeling giddily, started back up the hill. *Assegais* clattered on the rocks all about him; they fell farther and farther behind.

All danger passed—the warriors dared not leave the shelter of the rocks, neither dared they stand up, and he was out of range of their casts—he collapsed not ten yards from the stockade. Cockney, Jim and the others rushed out to him.

"Good old Jim!" he muttered as the Hottentot picked him up in his powerful arms and carried him into the mission.

"I never can finish what I start," he said with a whimsical smile as they put him down gently on the bed Audrey had quickly prepared for him. "I start things but good old Jim always has to finish them for me." Then he closed his eyes and seemed to sleep.

About the same time the trooper—they had put him on a pile of blankets in the kitchen—returned to consciousness and looked into the eyes of Cockney.

"Hell!" he muttered. "What a cropper I came. How—who—" he rubbed his eyes. "Oh, I remember." He sat erect. "I arrest you all in the queen's name," he said in a quavering voice. "And I warn you—"

"Ow shut up," Cockney interrupted gruffly. "Hif it 'adn't 'a' been fer hus—and 'specially the Major—you'd be so full of *assegais* that you'd look like an old maid's pin cushion. 'Ere! Drink this!"

He gave the policeman a stiff drink of brandy and nodded with satisfaction as he saw the color flow back into the other's cheeks.

"My name's Stephens," the trooper said presently. "I know yours. And a nice little war you've got on here, I must say. What's it all about?"

And Cockney told him, quite briefly for Cockney, all about it.

"I see," the policeman said slowly. "And you knowingly poked your nose into old Sayre's *indaba*, eh? Well, that's the sort of thing the Major would do."

"You know 'im then?" Cockney asked.

"Hell, yes. Who doesn't?"

"But wot I wants ter know is," Cockney continued, "wot are you a-doin' 'ere?"

"I came to arrest you and the Portuguese."

" 'Ow did yer know the Dagoes was 'ere?"

Stephens laughed. "We suspected there was something in the wind down this way. That's why I was sent—partly. And as soon as I got into this district the niggers had plenty to tell me about parties of strange white men who were fooling about the place. They were worried, the niggers were."

"An' they didn't tell yer about this little affair up 'ere?"

"No! They keep matters like that strictly a family affair."

Cockney laughed. "And so you comes to arrest the Major and hus and the Dagoes, eh?"

" 'Specially the Portuguese," Stephens said.

"W'y 'specially them?"

"Because my captain heard they were planning to do the Major in—and they're dangerous otherwise."

Cockney laughed harshly. "Us'll be lucky if any of hus are alive this time termorrer. Ammunition's short."

The trooper whistled softly. "Bad as that, eh? Well, look here, I wasn't going to tell you this—afraid you might bolt. But I sent a message back as soon as I found what a lot of Portuguese were wandering about loose. There'll be a big force coming along pretty soon—tomorrow, maybe. I ought to have waited for them."

"I wish ter 'ell yer 'ad," Cockney interrupted bitterly, "instead of gettin' in a mess which the Major 'as ter pull yer hout of."

He jumped to his feet as Audrey Sayre came into the room.

" 'Ow's the Major, miss?"

She shook her head doubtfully.

"He's lost a lot of blood and he's very weak. But that would be all right, nothing to worry about, only—"

"Yes, miss? Honly?"

"He's got the beginnings of an attack of malaria on top of it all."

Muttering something about damn' fool policemen Cockney rose and hurriedly left the room.

The soldiers who had clustered about the door, anxious to hear of their baas' welfare, wondered why the little man's voice was so harsh when he ordered them back to their posts.

THE NIGHT passed. The darkness which heralded the coming dawn dropped upon the mission. Men strained their eyes to pierce the gloom, their fingers rested on the triggers of their rifles. But the dreaded attack did not materialize.

The darkness lifted. Black gave way to somber gray, the gray to fleecy white clouds which scurried across the sky and lost themselves in the golden glow of the rising sun.

And still the men waited for the fierce yells and the savage onslaught they were so sure must come. They waited and watched with such intensity that it seemed as if the rocks must dissolve and disclose hidden warriors.

Nothing moved. There was no sound. And gradually the men relaxed, confident that all danger had passed, that the Swazi had returned to their *kraals*. Some of the men left their posts, others followed quickly, and busied themselves about preparing the morning meal.

Jim, his face drawn, his skin tinged with the gray of fear—fear for his baas—still kept watch. Occasionally he turned to look at Cockney who leaned disconsolately nearby.

"If he dies, Jim," Cockney said slowly in the vernacular, "I'll kill that fool of a policeman."

"Yah, little baas," Jim said absently. He was very tired and had relaxed somewhat from the strain of the long night's watch. Otherwise he would have looked still closer at the rocks which cluttered the ground about the stockade. And when one has been staring into the dark, endeavoring to see great distances, it is hard to see things close at hand in the brightness of a new day.

Death was very near the stockade.

In the before dawn darkness, fifty warriors—each one had taken oath to kill a defender of the stockade before himself meeting death—had crawled up close and waited now, hidden, their bodies painted the color of the veld, for the entire lack of lookouts which, they reasoned, would follow the long uneventful night's watch.

It was a daring plan. It would have succeeded had not one of the warriors wriggled his cramped toes, sending a little spiral of dust into the air.

It was a very little thing, but it was sufficient to focus Jim's attention. "The Swazi!" he yelled and fired at the dust.

The others ran quickly to their posts and fired blindly at nothing. And they kept on firing. The suddenness of Jim's warning, the swift transition from fancied security to threatened danger, had created a panic. Nor would they cease firing when Cockney ran up and down, cursing them and Jim.

The warriors remained hidden. They dared not rise to meet that hail of bullets which swept over them.

"Gord! 'Ere's a go!" Cockney yelled as Stephens and the two women rushed out of the mission. "The niggers 'ave got their wind up. They're firing cartridges as if we'd got a store 'ut full of 'em. And they're firing at nothink, the fools!"

He forcibly wrested a rifle away from one of the men. "You'll wake the baas!" he shouted now. " 'E's sick an' 'e'll fink 'e ought ter be out 'ere."

At that the firing slackened somewhat.

Now a volley of shots sounded far down the ravine.

They saw a wagon drawn by sixteen mules coming slowly up the road. A white man was driving, flourishing a long whip; a stupendously fat native sat beside him; natives in the back of the wagon were firing into the air.

"Bli'me! Hit's Yank!" Cockney shouted joyously and ran to the opening in the stockade.

But Jim the Hottentot forcibly restrained him. "There are Swazi warriors just outside, little baas," he said.

Warriors rushed at the wagon. *Assegais* flashed in the sunlight.

"Lumme!" Cockney groaned. "W'y doesn't Yank drive through? W'y don't 'is niggers shoot? Let me go, Jim." He struggled to release himself.

"Wait, little baas," Jim said gravely. "Watch!"

And they saw the warriors suddenly discard their spears and drop abjectly to all fours, their heads bowed down to the ground. "Greetings, O Earthshaker," they shouted. "Mercy!"

The wagon passed slowly on. Other warriors came from their place of concealment. "Greetings, O Earthshaker! Greetings and mercy!" Men sprang up almost within arm's length of the stockade and joined in the chorus of greeting and appeal for mercy to the fat, inert mass of flesh who sat on the driver's seat beside Yank; they asked for mercy of a man who was so fat that it was a torture for him to walk, who spent most of his time dozing in the sun at his *kraal*. But he was their king!

"Bli'me!" Cockney cried again. "You was right, you old 'eathen, abart the Swazi bein' close at 'and. Yank 'ud 'ave been too late, I'm finking—'im an' that tub o' lard you calls a king—hif yer 'adn't 'ad yer eyes peeled. Is it safe to go out now?" he concluded humbly in the vernacular.

Jim shook his head. "Not yet, little baas. First I think the king will want to speak to his people. See!"

The wagon had come to a halt and Yank was making motions for the defenders to remain in the stockade. The warriors had gathered about the wagon.

"You are fools!" The king's voice was powerful. It had a bite to it.

"Truly we are fools, O Earthshaker," they replied sorrowfully.

Jim grinned. "He will make them pay heavily for their folly. I hope I did not hurt the little baas when I held him. Now I go to tell my baas of the king's coming. Maybe it will cure the sickness!"

BUT THE MAJOR was not to know that day the tale of it all; of how Yank had captured the wagon from the Portuguese and driving on to the royal *kraal,* with great tact and diplomacy, had persuaded the obese king to return with him at once to the mission; of how, after the Swazi had been dispersed by their ruler, other Portuguese had come to the mission and of how, hard following them, rode a troop of the mounted police who made all prisoners—including Yank, Cockney, Jim and the soldiers who had followed the Major's fortunes.

All this, and more, the Major learned two weeks later when, the fever having left him, he had querulously voiced his wonder at being left alone to the ministrations of the two women, Lola and Audrey.

When they told him, he groaned aloud and turned his face to the wall, feeling that he had deserted his friends; that his weakness in giving way to the ravages of blood loss and malaria had been the cause of their arrest. In his despair he visualized them working on the Breakwater at Cape Town.

Here he was, lying on a soft bed, being administered to, read to, talked to, sung to and fed by women!

He summoned his reserve of strength. He tried to sit erect, partly succeeded and then fell back against the pillow. He groaned again.

"Of course you are very weak, Major," Audrey said quietly. She looked very cool and capable. But her voice— it was low, melodious and should have soothed him— affected him strangely. "Soon we will have you outside and then your strength will come back to you. Now you must drink this."

He protested weakly, but when she held the cup to his lips he gulped down the bitter abomination it contained. "Thank you, dear miss," he said.

He put his hand to his cheek and an alarmed look came into his eyes. "May I have a mirror, please—and—er—my monocle? I must be a frightful looking object. I need a shave and—" His hand fell limply back on the cover.

"I will shave you presently, when you are stronger," Lola said and taking his hand in hers stroked it gently. "And soon I am going to take you away."

"I think I could sleep now," he interrupted hastily, draw- ing" his hand away. "Perhaps if you dear ladies left me alone for a little while— I'm sure you should get a little fresh air. You both look a little pale if I may say so. And it must be frightfully boring waitin' on a stupid invalid like myself. Please go. Go for a good long walk. Climb to the top of the *kopje,* please! And come back with roses in your cheeks and all that sort of thing."

Audrey, a look of understanding and regret upon her pretty face, opened the door and stood there waiting. She caught Lola's eye presently and beckoned. Lola rose then and together the two women left the room.

" 'Pon my soul!" the Major ejaculated feebly.

The minutes passed by swiftly.

He tried to sit up again—succeeded! He threw back the covers and sat on the edge of the bed. The walls revolved furiously about him; the floor and the ceiling seemed to be coming together; black specks shot with flashes of light danced before his eyes—

Presently the dizziness passed. He sat in a sort of stupor, unable to move; in his mind was the fixed idea that he must get hence, must seek out the others that their punishment might be his.

There was the sound of wheels outside the window; a horse neighed; a voice scolded. The Major raised his head; his eyes glistened. Then he crept dismally under the covers and buried his head under them, sure that the delirium of fever was returning.

Hasty footsteps sounded outside the door. The door opened and Jim the Hottentot—a resplendent, beaming Jim in a suit of spotless white duck entered. "Baas!" he cried happily and set the tin uniform case he was carrying down on the floor. "Baas!"

The Major threw back the covers and sat up with a sudden access of strength. "Jim!" Color flowed back into his face, his eyes sparkled. "Is it really *you?* Come here, you bally old heathen. You are not a ghost, are you?"

"No ghost, damme, no, baas," Jim said, beaming happily, but there was a queer drag in his voice, his eyes clouded mistily as he looked at the Major's thin cheeks, his sunken eyes.

"But I thought, Jim," the Major's voice was very weary; the vernacular came haltingly, he could not give the *clicks* their proper value. "I thought the policemen had taken you all to *trunk?*"

"They took us away, baas. They could not let us stay here. But over the border they released us, making Baas Yank and the little baas promise not to return. Me they allowed to come back for you. The Portuguese they have taken with them; there will be a great *indaba*. The fat man wailed loudly. And so I have returned for you."

"Good old Jim. It was time; the pestle and the mortar were grinding me thin." His eyes clouded with anxiety. "But our soldiers, Jim? What of them?"

"They have gone with the policemen, baas. At first the little baas made great talk of fighting and our soldiers were with him. They said they were your men and owed no allegiance to no one else. But Baas Yank counselled other things—he is very wise, that one—and so our soldiers are going to join the black soldiers of the white queen. With that they are content. Baas Yank arranged that, pleading their case before the white officers of the police. He said that was how you would wish it."

The Major nodded, well satisfied. "And now what, Jim?"

"Is the baas well enough to trek?"

"Ay, Jim. Anywhere. This is only fever weakness. It will pass with time and food and peace. Honey is good, Jim, but too much of it sickens a man. There are times when a woman's softness is to be desired above all other things, but too much—"

"True, baas. Then we will trek. Look! Is it permitted?"

He picked the Major up and carried him to the window. Outside stood the Major's wagon drawn by six mules; tied to the back of the wagon was a coal black stallion.

"Satan!" the Major called and almost cried when the horse whinnied a soft welcome; laughed when the spirited beast reared and struck out playfully with its forefeet.

Jim placed the Major in a chair beside the window.

"Tomorrow we will go, baas."

"No. Today—at once, Jim."

"The baas is strong enough?" Jim asked doubtfully.

"Truly. Almost I am well enough to ride. Now shave me."

Jim hesitated a moment and then, opening the uniform case, got out an array of toilet articles and without further comment shaved his master.

"Now dress me, Jim."

Again Jim obeyed.

"Where do we go, Jim?" the Major asked as the Hottentot guided his arms into the sleeves of a well tailored tunic.

And Jim told of a shady spot he had discovered not many miles away, just over the border. A little *spruit*, its water crystal clear, burbled through the heart of it; all manner of buck came there to drink and the nearby *kopjes* swarmed with *klipspringer*. And there Yank and Cockney had built a camp, and waited.

"Hurry, Jim!" the Major breathed happily, and tried to help the Hottentot pull on the well polished brown polo boots. Presently he was dressed.

"All ready now, baas?" Jim asked.

"Wait! Those two dear souls! I should have died if it had not been for them, Jim."

"True, baas. They cured you that they might have the killing of you," Jim said cynically.

The Major laughed softly. Paper and pencil were on a table nearby. Reaching for them he wrote two letters; letters which required intense concentration. The writing of them tired him and he sat looking listlessly before him when he had finished.

Jim regarded him anxiously. "Perhaps the baas had better wait a little," he suggested. "Tomorrow, or the next day—"

The Major roused himself. "No, Jim. Today—now!"

Holding on to the window sill he pulled himself to his feet and stood tottering there. Jim handed him his helmet—it had been freshly blancoed, and its whiteness was dazzling.

The Major put it on his head. "Ready, Jim," he said and put the two letters on the pillow.

He was but a shadow of his old self; the tunic hung loosely about him; his riding breeches flapped baggily about his pipe-stem legs; his face was the color of dead ash.

"Better let me carry you, baas—or go back to bed," Jim said miserably.

The Major's lips trembled, for he was very weak. His hand fumbled in his top left tunic pocket. His fingers closed on a monocle. He pulled it out and fixed it in his eye. His lips set firm, his jaw muscles tightened, his eyes cleared.

"Out of my way, you bally old reprobate," he drawled and walked slowly out of the door.

THE BLACK-NECKED COBRA

IN CONNECTION with the mishap of the Major related in this issue by L. Patrick Greene, the author offers a further description and explanation of a particularly disagreeable and dangerous species of reptile.

"One of the commonest snakes of South Africa—especially in the Sabi Bush of the Eastern Transvaal—is the black-necked cobra, more commonly called the "spitting snake." This very unpleasant reptile likes to take up its abode in the thatched roofs of huts. I have a very squeamish memory of one falling from the roof and sliding down the folds of mosquito netting which covered my bed, to the ground. I know I watched its descent breathlessly, hoping that it wouldn't strike a rotten patch in the netting, and didn't move until it hit the floor and then I yelled for my 'boy.' He came a-running and killed the thing with a stick. I had the roof of my hut beaten every day after that. Couldn't afford to have a ceiling of board of canvas.

"These snakes inflict a very dangerous bite, but that's not the sum total of their cussedness. They can and do eject venom from their fangs a distance of several feet! A friend's dog was blinded by one, and I know of two cases where natives completely lost their sight through the action of the venom. In each case the natives were alone and far from any *kraal* when 'sprayed' with the poison.

"The experience of Major Hamilton is the best authenticated case on record. He says, 'I was in a dark outhouse one morning when I suddenly felt a spatter of moisture first in one eye and then in the other. Smarting was followed in a minute or two by intense pain, and *complete loss of sight!* Fortunately, assistance was at hand, and my eyes were treated continuously for three hours with fresh milk squeezed liberally into them. The clot of blood with which each was covered then came away, and the surface, though much inflamed, became visible. It was a great relief to discover that I was not permanently blind, but bandages were necessary for a couple of days, and blue spectacles for a month. At the end of that time recovery seemed complete; but then there came a relapse, the left eye, which had received a double dose of poison giving way, and causing me considerable inconvenience for a long time. The snake, which was killed and skinned, proved to be a black-necked cobra.'"

CORRESPONDENCE

THE DELAY occasioned in printing this letter from a South African friend and well-wisher, in no manner voids the interest—or dulls the point of his criticism.

Editor, SHORT STORIES,

DEAR SIR:

As you see, I live in South Africa and, apart from their great merit as stories, I find those yarns of Mr. Greene's about the Major extremely interesting. I must confess, however, that Mr. Greene puzzles me sometimes.

I've just finished reading "Concessions" in the early April number and gather that on the morning on which the story opens the Major was camped within a few miles or so of Kimberley, or, at least, about a mile from one of the diamond mines there. As soon as he got up he had a swim in the river and a crocodile thought to have him for breakfast.

Now, the only river near Kimberley in which the Major could enjoy a swim is the Vaal, and that is about fifteen miles away and there aren't any crocs left in it—not now, at any rate, whatever there may have been in it in the very remote past.

After arranging his little trap for Smithy, the Major pushes off to a native *kraal* in a district nominally under Portuguese jurisdiction. That, as you Americans would say, would be "some" trek, for Portuguese territory is a devil of a distance from Kimberely and in a direction decidedly not east. There may be crocodiles down that way—I'm not sure about that—but there are certainly lions. Only this morning I read in the newspaper that a flock of them, or covey or herd (or whatever it is that lions go about in when they want company) has been slaughtering cattle a few nights ago.

I don't want you to think I'm "grousing" about Mr. Greene's stories. I'm not. I like them immensely and wish that I could write such tales myself. As the late Mr. Shakespeare would perhaps have said had he written short stories instead of plays: The story's the thing; and small geographical or other inaccuracies don't matter very much if the story itself is otherwise good.

It is very evident that Mr. Greene has lived in this country, and for some time, too. Does he still do so? Perhaps some time you could let us have a paragraph about him, unless you've done this before? I've only been reading SHORT STORIES for a couple of years so I may have missed it.

My wife and I like the magazine very much indeed—more than any other magazine we get, and we do read a lot of 'em. We prefer complete stories to serials, however, and should like to see you drop this feature; but in this you are guided by the wishes of the majority of readers, and, since you are continuing to print serials, I suppose the majority want them?

B.H. BEARDWOOD,
106 Relly Street
Pretoria, Union of South Africa.

Mr. Greene's reply:

MY DEAR MR. BEARDWOOD:
Your letter of April 12, 1924, to the Editor of SHORT STORIES, has been forwarded to me.

First let me thank you for the kind things you say about my

stories and then admit—most freely—that you have caught me napping.

About the crocodiles in the Vaal River: When I first crossed that river, years and years ago, an old-timer pointed out something in the water and said, "Look at the crocs!" I looked and saw something I thought were crocs—perhaps because I was green and wanted to believe him. Anyway, I stand convicted of carelessness, because from that day to this, I've always believed there were crocs in the Vaal and would have been ready to bet my shirt on it. I *ought* to have made sure!

It is, as you say, a devil of a trek from Kimberely to Portuguese Territory, but surely the direction is decidedly east, or at least east-by-northeast, or even "Easter" than that. At the same time, it would have been much better had I placed my *kraal* on the Basutoland border: That would have made the Major's trek much more plausible.

Now there's a country I want to write a novel about some day—Basutoland. Its history is fascinating; its potentialities enormous. I am rather hazy as to its present political status. Is it still a Protectorate, or has it been taken in by the Union?

I've always thought of Basutoland as a volcano. If it ever erupts and sends out its thousands of armed warriors, there'll be one hell of an *indaba.*

I hope you will sometime soon take typewriter in hand, as it were, and drop me a line. The "lure of the veld" still has me fast and I'm promising myself to come back some day. But, until that day, letters help me a great deal.

If you'll let me, I'll send you a presentation copy of my new novel of the Major. I'm expecting copies from the publisher almost any day now.

L. Patrick Greene.

CPSIA information can be obtained
at www.ICGtesting.com
Printed in the USA
LVHW111520151219
640579LV00001B/70/P